IN THE BEGINNING . . .

Alan, being Alan, assumed she was looking at him. I, being me, was sure she was looking at him. But I looked at her anyway.

She was a real beauty. She had the drink in her right hand and her left hand was closed in a fist. It was nervously tapping against the edge of the bar. Like someone was standing her up and she was going to give it to him with both barrels if he ever got there. The way she looked I figured he'd turn out to be enough to give Robert Redford a run for his money.

He'd better get there soon. Her eyes had a desperate and hungry look.

And then she looked at me . . .

Other Avon Books by
Brad Solomon

THE GONE MAN
THE OPEN SHADOW

AVON
PUBLISHERS OF BARD, CAMELOT AND DISCUS BOOKS

AVON BOOKS
A division of
The Hearst Corporation
959 Eighth Avenue
New York, New York 10019

Copyright © 1979 by Brad Solomon
Published by arrangement with The Dial Press
Library of Congress Catalog Card Number: 78-23926
ISBN: 0-380-52969-6

All rights reserved, which includes the right
to reproduce this book or portions thereof in
any form whatsoever. For information address
The Dial Press, 245 East 47th Street,
New York, New York 10017

First Avon Printing, December, 1980

AVON TRADEMARK REG. U.S. PAT. OFF. AND IN
OTHER COUNTRIES, MARCA REGISTRADA, HECHO EN
U.S.A.

Printed in the U.S.A.

For my parents
and Steve Haberman

THE first time I saw her, she was sitting at the bar in the main room at The Dancers. She was sipping a drink.

No, she wasn't sipping. She was gulping. It was a good-sized drink. Probably a double. It could've been a triple. It would've been Jack Daniel's, but I wouldn't have known that then. Between gulps she was looking in our direction.

Alan noticed her first and pointed her out to me. "Wouldn't mind giving that one a try."

"You wouldn't mind giving anyone in the room a try."

"Wouldn't mind giving that one a couple of tries." He grinned his usual grin. Alan, being Alan, assumed she was looking at him. I, being me, was sure she was looking at him. But I looked at her anyway.

She was a real beauty. She had the drink in her right hand and her left hand was closed in a fist. It was tapping nervously against the edge of the bar. Like someone was standing her up and she was going to give it to him with both barrels if he ever got there. The way she looked I figured he'd turn out to be enough to give Robert Redford a run for his money.

He'd better get there soon, she definitely didn't like waiting. She crossed her left leg over her right knee so that her left foot could swing freely. It began to swing in a steady and unbroken rhythm. Her dark hair fell loosely down to her shoulders. It covered them as softly as the Pacific washes over the beach in Santa Monica on a cool quiet night. She seemed different now. Her eyes had a desperate and hungry look. They were still strong and striking, but a little bit lost. She turned and looked at us again.

Then two thin girls with toothpaste smiles came over to ask Alan for his autograph. I stubbed out my cigarette, picked up my fork and went back to eating my sand dab. Alan whipped out the black felt-tip marker he'd begun to carry. He loved the way it made his autograph come out three times the size of anybody else's.

His hand scribbled quickly. His mouth was smiling its killer smile now. His eyes were dancing with the skill of Fred Astaire's feet. The girls filled the air with giggles, collected the autographs and went away.

"Brother, you hit in this town, you hit fast." Alan's eyes flew around the room again. He was making it big in the business, and I wasn't.

It's hard, when you're trying to make it and you aren't. And those around you are. It makes you feel second rate. No, not even that good. It makes you feel worthless.

"By the way, Jake, my agent renegotiated my contract. Twelve thousand an episode from now on."

That was Alan all right. Always good at speaking without thinking. He was damn lucky it was me he was saying it to. Ninety-nine percent of the other actors in this town would've knocked him off his chair. I'm afraid I came pretty close to doing it myself. Feeling worthless didn't stop me from feeling mad.

"Cheer up, Jake. Your time'll come."

Would it? Sure. I shrugged and said nothing.

Twelve thousand an episode. God. At twenty-two episodes a year that was over two hundred and fifty thousand dollars per season. And I bet it hadn't been his agent who'd renegotiated his contract, he'd probably done it himself. He was that good.

I gave him a laugh that sounded almost honest, if

you didn't pay too much attention to it, and drained my wine glass. I would've drained the bottle but it was already empty. I watched his eyes dart around the room again.

But the way he was acting worried me a little. It wasn't just that people in the restaurant—people all over town for that matter—had begun to look at him. He'd begun to *need* them to look at him. It was happening to him that way so soon, that was the scary part. I reached across the table and tapped his hand. "Careful, Alan. I heard a rumor it doesn't always last."

"Hell, Jake, I know that! Let me enjoy it while it's here!" He looked toward the girl at the bar again. "Christ, see the looks I'm getting?"

"A blind man could see them." I pumped ketchup over my french fries as if I had some interest in the operation. "Pretty soon you'll have the Rolls, the new mansion on the hill, the mortgage payments on the new mansion on the hill. The gold faucets on the bathtub, the indentured servants." I watched him to see if he'd give any reaction at all. "The tax lawyers, the investment counselors. They'll be busy getting rich off *your* taxes and *your* investments. Any time I want to see you, I'll have to talk to some underfed fashion model first."

"Doesn't sound bad, Jake."

"Never does, till you get it. But once you get it, you know you can lose it. Guys become stars, next thing you know they're spending all their time counting their millions, just to make sure their millions're still there. And popping vitamins 'cause they're suddenly hypochondriacs and they're worried they're going to lose their health, their looks, their girls and their sex appeal." I paused. "And every time they go into a restaurant, they find they can't stop looking around to see who's looking back."

That seemed to ring a bell. He took a deep breath, held it and pushed his half-eaten dinner away. "Okay, Jake, let's say it happens to you tomorrow."

"I don't think tomorrow's the day it's going to . . ." I lowered my eyes. I tightened my lips against my teeth.

"Let's say it does. It could. Why not?"

I knew why not. It hadn't happened yet. I'd been in L.A. for two years and it hadn't happened. It wasn't going to. It just wasn't.

"If it does, you going to handle it any different?"

My hand began to shake. I tried to hide it by making a big thing of brushing crumbs off the table. "Probably not." I looked up at him. "I just wish it'd happen so I could find out!"

"The fame game, my friend. We all end up handling it the same way. We don't handle it at all. It handles us."

Handles *him*, he meant.

The fame game wasn't even what I wanted. Just a chance to act. And maybe get paid for it. Subsistence wages would be fine. Just a chance to *act!* For someone to realize I could *do* it!

Alan ran a finger around the base of his wine glass. "What the hell, they'll knock me out of the box some day, happens to everyone—but at least they'll know I was there for a while. When you make it, you better do it the same way." He rubbed his hand across his mouth and looked around the room again. "What would you give to make it?"

"Whatever they want."

"No, Jake. You wouldn't." He hesitated a moment. "That's your trouble."

I tapped the table with my unlit cigarette.

"Jake. . . . Reason I wanted to meet you here. . . . We got to talk about something."

The way he said it I knew I probably didn't want to hear what it was.

"Jake. . . . I'm moving out to Malibu."

It hovered over the table like something neither of us wanted to look at. Considering what our rented house was like, considering what Alan was becoming, considering how pleasant I'd been to live with the past couple months, it wasn't a big surprise.

I started thinking about being on my own again. I got rid of that quickly and started thinking about more concrete things. Like what I laughingly called my bank account. I hadn't had a decent piece of work in three months. The only thing that'd been keeping me afloat was a toothpaste commercial I'd done two and a half years before. I'd come out to L.A. and been here only three weeks when I'd gotten the spot. It wasn't much, no lines, just a quick reaction shot in the midde of the ad, but it was a good shot of me and enough to make you remember I'd been there. I'd gotten that commercial so damn easily I'd thought things were going to work out in L.A.

They hadn't. It had been beginner's luck. The toothpaste commercial had gone on the air, then off. But for some strange reason it had gone on again three months ago. I'd started getting checks again. Not much, but enough. Enough to cover half the rent. I'd been able to count on Alan for the other half. Till now.

"Jill pulled me out there Monday. Malibu. We signed a lease on a house. You know Jill, she wants something, you can't talk her out of it."

"You mean *you* can't talk her out of it." I was feeling a little mean, though I didn't have a right to. I tried to control it. "All right, so you're moving. How soon?"

He turned a little red. "Jill's already there."

"Oh." I forced a quick laugh. "That means *you're* already there, right?" I looked at my wine glass. It was empty. I looked at it anyway.

"Haven't got that much stuff to take out of our place, Jake. I mean, just the clothes are all I'm going to take. Be buying everything new for the house."

"Good for you! Help the economy along!" Then I shut up.

"Jake? You going to be okay? I mean, by yourself?"

I laughed again. I clinked my empty wine glass against his. I don't know why. I just wanted to hear a nice sharp clink. But then Alan's face looked a little bit miserable, and that didn't do either one of us any good.

"Don't worry, I'll be okay. If I were you, I'd do the same thing. You're on your way, you can't afford anything but the best, right?"

"Jake, next month's rent, I'll pay my half of it. You don't have to worry about that. And if you have any trouble finding someone to move in, I'll split the month after with you, too."

That was the wrong thing to say. It got me so mad at both him and myself that I came out with one of those stupid statements only a man who's been brainwashed into thinking he's got to prove he's a man could come up with.

"I'll handle the rent. Forget it." Sure. I'd handle the rent. I'd go to the poor house.

"Jake? You mad at me?"

"No."

"I can never tell with you. You always keep everything bottled up inside. I'm never sure what you're thinking."

I nodded a couple of times.

.. He gave up and looked toward the bar. It seemed like an excellent idea, so I tried it myself.

The girl was still there, the one with the drink. And the hair, and the eyes. Robert Redford hadn't showed yet. Her drink was a new one. It was big as her first. The way she was going at it, it wasn't going to last long.

Alan put money on the table. "I was the one who said let's go out to eat. Let me pay for it."

I stared at his money. And my empty plate. It figured. My dinner, including the wine, must've come to a good three and a half bucks. Next time he wanted to take me out to dinner, I hoped he'd tell me ahead of time. I'd order steak, not sand dabs.

His eyes scanned the room again, as if there were something to see he hadn't already seen at least twenty times. And the girls were looking at him. All of them. Even the girl at the bar.

"I let myself get stuck with one of these girls, Jill will kill me. Must be a back way out. I'll make it look like I'm going to the men's room. Stay here a couple minutes—it'll look like I'm coming back. Okay, Jake?"

"You're a mess."

"What?"

It had slipped out. I tried to cover it. "You're a star, Alan! A star!"

"I am, ain't you heard?"

He flashed his killer smile. Maybe that's what I needed. His smile, or his eyes. Certainly not his acting.

He covered his mouth suddenly and yawned. He tried to get it over with fast so nobody would see it. He'd been shooting his series all day, and he was tired. He tried hard to keep it hidden.

Sure he was tired. I was tired, too. Everyone I knew was tired. Worn out. Scared. Broken and beaten, or almost broken and beaten. Those who had made it, like him. Those who hadn't, like me. I hadn't seen a pair of bright eyes, or a warm smiling face that was honest, or a genuine spark of fire in the two and a half years I'd been out here. I probably never would.

He yawned again. This time his eyes were dull and bleak. God, we weren't actors out here, we were dead men. It was just that nobody had had the energy to bury us yet.

I reached out and touched his arm. "Alan."

"What?"

"Be careful. I mean, in Malibu. It's a dangerous country."

"I know. I can handle it."

He walked across the restaurant like he didn't have a care in the world. When he reached the end of the bar, he stopped. He was right next to the girl.

He looked at her. Said something. The girl just stared at him. She picked up her drink, found there wasn't much left. She gulped it down and signaled to the bartender for a refill. She gulped the refill. She hadn't bothered to look at Alan again.

God, she must've really been sure of herself, to turn down Alan that way.

Alan picked himself up off the floor, dusted himself off and took his wounded ego toward the men's room. I looked at the girl another moment, then at my empty plate and the ashtray full of dead cigarettes. And the money Alan had left behind. His money only made me think of my bank account again. A pretty flimsy thought for that time of night.

I gave Alan time to make his escape, then paid the check and went out. I gave a half salute to the neon glowing across the front of the restaurant. The neon didn't seem impressed. I wasn't surprised. Why should the neon be different from the producers and directors and casting directors I met? I shrugged and turned my back on it and walked into the parking lot. I came around the corner of a car, and ten feet in front of me a young kid was down on one knee. He was trying to pick the lock on the door of a car. It was my car.

He didn't bother to look up, but he must've known I was there. You see these kids all over. You never know what they might be on or what they might do. None of them ever seems to give a damn about anything. It's not that they're brave. They're just young. Too young to think about consequences.

I spoke just loud enough for him to hear me but didn't move toward him. "Hey, come on. That's my car."

His eyes slid toward me. They saw me, measured my height and weight, didn't think much of either and casually returned to the door lock.

I could've walked away from it right then. Normally I would've. I wasn't the kind to let myself get trapped in something like that. I'd never seen the point of a fight. The last time I'd touched anyone with any kind of aggressiveness at all, aside from acting a scene in a play or a TV show, had been playing touch football in high school.

But that night I was fed up with the world. Fed up even more with myself. On top of that I'd had half a bottle of wine. I was like the kid. I didn't give a damn. I was out to prove something.

I stepped forward. "All right! Get away from the car!"

He turned suddenly and came up in a crouch. His hand swung away from the door. His hand held a ten-inch screwdriver. His lips drew back across his teeth and showed me a hard grin. "I don't wanna get away from the car. Why don'tcha try'n make me?"

I stood still. It would be insane to go at some kid who was anxious to show what he could do with a ten-inch screwdriver. Only a fool would try it. But it was one of those nights. I knew exactly how much of a fool I was. I stepped forward again anyway.

I didn't get far. Laughter came out of the shadows. Other boys surrounded me. One had a knife. Another had some kind of pipe. We stared at each other a moment, then I heard a chain rattle against the ground.

"Whatsa matter, mister? Someone fooling with your car?"

It figured. The first time in a year I'd made a decision to take a step, and this is what I'd stepped into.

I tried to think. I was wearing a thick belt with a heavy buckle. If I could pull it off and swing it at them, it might make them give me a little room. Enough to make a break for it.

I looked at them blankly and let my hands travel carefully toward my waist.

I never reached the belt. They came straight at me. One put his fist into my stomach and two others grabbed my arms. Before I could even swing at them I was down on the ground.

The thoughts that went through my mind. What if they did something to my face? It wasn't my life I was worried about. It was my face. An actor with a scarred face might never get a chance to act again.

Then I realized. Maybe that was what I wanted. An actor like me who couldn't get a job anyway, maybe a scarred face would be all I'd need. An excuse to finally get out of the business. Without having to admit the real reason. That I was a failure.

Crazy, stupid thoughts. But they made a crazy, stupid kind of sense. Suddenly I was yelling and snapping at them and trying to kick them. I knew it'd make them mad at me. I kept doing it anyway. Maybe they'd *really* hurt me. Maybe if they hurt me enough it'd at least show me I was still alive, if I really was.

Then it was happening. There was an arm around my neck and it was cutting into my throat so bad I could hardly breathe. I knew what was about to happen. They were going to kill me.

Suddenly everything stopped. It was quiet. I didn't understand. What was going on? They were holding me, but that was all. They weren't hitting me anymore. A hand was clamped tight against my mouth.

Finally in the quiet I heard what they heard. Steps. Coming across the parking lot.

The hand still covered my mouth, so I couldn't yell out. The steps came closer. They made a hollow tapping sound that filled the darkness. The only other things I could hear were my breathing and the blood pounding in my head.

The steps stopped for a moment, as if they weren't sure which way to go. Then they started again and came quicker this time. They were coming toward us. I could tell the kids were scared. None of them was moving. They were all looking toward the darkness. So was I.

She came around the corner of my car and into the light. She saw us. She froze. She didn't know what to do. Her eyes were as striking as before but now they were startled. Confused. Frightened. She couldn't seem to make sense of it. She didn't make a sound. She didn't turn and run.

One of the boys laughed. He took his hands off me and got to his feet, and began to move toward her.

I didn't even think. I just reached up and grabbed his leg and tried to pull him back. I tried to get my mouth free to yell for her to get away. The hand came back and covered my mouth tightly again as other hands pulled my head back and the arm tightened around my neck. Then I was lying flat and my whole body was pinned.

I heard cold words above me. "Hey, honey! . . . Come on, honey! . . . Let's get it on!"

Another boy laughed.

I was desperate now. I struggled again. It was no use. They had me. All I could do was turn my eyes and look at her.

She was half in shadow now. She had stepped back slightly and you couldn't see her face. Two of them were moving toward her. I began to cry. I knew I was helpless and couldn't do a thing. If only she would run.

The two kids separated to come at her from both sides. Another five feet and they'd have her. My heart was beating like a drum. If only I could bite the hand on my mouth. Then I noticed her right hand was in her pocketbook. It began to come out slowly. It seemed to be holding a small, dark object. I couldn't see what it was. But for some reason the two boys had stopped moving.

Her hand came up slowly, an inch at a time. Higher and higher. Finally it was in light. All of us could see the gun clearly now. It seemed to be shaking slightly. It was dead silent again.

I braced my feet against the ground. I strained and pushed for all I was worth. But there were too many hands on me. I looked at her again. Her arm had straightened. The gun was almost at shoulder level. It moved till it pointed directly at the face of the kid on her right.

The kid yelled suddenly. He turned and came past us. Then the hands left me. Bodies slapped against each other as they struggled to get away. I heard their feet running across concrete, but I didn't look at them. I kept my eyes on her.

It was silent again. I was still on the ground, lying on my back. She was still above me, her arm still straight out, her hand still holding the gun.

I opened my mouth and began to choke as if I'd forgotten how to breathe. Then I felt sick. I thought I was going to throw up. My stomach and chest went into a spasm, and I could feel it coming up. Then I could taste it. I tried to stay still. It went down again.

I waited, then rubbed my throat. I looked up at her. She still hadn't moved. She could've been made of stone. I tried to say something but I couldn't get the words out. I felt faint now and lowered my head.

Finally I got to my feet and waited for her to say something, but all she did was stare into the darkness where the boys had disappeared. It was as if I wasn't even there.

I felt dizzy again and almost lost my balance. As I moved sideways the movement seemed to startle her. Her eyes darted toward me and so did the gun. Then I had another spasm. I felt it coming up to my throat again. This time I couldn't stop it. I doubled over quickly and turned my head away and vomited.

The next thing I knew I was sitting on the ground with my shoulder against my front tire. I couldn't remember how I'd gotten there. My mouth was so dry. She was kneeling beside me and looking at my face.

Then she opened her pocketbook with a jerk and reached in quickly. She took out a small packet of Kleenex. She began to offer it to me, then hesitated. Her eyes looked as scared and confused as before. She put the Kleenex on the ground and pushed it toward me with one finger.

I took several Kleenex out of the packet and wiped my mouth. I felt a little better now. I took some more Kleenex and wiped my forehead. Then I looked at her. She was looking past me. I slowly pushed the packet back toward her. It made a sound and she turned. Her eyes stared at the packet briefly, then drifted away and looked toward the darkness again. For some reason I reached out to touch her. As I did, she jerked back.

I waited. She stopped moving. I reached out again. This time she let me touch her gently on the arm. When I did, I found she was trembling. Then she pulled softly away from my hands and stood up. She took one step backward and began to turn, and then she began to shake. Her shoulders shivered, then shuddered; she seemed to be almost out of control. Her feet moved awkwardly against the ground. It was frightening to see. As I started to get up, she closed her pocketbook and snapped the clasp and held the pocketbook tight against herself, as if that would help her keep her balance. She turned again and tried to walk away. I had just taken a step toward her when she dropped the pocketbook. She turned again to look at it, and then everything seemed to go still. She wasn't tottering anymore. She was looking at me. "My pocketbook. . . . Please?" She wrapped her arms around herself. "Please?"

I picked it up and gave it to her. She opened it again. She took out a small bottle of pills and her hands fumbled with it. She was too nervous to get it open, so I took it away from her and pried it open and spilled blue-and-red capsules into my hand. "How many?"

"One." She breathed in sharply. "Just one."

I got one in my hand and held it out to her. "You need some water?"

"No."

She took the pill and swallowed it. She threw her head back to do it. Then she was quiet a moment with her eyes closed. Another moment passed. She wasn't shaking so bad now. Her eyes snapped open.

Then I was trying to close the bottle, and this time I couldn't make it work. Suddenly she took it from me and closed it herself.

"I'll be better now. Just give me a minute." She looked into the darkness again. She shivered once. "I need a drink." She turned around quickly. She looked at the neon that said THE DANCERS. "Not around here. Some place . . . far away from here." She faced me again. Her eyes were going back and forth rapidly. "They came back. Last time."

"What?"

She gulped. "Something like this happened to me once before. I had to scare some kids off. In Phoenix."

Her eyes blinked several times. "But they came back. Later. Looking for me." She waited for me to say something. "Please! I need a drink!"

I spoke quickly. "There's a place I go to. Up on Highland."

"Highland?" She began to shake again. I stepped forward automatically to put my arms around her and try to hold her still, but as soon as I moved she jerked back the same as before. "You said Highland?"

". . . Yeah. But it'd take at least twenty minutes to—"

"I've got a car. I'll follow you." She looked toward the ground behind me. "Could you . . . ?" Her hand gestured toward the ground.

I turned and saw the Kleenex packet. I bent down to pick it up. Then I saw what was next to it. The gun.

I stared at it. Up close, it looked different. Real, but then not quite so real. I couldn't believe it was possible. I picked it up. I felt its weight in my hand.

I still couldn't believe it. I turned the gun slowly and pointed it at my car. I pulled the trigger. A thin stream of water shot out of the barrel. It squirted against my car, splashed down the side and dribbled onto the ground.

I looked up at her. She said nothing. Her hand was out.

I gave her the water pistol and the Kleenex and watched silently as she put them quickly into her pocketbook. Then she turned. The next thing I knew, she was thirty feet away. She got into a yellow Volkswagen and it seemed like only a second later that the motor started. The lights snapped on, and she turned and looked at me. I turned away from her and stood absolutely still, and for a second I thought I was going to throw up again.

I held it down and got into my car and put my key in the ignition and turned on the motor. I stopped and balled my hands into fists. I squeezed them as tight as I could. When I looked around she was still staring at me. I could tell she needed to get away from there fast. So did I.

I put my car into reverse, backed out of the space and circled slowly toward the exit. The yellow Volkswagen was only half a car length behind me. I could see her face in my rearview mirror. She seemed so frightened. I drove carefully onto the street and turned left.

EACH time we stopped for a light my eyes crept toward the rearview mirror. Her face was always there looking back at me. I wanted to keep looking at her, but I didn't have the nerve. When we finally reached Highland, I turned left and drove north two blocks. I pulled into the parking lot at Tulley's Bar. The yellow Volkswagen pulled in right next to me. She did it so fast I thought she was going to scrape the side off my car. She realized she'd parked too tight and put the Volkswagen in reverse. She pulled out and then pulled in again so she had enough room to get out on the driver's side. I got out and went around the back of my car. She got out and came toward me. She didn't seem so shaky now. Apparently the pill had calmed her down. I started to say something and reached toward her slightly, but when I did she moved away from my hand and looked at it as if she was afraid it was going to do something to her. Then she went past me and into the bar.

We found an empty booth. I asked her what she wanted. She said anything was okay. I suggested wine. She said that was okay. I got a pitcher of sangría and brought it back to the booth. When I did, she was smiling.

I filled a glass for each of us. She barely sipped the wine. She didn't gulp like I'd seen her do earlier. She drank almost like a sixteen-year-old girl who was taking her first taste of anything harder than a Coke. It made no sense at all.

She'd had me hooked from the first moment I'd seen her sitting at the bar at The Dancers. But I hadn't thought I would've had a chance with her. I'd never known how to approach a girl who looked like this. So pretty. Oh yes, she was pretty. Up close she was small and fragile and even more beautiful than before. She looked as innocent as morning. And strangely enough, she was acting now as if she was as shy as I was.

I've always been shy. It's always held me back. Not just with girls. It's stopped me from selling myself the way an actor has to.

And of course the shyness is probably the reason I'd become an actor in the first place.

She didn't say anything and neither did I. We just looked at each other. Then I turned away and started looking everywhere *except* at her. When I looked around the room I saw so many familiar faces I said, "You could fill five unemployment offices with what's in here right now. Come Friday it'll happen." I tried looking at her again.

Her eyes hadn't moved off me. They weren't as self-conscious as mine were. But she still didn't speak.

"This is an actor's hangout. Guy that runs the place, he's very sympathetic to actors. You need a free meal, he'll carry you on the books. Long as you don't ask him to do it too often."

She nodded. Her mouth turned up slightly at the corners as she sipped more of her wine. Then she stopped and looked at her glass. She laughed. "This what you like to drink? Sangría?"

"Yeah, I usually stick to wine." I fumbled for something else to say. "I'm not too good, it comes to hard liquor. So I—" Then it hit me, what she really meant. I moved toward the edge of the booth. "You want something else, I can get you whatever you—"

"No. This is fine."

I wasn't sure if she meant it or was just saying it to

put me at ease. I was still ready to get her something else if she wanted it but she sipped the sangría, so I slid back into the booth. I waited for her to say something else and she didn't. I tried to smile. "Wine doesn't give me too many problems. But too much of anything else, I can't handle it. Makes me sick. I try to stick to wine."

"Better off that way." She nodded calmly. She seemed completely at ease now.

I wasn't. I could still feel the parking lot all the way down to my shoes. I forced a laugh. "Wish it was different. There's times I'd really like to get high. Least once. See what it's like." Then I slid across the seat again. "Look, really, it's all right, if you want something else—"

"No. I don't. This is fine." It came out firmly. I stopped moving. Her eyes wandered slowly across the room. "You're an actor."

I hesitated. "I pretend I am." I hesitated again. "All actors pretend everything, it's all part of the game."

"I've seen you." Her eyes came back suddenly. "You're on TV."

"What? No. I haven't been in a TV show for—" Then I realized. "Oh. You mean the commercial. You've seen the TV commercial."

She nodded. Now I felt lousy. She probably figured everyone who had a commercial on TV was somebody. Some are. Most aren't. I wasn't. She probably thought I was. I took a big gulp of sangría. "I made it two and a half years ago. My only commercial. They just started running it again."

"The man you were eating dinner with. He's an actor too, isn't he? He looked familiar."

"Yeah. He's Alan DeVoss." I took another gulp. A bigger one.

"Alan who?"

I looked up. "DeVoss. He's on a series. Starring in it."

"Oh." She nodded. "Then he must be doing okay."

"Very okay." I put down my glass. "You could've been sitting with him tonight, instead of me."

"What?" Her forehead wrinkled. "Oh. Yeah. Back when I was at the bar." Her head shook quickly. "No, I don't like men like that, they're too pushy. I don't like pushy people." She was silent. "I remember now, I saw

16

his show once. He must be doing really well. Are you doing really well?'

"Not exactly." I picked up the glass again.

She leaned forward. "It must be a really exciting business."

"Yeah. It must be. If you're *working*."

I was sorry the whole thing of actors and acting had come up. I was sorry she'd thought I was something I wasn't, even for that brief moment. I knew nothing was going to come of sitting here with her.

"I guess it's tough? Acting?"

"Tough enough."

Her eyes stayed on me. "Why do you do it?"

I hesitated. I didn't know what I was going to say. But her eyes were so clear and patient I had to say something. "Recognition, maybe. I mean, I can act, I really can. I know I can." I paused. "But I guess I need people telling me I can. Or at least, appreciating that I can." I looked away. "I don't know. It's what I do. What I try to do. I need . . ." I looked at her. "I need an audience. Every actor needs an audience. They're born needing it. There's something sick about it, but that's the way it is." I shrugged and looked away again. I tried to shake off my gloom.

But she seemed to want to hear more. She didn't seem to disapprove. She seemed interested. I went on. "Couple years ago, I was in New York. Did a small part on Broadway." I immediately felt guilty about the lie I'd been almost ready to tell. I held up my thumb and forefinger so they were only a quarter of an inch apart. "Just a small part. Very small. Minute. Six lines." I smiled. "But one of 'em was a laugh line, so it wasn't bad."

She smiled back at me. "Everyone's got to start off somewhere."

"Yeah. Guess so." I laughed weakly. "Only problem is, some end up where they start."

I was really talking stupid. The Broadway part. If I was going to say anything to her about it at all, why didn't I say it *smart?* Why didn't I build it up and make it seem like it'd *been* something? *She* wouldn't know.

Because I wasn't the kind for that. Never had been.

But for some reason she was still interested. Or at least seemed to be. I leaned forward and even felt a little better. "Some people said I ought to give L.A. a try, so I came out here. First year, I got some work, here and there." Here and there had been TV, not movies. And the TV hadn't been the good shows. And the parts hadn't been the good parts. God, I felt rotten again. The same as always. "Then everything dried up. That's the way it is, huh? L.A. Things seem to dry up fast in L.A. I guess it's all the sun."

She laughed. Laughed?

I kept on. "I don't know what it is they're looking for. The people who do the hiring. Must be something, huh? Just whatever it is, I don't seem to be it." But even while saying that, I felt so good looking at her that I was smiling like an idiot. "Maybe if I was two inches taller, with darker hair!" I sat up straight. She nodded as I did it. "Or seven inches shorter!" I scrunched down. "And bald!" She laughed. "Or maybe, if I looked like . . ." I spread my mouth wide open and let my tongue drag out the corner. I crossed my eyes and made sounds like a monkey in a zoo.

People must have been looking at me, but I didn't care. She was laughing her head off. I kept making the sounds. When she finished laughing, she sat there grinning at me like I was the best show she'd ever seen.

I kept going. "Or maybe this is what they want!" I curled my lips in so I'd look toothless, then I started nodding my head up and down and swiveling it slowly from one side to the other, as if I were a turtle. She laughed even louder at this one. I could see a couple at a table looking at me as if I were crazy, but I didn't give a damn. I didn't know how many more faces I could come up with, but I kept at it. She seemed to love the third one. She clapped for the fourth.

Applause! God, it was the first time I'd heard it for over a year and a half! I almost stood up and took a bow!

I refilled her glass and refilled mine. We held our glasses up and she clinked hers against mine. "To making it!"

"Yeah! I hope I do! This is a hard city to crack! For everyone!"

Not for everyone. Not for someone who was sure of himself. Like Alan.

I was silent a moment. "This city." I inhaled. "It

knows how to pound you to bits. And soon as it does it, they roll a freeway over what's left of you."

I meant it serious, but she didn't take it that way. She laughed again like I'd made a joke.

So I pretended I had. I clinked my glass against hers. "Just got to find a way to stop it from getting to you. Right?"

"Right!" Her glass came back against mine so hard I expected them both to crack. "You found a way?"

That did it. I lost my grin. I put down my glass. I pulled out my cigarettes and rolled one between my fingers. She was still waiting for me to answer her. "Sure. I found a way. I believe in my talent."

But the way I said it, she must've known I didn't. It was pretty bad. All the tension I'd felt earlier when I'd been with Alan. Watching him sign autographs, watching him pay for dinner. Hearing about his renegotiated contract and his new Malibu mansion. Good ingredients for sending you home empty and confused and lost. Even her smiles and laughs couldn't change that.

Her hand crept across the table and touched mine. It surprised the hell out of me. Each time before when I'd tried to touch her she'd pulled away. I'd thought she didn't want to be touched. But now she was reaching out toward me. Her hand covered mine gently. "This town can get lonely, too."

I looked at our hands and then at her eyes. "Yeah. Lonely as they come."

We stayed that way, looking at each other. This time I didn't have the feeling I had to look away.

But then a voice said, "Hi, baby! Figured I'd find you here!"

"Tell me if I'm intruding, baby!"

"You're intruding." I said it as if it'd be worth something, but it was worth absolutely nothing. Ruth gave me a tired smile and enough of a shove to push me farther into the booth. She sat down next to me. Her fingers dragged slowly through her hair. Her eyes closed for a moment. The girl's hand wasn't on mine anymore.

Ruth's eyes popped open. She beamed at my glass of sangría. "Ah! Nectar of the gods!" She took it and drank some. She saw the cigarette in my fingers and took that.

She lit it with a flourish and puffed smoke. She looked across the table at the girl and smiled and then looked back at me. "What's the matter, baby? Aren't you going to introduce us?"

Ruth was doing her tough act, but I knew it was just an act. I could tell by her eyes she was scared the way she was always scared whenever she saw me with another woman. And as usual I didn't have any idea what to do about it.

I looked at the girl across the table from me again. "This is my agent, Ruth Shapiro. Ruth, this—"

"So! How you doing today, Jake?" Ruth laughed and drank sangría. She moved closer to me and puffed more smoke. She pushed the cigarette at me. I didn't take it, but she kept pushing it.

"Ruth, this is—"

"Yeah? Who?" Ruth cut me off again. She was really coming on. I was worried that Ruth being so aggressive with me would make me seem like less to the girl, but I couldn't stop Ruth from doing it. Once Ruth got going, nobody could stop her. Besides, I understood too well why she was doing it. She turned abruptly and stared at the girl. "Well? So what's the story? This is . . . ?"

The girl didn't say. She just sat there. I looked at her, Ruth looked at her, then Ruth laughed and looked at me. Ruth cocked her head to the side and looked at the girl again.

The girl spoke softly. "Katie."

"Katie?" Ruth's voice was full and open. "That all the name they gave you?"

The girl didn't answer.

Ruth stretched her arm over my shoulder so her fingers could caress my neck. The same way she'd done it that other time she'd walked into a restaurant and found me sitting with a girl. I'd pushed Ruth's arm away that time. It had taken me two weeks to get her talking to me again. This time I didn't touch her arm.

Ruth kept smiling at the girl. "You in the business?"

The girl looked startled and confused now, just like she'd been in the parking lot. She obviously wasn't used to people like Ruth. The kind of people L.A. was full of. I tried to move gently out from under Ruth's arm, but there was no room. "There's still some around town who aren't in the business, Ruth."

"Yeah? Who?"

I tried joking. "Cops. Dentists. Certified public—"

Ruth didn't laugh. She cut me off again. "Don't count on it! They're *all* in the business! Or *trying* to get in! *Every one* of them!"

Then the girl stood up. Her hand went into her pocketbook, came right back out, dropped two dollar bills on the table. "Excuse me."

She turned away quickly and left the booth. She walked toward the front.

I waved my hand at her. "Hey!" I tried to stand. Ruth wedged herself against me and trapped me against the inside of the booth.

"Hey, yourself." She grabbed my arm and pulled it down. I took a quick look at her face and knew what I was seeing there. But I still wanted to stop the girl.

I turned and could only see her head and shoulders now. She was moving quickly. I could've yelled her name out. Could've called to her. To come back. I could've. But I didn't. I just watched her walk toward the front door. I felt Ruth moving closer to me and touching my arm. And then it didn't matter. The girl was out the front door and gone.

A moment passed. Ruth moved slightly away from me. Her hand left my arm. She was embarrassed to look at me now. She toyed with the sangría glass. "Heard a rumor, Jake." I said nothing. "About Alan. He renegotiated his contract." I remained silent. "Twelve thou an episode."

I exploded. "I know! He's a star! So?"

I put my elbows on the table and leaned forward with my hands clasped in front of me. I spoke normally. "He's moving out. To Malibu. Not moving. Already moved. Didn't even have the guts to tell me about it till tonight."

"That's how it is, Jake. They make it, they start new lives. They leave whatever they used to have behind 'em."

"He isn't leaving everything. He's sticking with Jill." I couldn't stop myself from looking toward the front door again.

"Sure, Jake. He knows she'll kill him, he doesn't stick with her. Give him time. He'll dump her, too. Just wait." Ruth puffed hungrily at the cigarette. She watched me. I was still looking at the front door. Her voice got soft, the way it usually was. "All right, baby. I'm sorry. I get jealous easily."

I said nothing.

She bent forward so she could see my eyes. "I mean it. I apologize."

I didn't react.

She moved away toward the corner and looked down. "All right. What do you want me to do? Run outside and see if she's still in the parking lot?"

I ran my hand along the pitcher of sangría.

Ruth moved an inch closer. "Okay. Want to hit me?"

"Yeah. But I'm not a hitter."

"I know. That's why I made the offer." Her hand touched my cheek. "What do you think I am? A fool?"

She slid along the seat so she was nuzzled against me again. Her fingers tapped gently on my arm. I knew what she wanted. I put my arm around her. She quickly pulled it tight. She opened my hand and kissed my palm. I didn't react. She looked at me again. "Baby? You okay tonight?"

"Sure."

"Yeah? *Really* sure?" She paused. "Alan's off to Malibu. That means you're alone now." I felt a shiver go through me when she said that. She raised my hand so it was against her cheek. "You need company. *I* need company."

"I need work."

"Sure." She kissed my hand again. "I'm trying, baby. It's slimsville."

"Not for Alan, it isn't!" It started getting to me again. I turned and looked her in the eye. "I can act circles around him! He admits it himself!"

Her fingers touched my lips. "So what? He's got two things, Jake, enough talent to get by and enough luck to get the breaks when he needs 'em. You got more talent, but the breaks can be a hell of a lot more important. And they either happen, or they don't."

I chose my words carefully to strike back at her for

the way she'd just been with me and the girl. "Then what do I need an agent for, if they just happen?"

She pulled away an inch and puffed the cigarette evenly. "To *recognize* the breaks, when they happen."

She took the cigarette from her mouth and put it between my lips. I took it. "The Taper's doing *Othello*, Ruth. I heard they're still looking."

"Yeah. For Cassio. They had one, but he left to make a movie. No money at the Taper, Jake."

"So what? Can you get me an interview?"

My own words surprised me. An hour before, I wouldn't have asked her to get me an interview. An hour before, I'd felt half dead. But ten minutes ago a girl had laughed and applauded me and asked me questions about myself. As if she cared.

Now I wanted an interview. "Get me an interview, Ruth! I mean it!"

Ruth studied her cigarette. She took one more puff and then tapped it lightly against the ashtray and killed it. "First thing they'll say is you haven't been on a stage in two and a half years. You haven't done Shakespeare in four. Even if you got the part, the kind of money—"

"Don't give me that stuff!" I slammed the table with my hand. "I haven't been on a stage 'cause you don't want me tied up in case something good comes along! And nothing good comes along!"

"Hold it, Jake. I'm not finished." Her voice was firm but soft. "Five weeks of rehearsal. Six-week run. Think about it. That's eleven weeks tied up for no money. Don't tell me it's prestige—it's prestige for some star that's already made it and can afford to show everybody he still knows how to act. As if he ever could. This isn't New York, Jake. Let's not get you stuck in that kind of thing just to feed your ego. I'd rather find you something that'll feed this." Her hand patted my stomach. "Don't care what they say, baby. Stomachs are a lot more important to take care of than egos."

"I'll be happy, you find me something that'll take care of either one of 'em. God, Ruth, just find me some words to say! A part! Something I can do! I don't know if I can take much more of it!"

She nodded slowly. "I know. I'll find you something. I will."

But when?

Ruth drank what was left in the glass. She picked up the girl's two dollar bills and inspected them as if she doubted they were real. She put them down, opened her pocketbook and took out her wallet. "I'll get the drinks."

"You might as well. You drank 'em."

"Umm. They were delicious." She kissed my nose. She put down her money and slid out of the booth.

I looked at her money. "Glad you got a couple clients you're making money off of."

She held her hand out to me. "Look at it this way, baby. I make it off them, I can find a way to make it off you. Patience and persistence."

"They'll make that my epitaph."

I took her hand and we went outside. I stood by my car. The yellow Volkswagen wasn't parked next to it anymore.

Ruth leaned against my car and yawned. "Tough day, baby. Mel loused up a deal and started yelling at all of us. Wish he'd find someone else to take it out on."

"Bosses are all the same." I stared at the empty space next to my car. "Was it a good deal? The one you lost?"

"We didn't lose it. Mel almost did, but I saved it. Went over to Universal and argued my head off and got it fixed up. Ten men in the goddamn room and me, but I got 'em up to what we wanted." She laughed. "They didn't know how to handle a woman. Men never do." Her eyes closed. Her head shook back and forth. "But Christ, Jake, the way I got to act sometimes, the business is killing me! I'm not even a woman anymore!" Her hand rubbed her forehead. "I don't know what I am. This is a man's business, a lousy man's business." She yawned again. "No, I know what I am. Tired. Tired and worn out. Sometimes I think it's just ten years of doing it that *keeps* me doing it. I can keep dancing 'cause I know all the steps. But sometimes the dance can get awfully dreary."

I hated it whenever she talked that way. I needed her to be strong, strong as iron. Usually she *was* strong. But sometimes I wondered if she was strong enough. It scared me whenever it seemed like she wasn't.

She laughed bitterly. "Well, I've done the steps so far. I guess I can keep doing 'em. But sometimes I just don't know. It's starting to take a little too much out of me, Jake."

God. No actor wants to hear his agent sound that way. Confused and doubtful. If there's one thing an actor needs it's an agent he can rely on. He's dead without that.

Ruth read the look on my face. She straightened up and slapped her hands together. "Well! By tomorrow we'll be all moved into our new offices! Ought to bring us luck, Jake!" She touched my arm. *"All* of us!"

I nodded. I turned and unlocked my car door. She stepped closer. "Going to be lonely tonight, baby."

I thought of the girl again. The way she'd left. It was already lonely.

"You know, baby, Alan's gone. You'll be going home to an empty house."

That made me feel worse. I'd always lived with someone. At home. In college. In New York. Out here. I'd never had to face an empty apartment or house by myself before. I had no idea what being alone might be like."

"Want some company tonight?"

I hesitated. I looked at her.

Then I turned away. "No thanks." I opened the car door.

"Going to be *alone,* baby."

I froze. Then I spoke. "We're all alone, aren't we?" I paused. "I can handle it."

She nodded. But she stepped closer. She held out her hands. I looked at her a moment and then finally took her hands and pulled her close and kissed her, which was what she was waiting for me to do. She nodded again, kissed me on the nose and said good night. Then she went across the lot to her car.

I stood there a minute replaying the evening in my mind.

The girl. I could hardly remember what she'd looked like. I could remember the separate parts. The hair. The look in her eyes. The smile. But I couldn't fit it all together so it looked right. And I couldn't quite hear the sound of her laugh. The feeling she'd given me—it was almost completely gone.

I got into my car and drove to the exit. I was thinking about making it now, and the thoughts were giving me the shakes again. I sat there waiting for a break in the traffic when a car horn sounded behind me. I felt a sudden hope and looked quickly into the rearview mirror, and a face looked back at me. But it was Ruth.

I nodded at her. She nodded back. I turned right and drove onto Highland. I checked the mirror after half a block. Ruth was still there. I didn't look into the rearview mirror again, not once all the way home.

I pulled up in front of my house, turned off the motor and sat in the darkness. Ruth's car pulled up next to me. She got out and waited. I looked at her tired eyes and drawn face. The limpness of her hair. The way she slouched, like she always did at the end of the day.

"What're you doing, Jake? Worrying about the rent?" She slowly took out a cigarette and then didn't have the energy to light it.

I almost put my car into reverse and drove away. It wasn't that I didn't like Ruth. The truth was I liked her a lot. But it didn't go much further than that, and I knew it. Whatever it was that I needed, she just wasn't it.

"Listen, baby, you need money, I got a way you can make it. I'll talk to Mel, we'll set it up for you to come into the agency."

I breathed in sharply and got out of my car. "No thank you. I don't want to make money off of people like me." I went past her, unlocked the front door and went into the dark house.

"That's the attitude of a pauper, baby." Then she sighed. "Of course, with someone like Mel yelling at you all the time, maybe I ought to have the same attitude. God, sometimes I wonder why I stick."

Why did she always have to go *on* about it that way? I didn't want to hear about how hard it was to be an agent! I just wanted her to do her job! Get me some work!

We went down the hall and into the living room. She hit the light switch. The overhead light went on and there was a small pop. Ruth flipped the light switch back and forth quickly, but we remained in darkness. I looked up at the dead light bulb.

"You know I don't have any more light bulbs in the

house, don't you!" I raised my fist at it. "You been waiting till I came home late one night to do this to me, right? If that's what you want, all right! Put up your dukes and come down here and fight like a man!"

Ruth finally laughed a little, but it was forced. The girl's laughs hadn't been forced. Not a single one of them.

I could hear Ruth yawn. "He come down yet, Jake?"

"No. He's scared."

"Sure he's scared. Just like the rest of us."

I looked at her in the darkness. I felt mean and angry. And lost.

Then I changed. Okay, she had problems too. One of us was going to have to cheer the other up, and if she couldn't do it, I'd have to. I went to her and put my arms around her and growled. I bit playfully at her neck. "Come on, Ruth. Let's talk."

"Talk? About what?"

I held her tighter. "I don't know. About you. About me. But not about the business. Anything but the business. Okay?"

"Sure."

But she didn't talk. All she did was kiss me.

She kept at it, so I kissed her back. But then I walked away and flopped on the sofa and stared at the dark ceiling. She came over and knelt on the floor beside me. She kissed me again. It was better this time. I guess we both enjoyed it. I guess the darkness helped.

Then I started laughing. "Oh God."

"Jake?"

I sighed. "I don't know. I just don't know."

She tried kissing me again, but now it was no good. She gave up finally, walked across the room and turned on the table lamp. At least that bulb worked.

I wish it hadn't. She looked down at the stack of pictures on the table. "Going to get new pictures or not?"

That brought me back to reality. I got to my feet and shoved both hands into my pockets. Pictures. Pictures.

When you're an actor you've got pictures. You've always got pictures. You send them to casting agents and producers and directors. Assistant producers and assistant directors and assistant assistants. You send them to mailroom clerks. Janitors. Relatives of someone in the business. Friends of a friend who knows a girl who's a

27

secretary to someone in the business. You send them to anyone who might take an interest in you. And none of them ever does. It doesn't matter, you still send them out.

Pictures. I'd had these taken ten months before. I still had about a hundred left. I wished I'd had none. I'd reached the point where I could hardly stand to look at the damn things any longer. They'd become symbols of failure.

"Yeah. I'm going to get new pictures."

"Good! When?"

"Soon."

"Good! When's soon?"

I mumbled something.

"Been soon for about three months, baby."

"Soon as you get me a job and I get some money! Then I'll get some new pictures!"

She hesitated. "Maybe as soon as you get some new pictures, I'll be able to get you a job." I said nothing. "You want to be an actor? All right, then you got to play the game! *You* picked the game, Jake, not me!" I still said nothing. She came toward me. "Get new pictures, Jake! You got to learn to do things for yourself, damn it! You're as bad as three-quarters of the actors I handle! You expect too much of an agent! Your career's *your* responsibility too! If you need new pictures—"

"I'll get 'em! Lay off it, Ruth! I'll get 'em!"

She shut up. I guess we both felt bad about it. We'd both had a tough day. I'd had a day of nothing. As usual. No calls, no auditions, nothing. She'd had a day of Mel. Which was just as bad. And arguing her head off at Universal. It was a tough day on all of us. Even the light bulb.

Her fingers went to her neck and stayed there a moment, then floated downward. They reached the top button of her blouse and unbuttoned it. Then the next button.

I turned away and looked at the line of liquor bottles on the bookcase. They were Alan's bottles. I wasn't much of a drinker. But there was vodka there. Sometimes I drank vodka. When I needed it bad enough.

I reached for the bottle. "I got to find a new photographer first. A good one who works cheap. Very cheap. Ever heard of one?"

She didn't answer. She finished with the blouse and then unzipped her skirt. She stepped out of it. Just one look at her eyes told me how much she wanted me.

But I couldn't do it. All her talk of how tough it was being an agent. Telling me I had to take responsibility for my own career. I knew she was right, of course, but she should've known better than to say it that night.

I didn't go to her. I put down the bottle and went past her and down the hall to the bedroom. I emptied my pockets. Spilled wallet and coins and keys across the top of my dresser. I didn't bother to turn on the light. I could see well enough without it, and I figured, with my luck that night, I'd probably end up blowing another bulb. I put a cigarette in my mouth, then searched for matches.

"Going to be hard on you, baby. Without Alan. Being alone."

Alone! Why did she have to keep saying that?

"I know you, baby. You need someone to be with. Someone to get you going. Tell you what to do. Keep your spirits up. Besides, he gave you someone to compete with."

"Yeah?" I laughed. "That sure helped me a lot!" I tried again to shake off my fears. "It's all right, I'll get along without him."

"I'm not saying you won't. I think you will. I'm just saying it'll be hard. At first. Readjusting."

"That so?" I toughened my voice. "Consider me readjusted! As of now!"

"All right! That's what I want to hear!" But then she went quiet. "Don't worry, baby. Everything'll work out. Just a matter of time. Stick with me. I'll make sure you get there."

Would she? She sounded as scared as I was.

I lit a match. She was standing in the doorway. She wasn't wearing a thing now. The flame from the match did wonderful things for her. She knew it.

But that wasn't what got me. It was knowing that she needed someone as bad as I needed someone. I started to move toward her.

But then I stopped. "I want that audition, Ruth. *Othello.*"

"Jake, it's no use for you to go down there and—"

"I said I want it!"

We were silent. We kept looking at each other till the match burned out. Then neither of us moved.

"All right, Jake. I'll give 'em a call. Tomorrow."

I swallowed hard. I felt triumphant, but I also felt guilty about it. "All right. Then it's settled."

I moved toward her. I put my hand on her neck and then slowly stroked down along her shoulder. I stepped closer and brought my other hand along her side. She took my hand and raised it to her breast. I rubbed her gently. She just stood there. "Yes. Yes."

I wanted her to do something. But she just stood there. And let me stroke her.

I picked her up finally and carried her to the bed. She lay there passively as I began to kiss her. Her mouth. Her breast. Down across her stomach. I wanted her to do something, or at least say something, to tell *me* what she wanted *me* to do, but she didn't. She just ran her fingers through my hair and kept saying yes.

Finally her legs spread apart. I put my hand between them. Then she began to moan. "Oh God! That feels so good! Yes, Jake! Yes!" She turned and looked at me, and her eyes were full of love, or something very close to love, so I put my other hand on her breast and then her eyes closed and she began to moan louder.

It made me feel good making her feel this way, but what I really wanted was for her to *do* something. Something besides just *lying* there.

But all she did was keep moaning. Then she dug her feet into the bed and started lifting herself up against my hands.

When I entered her, she was wide open. She was warm and ready and smiling and happy and crying a little. I took it really slow because I knew she liked it that way. I knew it out of past experience. Not because she was telling me anything. Asking me to slow down or speed up. I'd been so shaken up by all the things that'd happened that night, I would've liked her to take control, but she didn't. She never did in bed.

She enjoyed it that night. Ruth was one of those who always enjoyed it. I enjoyed it too, even if it wasn't all I really wanted. I liked Ruth. Liked her a lot. And she was there.

It was a lonely town, Los Angeles. Maybe we'd made it a little less lonely for another night.

I was lying on my back, half asleep. Ruth was lying next to me with her leg across my stomach. Her fingertips were caressing my cheek. They did it gently, as if I were a baby. Every few moments, her lips would brush the side of my arm. It felt nice. Part of me wanted to respond again, but I controlled it and lay there quietly with just one arm around her. I tried to empty my mind and hoped for sleep. Then I felt her whole body tense up.

"Ruth?"

"Shh."

"What's the—"

"Shh!" She moved slightly. Her voice was scared. "There's someone at the window."

"What?"

"Just now! Didn't you hear it?"

I began to sit up.

"No, Jake!" She reached for me. "I just saw someone out there! I'm sure!"

All I could see was darkness. I waited a moment, then moved away from Ruth. I got off the bed. I waited again. I slipped along the wall toward the window. I reached it, hesitated, then moved so I could look directly through the glass. There was nothing there. The window was a few inches open. I set my right hand under it and pushed up gently. It squeaked.

"Jake—"

"Shh."

I got the window open far enough so I could put my head through the opening. I couldn't see anything except bushes and trees and the half moon. I pushed the window farther up, balanced on the sill and leaned out. My shoulder brushed the window and it made a small noise, and then I heard another noise to my right.

Maybe it was a twig snapping. Maybe it was something else. Whatever it was, something was out there. Moving, I pulled myself back into the bedroom and pressed my back against the wall. I felt as scared as I'd felt in that parking lot when those kids had come at me.

But I had to do something. I pulled on my pants and found my sneakers. I jammed them on my feet.

"What're you doing?"

My mouth was dry. "I'm going to take a look."

"What if there's someone out—"

"Nobody's out there! . . . I'll look, just in case, but nobody's out there. Stay here and stay quiet."

I left the sneakers untied and went slowly across the bedroom.

"Jake? You got a gun or something? A knife?"

"God, no."

"Take a baseball bat or something."

"I don't have a baseball bat. Be quiet."

I went down the hall and into the living room. My mind was racing. I had a flashlight. The flashlight was in my car. My car was in front of the house. I sure wasn't going outside with a candle. As for a weapon, I didn't even have a fly swatter. It made no difference. I wasn't going to go out there. I'd look through the windows, that's all.

I looked through the living-room window and saw nothing.

Then I knew I *was* going to go out there. It was a stupid thing to do. I knew it was stupid as I thought about it. And I knew I was going to do it. If Alan had been there, he would've done it. But he wasn't there. So I had to.

If I went out the front door and there was someone out there and they heard me and they wanted to get away, which way would they go? Right to where I'd be. The front. But if I went out the back door, that would leave the front as a way for them to escape. I was more interested in letting them escape than trying to catch them. Catch them? I didn't even want to see them.

I should've played it smart and just sat in the house. Called the police. Waited to see if the police gave a damn. But I was stupid and didn't do that. Thank God. I went into the kitchen and unlatched the back door, stood there a full minute trying to get up some courage, then stepped out softly.

I looked this way and that. I saw nothing. I let go of the door and stepped out into the small yard but stayed close to the house. I looked toward the woods. Saw nothing. Heard nothing. And knew someone was there.

I went slowly to the ground. My hand swept the grass and found some small rocks. I stayed low. I tried not to breathe. My hand swung up. The rocks sailed at the woods. Some of them hit trees. Immediately, there was movement. It was at the side of the house, farther away than I'd expected.

From the bedroom window came, "Jake?"

"It's okay, stay inside."

I was crouched on the ground. I had decided I wasn't going to move again, but it didn't work. My curiosity got the better of my fear. I got up and went around the corner toward the front yard.

It was the same thing again. I saw nothing, heard nothing. Seconds passed. Minutes, it seemed like. It couldn't have been that long. It always seems longer when you're scared and don't know what you're up against. And don't know how long it's going to be before something happens. Or stops happening.

I heard a noise ten feet away. I jumped before I realized it was only the front door opening. Ruth was there, wearing my robe.

"Jake? You all right?"

I almost screamed. "I'm okay! Close the door and—"

A car engine started down the road. It sounded like it was at least fifty feet away. Without thinking, I ran from the house. I crossed the front yard and went onto the dirt road. I ran straight toward the sound. I kept running faster and faster. I got close to the car. Close enough to see it pull away. Close enough to see that it was a Volkswagen, and yellow.

I stood there a long time. I watched the car's taillights get small. Disappear in the darkness.

Finally I heard Ruth calling to me from the house. I went back up the road to her. When she asked me what I'd seen, I said I'd seen nothing, just a car driving away. I said it must've been some kid.

I held Ruth till she calmed down, and then she slept. But I didn't. Not a wink all night. She woke up around six, and when she began to move I closed my eyes and stayed quiet. She dressed silently so as not to wake me and then bent over the bed and kissed me on the forehead. I still stayed quiet. As soon as I heard her car pull away, I got up and put on some clothes and went out to the kitchen. I wasn't hungry, but I made coffee anyway. I figured I ought to have something, and coffee was at least a gesture toward food. I sat at the kitchen table for about an hour and stared at the coffee and burned my way through cigarettes. I heard a noise at the front door, and the suddenness of it almost made me jump out of my skin. Then I realized it was the sound of a key in the lock. Feet wandered through the house and came down the hall to the kitchen. When they reached the doorway they stopped.

"How you like it Jake?" He was wearing a T-shirt with his picture on it. He puffed out his chest and turned so his image was glaring straight at me. As sure and as proud of himself as ever. "Goes on sale end of the week! I get two cents, every one they sell!"

"Twelve thousand an episode isn't enough for you, huh?"

"Hardly!" He laughed. He looked at me with his killer smile. Then he saw what I looked like, and his hands opened up apologetically. "Sorry. I'm not trying to rub it in."

"I can see that. Thanks a lot."

"What's the matter, Jake? Come on! Snap out of it! Day's just beginning!" He rubbed his hands together with the energy of a football coach sending his team out to meet a team he knew they could beat.

Mornings with Alan were always like that. Alan was always ready for whatever was coming, and he tried to get me to be that way too. Sometimes it worked, but it wouldn't work any longer. He wouldn't be here in the morning any longer. It'd all be up to me.

"Hey! Come on, Jake! Cheer up!"

"Yeah? What've *you* got scheduled for today?"

"Ha! Too much!" He looked at his watch. "Got to be over at Universal in an hour. Probably be shooting till eight tonight."

"You got my sympathy. You got a very tough life. I can see how it's getting you down."

"Hey, Jake! Come on!"

I shrugged and said nothing. He leaned against the wall, crossed his arms over his chest and gave me a look. "That's the way you want to be this morning?"

"Yeah." I took a long drag on my cigarette. I tried to get my mind onto the yellow Volkswagen again. But I couldn't. Not with Alan's face on his T-shirt staring at me that way. "Got an interview this afternoon. Commercial."

"Hey! That's great!"

They were only three words, but he said them with such enthusiasm, such excitement, such lack of fear. I knew that when I went to the interview that afternoon there'd be an actor just like him who'd come in with that same kind of enthusiasm and excitement and lack of fear. *That* actor would get the job. That actor wouldn't be me.

I took the dying cigarette in my fingers and sneered at it. "What the hell's so great about it? I won't get the damn thing."

I said it as if my acceptance of the inevitable failure

meant I was prepared for it. I didn't give a damn. Of course I *did* give a damn, and Alan knew it. He kept looking at me.

I flipped the cigarette into the air. It made a perfect arc and landed just where I wanted it. In my half-empty coffee cup. It sat there in the dimly colored liquid. I waited for it to soak up enough coffee to drown, but it didn't. It just floated on the surface like a piece of rotting wood in the middle of an unfriendly ocean.

I went into the living room and still felt masochistic, so I stood by the table and looked at my stack of pictures. God, I hated them. They were the things I sent out to get me jobs. They didn't get me jobs. I wanted to incinerate the damn things.

I settled for the destruction of just one picture. I took it by one edge and ripped it straight down the middle. I put the two pieces together, one on top of the other, and ripped again. Then I ripped the four pieces. The eight pieces wouldn't rip so I took them into the kitchen and used a scissors on them. I singed them with a match, then blew out the flame and dumped the mess in the garbage. I put away the scissors and returned to the living room. I picked up the rest of the stack but was smart enough not to start the process again. I couldn't afford to throw away a good-sized financial investment. I tapped the pictures lightly on the table till they were lined up and squared off and put them in the exact center of the table, as neat as neat could be. I sat on the sofa and brooded for a while.

Alan came in with a suitcase and cardboard box. He put them down and looked at me. He understood exactly what he was seeing. He was enough of a friend to be concerned. He spoke gently. "You all right?"

He was so damn genuine about it I couldn't stand it. I hated myself. Why couldn't he hate me, too?

"Sure I'm all right! Go off to your TV show! Go off to Malibu! Go off to wherever the hell you go off to when you make it! Never-Never land! Nirvana! El Dorado! Just go already!"

It didn't bother him at all. He'd been through it himself. Only one difference. He'd found a way to get through it. And past it.

He sat in the chair and gave me a moment, then he said, "You got to stop it, Jake."

"Do I?"

"Yeah. You're letting this place beat you."

"What place?"

"L.A. You're scared of this town."

Sure I was scared. I knew what he knew. That I wasn't going to make it.

I rubbed the side of my neck and looked blankly across the living room.

"You're letting yourself get scared of everything, Jake. Your confidence is gone. Everyone knows it. You make sure they know it. You're turning yourself into a loser." He paused. "You didn't used to be like that. You used to be a hell of a lot stronger. You could be again."

Could I? All right! I'd show him stronger! "Easy to make speeches when you're pulling in twelve thousand a week, isn't it? You ought to be spending that much on acting lessons, but they probably wouldn't help much, would they?"

And then I laughed at him. A good strong laugh. It was nice and bitter and I enjoyed it. I could see by his face I'd gotten to him. He knew he was a mediocre actor, and he didn't like anyone else reminding him of it. I knew it would stop him from feeling sorry for me and it happened. He struck back like I wanted him to.

"Jesus Christ, you know why I'm making it? 'Cause I got enough balls to make it! I know how to push and shove and hustle! And I don't give a damn what anyone says about me! So I been turned down a couple times myself, you know! So what? I don't let it stop me!" He was out of his chair now and his arms were waving. "You know why I'm moving out of here?"

"No! Tell me!"

" 'Cause I can't take *you* anymore! I can't take getting depressed watching *you* get depressed! I've gone that route! I've gone through a year and a half of it! It doesn't get any of us anywhere! It's just a stupid waste! As far as I'm concerned, it's over! I'm past it! I'm finished with it!"

He did it nice and loud like I thought he would. Actually, it was the first decent performance I'd ever seen him give. And I was glad. Now *I* could get nice and loud. He'd given me all the excuse I needed.

I stood up and stepped forward like a leading man taking center stage. I pointed a finger at the smiling face on his T-shirt and let him have it with every ounce of talent in me. "Good for you, sweetheart! I can't tell you how happy I am for you! Tell me when you're ready to incorporate and open yourself up to the public, I want to buy shares in you! Then I can watch you make it all the way to the top! I can collect a nice yearly dividend off the profits!"

We stared at each other. He laughed. What was he laughing about?

"Christ, Jake! If only you could do that in front of a director, in front of a camera, you'd be as big as anyone in this city!"

That cut it. He'd seen right through me. That really got me mad. "This isn't an act, goddamn it! I mean this!" I held up my fist. I wanted to hit him. "You know what I want? What I *really* want? To be a good actor?" I paused for barely a second. "No! Not on your life! I want a little bit of the fun!" I watched his reaction. "That's right! The money! The TV shows! The T-shirts! The houses in Malibu!" I laughed. "Yeah! The groupies who want to measure you for a plaster cast. The gravy! The green stuff! Easy Street! That's what I want!" I stepped closer to him. I was getting to him now. This time he *did* believe me. I went further. "Wasting time in New York? Doing off-Broadway? Off-off-Broadway? Going out to Podunk to do off-off-off-Broadway? The hell with it! I don't want that anymore! I want to do it your way, Alan! The quick way! No stage work, no nothing! Just make the rounds, huh? Kiss some ass, huh? Smile a lot! Nod your head! Find some hungry women with connections! Sleep with 'em whether you like 'em or not, and pretty soon they get you into your own goddamn TV show! You're king of the mountain, right? And the hell with anyone who isn't king!"

Then I turned my back on him and shut up.

Alan and I had lived together for pretty close to two years. You say lots of stupid things to a guy in two years. But I'd never said anything as stupid as this. Another time, another place, another mood, I'd have laughed at myself for flying off the handle. I think he would have laughed too. We both knew the ways bitterness comes spilling out of you before you can stop it.

But right then neither of us laughed. One of us had made it. The other never would. There was no laughing about a thing like that.

I hated myself. I stared at the wall. "You're right, Alan. I'm a loser. I've turned myself into a loser, you've turned yourself into a winner. Better get away from me. What I've got is probably contagious. You don't want it. I don't want to give it to you." I moved away.

He started to say something but I cut him off. "Aw, what the hell, huh? Take it while you can get it, right? Good luck!"

He grabbed my arm. "Come on, Jake! You're not going to get anything! Not as long as you got the smell of fear on you!"

"I know!"

"Then do something about it!"

"I've been trying to!" I tried to move away. "It hasn't been working!"

"Jake! If I can make it, you can make it too!"

"No I can't!"

I knew the tears were about to start. I tore away from him and went into the kitchen. I heard him coming after me, so I went out the back door. Into the woods. When I heard him at the back door, I went farther through the trees. I stood where he couldn't see me, like a dog who wants to hide under a bush so nobody will know where he is while he waits to see if his sickness is going to go away or kill him.

I wasn't completely gone. By eleven o'clock I'd pulled myself together well enough to shave without slashing my throat. I'd dressed myself so well I could probably even walk the streets without getting picked up for vagrancy. I'd fed myself. Smoked another cigarette. I'd gone back to the bedroom for another look at myself in the mirror. When I saw myself, I tried to copy Alan's killer smile. But I couldn't copy his eyes. Or his confidence. Or his ego.

I thought about all the things I *might* be able to do.

I didn't do any of them. I didn't put on my best suit,

didn't even put on a cleaner shirt and better pants. Didn't go out and get the haircut I needed. I looked all right the way I was. If they really wanted me, they'd take me, even looking like this.

No, I wasn't fooling myself. I knew I should've changed my appearance *and* my emotions. But something inside me knew if I did make the effort to look as good as I could—if I did get a haircut and put on a better shirt and splash expensive-smelling cologne on my face and put a twinkle in my eyes and a killer smile on my lips—if I did *all* that stuff—and then they *still* didn't take me—it would hit me so hard I probably wouldn't be able to handle it. I knew what actors did to themselves in this town when they couldn't handle it.

But if I went there looking like hell and *then* they turned me down, I'd be protected. I'd be able to say there'd been something other than my talent and personality that was responsible for the rejection. My lack of a killer smile. A wrong pitch to my voice. A wrong look in my eyes. But not my talent.

And there was that other thing in the back of my mind. I must still have *some*thing. I'd been good enough to get that girl laughing at me the night before.

Interviews are tough. First you sit in a too-small room with lots of other people who all look the same as you, but better. They all look nervous. Just like you look nervous. For some reason they never look *as* nervous. Maybe some day an actor would have a fit right in the middle of the waiting room and then I could finally say, Hey, I'm not in such bad shape. Look at this guy. He's busting out at the seams.

We sat there, all of us, and waited, as we do. Time passed, as it does. The casting people were behind schedule, as they are. And the fear in me got bigger.

Finally, a girl who was too tired to act pleasant came out and yawned at us. "Mr. Bolin?"

I nodded and stood. I didn't even have the strength to answer her. But then I thought again of the girl. I tucked my portfolio under my arm and went down the hall. I found a closed door. I knocked. Half of me hoped there wouldn't be an answer, but there was, so I went in.

There were two of them. Neither of them looked at

me. One of them turned to the other. "How far behind?"

"Forty-five minutes."

"Terrific." He waved fingers at me without looking.

I acted like his lack of interest didn't bother me any more than the high-priced Guccis on his feet bothered the cut-rate Keds on mine. I had my picture and résumé in my hand. I walked forward even though I wanted to run away, and I opened my mouth to say something that might even turn out to be pleasant. Then the first one said, "Bolin?" without bothering to look up from a list. And before I could answer him, I was looking down at the list, and there were names all over it. A sea of names. My name wasn't enough to make the slightest ripple in it.

"Well? You Bolin?"

". . . Yeah. Jake Bolin." I put my hand out and made my voice sound as nice as I could. "Glad to meet you."

It didn't make any difference. They didn't care. It was already too late in the day for them to care. The first one took my picture. Sometimes they're nice enough to turn your picture over and look at your résumé and pretend they have some interest in it. But these guys were running forty-five minutes late. The first one put my picture on a stack that was almost as tall as I was. The second one handed me a sheet of paper.

"Okay. Read this."

There was no "please" in his request, but I didn't mind that. They hadn't asked me to sit down, and I didn't mind that either. I was thankful nobody had asked me to leave yet.

I looked at the paper. It was copy for a commercial. I read it over in my mind and tried to decide quickly what phrasing choices I was going to make.

The copy was bad. It usually is. If actors acted as poorly as some of these copywriters write, TV commercials wouldn't sell ice cubes in a heat wave. But most copywriters make money, even if they're bad. Most actors don't, even if they're good. It's a fact of life, like many others. It's not how much talent you've got, it's if you're lucky enough to have the talent there's a market for.

I started to make my choices. How I was going to approach the copy. It needed a firm, quick opening, then a short pause, and some lightness. The third line was meant to get a laugh. It might, if the audience were stoned. Even then, it would be iffy. Maybe if I put the right look in my eyes, waited half a beat, and shrugged. Maybe if I used one of those faces I'd made last night for the girl. Yeah. That might get a chuckle. Even from these guys.

Yes! And then I could drive straight through to the end and give the same look and shrug again!

I was starting to feel sparks. I wanted to make it. Something was pushing me forward. Maybe it was knowing that Alan was pulling in twelve thousand an episode and the T-shirts were going out with his face on them. Two cents in his pocket on each sale? Maybe I wanted some of that. Maybe I wanted girls laughing at me some more. I looked at the copy again, and I didn't care what it looked like. I was going to give these guys an audition they'd remember for the rest of their lives.

If that feeling had lasted half a minute more, I might have made it. But one of them said, "We got anyone interesting coming in later?" and the other one said, "Tom Halloran" and the first one said, "Thank God," and I knew who Tom Halloran was. He was good.

Desperation hit. The fear. The panic. I fell into my funk again. I stopped thinking. I asked the one question every actor knows you never ask.

"There a particular way you want it read?"

Never ask them that. *Never*. Why? Because they don't know. The one thing in the world you can always be sure about—*they don't know how they want it read*. They sit there and pray till their hearts turn blue that some actor will come in and *show* them how it should be read. They also pray they'll be smart enough to know he's showed them when he shows them. If an actor is stupid enough to ask them how they want it read, they know he's not the actor they're waiting for. So I was sunk. Finished. And I'd done it to myself.

The first one kept his mouth shut and looked at the windows on the other side of the room. The other one leaned sideways and draped an arm over the back of his chair. "A particular way we want it read? No, I don't think there's a particular way we want it read." He took out a gold-plated cigarette case and flipped it open. He snapped out a cigarette and tapped it against the case.

He was the actor now, and he was enjoying it. "We just want it read. Quickly. Think you can do that?"

I read it as quickly as I could. Then I went out. One day, maybe it'd be different. But not that day.

I stopped by Schwab's and picked up a *Hollywood Reporter*. I had a perverse wish to see who was working while I wasn't. I checked the Travel Log and saw who was traveling, the Stage Notes and saw who was doing theater around the city, the Regional Theatre and Stock and saw who was doing theater out of town, the Briefs and saw who was making money in TV, the Feature Casting and saw who was making better money in movies. I checked the Personal Data and saw who was being born, who was getting married. There were no death listings today. Maybe nobody had died. Maybe this was Hollywood, and when someone died we ignored it.

I thought about *Othello*. I'd told Ruth to get me an interview. She probably hadn't. I could call her up and give her hell and demand she do it right away. I could be as tough about it as I'd been for that moment last night. Or else I could ignore it.

I ignored it. I walked around a little, had a cup of coffee and looked at the *Reporter* again.

Half an hour later I called my service and found out Ruth *had* gotten me the audition for *Othello*. I got back into my car and sat quietly and waited for my stomach to get itself together. When it almost had, I drove to the Mark Taper. When I got there I had to sit and wait for my stomach again. It took a while.

I finally walked over to the office and met the casting director. Ruth was right. He spent two minutes talking to me and let me read a short scene out of courtesy. It didn't matter. He'd already made up his mind when he'd seen my résumé. I hadn't been on a stage in two and a half years.

He thanked me for reading, we shook hands and I left. I drove up Hollywood Boulevard and took a look at the new building Ruth was in. It was modern and new and sparkling and very impressive. When I walked into Ruth's office, my feet sank three inches into the carpet. The wax shine from her desk came close to blinding me. The paintings on the walls and the aroma of leather from the chairs told me exactly what kind of commissions her other clients were bringing her.

She was talking on the phone. She looked up, smiled, motioned me to sit. She wouldn't have smiled if she'd known what I was doing there. I wanted to throw something, and she was about to be my target.

She talked into the phone. "Yeah, baby, I read the script. Got an actor I want you to see."

I waited silently. My stomach did flip-flops as I wondered if she was going to say my name.

"Tim Garrison. New face in town. Going to hit ... Ought to take a look at him, baby. You don't want to take a look, no skin off my nose. None off his, either. ... Garrison. Tim Garrison."

I wondered what Tim Garrison looked like. I wondered if he needed a new suit and a haircut. A multivitamin shot of ambition and self-confidence. I wondered if he could act. I wondered if it made any difference.

"Yeah, baby! Ten-forty's fine! He'll be there! Talk to you!" She hung up the phone. "God, Jake, you wouldn't believe today." Her hand dragged across her forehead. "Mel's been on a rampage. Yelling at me half the morning. Yelling at everyone." She shook her head. "Well, the hell with that. Right?" She opened her arms wide and waved her hands in the air. "How do you like the new office?"

I sat stiffly, with both feet planted firmly on the floor. "Very useful interview you sent me on."

She held on to her smile. "The commercial?" I nodded. "You could've dressed better, you know."

"I could've gone in there naked with my head shaved! Then they might've noticed me!" I leaned forward angrily. "How much commission you make for keeping your clients out of work?"

She sagged in her chair. "All right, Jake. What happened?"

I saw she couldn't take it, but I gave it to her anyway. "Nothing happened! Slightly more'n three hundred of 'em were just under six feet! A hundred sixty pounds! Dark hair! I was sitting in the goddamn waiting room looking into a bunch of goddamn mirrors! What the hell chance did I have?"

She was silent. Her fingers pulled slowly through her hair. "Were you polite, at least?"

"I was extraordinarily polite! The agency people, on the other hand, were not at all polite! I guess they're trained not to be polite!"

She didn't answer. Her eyes had left my face and she looked past me. A voice said, "What the hell's going on in here?"

I felt awful when I realized what I'd done. I sat still.

Ruth smiled. "Nothing, Mel. Just the usual."

"The usual's making money! We making money?"

"We're trying." Ruth held her smile.

Then I turned and looked at him. The slightest flicker of recognition played across his face. It took him a moment to connect it with a name. "Bolin? Right?"

"Yeah. Jake Bolin."

"Yeah. Sure." He stuck out his hand to shake mine. "How's it going, Jake?"

A shrug was the best I could give him. He didn't like it. If there was a thing in the world Mel did like, I'd never seen it. Except yelling at the agents who worked for him. He seemed to like that.

"All right, let's start making some money! Okay?" His eyes dropped to me again. I suppose he still had some compulsion to say something, but the compulsion wasn't strong enough to tell him what to say. He nodded and left.

Ruth waited a moment, then went to the door and closed it. She came back to the front of her desk and leaned against it. She looked bad.

"Advertising people make a lot of money, Jake. They can afford to be as impolite as they want. They can afford to lose their tempers. They can afford just about anything."

"I know. One of 'em flashed his gold-plated cigarette case at me. The cigarettes were gold-plated, too."

"You got to be smart. Got to know what you can afford to be, what you can't."

"What's that mean?"

"If you're stupid enough to want to be an actor, you got to be smart enough to know how to go about it. It's a rotten business and you don't have a chance, so the only chance you might have is to take the punch they throw at you, roll with it, apologize for getting in the way of their fist and keep smiling."

"Like you with Mel?"

"Like me with Mel."

I grunted. "All right. Don't worry, I still got a few smarts left," I smiled, or at least half smiled. "You notice, I saved it up and gave it to you. I knew I could get away with it, with you."

She leaned forward and kissed my forehead. "That's right, baby. Just don't forget. How was the Mark Taper?"

"You were right. Bad day all around. Even had an argument with Alan this morning. No reason at all. Told him how now he's making good money, he ought to spend it on acting lessons."

She ran her fingers through my hair. "He must've loved that piece of advice. Think it got you anywhere, talking to him that way?"

"Hope not, for his sake. He ever goes to an acting class, he'll start to see how much he's got to learn. Screw him up so good, he'll never be able to work again."

She put her hand under my chin and raised my face till I was looking at her. "Can't say what you really think, Jake. Not to Alan, not to anybody. They don't want to hear it. They want to hear the things they expect to hear. Give it to 'em."

"Lie?"

"Right. Keep the truth to yourself." She looked toward the closed door. "Gets you further."

I opened my mouth, but she put her fingers against my lips. "Being a little too honest'll get you screwed, Jake. People don't want to hear the truth. They're scared of it. Just remember, nobody ever lost a friend by telling him what he wanted to hear."

"I don't like your rules."

"They're not my rules. They're just the ones I follow."

"No difference."

She smiled at me. "You're hopeless."

"I feel hopeless."

"Okay. Anything else you got you want to get out of your system? Go ahead, baby. I can take it. I can take Mel, I can sure take you."

46

I had about five gallons of it left, but before I could let it out, the door began to open. Ruth stiffened but then relaxed again. Donna, another agent in the office, came in.

"Jake! How you doing?"

"Don't ask."

"Oh."

Donna let it pass. Agents have to understand what it's like to be an actor. They have to put up with it or they won't get anywhere. Donna put a hand softly on my shoulder and threw a magazine at Ruth's desk. "I read the Christolf interview."

Ruth laughed acidly. "What'd you think? Spreading it pretty thick these days, huh?"

"Least we know what he wants of life. A woman who can outlast him."

"None will. Stamina is one thing Jack always had. He rated very low on devotion, very high on stamina. I told him he ever needed money, he could always make it at a sperm bank."

Christolf was Jack Christolf. His picture was on the cover of the magazine. He was on lots of magazines these days. He was famous, and he was good. He was a rarity. A star who knew how to act. He was also a son of a bitch. Everyone agreed on that, even Christolf himself. But he pulled in the audiences, so it didn't matter.

Ruth had been his agent once. She'd helped him make it. Then he'd left her.

Donna turned to me, looked at my face and smiled. "Cheer up!" I kept my face the way it was. She cocked her head. "Come on, won't you cheer up?" I laughed halfheartedly and gave her a small smile. She frowned. "Come on! More! Please?" She smiled again, and this time it made me remember another smile. I gave her more. "Better!"

She went to the doorway and looked into the hall. "Better get going fast while the coast is clear, He's really been lousy today."

Ruth nodded. "Maybe if he was making the kind of deals the rest of us are making he might be a little better."

She closed the door behind Donna and came back and touched her hand to my neck. "Just wait, Jake.

We'll make you as big as Jack Christoff. Then you can get mad at anyone in this town you want to get mad at."

I looked up at her. "Let's hope I make it, but not like Jack Christoff."

"Amen."

The phone rang. Ruth picked it up. She spoke with her agent's voice. "Hi, baby!" She listened. Then her eyes lit up. As soon as they lit I knew it had nothing to do with me. "Hold it, baby. Not so fast. Sure, you can have him, but it's going to cost you *forty* thousand." She listened. Her eyes got bigger. Her mouth grinned. "That's right, baby. The big four." Her lips tightened. The grin was gone now. She was quiet. Her hand closed in a fist. Her eyes looked desperate, but still she spoke as casually as if she were discussing the odds on the sun coming up the next morning. "Up to you. We got other people to talk to. Talk to you, baby. When you're *ready* to talk." She hung up. She stared at the far wall and let out a deep breath.

Then she looked at me and her expression changed. "Sorry about the commercial, Jake. Didn't know it'd be one of those. The way you been acting the past week, I was just trying my best to get you something I thought might be—"

"Your best's supposed to be better, according to your reputation." I was feeling mean again. And I knew the door was closed. I slapped my leg. "Well? Isn't it?"

I really said it harshly. It was just her saying forty thousand dollars that way. Me knowing it was another actor she was negotiating for. The whole thing had started to get to me again.

But she stayed calm. Sometimes she was so good at that. "We all make mistakes, baby."

"Make 'em for someone else! Don't make 'em for me!"

"Don't be bitter, baby."

I got out of my chair. "Don't you tell me—"

I stopped and let it hang there. I didn't want to continue. She had enough problems.

I sat down again. I tried to make a joke of it. "Can't even pull off a little of the Mel stuff, can I?" I breathed in quickly. "I'll never get to be a big man like him, huh?"

She watched me, then relaxed. She laughed weakly.

48

"You're okay, baby. Just don't lose your sense of humor."

"Lose it? Didn't know I had it!"

We both laughed. We both needed to laugh. She came around to the front of the desk. "Next time I send you out, it'll be something better. I promise." She put out her hands. But I didn't take them. "Come on, baby! How about a kiss?" I didn't kiss her. "Come on, baby. What's the matter?"

There was the smallest crack in her voice. As soon as I heard it I understood why it was there. I stood up and kissed her. I was still mad at her. I wanted her strong enough to take it. Me and my anger. But just then she wasn't strong enough, so I had to kiss her.

"That's it, baby. All made up, huh? How about I buy you dinner tonight?"

I didn't want that at all. Not after that lousy interview she'd sent me on. I wanted to get away from her.

But she needed a friend. So did I.

I also needed an agent. "Sure, you can buy me dinner. Struggling actors don't pass on free dinners. It's a union rule."

I kissed her again. I even laughed. She smiled. The phone rang and she picked it up. "Hi, baby!" She listened. Her eyes got big again. This time I thought they were going to pop out of her head. "That was fast! Sure! Send me the contract! Soon's I got it on paper, you got him!" She covered the phone with her hand and looked at me. "Another twenty minutes, Jake. If Mel doesn't come in and waste my time anymore. Hey, why don't you stay and watch me work?"

"No thanks. I'd just's soon not know how much work your other clients are getting."

She realized how I felt and tried to make up for it. "I can get it for them, I can get it for you!"

"Yeah?" I laughed. "Let it happen."

I waited for her on the street outside the building, and a funny thing happened. A yellow Volkswagen drove by.

It drove by very slowly. I could see the driver was a girl but I couldn't see if it was *the* girl. The Volkswagen went as far as the corner and then had to stop at a red light.

I started walking. Just normally, not especially fast or slow, I was twenty feet away when the light changed. The yellow Volkswagen went forward.

I ran, I didn't yell, didn't wave my arms or anything, but I ran. And as it happened the light at the next corner turned red. The yellow Volkswagen had to stop again. I caught up with it. The driver turned and looked at me. She had a beautiful face, but not the face I wanted to see. She looked at me and smiled. I nodded sheepishly and turned around. I walked back toward Ruth's office. I stood there quietly and watched more cars go by. None of them was a yellow Volkswagen.

Five minutes later Mel came out. He was shaking his head. I smiled and nodded. He paused for a second and nodded absently and then kept walking as if he'd never seen me before. That made me feel good. I was obviously an actor nobody ever forgot.

I stood and watched cars. Another ten minutes passed. No yellow Volkswagens. Ruth came out and took my arm. "Okay, baby! Dinner! Anywhere you want to go! Name it!"

It took me half a second. "The Dancers."

All during dinner I kept looking toward the bar. I don't know if Ruth realized it or not. At one point she said, "I would've popped for the most expensive eats in town, baby. Why'd you pick this place?"

I shrugged and started talking about something else.

We sat a long time over coffee. I wanted to really talk, but all she wanted to talk about was the business. Finally she got restless and called for the check. I watched her sign the credit-card receipt. It was getting awfully easy for me, watching her pay for things. We went out and into the parking lot. I looked around. My whole heart was hoping I'd see a yellow Volkswagen. Either Ruth caught on that there was something eating me or it was just the effect of the two bottles of wine we'd gone through—she hung pretty firmly to my arm.

"What's the matter, baby? Looks like you're looking for something."

"Fresh air. Know where I can find some?"

"Give you something better." She took my face in her hands and kissed me. Kissed me again. There was a lot of hunger behind it. I liked her this way more than I'd liked the way she'd been the night before, so I kissed her back. Her mouth opened wider and her fingers spread through my hair. Her voice was only a murmur. "How about my place tonight?"

She seemed strong now and I was feeling pretty lonely, so I said yes. She got in her car and I got in mine, and I followed her to her apartment. Five minutes after we got there we were making love. I enjoyed it when it started. She was tearing my shirt and pulling at my belt. But then as soon as I was undressed, she just lay back on the bed and waited for me. The same as always.

I made love to her. I didn't feel right about it, but I did it anyway. She wanted it so much. In a way so did I. But for the first time making love to her hurt a little. Not physically. We knew each other too well for anything to go wrong there. I put my hand between her legs at just the right moment and began to kiss her breasts, and then she wrapped her arms around me and held me tight with her legs. Technically it was perfect. But anything beyond the technical—it just wasn't there. After it was over I felt weak and tired. So much effort. So much of it mine.

She lay back against the pillow and lit a cigarette. She passed it to me. She lit another for herself. She was smiling. She was my agent. I'd made her a little happier. She'd tried to do the same for me. But for me it hadn't worked. And I knew it.

I'd known it for a long time. And I still hadn't said anything about it. That was beginning to hurt too.

"Ruth, let's talk."

"Sure." She yawned. "What about?"

"I don't know. But not about the business. About the way things are."

She laughed. "The way things are *is* the business!" Her eyes closed. "Everything's the business, Jake. Don't you know that?"

I turned on my side. "How'd you get into it?"

She yawned again. "By mistake." She put the cigarette in her mouth. "God, I'm tired." He eyes were still closed.

I lay there and looked at her. I knew she wouldn't need to do it again. Make love. Ruth never did. I sat quietly for a moment and realized she was drifting off. I made some excuse for why I couldn't stay the night. She was so tired from the wine and the lovemaking that she didn't have it in her to give me much of an argument. I left her place around one o'clock. I wasn't sure what I was going to do with myself. The house would be empty. Then I realized it wouldn't. There would still be Alan's bottle of vodka on the bookcase in the living room. I knew I'd have plenty of use for it by the time I got there.

I drove home and sat silently in front of my house with the motor turned off. As I'd driven up the road, I'd kept looking to see if there might be a yellow Volkswagen parked somewhere. I'd even driven past my house and farther up the hill to see if it might be parked there. But it wasn't.

I finally got out of the car and went into the house. I turned on the light switch in the living room and heard the click and nothing happened, and then I remembered I'd forgotten to replace the burned-out bulb from the night before. I wasn't in the mood for a room full of darkness so I turned on the table lamp. I looked down at my stack of pictures. Something struck me as strange. I thought about it another minute, and then I knew what it was. The pictures were still in the same nice neat pile I'd left them in, all squared off against each other, but there was one difference. When I'd left them there that morning, I'd put them in the center of the table. Now they were at the side.

I went all over the house searching for anything else that might've been moved. But it didn't matter. The one thing I was sure about was the pictures. They'd definitely been moved. There was no question about it. When I came back to the living room, I picked them up and put them back in the center of the table. That's when I realized the second thing. The stack wasn't as thick as it had been that morning. There must've been ten, maybe twenty pictures gone.

THE next couple of days, every time I saw a yellow Volkswagen I thought I was going to explode. Every time I didn't see one, I felt the same way. It was really getting bad. I did a lot of driving. Whenever I didn't have auditions, which was most of the time, I was always on the move. I stopped by The Dancers a lot. She was never there. I finally went up to the bartender and described her to him, but he didn't remember her at all. He said if she'd been in that night she probably hadn't been there before or since. I decided the smartest thing to do was stay home at night in case she showed. But she didn't. It was driving me nuts.

I was on Hollywood Boulevard one day so I stopped in at Larry Edmond's place. It's a movie bookstore, always full of actors who are hoping a director who's looking for a book will see them and offer them a job. Directors do stop in, but all they ever seem to pick up are books and an occasional companion for the night. However there's always that chance—one of them might give you a second look, talk to you, it might lead to something

—so actors keep going back there. There and thirty other places.

I'd just been through another worthless interview. The only one Ruth had gotten me that week. I was so low I would've been just as happy if she hadn't gotten it. The interviewer had been twenty years old at most, dressed expensively, and stoned out of his mind. His speech had been mostly incoherent. It wasn't unusual. You saw people, especially casting people, stoned all the time. They all wanted to be in some other world, and most of them usually were. I knew if they didn't kill themselves on drugs during the next five to ten years, they'd all end up as TV network vice presidents or heads of the movie studios. Knowing this, I treated them with respect.

This one had straightened himself out long enough to tell me to read for him, which I did. I wasn't at my best, but it didn't matter. I was sure he didn't hear a word. When I'd finished I'd shaken his hand. It had felt limp as a jellyfish.

I found some books at Larry Edmond's I would've bought if I'd had some money. I looked at pictures of old stars. I guess they went through it, too. Making the rounds. Collecting the rejections. It had been worth it for them they'd made it, they'd hit. I wondered if it had been worth it for the ones who hadn't made it.

Yeah. I was in great shape that day. No question about it.

I made small talk with other actors and then went out to the street. Instead of going back to my car I decided to walk a few blocks. They say exercise can help get you out of depressions. Even walking, if you do enough of it. I was ready to walk to the ocean. I pointed myself in that direction and started strolling. I looked around at the other people on the street. Then I realized there was a yellow Volkswagen half a block behind me.

I didn't know if it was the right one. I'd seen so many that weren't. But I had a feeling. I stopped in front of a store and pretended to be interested in the shoes on display. The window gave me a perfect reflection. I could tell it was her immediately.

I stood still. The car was inching forward. I could see her behind the wheel. She was looking at me but didn't realize I knew it. I was looking at her but she didn't realize that either.

I stared at the window. The Volkswagen was coming closer. It pulled over to the curb. Its horn honked.

I didn't move. I just stood there. God, why was I so scared?

The horn honked again. I turned suddenly. I let my eyes sweep the street as if I didn't expect the horn to be for me, then I did a slight take and pretended to be surprised to see her.

"Hi!" She had that same smile again.

". . . Hi."

"Thought it was you. How you been?"

I shrugged. "Not bad. How about you?"

"Okay." She turned sideways on her seat. "How's the acting business going?"

I laughed. "Slim as always."

She nodded. Her eyes twinkled. "Ah, don't worry. You'll get something pretty soon. You're talented, right? And you sure are funny."

I smiled. "I think you're the only one who thinks so."

"I can't be." She slid into the passenger's seat. "They must be crazy if they don't see it!"

"They *are* crazy." I shoved my hands into my pockets. I still didn't move toward the car. "But they got money, so it doesn't matter."

She rested her arm on the window. "Then they're not as well off as you. You can lose money. You can't lose talent." Her eyes lit. "Hey, I been dying to see some more of your faces. How about it?"

"Okay." I squinched my eyes tight together and slanted my mouth to one side. She started laughing. When I heard that I exaggerated the look further. Then I began a Walter Brennan walk toward her car. I knew people must be looking at me like I was crazy, but I didn't care. I was even getting ready to try to imitate Brennan's voice.

Then everything went wrong. A voice up the street yelled, "Jake! Hey, Jake!"

It startled me. I turned. A beautiful girl in short shorts and a halter top was running down the street. She threw her arms around my neck and hugged me and kissed me. It was a million-to-one shot, and it happened at just the wrong moment. By the time I turned back to the Volkswagen, the girl had slid back into the driver's seat and was shifting gears. Her head turned for a brief second. "See you some time." Her head snapped forward again. The car pulled into traffic. It picked up speed fast and went on through the intersection.

"Jake, how've you been?"

I kept my eyes on the Volkswagen. "Fine, Jill. You?"

"Great! Who was that?"

". . . A girl."

"Pretty."

"Yeah."

The Volkswagen kept moving. It was almost down to the next intersection now.

"You look good, Jake!"

"Do I?" I probably *did* look good. I'd started smiling when the girl had laughed at me. I turned back to Jill. "So how're things in Malibu?"

"God! The house is a mess! Alan's so busy shooting the series, I've got to do everything myself! I was putting up wallpaper all morning!"

"Sounds exciting." I looked down the street again. The yellow Volkswagen was four blocks away. It turned a corner and was gone.

Jill and I went into a restaurant and traded gossip over hamburgers. She gave me all the latest news on Alan's career. She said he was doing great! Terrific! Fabulous! The house was great, too. Terrific. Fabulous. And of course so was Malibu.

But it didn't depress me. The girl had said, "See you some time." Now I knew all I had to do was wait.

It was two days later, and I was pushing a grocery cart down a line of canned goods. I had just reached up for some green beans when another cart came around the corner. She was pushing it. She tried to look surprised. "Hey! We're really running into each other, aren't we?"

"Yeah. Small world, isn't it?" I smiled and acted as surprised as she did. I could've said something about how I wasn't surprised at all, but I wouldn't have done that for a million dollars. Let her play it whatever way she wanted. I didn't care.

I got her last name out of her. It was O'Hanlon. At

least that's what she said it was. I did some more faces for her. She laughed at all of them. We went through the checkout line together and out to the parking lot and into our separate cars. We both ended up at my place.

It was five-thirty by then, so as soon as we walked into the house I invited her to stay for dinner. I led her into the kitchen, put whatever needed to be frozen into the freezer, pulled out a baking dish and poured some oil into it. I put in some chicken and gave it celery salt and pepper, onion powder, garlic powder, lots of dill. I poured wine over it, and it still looked a little lonesome so I sliced an onion and stuck that in there too. She was snapping her fingers then and watching me restlessly. Suddenly I realized I'd forgotten to light the oven. As I reached for the matches, she opened the refrigerator. "I'll make the salad."

Before I could answer, she'd taken out lettuce and celery and tomatoes. She spread them out on the counter.

"Better wait on the salad. Going to take at least an hour yet. I forgot to light the oven."

"Oh!" She stared at me. "Well . . . all right." She immediately put the lettuce and celery and tomatoes back into the refrigerator. Then she looked at me still standing there with the baking dish in my hands. I didn't know what else to do so I laughed. She started laughing too. I don't think either of us knew why we were doing it. I guess we both just felt a little foolish or something, so we laughed. It was nice. We were both acting like thirteen-year-old kids who were holding hands for the first time and wondering if we knew what it might lead to. At least I was.

I tried to break through my shyness. I remembered the way she'd been drinking when I'd seen her sitting at the bar at The Dancers. At least that gave me *something* to say. "How about something to drink? Whisky?"

"No! . . No, thanks." Her hand went lightly to her hair. She flicked some of it behind one ear. "Could I have some milk?"

"Sure." I moved toward the refrigerator.

"No, it's okay. I'll get it." And she laughed again. I still had the baking dish in my hands. It hadn't seemed to occur to me that I might be able to put it down somewhere.

She took milk from the refrigerator and poured herself a glass. She held the glass but didn't drink. As if she were waiting for something. I didn't know what. I couldn't figure out anything that might be on her mind. As long as she had me wondering that way, she really had me.

Then I realized it must've been that she was uncomfortable because I was staring at her, so I bent down and lit the oven. I blew out the match and threw it away, and when I looked at her again the milk was two inches gone.

She looked around the kitchen. "You said that other actor used to live here with you. Alan . . ."

"DeVoss."

"Yeah. DeVoss." She sipped her milk. "The star."

"That's the one. He moved out to Malibu, with his girl." I leaned against the counter. "This is the kind of place we all want to move out of."

"Oh?"

I nodded several times.

"What's the matter? You don't think you ever will?"

The directness of it stopped me for a second. "I don't know. I'm beginning to wonder."

"Oh." She took another small sip of milk. "What do you want most in the world?"

". . . What do you mean, what do I want?"

"What're you after?" She moved closer. "What do you want most in life? What do you dream about?"

I'd been dreaming about her the past two nights, but I couldn't tell her that. "I dream about making it."

"Making it. As an actor."

"Yeah. Afraid so." I looked away. "Not much to want in the world, but it's what I want, God help me."

She moved a step closer. "No. Don't be afraid of it. Or sorry. There's nothing wrong with wanting that. If it's what you want, you want it."

"I don't know." I moved several steps away from her, leaned against the window sill and looked at the floor. "It's a rotten business. Maybe you have to be a little rotten to want to be part of it."

"Who says it's rotten?" She came farther toward me. "And even if it was, *you're* not rotten! You're nice! You're talented. That's what's important. And people

58

love actors, they love to watch movies and TV. It's wonderful that you want to be an actor."

I finally looked up at her. "I don't want to be just an actor. I want to be the best actor I can be."

"Good! That's good! You know exactly what you want! That's the best thing in the world!"

"Well . . ." I looked down again. "I don't know if it's the best thing or not, but even if it was, I don't seem to be getting anywhere at it."

"You will." She moved closer. "The important thing is, you've made your choice. You know what you're after. You're committed to it."

I was silent. I was looking at her feet now. I raised my head and let my eyes come slowly up her body. I looked into her eyes. "I guess so. Something inside me must really want it. Some part of me must still believe I've got the talent to do it, or I wouldn't still be out there knocking my head against the walls. Huh?"

She didn't answer. But she looked so convinced I was right. And then something about the intensity of her look got to me. I had to do something, so I turned slightly and did a bit—pretended to be knocking my head against the wall.

She laughed.

I laughed too. "I just wish I could find a way to sell that belief to someone who's got an inclination to pay for it."

"I thought that's what your agent's supposed to do. Sell it."

". . . That's what she's supposed to do." I grinned. "I'm supposed to sit tight and wait for her to do it." I put one hand behind me and tapped my fingers against the window. But I did it very softly so it would make no noise. This was the first I'd thought of Ruth all day. Right now I didn't want to think of her at all. "Sitting tight—it ain't the easiest thing in the world."

"Of course it isn't. It never is. Not for anyone."

She still had the milk in her hand. She finished it in one big swallow and went to the sink. She ran the water and put the smallest dab of soap imaginable on a sponge and soaked the sponge with just enough water to get some bubbles and cleaned the glass till it was spotless. She put the glass in the drainer. Then she cleaned the sink. She sponged off the counter. Then she looked at me. "So he moved out. DeVoss. You find a new roommate yet?"

"No. Haven't looked for one."

She nodded. She lined up the soap, the sponge and the bottle of detergent against the back of the sink. "I got the same problem. The girl I've been living with. She just got married."

It didn't mean a thing to me. I assumed she was just making small talk. "Didn't know people were still doing that. Getting married."

"She is. She comes from a very proper family."

There was a whole line of spice bottles sitting on the counter. Her fingers played with them. She lined them up straight as soldiers and adjusted them methodically till the spaces between them were uniform. "My apartment, it's bigger than I need. Rent's pretty high."

I refused to believe it. This kind of thing didn't happen to me. And if it ever did happen, it wouldn't happen with a girl that looked as good as this. It had to be just small talk.

Suddenly she came over to me and reached for the baking dish. "Oven must be ready by now. I'll put it in." She pulled down the oven door. She slid the dish onto the middle rack and closed the door. She stood up and looked at me.

I looked at my watch. "All right, in precisely forty-five minutes, we eat like rich people." I waited a beat. "Or poor people who've read a cookbook."

Maybe she really thought it was funny. Or maybe she liked the way I smiled when I said it. Or maybe my timing had really been as good as I'd hoped it would be. Anyway, she laughed.

We went into the living room. She straightened that up, too. I think she would've vacuumed the rug if I'd had a vacuum cleaner. And a rug. She went to the table with my pictures on it. The pictures were sitting in the center of the table, the way I'd had them originally. Those that were left. I didn't say anything about that. I watched silently as she picked up the top picture. "I like it." She turned it over. "What is it?"

"Pictures and résumés. In the army, you get caught,

the enemy takes your dog tags. Here in Hollywood, they take your pictures and résumés."

She turned it over again and looked at the picture again. "I like it! It's very nice!"

"No, it's no good. I got to get new ones taken."

"Oh?" She put the picture down. Her face slowly frowned. "I see."

"Soon as I can find a good photographer who doesn't charge an arm and a leg." I waved a hand at the air. I was feeling much looser now. "See, an actor who can't get work, he gets new pictures. Till he gets 'em he can tell the world that's the reason he can't get work. 'Cause he hasn't got his new pictures yet."

"You mean it's just an excuse?"

"One of the many. You're an actor, you aren't making it, you need all the excuses you can find."

It was the kind of thing I didn't even like to admit to myself, but for some reason I felt I could admit it to her. I knew she'd understand. I knew she wouldn't look down on me for it. Like most people would. That's what she was, all right—understanding. And sympathetic. And warm. And open. And very, very pretty. But now that I was really talking to her, the prettiness didn't even seem important.

I found I had a cigarette in my fingers. I had no idea how long it had been there. I put it into my mouth and lit it. I watched her eyes search the room as if she were memorizing everything that was there. Finally her eyes came back to the table and focused on the pictures. "So then, these pictures, you don't like sending 'em out. You don't think they're any good."

"No. Matter of fact, I hate 'em."

She nodded.

I offered her wine during dinner. She refused it and asked for another glass of milk. I asked her again if she wanted whisky but she said no, milk was fine. I moved toward the refrigerator, but she beat me to it.

I was lucky, the chicken had turned out well. Actually, if it had turned out terrible I don't think it would've made any difference to either one of us. I was telling jokes and she was laughing. We were both enjoying ourselves. I really felt at ease. And I hadn't had to drink any wine to get me feeling that way.

When we finished eating, she insisted on clearing the table. Then she started washing the dishes. I told her to just put them in the drainer to dry, but she insisted on stopping to dry each one herself, immediately. I couldn't let her do that, so I took a towel and almost had to fight her for the right to dry them. We carried out the operations, her washing, me drying, in absolute silence.

It probably sounds screwy, but working side by side in silence that way, it was pretty erotic. I guess it was just being able to stand next to her, our bodies touching slightly every once in a while. I considered getting more dishes out of the cupboard.

She went back to the table then. So did I. I took out my cigarettes and offered her one. She declined it and turned sideways in her chair. There were about a month's worth of old newspapers in a pile on the floor. Something in the top paper caught her eye. She picked it up, and then looked upset.

"Katie? What's the matter?"

She didn't answer. I looked across the table and read the headline MIDDAY ROBBERY ON FAIRFAX. I grunted. "Yeah. All over the place. Like those kids the other night. At The Dancers."

She nodded. She put the paper down. I reached across for it, but she picked it up again quickly. "It says someone went into this butcher shop, right in the middle of the afternoon. They wanted money."

"Don't we all?"

She didn't laugh at that one. "It says the butcher, he'd been robbed three times in the last year and a half. So he had a gun. But the thief grabbed one of the carving knives and made him drop it."

I smiled. "I thought acting was a tough business. Glad I'm not a butcher."

She still didn't laugh. "The thief took some money from the register, and the gun, and went out." She put the paper down. "God, Jake. Middle of the afternoon. Broad daylight." She pressed her lips together, then looked at me. "They could've killed each other! Over a little bit of money! What's the sense in that? Why do people do things like that to each other?"

I was silent a moment. I thought she was going to cry. I tried to think what to say. "People want things. Sometimes, they do funny things when they want things. Sometimes, they don't seem to care what they do, long's they get what they want."

"Something like this shouldn't happen! People shouldn't treat each other this way! It's wrong!" She slammed the paper back on the pile. I was sure she was going to break.

But then she changed and was quieter. "I'm sorry. This is foolish. I shouldn't let something like this get to me. There are plenty of other things to worry about."

She looked so shaky now. Like she'd looked in the parking lot with those kids. Before I could stop myself, I'd reached across the table and touched her hand. She flinched slightly, but then left her hand where it was. Her eyes traveled up to my face, then away. Then across the room. But her hand didn't move.

Not too much else happened till we got outside. We talked for a while, and then she said it was late, she really had to go. I said yes, I guessed she really had to go. We walked through the house. Without touching anymore. We went into the front yard. We stood in the night air. Neither of us knew quite what to say. It was the beginning of the evening all over again. I was shy, I was nervous. It seemed like she was, too. If we'd been two other people we would've been in bed by then. But we weren't two other people, we were us.

She opened her pocketkbook and took out her wallet and looked inside. "Could I borrow ten dollars?"

"Sure!" I dug out my own wallet and took out two fives. She could've borrowed a million that night if I'd had it. "What do you do? You work? Got a job?"

She nodded, that was all.

I gave her the fives. She ran the bills gently through her fingers and straightened out the wrinkles. She put them carefully into her wallet. It was dark, I couldn't be sure, but it looked as though there was money already in there. But if she needed another ten dollars for something, I wasn't going to ask her why. She said, "I work for an insurance company. Allstate."

We were silent again. She started for her car.

I couldn't just let her go like that. "How about giving me your phone number?" She turned abruptly. I smiled. "So I'll know I can get my money back."

"Don't worry, you'll get it back."

I didn't know what else to say. I waited for her to turn toward her car again, but she didn't. Then I stepped forward slowly. "It was nice, being with you. Tonight."

"Yes. It was nice for me, too."

"What I mean is . . ." I felt younger than I'd ever felt before. "I'm tied up tomorrow. Working on a movie. Extra. Might take all day."

She nodded.

"What I mean is . . ." I was trembling. "I'm free on Sunday. Maybe we could get together. If you'd like to."

"Maybe. . . . I'll let you know."

"Yeah."

We looked at each other. I couldn't take any more of it. I reached forward slowly and took her hands. I was scared she wouldn't let me, but she did. She looked down at her hands in my hands, and then she looked back up. I leaned forward very slowly and kissed her.

She let me do it, but I can't say she helped me. I let go of her hands and stepped back. I waited for the ground to yawn open and swallow me. But before it did, she stepped forward and put her hands up to my face and kissed me.

Then I felt something funny. I realized she'd bitten me gently on the lip.

She stepped back. Looked at me. I didn't move. Then she came forward and kissed me again. It was so sudden this time. Before my mouth could even open her tongue was pushing inside it. Firmly but still gently. Then her arms were around me. Her body was straining against mine.

It was wonderful. It was a long, strong kiss. I closed my eyes, and we both rocked back and forth.

Then she bit me again.

She stepped back. Looked at me. And laughed. That small, quiet laugh of hers that always sounded so warm. A second later she turned and got into her car. She turned on the motor and snapped on the lights and drove off. I watched the yellow Volkswagen go down the dirt road.

I took a deep breath. I felt my lip where she'd bitten it. I went into the house. I rinsed my mouth with water and got rid of the last taste of the blood.

I got through Saturday all right because I had to spend most of it working on that movie. Extra work. A lot of standing around doing nothing. Going through dozens of cigarettes. Drinking gallons of weak, tasteless coffee. Keeping quiet. Being where they wanted you, when they wanted you. And for me, keeping my face turned to the side of my mouth where the lip was puffed up slightly wouldn't show to the camera.

Movies. You see the way they're shot, you wonder how they make money on any of them. The truth is they make money on damn few. They still end up shooting the next movie the same way. More standing around, more waiting, more doing nothing.

Extra work isn't glamorous or fun. It's a bore. But it's part of the business, and it's worth a couple bucks. It gives you a few hours to fool yourself into believing you really are part of the business. You're not just walking around saying you are. Fooling yourself is very necessary out here. You stop doing it too long, you'll crack.

I really needed it that Saturday. It meant people around me. And talk. Stupid talk, mostly. Sometimes that's the best kind. Gossip. Ugly rumors. But communication. With people in the business. People who were just as bad off as I was. Who understood the problems. But that day, even that wasn't enough. I'd been spoiled the night before. I'd talked with her.

When I got home, I called the service. She hadn't called.

Sunday was hard. From the moment I woke up I was thinking about her. I went through three cups of coffee and four cigarettes. Didn't eat. Wasn't hungry. Couldn't decide if I could dare leave the house or not.

I shaved. I looked in the mirror at my lip. The swelling was almost completely gone. It didn't feel tender anymore.

I sat in the living room. And waited.

I couldn't sit. I finally put a note on the door—BE RIGHT BACK—and jumped in the car and drove down the hill for the Sunday papers. I got back to the house within ten minutes. All I found was the note staring at me. I called the service. No message. I sat down and waited.

Now that I had the Sunday papers I wasn't interested in reading them. I suppose I'd gone to get them just so I'd see a human face. As it turned out, the only face I'd seen had been sour as a lemon. Its owner had taken my money, thrown my papers at me and gone back to its portable TV without a word.

I flopped the papers on the table next to my pictures. All that did was make me think of her again.

Enough. I pulled open the phone book and turned pages. Found *O'Hanlon Kate 505 Federal Ave. H05-6241*. I stared at the phone for a minute and then dialed the number. It rang. Nobody answered.

I went through two sections of the paper. Two more cups of coffee. Three more cigarettes. I stared at the phone again. Dialed. No answer.

I took a stroll into the back yard, a little ways into the woods. I didn't go too far away from the house in case the phone rang or someone drove up to the front.

Neither happened.

I leaned against a tree and noticed a bird on a branch about twenty feet away. It was singing but the song seemed sad. The bird flew to another branch where there was another bird. The two of them sat a moment, then the first bird chirped, and then they both flew off together. That did it. I went into the house and dialed the number. When I got no answer I took a piece of paper and wrote down *505 Federal* and put the paper into my wallet and went out the door and was standing next to my car trying to decide if I should leave another note on the front door or not when I heard a car coming up the road. My heart almost jumped out of my chest. It was her.

We set up two folding chairs in the back yard and sat

in the sun. I don't know what it was, but she seemed a little distant today. She didn't seem to want to touch me, much less kiss. I guess it was just that she was shy again. But she was very animated. She gestured a lot with her hands as she talked. I was drinking wine. I had offered her that or whisky but she'd declined both. She'd said she'd taken a pill and didn't want to mix it with liquor. She'd opened up the refrigerator and gotten herself a glass of milk.

We talked for an hour about nothing much at all, which was still worth more to me than talking to anyone else about anything. Actually, she was doing most of the talking. I was just listening to how beautiful her voice was. I said a few things sometimes and sometimes made her laugh. Then she hit me with it.

"You ever heard of a man named Antonio Calisi?"

I laughed. It was a little like asking me if I'd ever heard of Wilshire Boulevard.

"Sure. Calisi's got a rep as one of the best photographers in the city. I've seen his work, his rep's accurate. I've seen his prices, too. For what he charges, he must be rich enough to own streets in Beverly Hills."

She looked toward the woods. "I was thinking, yesterday. Calisi's got an insurance policy with us."

I took a long sip of wine and looked toward the woods myself. I wanted to see if those two birds were back on their branch.

Things happened fast, as they often seemed to with Katie. Within forty-eight hours I was sitting on a stool in the middle of Calisi's studio. She'd left me half an hour later on Sunday telling me she couldn't stay for dinner, she had an appointment to meet someone. But then she called me Monday at six-thirty and said everything was all fixed up with Calisi for Tuesday morning at ten. She'd said I better get a haircut first, I needed one. I laughed. I'd known I needed one for almost a month.

I got up early Tuesday morning and went to a shop on Sunset. I was the first one there when they opened the door. It was nice, sitting in the barber's chair, having my appearance looked after. Caring about how it came out. The first time in a long time I'd cared. I really liked having the guy fuss over me. God, I felt worth it!

Calisi's studio could've passed for a mansion, even in L.A. There was enough wood paneling in the outer office and enough gold on Antonio Calisi's fingers and wrists to show I was in the presence of a fifty-percent tax bracket or better. Calisi was a real professional, as good as I'd ever seen. Even with my new haircut I didn't look good enough for him, but he masked his thoughts awfully well. He looked at me carefully, made no comment at all and went into another room.

A few moments later someone came and got me and took me into the make-up room. They fixed me up in there. Nobody said a thing about how badly I needed the fixing. They just did it. They did it fast. They didn't give me enough time to worry that maybe there were things wrong with me. They took what was wrong and got rid of it the best they could.

They took me into the studio. Katie was there. Calisi let her sit in on the shooting. I got the impression he didn't let everyone do that, so I figured they must know each other pretty well.

Calisi moved around me quickly, with a great deal of sureness. He knew exactly what he wanted and exactly what to say to me to make me give it. He spoke gently but firmly. Treated me like he loved me. I knew he must treat everyone he photographed that way, but it made no difference. He was sincere about it. If it wasn't sincerity, he was a better actor than I'd ever be. And besides him, I had her. Every time I got the chance I looked at her, and every time I looked at her it was like a shot of electricity going through me.

Calisi shot three rolls of film in twenty minutes but it was no rush job. Twenty minutes with him was better than three hours with the photographers I'd gone to in the past. I wanted to kiss him. I wouldn't have done it, of course. I wouldn't have done it even if he'd been a girl. All I mean is, the feeling to do it was there. The way he treated me. Like we were lovers. He really knew his business. When he finished I got off the stool, and I didn't kiss him but I did kiss her.

I kissed her all that night too. When she threw her head back and sighed and seemed ready, I put my hand gently between her legs and rolled over on top of her. But then she stopped me. For a second I didn't understand why. Then she brought her head up and kissed me on the neck and put her hand softly against my chest and nudged me over so I was on my back. Her leg came slowly across me and she was kissing me on the mouth, and then she was on top of me.

I let her do it. It was fine with me. I didn't care how we did it. Besides, I'd always read women got more enjoyment out of it when they were on top.

She really seemed to like it. She was sitting so her legs were bent along my sides and her hands were on my shoulders. She began to rub herself softly against me. Not roughly. Very tenderly. Very slowly.

Then she started to laugh. Suddenly I was laughing, too. She smiled and reached down between my legs and took me and put me inside her. It was nice, the way she did it. So easy. So sure. We had none of those nervous few seconds when I'd be fumbling around. It was just done. She'd done it for me. I was inside her.

She rode on top of me, rolling so slowly back and forth. Then she straightened as if a shock had gone through her and her fingers tightened on my arms. Then she sighed. Then she laughed again.

I let my head go back against the pillow. I held her at the waist. Then I stroked her gently with my fingers, down her hips, across her legs, then up to her waist again. She murmured for me to keep doing it. Her hips swirled in a soft circular motion, slowly increasing the speed. I arched my back slightly and circled with her. Then an involuntary twitch snaked through me. She moaned when it happened.

I looked up at her and her mouth was open. She stopped moving for a moment, but then she looked down at me again and smiled and began to move slowly back and forth. She knew just how much to pull back till she almost lost me, then come slowly forward till we were tight against each other. When she was forward, I brought my head up and kissed her on the lips. We held there a moment and then she drew back in that same slow, gradual, tantalizing way. It was wonderful. Incredible. She came forward again. I kissed her again. We held it a moment and she drew back again. We did it one more time that way, and then when she drew back I suddenly pushed off the bed to get farther inside her. Her eyes opened wide. Her mouth was open, too. I could tell by her eyes that she knew exactly what it meant. Her whole body came right back down on me and her arms and legs gripped me. She screamed several times and was tight against me as I came. It was perfect.

Half an hour later her hand stroked gently along my thigh, moved up and found I was hard again. She gasped. I thought she was alarmed by it the way Ruth would've been, but it turned out she wasn't alarmed at all. She laughed. She was ready again, too. We were lying there side by side, smiling at each other, and suddenly she'd swung her leg over my hip and again I didn't have to do a thing. As I reached down she reached down, too, and carefully guided me into her.

It was even easier this time. She was even more ready this time. She guided my head down and had me kiss one breast, then the other. Then she took my hands and put one on each breast and showed me how she wanted them touched. Then we kissed on the mouth. We pushed against each other in a slow and perfect rhythm.

Then she started moaning and seemed out of control. Her arms were tight around me. I felt her nails scratch my back. It was the first time a girl had ever done that to me. It didn't hurt, it felt sensational. Finding someone who had so much passion in them. And for me. A woman who was strong enough to know what she wanted and sure enough of herself to let *me* know exactly what she wanted. And since she could do that, I was able to give it to her. She was on top of me now. I bent my legs at the knees and pushed up off the bed, and suddenly I had her in the air. She screamed louder than before but it was the kind of scream that didn't want me to stop. Her legs had tightened around me and her fingers had gone up to the back of my neck. She pulled my head forward so our faces were mashed as tight against each other as they could be, and then I was flat on my back once more. She kissed me so hard I thought I would die, or at least pass out. Then her pelvis began moving in short spasmodic jerks, and this time we came together.

It must've been at least an hour later when I felt her hand against my cheek. At first, I didn't know if it was a dream or actually happening. Her hand stroking my forehead. Her fingertips gently touching my cheek again. Her voice seeming to say something. Her fingernail tracing a circle on my chin. I just lay there with my eyes closed and didn't make a sound. I didn't want to break the spell.

Then I must've fallen asleep, because when I heard her say "Jake," it was so soft and distant I was sure it was only a dream. She couldn't be trying to wake me. Not again. So I didn't react. I just lay there peacefully and felt her soft warm hand against my cheek.

Then her hand left my cheek. Then it came back. But when it came back, there was a sharp stinging sensation and a crack.

I opened my eyes and sat up with a jerk. I suddenly realized she'd slapped me.

But her hand touched me softly again. "I'm sorry. Did I hurt you?"

I blinked my eyes.

"I'm sorry, Jake. You were asleep. I just wanted to wake you up." She pushed against me gently and nudged me down again. "Jake? Are you all right?"

Her words were soft as fur, but my cheek still tingled.

"Jake? Do you think you can?"

I didn't know what she meant. Then her hand was on me again. It went lightly across my chest and down to my stomach. It went lower. "Jake? Can you?"

"I don't know."

She stroked me. "Please? Can you try?"

Then I was inside her again and she was on top of me and her hips were making that slow, circular motion.

Her head came down to mine. Her mouth was against my ear. "Jake? You all right?"

I mumbled something. Her whole body wriggled sensuously against mine so that her hard, taut nipples were skimming the surface of my chest. Then she seemed to want me to kiss them again. Her breasts. I kissed them and sucked them. She moaned. She rolled back and forth. I'd never been with anyone like this before. It was like a dream. I knew she was on the edge of another orgasm. I thought I could've held her there forever. I felt like the strongest thing in the world.

But then suddenly I began to feel strained.

"Jake? You all right?"

I tried to choke out some kind of answer. I didn't know if I was all right or not. I'd never done it three times in one night before. Now I wasn't sure if I could.

But she was sure. And patient. And careful. And confident. And very, very gentle. And though it seemed to take forever, when it finally happened it had more power in it than the first two times.

She collapsed on top of me. She drew my arms around her. Her head turned and her lips pressed against my neck. Her mouth opened and her tongue licked me and then she moved higher and her teeth played softly against the edge of my ear. Then she laughed and began to bite it. I laughed, too, and quickly turned my head to get my ear away from her. Then I took what strength I still had and kissed her. We did that for a long time, and then she drew back. I tried to catch my breath.

"Katie . . . I think that's it for tonight . . . Okay?"

She laughed her soft laugh. She nuzzled against me. "You're wonderful, Jake!" She kissed me on the chin. "God, you're just wonderful."

A small, cool breeze came through the open window. It felt very nice. It made me even more aware of how warm she felt against me. It was exactly one week to the day since I'd first seen her standing at the bar at The Dancers gulping whisky. I thought I loved her. God, I was sure of it. I felt ready to give her everything in the world I had to give to another person.

But no more lovemaking. Not that night. It would've killed me.

We finally both fell asleep with our arms around each other.

When she moved in the next day, she brought two suitcases, three armfuls of clothes, a bottle of Jack Daniel's and the promise of enough money to cover half the rent.

THREE days later, the pictures were ready. I thought they looked terrific. They made *me* look terrific. I felt so confident, I was ready to go after almost anything in the world. I spent all morning going through the pictures and that afternoon I took them to Ruth.

It was the first time I'd seen Ruth in days. I hadn't called her at all and I guess she'd been busy, she hadn't called me. She put the pictures on the desk in front of her and went through them silently. I held my breath and waited for her response.

Donna came in. She said hello and squeezed my shoulder and went behind Ruth's desk to look at the pictures. "Jake! These are fabulous! Best pictures you've ever had!"

I felt so, too. But I waited. Waited for Ruth to say what she thought. She remained silent.

I looked up at Donna. "Usually takes me hours to find the two or three I think I can use. With these, took me all morning to decide which two or three to discard. I'm still not sure."

Ruth still said nothing. I began to squirm in my

seat. Even if Donna liked them, I was nervous. My stomach was starting to bother me like it always did.

Then Donna said, "Ruth? What do you think?"

Ruth's eyes stayed on the pictures, but her words were exactly what I wanted them to be. "You're right. They're fabulous."

I'd thought she would think they were good, but I'd needed to hear her actually say it. Now that she'd said it, I could finally relax. Ruth's judgment was good. The best. But now I realized I still didn't have anywhere near as much confidence in my own judgment as I needed.

Confidence? God, a week before I'd been ready to throw in the towel on the whole thing. Quit the business. Quit L.A. Quit on everything.

But I didn't feel that way now. Not at all.

Not at all!

Ruth's fingers continued turning from one picture to another. Donna said, "Who took 'em for you?"

I laughed. "Antonio Calisi!"

Ruth's eyebrows went up. "Calisi? Who died and left you money?"

I chose my words carefully. "They were freebies. I know someone who knows him."

Ruth nodded absently. "Must be a good connection, baby. Calisi's not a freebie type of guy."

I felt like yelling. "He's the best I've ever been to, Ruth! You should see the way he works! He makes you feel like the two of you are lovers!"

She looked at me. Her mouth turned into a big smile. "That's the way it felt, I'll have to get myself a camera."

It did something to me. Froze me. I waited a moment and let her comment pass. Then I said, "Things're going to change, Ruth. Starting here, starting now. Everything's coming up roses." I laughed. "Roses! Daffodils! Carnations! Bushels of 'em! Better order a case of vases!"

Donna put her hand on my shoulder. "Know who you sound like?"

"Who?"

"You!" She laughed. "Like you *used* to sound, when you first hit town!"

Yeah, Maybe she was right. Maybe I really had it back. If I didn't, at least I was finally on my way to getting it back. I took her hand. "One difference, Donna. This time the town is going to know it's been hit!" I closed my other hand in a fist and swung it at the air. "Knockout! We're going all the way!"

Donna's hand tightened inside mine. "Whatever you say, Jake! We like taking those kinds of orders from our clients!"

She leaned down and kissed my cheek. She'd never done that before.

Don't believe what they tell you about agents. That they're just in it for the money. That's a lot of crap. If all they wanted was money they'd be out selling real estate. They care. Damn right they care. They wouldn't be in the business in the first place if they didn't care. They'd never be able to put up with actors if they didn't care.

Donna squeezed my shoulder again and looked at Ruth. "See? I told you he still had it in him!"

Ruth didn't answer.

Donna went out. Ruth put the pictures into a neat stack and slid them carefully into their envelope. She came around the desk and handed me the envelope. Then she leaned against the desk and looked at me and smiled. "Well I guess you *are* different, Jake. You're feeling it again."

"That's right! A week and a half ago Alan told me I was turning myself into a loser! I wanted to hit him! I knew he was right! Okay! That was then! It's behind me now." Both my hands came up in fists. I wished I had a camera in front of me. I'd give it a performance it would love to put on film. "I was a good actor, a couple years ago! I knew I was a good actor! But I started letting people talk me out of it! They can talk you out of all kinds of things in this city, if you let 'em! I'm not going to let 'em anymore!"

The only trouble was, I was still doing it a little bit like it was a performance. Because of course it was. I was saying it like I believed it, but I still didn't believe it. Not yet. I felt the urge to make it now but I still didn't have anywhere near enough self-confidence.

So I had to act it. Pretend it. Do it with bluff and bravado. Hope if I said it well enough, someone, *anyone*, might say I was right.

And if someone like Ruth said it, maybe that would be enough to give me the self-confidence.

So I waited for Ruth to say something. But when she finally spoke, what she said was what I didn't want to hear.

"I love you, Jake."

She was leaning against the desk again. Her hands were coming out. She was waiting for me to stand up and take them and kiss her like I always did. And this time, for the first time, I didn't do it.

It really bothered me, driving home. A kiss wasn't much. Why hadn't I given her one?

I knew the answer. I didn't want to think about it. I knew what it might lead to.

I parked in front of the house. I went to the front door and went into the living room and sat on the sofa. I sat there a long time. I was about to light up a cigarette when I heard a car pull up out front. I put the cigarette into my pocket, and a moment later the front door opened. Katie came in.

She looked radiant, as always. Her fingers were snapping against each other quickly like they sometimes did when she was really full of energy. She was smiling and seemed so terrifically alive. It wiped my worries right out of my mind.

"I called Calisi this morning, he said you'd picked up the pictures! He said they turned out great!"

"They did! Come here and look!"

She sat beside me and threw her arms around me. We looked through the pictures together. They excited her so much she kissed me on the cheek. That excited me so much that pretty soon we weren't looking at the pictures anymore.

Then I heard the doorbell. I gave Katie another kiss and started to get up. She pulled me back down by the neck and gave me another kiss. Then we both laughed and I left her and went to the door and opened it.

"Hi, baby. Mind if I come in?"

I knew it was bad. She already had that tough edge to her voice. Her business voice. Her agent's voice. I didn't know what to do.

Before I could do anything, she'd pulled the door all the way open and had come past me and walked into the living room.

It was about as noisy as a funeral parlor. I cleared my throat and then hesitated, then finally found a way to get a few words out of my mouth. "Ruth, you know Katie.... You met her last week at—"

"Sure. I know Katie." Ruth nodded several times. "The girl without the last name." She nodded again. "How you doing, baby?"

It was silent. I had to do something.

Then Katie's fingers snapped. She spoke, but very quietly and very measured. "I'm doing all right, Miss Shapiro." Her eyes were steady. "How are you doing?"

"Me? I'm doing fine!"

It was still again.

Katie's fingers snapped one more time as if they had wills of their own. Then they were silent.

I started to move forward.

Katie jumped up from the sofa and walked across the room to the bookcase with the liquor bottles. When she got there she stopped. She stared at them blankly. Then she reached forward suddenly and took her bottle of Jack Daniel's. She poured herself a glass. It was the first time I'd seen her take whisky since that night at The Dancers.

She held the glass and looked at it. She raised it toward her lips.

Then she stopped. Her eyes turned uncertainly toward Ruth. "I'm sorry. Would you like a drink?"

"No." Ruth looked at me, then away. It was sudden, but just long enough for me to recognize the look of fear and uncertainty in her eyes.

Ruth wrapped her arms around herself. "Only five-thirty." She laughed. "I try not to hit the stuff, this early in the day." Then she seemed to shiver. It wasn't her agent's voice anymore. It was a good deal weaker.

She looked toward Katie again. "But don't mind me. Help yourself."

Katie nodded. The glass in her hand seemed to be shaking as much as Ruth's voice had.

Katie raised the glass again and this time got it all the way up. "Well ... cheers." She drank.

Then Katie stepped halfway across the room as if she weren't quite sure where she wanted to go. She looked toward the table by the sofa. "Did Jake . . . Did Jake show you his new pictures, Miss Shapiro?"

"Yeah. He did." Ruth moved toward the window, increasing the distance between them. "I thought they were terrific."

"I thought so, too." Katie drank again. Katie kept her eyes on Ruth and moved slowly back to the bookcase. Her hand came out slowly and took the bottle again. She refilled the glass almost to the top. When she put the bottle back on the bookcase it rattled slightly. All three of us looked at it.

Katie drank. She moved quickly across the living room. She sat on the sofa. She reached for the pictures with a trembling hand. She spread them on the table so they faced Ruth. She looked up with a weak smile. "Jake ought to be able to really do something now. Now that he's got decent pictures."

"It's not pictures that get you the work, baby. They help, but it takes more than pictures, no matter how good they are." Ruth's voice was her agent's voice again. "Takes talent. That's what lets you make it."

"That, and someone who knows how to sell the talent. Right?" Katie lifted her glass in a toast. This time the glass didn't shake at all.

Ruth didn't move. I didn't move either, but I was really on edge. Then Ruth half turned away and looked at me, and her voice came out softer again. "Didn't get to talk much at the office, baby. Maybe we ought to get together. For dinner or something." She took a deep breath. "Little extended conversation."

I didn't know what to say.

Katie stood up suddenly. She stretched her arms and yawned. "I'm tired, Jake. Really had a tough day." Her hand came up and covered her mouth. Her eyes slid sideways and stared for a moment at the back of Ruth's head. "I'm going to lie down for a little while." She hesitated. "Better check me, about twenty minutes. In case I fall asleep. Okay?"

Katie stood there and waited. Finally I nodded. Ruth saw it.

Katie came across the room and stopped as she

reached the arch. She turned and looked briefly at Ruth. "Excuse me. I really am tired."

Ruth didn't answer. Katie went down the hall and into the bedroom.

I felt like disappearing through the nearest wall. For all the words I spoke I could've been a dead man.

Ruth moved aimlessly toward the sofa. She looked down at the pictures and stared at them a long time. Then she moved toward the bookcase. Looked at the Jack Daniel's. "Well. She likes her whisky."

I cleared my throat. "Yeah. Guess she does."

Ruth's eyes snapped at me. "Well! Finally got your voice back! Huh, baby?"

She turned and paced the room. She looked down at my pictures again. "She likes her whisky. And she likes you. Huh?" She paused. Turned toward the window. Her voice lowered. "Question is, do you like her?"

I held my breath. What could I say?

"I think I like her a lot."

Ruth's head nodded absently. She wandered to the other side of the living room again. Her voice came out the softest yet. "She actually moved in here yet? . . . Or she just hinting at it, so far?"

I put my hands in my pockets. "She moved in. Couple days ago."

Ruth's head nodded once more. Then she turned. She kept her eyes off me and walked past me and out the front door.

I followed Ruth to the front yard. We looked at each other for a moment, but neither of us found anything to say. She got into her car. I watched her back into the road and turn and go off. I stayed in the middle of the yard. Minutes passed. I heard the front door open behind me.

"Jake?" She waited for me to answer. "Jake? What's the matter? Why're you standing out there?"

I didn't turn to face her. I rubbed the back of my neck and kept looking at the empty road. Then I couldn't hold it in any longer. "She's one of the best agents in this city."

"So?"

". . . So, you're dead in this town without a good agent."

I still didn't turn. I was scared and was trying to hide it. I walked across the yard and into the road.

When I finally turned, Katie wasn't there. I went into the house. She wasn't in the living room. I found her in the bathroom standing by the sink. She was drinking water from the glass she'd had the Jack Daniel's in. She took a big gulp and threw her head back. I didn't give it a thought. My thoughts were still on Ruth.

"I'm sorry, Jake. If I made any trouble for you . . ."

She seemed so very small. So very frightened. The same way she'd been that minute or two in the parking lot at The Dancers right after those kids had run off. I wanted to hold her and tell her it was all right. But I couldn't. I had too much fear in myself.

She came past me and went into the living room. She poured more Jack Daniel's into her glass. Then I went to her and took her in my arms, doing it as if I were acting a part. "It's not that important. Don't worry about it. It won't mean a thing."

Then I realized. It was one of the few times I'd reached for her that she hadn't stepped back. Usually she liked it if she was able to touch me first. But this time she hadn't resisted.

I held her firmly and kissed her. I was trying to act strong, but I didn't know if it was good enough to fool her or not. After we kissed she moved away. She held the glass in one hand and the bottle in the other. She kept her back to me now just like I'd kept mine to her, before, outside. We weren't connecting at all.

She went down the hall toward the kitchen.

I sat on the sofa and stared at my pictures. They didn't seem so important now. My mind drifted off to nothing. Minutes went by, and suddenly she came back. She sat beside me and put her hand on my arm. "Why're you so worried about her?"

"What?"

"Come on, Jake, tell me." Her hand tightened on my arm. "You're acting like there's more to this than I thought there was. Do you love her?"

"What? No!" Then I was quiet. I tapped the pictures together till I had a tight stack. "I like her. Very much.

But that's all there is to it. All it's ever been, far as I'm concerned."

"Far as *she's* concerned?"

She was leaning right up next to me. I leaned back against the sofa and crossed my arms on my chest. Then I reached forward and put the pictures into their envelope. I tried to speak calmly. "She's a good agent, Katie. It's tough, to get someone like her to represent you."

"So?"

"So . . ." I felt all the feelings I'd had the week before coming back at me. "So she took me on in the first place because she went for me a lot more than she went for my acting. And I . . ." I ran my finger along the edge of the envelope. I felt rotten enough and hated myself enough to hope the edge might cut me. "And I've been able to keep her, because of that."

Katie nodded. She moved back. She drank more Jack Daniel's.

I rubbed my neck. "She's good, Katie. She's awfully good. She used to handle Jack Christolf, couple years ago. He wasn't big then. He was just starting out. Way I heard it, it was a pretty tight relationship. So all the time he wasn't making it, she stuck with him." I flipped the envelope at the table. It slid toward the corner and almost went over but stopped in time and balanced on the edge. I wanted to give it the nudge it needed to fall to the floor. "Then he started making it, and he dropped her cold. Professionally and romantically."

Katie's hand dropped softly across my knee. "You mean you wanted her to feel about you the same way she'd felt about Christolf."

I closed my eyes tight. I said nothing.

Her hand left my knee. I opened my eyes and watched as she took the envelope. She pulled it back to the center of the table. "You're an actor. It's hard, being an actor. Any actor would've done what you did."

I closed my eyes again. "I'd like to think I'm not just the same as *any* actor. That maybe I wouldn't do the same things, to make it."

Her hand was on my knee again. "Don't be so hard on yourself. We're all human. We all do things we shouldn't."

I shook my head and turned away. I felt her fingers

on my neck, stroking it gently. It felt good. I hated it for feeling good.

"There's another thing to think about, Jake. About her. As an agent." She moved closer to me on the sofa. "If Christolf left her, maybe it meant she wasn't doing enough for him. As an agent. He wanted someone better!"

I opened my eyes and looked at her. "Katie! For God's sake! They don't come any better!"

"No? Think about it." She waited a moment. "She's not doing anything for you. She hasn't gotten you—"

"Katie, she's a damn good agent! God! She's one of the best!" I turned away again. I found the cigarette I'd put in my pocket before. I stuck it in my mouth and took out a match. I still felt scared and guilty but suddenly I felt a little angry, too. Hearing *her* tell *me* about the business! "Katie, this is a small world out here! A good agent's one of the hardest things there is to come by!" I burned almost half an inch of the cigarette trying to get it lit. "A guy like me, with no credits worth talking about—"

"You've got credits! You did that part on Broadway! You—"

"That was nothing! I don't have the kind of credits that matter out here!" I took a deep breath. It was filled with smoke. "A guy like me, I'm lucky if I can get any agent at all!"

Katie stood up. She moved away several steps. She raised her glass. But it was empty. She lowered it, hesitated, then went down the hall. A moment later I heard water running. Then it stopped.

I stared at my cigarette. A few minutes passed, and then Katie came back. "We made an agreement, Jake. You weren't going to waste your time getting yourself depressed anymore."

I grunted. I found I still had the dead match in my hand. I flipped it at the ashtray. I took another strong puff on my cigarette.

"Jake?"

I didn't answer.

Katie turned away. A moment later she turned back, and now she was smiling and her fingers were snapping. "No. I'm not going to let you get away with it."

"Get away with what?"

"I'm not going to let you get depressed. You're going to put all your energy into one thing, Jake. Making it. Right?"

I didn't answer.

She came forward. "Well? Right?"

". . . Easier to say it than to do it."

"So? Do it anyway. Come on, Jake! Do it! The only way to beat it is to do it!" She reached down for my arm and pulled me to my feet. I don't know where she got the energy, but she was so strong I couldn't resist her. Three seconds later she had me at the front door. "Come on, Jake! We're going somewhere!"

"What? Where?"

"I don't know yet! To cheer you up! That's where!"

What she found to cheer me up was nothing fancy. She took me to the empty-minded heaven of a junk-food maniac. Greasy french fries and undercooked hamburgers and thickly foamed, oversugared milkshakes. It was terrible. It was terrific. It was young, it was cheap, it was grunchy. It was fun, just like she was. She paid for it. What we needed next was a carnival roller coaster, a really dangerous one that'd make us sick to our stomachs. There was none available so we settled for an ice-cream place in Westwood. She treated us both to triple-decker cones.

We were acting higher than kites by then. My mind was God knows where. I wasn't worried about it. I didn't care. We came out of the place with two matched cones, each containing a scoop of pistachio and a scoop of banana nut and a scoop of something they called mudpie.

We slurped our way across the street, and we were almost dancing. I took her hand and twirled her around. She must've liked it 'cause she started to sing.

I laughed. "What's your secret?"

She stopped singing for a second. "I got lots of 'em! Which one you interested in?"

"You're so young! You got so much energy!" I had to stop waving my arm so much. I was almost losing the top of my ice-cream cone. "How do you keep from letting things get you down?"

She stood still a moment. "You're my secret on that one." She came close to me and kissed me.

This time I backed away a step. The dancing was

okay, but I didn't want to kiss. Not that way, in the middle of the street. It didn't matter how high I was. Lots of eyes were watching us now. I felt so self-conscious about it.

It's such a stupid thing! I'm an actor! I must want to be an exhibitionist or I wouldn't be an actor! But when it comes to showing private emotions in public, I've never been able to do it. Not unless there was an audience out front, or a camera on me. I've been able to do the expected things. Holding hands, a kiss on the cheek. Everybody does that. And the dancing, it was a spur-of-the-moment thing. I'd done it without even thinking about it. But the way she squeezed against me and started kissing me right in the middle of Hilgard Avenue with people all around us, the way she was suddenly almost clawing at me—I wasn't much for that. Only someone as free and young and vital and open as she could do that.

But then she stepped forward and squeezed against me again and kissed me again, and that time I didn't back away. I went with it.

Because it was her. Because I was with her. Because I was high. Because she seemed high. Because she didn't seem to care where we were or who was watching. Because all of a sudden I didn't care where we were or who was watching. I didn't care *what* we did. Where we did it. Who saw it. All I cared about was her. And being with her. I'd never met anyone else in my life who was like her.

We finally stopped long enough to get both ourselves and our ice-cream cones into her car. I held both cones as she drove onto the freeway. She was laughing more than I'd ever seen her laugh before. She asked me to make my faces for her. I did. She screamed, "I feel happy, Jake! For the first time in my life, I feel really happy!"

It thrilled me to hear her say that. "Oh God, Katie! So do I!"

Soon she was driving fast. I paid no attention. I didn't care.

"The past year and a half, Katie, out here, it's been like I've been paralyzed! Half dead!" I turned toward her. "I've been scared! Yes! Scared of everything! God, I've been so frightened!" I leaned over and kissed her cheek. "You know what?"

"What!"

"I don't feel scared of anything anymore!"

Her mouth smiled and her eyes flashed at me. "That's what I want to hear!" She looked front again. "Hey! You scared of going faster?"

"No! No! I'm not scared of anything when I'm with you!" I was laughing so wildly I almost dropped one of the ice-cream cones.

She pulled the car into the extreme left lane and gunned the motor. We shot forward like a rocket. Faces in other cars turned to look at us as we raced ahead of them. I waved an ice-cream cone at them. Katie began switching lanes. It seemed okay, she seemed in perfect control of the car. She found a patch of open road and hit the gas pedal again. She began to yell. "It's different, Jake!"

"What's different?"

"Me and you! I've always wanted to be with someone! But with you, it's different!" Her head turned for a split second. "With you, it's not just being with *someone*! It's being with *you*!"

I loved the sound of her voice and the things she was saying, but I was finally aware of how fast she was going. The speedometer was past seventy.

"Katie!" I laughed. "I'm not scared—but let's not push it!"

"What?"

"You're going too fast! Slow down!"

"Why?" She couldn't stop laughing.

"Katie! Please! Slow down!" I looked through the rear window. "There're probably cops along here!"

"What?"

She swerved the car sideways. I almost fell against her. She'd suddenly begun to angle straight toward the extreme right lane. Thank God there were no cars near us. She was still going well over seventy. Without slowing down, she went straight onto an off-ramp and along a curve and down toward a stop sign. She braked. I went forward and had to slam my forearm against the dashboard to stop myself. When I turned to look at her, she was turned so she could see through the rear window. I started to say something, but she turned front and gunned the motor and we went forward again. I fell back into my seat. She took the first turn we came to and then we were in a dark, empty street. She pulled over to the curb and stopped the car. She was breathing heavily now. She looked through the back window again. "You said you saw cops. . . . I don't see any cops. . . ."

I looked down and found my pants were covered with the pistachio, banana nut and mudpie ice cream. I felt too high to do anything about it but laugh. "Katie! Look what you've done to me!"

". . . What?" Then she saw it, saw my face, and she began to laugh, too. She leaned over and kissed me.

I said, "Let's get married!"

"What?"

I took her arms. "I mean it!" I kissed her. "God, Katie, I really mean it! I've never felt this way before!" I kissed her again. "I love you, Katie! You say you feel happy for the first time in your life! I feel that way too! Come on, why not? We can do it right now! Let's drive to Vegas! We can—"

"NO!"

She pushed my hands off her arms.

Everything had changed completely, just like that. We sat silently. She was staring straight ahead. I became aware of how wet and cold the ice cream felt, soaking into my pants. I didn't do anything about it. She'd brought me down pretty quick and pretty hard. I had no idea why.

She seemed to feel bad about it, too. Her hands fumbled at her pocketbook and opened it up and dug inside. She took out her pill bottle. The one I'd seen before. She pried off the cap and spilled a red-and-blue capsule into her hand. She popped it into her mouth, swallowed, waited a moment and then snapped the top back on the bottle and threw the bottle into her pocketbook. Then her hand covered mine. "Please, Jake. I love you too. I really do. But don't ask me to marry you. Please." She looked at me. "I can't."

". . . Why not?"

She looked away. "It wouldn't work." Her head shook back and forth. "I don't know why, it just wouldn't."

I spoke evenly and slowly. "If I love you, and you love me, it can work."

"No!" Her hand left mine and began to rub the side

of her face. "I was married once." Her eyes closed. "It was wrong. Made me feel trapped." Her head bent forward. She began to rub her forehead. "I don't want to be married again. I'm afraid of it." She put both hands in her lap and clasped them together. Her eyes opened. She took a deep breath. "He's dead now. My husband. Someone killed him."

She finally put the car in gear. I watched her carefully. Her hands were shaking on the steering wheel. There were tears on her cheeks.

"Katie? Maybe I better drive."

She shook her head back and forth. She hit the gas. The car shot forward. We went about a block.

"Katie? . . . How long ago were you married?"

She was silent.

I asked some more questions. She didn't say a word, all the way home. She didn't say another word all that night. When we got home, she went into the living room and took the bottle of Jack Daniel's. She poured herself a full glass. She drank about a third of it. Then she put the glass down and came across the room and put her arms around me and hugged me very tight.

But then she let go of me and went back to the Jack Daniel's. She drank a good deal more of it. She went into the bedroom and quickly undressed. She stayed on the far side of the room, keeping a distance of several feet between us all the time.

It was a cold night now. I didn't know what to do about it. We got into the same bed we'd been getting into for the past four nights, but this time we did it without touching. She stayed far over on her side of the bed and curled up in a ball almost at the edge. She seemed to fall asleep after half an hour or so. The glass on her night table was completely empty by then.

I must've fallen asleep some time after that. It was a very bad sleep. I woke up very tired the next morning.

Katie had her insurance office to go to the next morning. I had nothing. I sat around the house and waited for the phone to ring, and of course it didn't —it never does when you want it to. I couldn't sit still. The mail came. Mostly nothing. There was a card from Alan, inviting me to a Charlie Blow party at his house in Malibu. Charlie Blow meant you didn't have to bring any drugs, he was supplying. The party was for that night. If the card was just coming this morning that meant he probably hadn't planned to invite me but had sent the card as an afterthought. Or maybe Jill had told him he'd better invite me. It didn't matter. I didn't want to see Alan, his house or his party.

Around noon I was really climbing the walls. I went for a ride. Around twelve-thirty I found myself on Highland. I stopped in at Tulley's Bar. I didn't feel like eating, so I just ordered a glass of wine. There were plenty of actors there but none I knew well enough to have to say much more than hello to. I said my hello, they said theirs, they continued their gossip, I left them alone. I sat in a booth and didn't even eavesdrop. For the hundredth time

I went over in my mind the way Katie had been in the car the previous night.

I don't know if I stopped at Tulley's on purpose, on the blind chance Ruth might come in there for lunch, but as it happened she did. She saw me and came to the booth. She looked tired. Her face was tight and drawn. She sat down across from me and ordered lunch. She took out cigarettes and put one in her mouth and lit it. She left the pack on the table. I didn't touch it.

"Been a lousy day." She shook her head. "Mel had us all in his office for a meeting. Telling us he just got the figures for the quarter. We didn't pull in as much as he thinks we should have." Her eyes passed briefly over my face. "He pulled his weight, maybe the rest of us would have it a little easier." She played with the cigarette pack. "God, never work for anyone else. All it does is keep you up at night." Her hand stiffened. Her eyes came up again. They were dull and glassy.

But then there was a spark in them, and when she spoke I knew the spark was anger. "Your friend came in to see me this morning."

"What?"

"That's right. Dropped by my office. She wanted to talk."

But then Tulley came over with her lunch. Ruth sagged against the back of the booth, and we both watched as he set her up with a bowl of chili and a salad and a martini. He looked at my glass. Asked if I wanted more wine. I said no. He went away.

Ruth's hand finally came forward and touched the martini, but she didn't pick it up. Her voice was tired again. "Want to know what she came to see me about?"

I coughed. "Up to you. If you want to tell me."

"Said she wanted to know something about you." Ruth paused. "I said sure, ask away. She said why wasn't I getting you any work." Ruth paused again, in case I wanted to say anything. I still didn't. I kept my face blank. Ruth leaned forward. "I told her it's a tough business! I told her we try! Then she asked me, did I think you have any talent!" Ruth looked me straight in the eye. "I told her yes, I thought you had a lot of talent." Ruth paused. "She said if I thought you had so much talent, why wasn't I selling it."

I kept absolutely still. Kept my teeth clamped and let myself show no emotion at all.

Ruth went on. "I told her there's plenty of sellers in the business, but there aren't so many buyers."

Ruth paused again. I picked up my wine glass and finished off what was there.

"Drinking wine, huh?" Her head cocked to one side. "Jake? What's the matter? You okay?"

"I'm okay."

"You sure?"

I nodded. I picked up Ruth's pack of ciagrettes and took one out. I could've taken one of my own, but I knew it would make us both feel more at ease if I took one of hers. I rolled the cigarette in my fingers. "What you told her, just the facts of life. Didn't tell her anything I didn't hear myself, long time ago."

"Yeah?" Ruth dipped her spoon into her chili and stirred it once, then looked at me. "I know you've heard it, Jake. I've never known for sure if you've understood it."

I nodded slightly.

I heard voices from another table. Actors. Talking about other actors. About the jobs the other actors were getting. About jobs *these* actors *weren't* getting. If they'd been getting them, they wouldn't have been sitting here talking about it.

And I wouldn't be sitting here either.

"All of us know what the odds are, Ruth. None of us can be sure if we really understand 'em or not." I tightened my lips and looked at the floor. I tried to go on with it. "Probably, the time ever came we really understood 'em, we'd quit."

She let go of her spoon. "What's that mean? You're getting ready to quit?"

". . . No. Not yet." I immediately hated myself for tacking the "Not yet" onto it. I straightened my back. "No! I'm not quitting!"

Ruth's eyes wandered across the room toward the bar. Her head nodded. Then she turned to her chili and started spooning it up. "She says to me, your friend, says she heard I used to know Jack Christolf pretty well." Ruth paused. "I said yes, I used to know him. Pretty well."

I turned my head and kept my eyes off her.

"Well enough to know he's not all he pretends to be. She says, your friend, says she heard it took Jack a long time to make it. I said yes, it did. I said fortunately for him, I'd known how to nurse him along when he wasn't making it. I got him there. She said maybe Jack Christolf would be willing to help someone else who hasn't made it yet."

Ruth looked up for my reaction. I shook my head and smiled. "Sure. Jack Christolf. He knows how to help one guy. Jack Christolf."

"Almost word for word what I told her." Ruth pushed at her salad so the dressing would mix through. "Sometimes amateurs take a look at the business, they get ideas, Jake. They start shooting their mouths off. Don't let her talk you into thinking crap. Like someone like Jack Christolf's going to give two cents' worth of a damn about helping someone like you." Ruth's mouth tightened. "I was a little worried—the way she asked me—maybe she was saying it because of something you'd said to *her*."

"No. Don't worry, I know what the odds are."

"I thought you did, but I'm beginning to wonder." Her voice changed. "Maybe you think there *is* a chance something like that might happen! That I *might* be able to get someone like Christolf to do something for you!"

I laughed. "Only time Christolf would help another actor is if the guy's friends are taking up a collection to pay for his burial."

Ruth studied my face. Then she settled down. "Not even then, Jake. Not even then." She sipped her martini. "It's bad odds in this town. Bad odds for everyone."

But then she put down her drink and changed her expression and smiled. "Hey! I didn't ask! You had anything to eat? Haven't had lunch yet, I'll treat!"

". . . No thanks. I've eaten."

"Oh!" She thought. "Another glass of wine?"

"No thanks." I stuck the cigarette in my mouth and lit it. I turned away. I had a feeling my face looked pretty bad by then. "So what else happened? I mean, she say anything else to you?"

"What? Oh. No. That's about it." Ruth paused. "She looked sort of screwy, though. Very still. Very quiet. *Very* quiet."

I thought of the way she'd been the night before. When I'd asked her questions in the car, and she hadn't answered. When we'd gotten home. "Yeah, I guess she gets like that. I guess we all do, sometimes."

Ruth didn't answer. She finished her chili and drank the rest of her martini. Then she set the glass down in the exact center of her napkin and looked across the table at me. "She's a very attractive girl, Jake. Most men would be attracted to her."

I stayed silent.

"I mean . . . I'd like to know. Is that what it is? Her looks?"

I put my hands on the edge of the table and gripped hard.

"Well?"

"No. It's not her looks."

Ruth hesitated. "Well? Then what is it?"

I couldn't shake Ruth's eyes. "She's not like us, Ruth. She's normal. A real person."

"What're we? Freaks?"

"Sometimes I think we are." I held up my hands and gestured. "I don't know what it is. It's so many things. She's not tired. Us, we always seem so tired. All of us. But her, she's so full of energy. She seems to want things so much. She's got so much feeling. So much emotion. She doesn't let things get her down. Or stop her. It's . . . She's so alive!"

"Aren't the rest of us alive?"

"No! I don't think we are!" I looked down. "Maybe we were, once. But we aren't now. Maybe we've been through too much. Seen too much. Been beaten, too much." I looked up and leaned forward. "But her, she's young! She's fresh! She knows how to laugh at things! I mean, *really* laugh! And she's . . ." I thought of her coming into Ruth's office. The guts it must've taken. "She's so damn *sure* of herself!"

Ruth sat still. She said nothing. She looked across the room vacantly.

Then she exhaled and shook her wrist loose from the sleeve. She looked at her watch and sat up straight and smiled. "Well! Time for my irresistible force to meet those old, tired, immovable objects before they take their afternoon siestas, huh?"

She jumped out of the booth. She swung the strap of her pocketbook over her shoulder with a flourish. Then she stopped. She sat down again. "Look, damn it. I may be older, I may be a little tired sometimes, I may be a little worse for wear, but I care about you, Jake. I'm talking about the kind of care that doesn't go away. You understand that, don't you?"

I began to squirm in my seat.

She jumped up again. "Okay. Settle down. Let's not get heavy about this thing." She laughed. "Especially not in the middle of the day." Her head shook back and forth. She reached down and took the cigarette from my mouth, put it into hers, took a long drag, and then gave it back to me. "Okay, baby. I've been around. You like her? Okay. Maybe you got to get her out of your system." She looked at the empty wine glass next to my hand. "Paid for that yet?"

". . . No."

"Wouldn't let me buy you lunch, least you can do is let me pay for a glass of wine. Okay?"

". . . Okay."

She smiled. "Chin up, Jake. We'll come through."

She went across to the bar and talked to Tulley. Her hand gestured in my direction. Tulley looked at me and nodded. Ruth took out money and gave it to him. I dropped my eyes toward the table.

At four o'clock I stopped by the photographic reproduction place where I'd taken my top choice of the Antonio Calisi pictures. They had my copies ready for me. Five hundred eight-by-ten glossies. It was unusual that I was able to get them that fast. Usually it takes at least a week, and that's if you're lucky, because usually when you go down to pick them up they aren't ready, and then when you come down again they still aren't ready. But you say nothing about it, because if you did it would get you nowhere.

But I had a connection at this particular company. His name was Steve. We'd been actors together in New York years before. He'd come west before me and hadn't been able to get a thing. Los Angeles had chewed him to pieces. Eventually he'd needed money, so he'd gotten the job with this company. Pretty soon he liked the steady salary. Soon after that his ambition was gone. He dropped out of the business completely. He wasn't an actor anymore. Except in that screwy way all of us are actors, and stay actors, whether we make it or not. 'Cause we've got it in our blood, right up till the day we die. But for all practical purposes he was no longer an actor. He was an upstanding, wage-earning, respectable adult. It was just an accident of fate that he happened to earn his wages in a town called Hollywood.

He'd completely given up on his dreams, and he knew it.

But he was one of the lucky ones. After two years he'd managed to get past most of his bitterness and despair. He'd been able to remain friends with those of us who were still in the business and still trying to make it. Been able to look at us without wishing we were dead, or at least beaten like he was. So when I came in with my Calisi picture, he was strong enough to look at it and say he thought it was good, and strong enough to mean it. He made it a rush order.

Most people in his position wouldn't have done that. I admired his strength.

I picked up the eight-by-ten glossies and drove home. I sat in the kitchen and stapled résumés to the backs of the glossies. I heard the front door open.

"Jake? I'm home!"

"In the kitchen!"

I could hear her in the living room. I didn't go to look. I stayed at the table and continued to staple. When she came in I half expected to see a glass of Jack Daniel's in her hand, but her hand was empty.

"Hey! You got the pictures!" She came over to the table. She kissed the top of my head and put her hands on my shoulders. She looked at the glossies. "Oh, Jake, they really look terrific." She kissed me again. Then she went to the refrigerator and poured herself a glass of milk and began to drink it.

I decided I couldn't put it off. "Katie, I ran into Ruth today."

"Oh?" She stood absolutely still. Then she opened

the cupboard and took down a bag of chocolate-chip cookies. She munched a cookie and then dipped a second one into her milk and began to eat that one.

I put the pictures aside. "Ruth told me you were in to see her today."

"Yeah." She chewed another cookie. "She's got a nice office. Just moved in there, huh?"

"Yeah." I rubbed the back of my neck. "They've been doing pretty well, this past year. The boss decided to expand the agency." I watched as she took out another cookie. "Why'd you go to see her?"

She shrugged. "No special reason. Happened to be in the neighborhood." She dipped the cookie into the milk. Then she faced me. "I asked her why she wasn't getting you any work."

"I know." I rubbed my fingers gently across the top of the stapler. "It's a tough business, Katie. She's trying."

"Is she?" Katie put down her glass. "You sound just like her, Jake. It's a tough business. It's a tough business."

"It is!" I pushed the stapler aside. I noticed my fingers were trembling slightly. "Did you ask her if she could get Jack Christolf to help me?"

She started to say something. Then her hand waved at the air and her mouth closed and her hand came down and dug into the bag of cookies again. Then she stopped. "Jake? Why're you letting me eat these things? You know they make me fat." She closed the bag tightly. She opened the cupboard and put the bag inside it. She closed the door and suddenly faced me again. She had a smile on her face. "Will power. Right? I just got to stop it. Right?"

I didn't answer her. I'm not sure why.

"Right! *Will* power!" She walked across the room. She looked at me again. "Yes, I said something to her about Christolf. Why? You said she used to handle him. It was just a thought."

I tapped my fingers on the table. "Doesn't work that way. Not in this business. Maybe not in any business."

"No? Well . . . maybe not." She went back to the counter. She picked up the milk and drank it.

She immediately washed the glass thoroughly and put it upside down in the drainer. She took it out again and wiped it dry with a towel. Then she turned to me. "Look, Jake, it doesn't hurt to ask a couple questions when you get an idea, does it? I mean, people ask people to do favors all the time."

"Let me tell you something about Jack Christolf, so you won't get any more ideas about him. The only person he's interested in is himself."

Katie moved back a step.

"Katie? What's the matter?"

"That's what *she* said! You *are* sounding like her!"

I chewed my lower lip. "I'm sounding like someone who knows the business. And the people who're *in* the business. They've got their minds on one thing. Themselves. They haven't got room for anyone else."

"Oh . . . I see. . . ." She moved back another step. Her eyes left me. "Is that the way *you* are? The same as *them?*"

That stopped me.

The next thing I knew my hands were searching my pockets for cigarettes. I found one and held it in my fingers and stared at it. "No. No, Katie. I'm not that way."

But what I was thinking wasn't pleasant. I knew that business too well.

I laughed to hide my thoughts. "Haven't made it, yet. Right? Maybe, I get lucky enough to make it, *then* I'll be that way."

She looked at me again. Her face was as soft and innocent as a helpless baby's. "No, Jake. You are what you are. You're not going to change." Her mouth broke into a big smile. "I can see that."

I laughed again, but I didn't like the laugh. It was lousy and forced. "You're seeing things, do you see if I'm going to make it or not?"

She moved behind me. Her hands took my head and pressed it gently against her. "Of course you're going to make it. You're good, Jake. You're very good. So stop it. Don't let yourself get depressed." Then my head was against her stomach and I could feel the big breath she took. "Please, Jake. I can't stand it, when you let it get to you like this. Believe in yourself." Her fingers tightened against the sides of my head. "Please, Jake. You got to believe in yourself. *I* believe in you. You know I do, don't you?"

I didn't answer. I didn't move. But then I slowly got my head free and leaned forward and put the cigarette in my mouth and lit it.

She knelt beside me suddenly and grabbed both my hands. "I mean it, Jake. I believe in you. And you've got to believe in you. It's important. You haven't got a chance, you don't believe in yourself." Her grip tightened on my hands. "I know what I'm talking about. Nobody'll *ever* believe in you, you don't believe in yourself. Don't let it happen to you, Jake. Beat it. *You got to beat it!*"

I'd never seen her like this before. "It's all right, Katie. Don't get so excited."

"Please! *Listen* to me! Don't doubt yourself! Your mind can play tricks on you! You can't let it do it! It'll kill you. Don't let *anyone* put doubts in your mind! You've got talent! You can make it!"

"Okay. I agree with you. I'll make it. Settle down."

She stood up abruptly and went to the sink. She ran water into the glass. She opened her pocketbook and took out her pill bottle and poured one of those blue-and-red capsules into her hand.

I stayed in my chair. "Katie? You all right?"

"What?" She looked around. "Sure. Sure." She popped the pill into her mouth and took a quick gulp of water. She threw her head back.

She capped the bottle and put the bottle in her pocketbook and washed the glass again and dried it and then turned her back to me. "I asked her if *she* believed in you." Katie paused. "She *said* she did. So I asked her was she going to help you make it? You know what she said to that?" It hung there a moment. "Nothing, Jake. She wouldn't even answer me."

I shook my head. "She's trying her best, Katie."

"Is she? I saw her try. You ever been in her office? The phone was ringing all the time. I was there ten, fifteen minutes, she made a big deal for some actor. A movie. Fifty thousand dollars." She turned and faced me. "That could've been *you* she was making that deal for!"

I looked away. I reached for my stapler. I grabbed another picture and résumé. "Not if the people with the fifty thousand didn't want me."

"Don't think like that! They *could've* wanted you!

She could've *made* them want you! Jake, it's her *job* to make them want you!"

She caught herself. She took the glass and pushed the corner of a towel into it again. She dried it again and then dried the outside again.

I went to the sink. "You sure you're all right?"

I started to put my arms around her. She started to push me away like she usually did when I make the first move. But this time I didn't let her. Suddenly she changed her mind and squeezed close against me and huddled in my arms.

"Please, Katie. Do me a favor. Far as Ruth goes, you better stay away from her."

"What?"

I realized immediately it was exactly the wrong thing to say. Katie burst out of my arms. "She was right!"

"What?"

"She was right! She's really got you!"

"What're you talking about?"

"Nothing!" Her hands flew up, then down. "Nothing. Just something she said . . ."

"What do you mean? What'd she say?"

Katie didn't answer. I reached for her again. "Katie! Tell me what she said!"

"She said if you knew I'd been in to see her, that'd be the end of me."

"What?"

Katie began to shake again. "She said actors know they can't exist in this town without an agent! That if I tried to make any trouble between you and her, you'd kick me out!"

I moved back to the sink. I couldn't be sure. It didn't sound like Ruth.

But Ruth was smart. Clever. Tough. At any moment she might say lots of things you'd never think she would say. That's what made her such a good agent.

Katie's eyes were wide open. "Jake? Was she right?" She came halfway back to me. "I wasn't trying to make trouble for you, Jake! I was just trying to help! Is that what you'd do? Kick me out?"

"No! Of course not!"

Again I wanted to reach for her. But this time I didn't do it.

I sat at the table and thought about it. Maybe Ruth *had* said something like that. And not just to scare her. Maybe Ruth had really meant it.

Ruth knew me well. She knew the business. The way people in the business act. How they react to the things people around them do. How they turn on each other, how their relationships fall apart at the blink of an eye.

How they put their eyes on their dreams and push aside anyone who gets in their way. How they get hungry, so hungry they don't care if someone gets hurt. How they want it so badly they use people—everyone around them —even themselves.

Did I really think I was immune to it? The exception to the rule?

Yeah. Maybe Ruth *had* said something like that.

"You got to understand, Katie. Ruth, she was telling you the truth." I stared at the table. "I mean . . . maybe . . . maybe not about me, but about most actors. They'll—"

"I'll tell you what she thinks about most actors!" Katie pulled a chair next to me and sat in it. Her eyes were blazing. "When she was talking about Jack Christolf. She said he's not all he pretends he is."

"That's the understatement of the century."

Her hands gripped my arm. "No, Jake! That's not what she meant! She said *most* actors aren't what they pretend they are!" Her fingernails dug into my arm just above the elbow. "She meant it, Jake. That's what she thinks of actors. She wasn't just talking about Christolf."

I said nothing. I covered her fingers with my hand. But I wasn't looking at her now.

"She told me she's one of the best agents in the city, Jake."

"She is."

"She said," Katie hesitated, "she said if Jake Bolin or any other actor can't make it through her, they can't make it through anyone."

I swallowed hard. "She's probably right."

"No! Jake! Please! You can't let yourself think that way!" Her hand grabbed my chin and jerked my head around with more force than I thought a girl her size could possibly have. "You can't."

I stared at her. "I'm afraid I *have* to think that way. It's reality. I've got my illusions, like we all do. I probably got too many of 'em for my own good. But, somewhere in the middle of it, I've got to hold on to a little bit of truth." I breathed in sharply. "I don't do that, I won't have a chance at anything."

She let go of my chin. Her hand slipped off my arm.

I sat still a moment and then turned and slowly began stapling my pictures and résumés together again. She watched me for a minute. I didn't say a thing to her. Then she got out of her chair and left the kitchen.

About twenty minutes passed, and then she came back. She was different. She had a bounce to her step and her fingers were snapping. She held that card Alan had sent me. "You're invited to a Charlie Blow party."

"Yeah. Cocaine's on the house."

"I know. Who's giving the party?"

"Alan. He's celebrating his new house. Showing off his new money."

She thought that over. "Tonight. Eight-thirty."

I grunted.

"Jake? What's the matter?"

"Forget it."

"Why?"

I grunted again. "I don't like those things. And I don't need to see his new life close up, either. Bad enough hearing the gossip and reading the magazines."

She snapped the card onto the table in front of me. She tapped it several times with her finger. "He's making it, Jake."

"Don't have to tell me he's making it." I laughed. "The world knows he's making it."

"That's not what I mean." She knelt beside me. "He's a connection for you, Jake. That can mean something."

"I don't care what it means."

She looked at me some more. I stapled some more. Then she gave up on it.

She wandered across the kitchen. Her fingers tapped against the counter. "He must've really wanted to make it, to get where he's gotten. His TV series, being a star. What do you think kept him at it?"

"He didn't have to keep at it very long."

"He had to keep at it for a while. You told me he lived with you here for almost two years."

I continued to staple. I hoped she'd stop.

"Why do you think he kept at it, Jake?"

"He kept at it 'cause he wanted what we all want. Recognition. Approval. Success. Someone to tell us . . ."

I looked at her for another second, and then I looked away. She stayed silent and waited. I became aware of exactly how silent the kitchen had become. I stapled another résumé to another picture. This time I banged the stapler as loud as I could.

"Someone to tell you what, Jake?"

"Nothing."

She sat next to me and put her hand on my arm. "You feel like you have to prove yourself, don't you?"

She didn't really ask it as a question. She said it more as a statement. And she was right—it was a statement. I shook my head. "Yeah, I guess so. I don't even know to who, anymore."

"What's that mean?" She gave me a moment. "Did you used to know?"

Yeah. I used to know.

It was funny. As soon as she touched my arm I knew I was going to tell her about it. I wasn't quite ready yet. I still needed another minute or two. But I knew I was going to do it. I don't know what it was about her. How she managed to make me feel that way. But she always did. She made me feel so open. I could be honest with her. I didn't have to hide things from her. No matter how stupid.

Because she never judged. I'd known it that first night, when she'd asked me why I was an actor. They'd been asking me that question for years. They always asked it. Everyone who wasn't in the business asked it. *Why are you an actor? Why do you want to do that with your life? Don't you want to do more than that?* As if it were a crime to want to be an actor. As if it weren't a decent thing to want to do.

God, even Ruth looked down on actors. And she *handled* actors.

But Ruth looked down on the whole business. And kept saying how rotten it was. And ugly.

All right. Maybe it *was* rotten and ugly. That wasn't important. What mattered was, acting was what I wanted to do. I had a right to want that.

It *was* a decent profession. It *could* be. If you did it right. It could be a wonderful thing to do. It could give people enjoyment. Relaxation. Escape. Happiness. What in the world could be better than that?

"Who were you trying to prove it to, Jake?"

I took a quick breath and then spoke even quicker. "My father, I guess, but it doesn't matter anymore. He's dead."

She looked at me. Then she nodded. "Sure. Your father. Of course." Her hand went up to the back of my neck and rubbed it softly. "What was he like? Your father?"

I spoke slowly now. "I don't think he was very happy."

"Why?"

I hesitated. "He had a tough life. He came over from Germany, before the war. He didn't know much English. He needed a job, he had to take any job he could get. He became a plumber's apprentice. Then, eventually, he became a plumber." I shook my head. "He had his own little company. Three men working for him. I mean, it was a good, respectable job!"

"Did *he* think it was respectable?"

"No. He hated it. He was always thinking of what he could've done with his life, if he'd had a chance. He felt he'd been forced into taking the first thing that had come along. He always talked about what he *could've* become, if he'd had a choice."

Her face seemed confused. "But then, didn't he want you to have that choice? To do what you wanted to do?"

"You'd think so, wouldn't you?" I began to feel cold. "No. He wasn't like that. He had a very narrow view of the world. He felt if he'd been forced to take the first thing that came along, then everybody ought to be up against the same thing. That was the way the world worked. Nobody had a right to waste their time searching for what *they* wanted to do. The world was simple. You were supposed to find a decent job right away, you were supposed to settle down, you were supposed to get married, you were supposed to have children, and that was it."

"You weren't supposed to be an actor."

"Trying to be an actor, that was the last thing in the world you had a right to waste your time on!" I put one hand tightly around the other.

She moved closer to me. "Were you close? You and your father?"

"Hardly. We were never very physical in my family. We didn't touch much at all. Not my father and me, not even me and my mother. I think she wanted to, sometimes, but my father wouldn't allow it. He seemed to think showing emotion was a sign of weakness."

Katie nodded. "A lot of fathers seem to feel that way."

"He never congratulated me on anything. I came home once with a report card. I was in junior high school. I had all A's except for one B. It was the best report card in the class. I thought he'd finally tell me how well I'd done. So he looked at it, and he nodded, and then he asked me how come I'd gotten the B." I turned away. "Aw, it's so stupid."

"No, Jake. It isn't stupid." She took my chin and turned my face so I was looking at her. "It's important. If you're still thinking about it after all this time, it's very important."

She was right. It *was* important. It was idiotic and childish and immature. But if I still remembered that stupid report card, it was important.

And she understood.

I felt so close to her. Closer than I'd ever felt to anyone in my life.

"He was always like that, Katie. He never changed. No matter how well I did on something, he always asked me why I hadn't done a little better. Nothing was ever good enough for him. Not unless it was perfect. Even then it wouldn't have been good enough."

"You always wanted his approval, and you couldn't get it." Her fingers stroked my cheek. "And now he's dead. You'll never get it. So now you need to get it somewhere else."

I was silent.

"There's nothing wrong with wanting approval, Jake. We all want it. We all need it."

"It's stupid."

"It's not stupid. You need what everyone else needs." Her fingertips brushed my lips. She leaned forward. Kissed me gently. "But you're not like everyone else, Jake. You're different. You're special. Very special."

"No, I'm not."

"You are!" She looked into my eyes. "You know what you're trying to do. Most people don't. But more than that, you don't want to just *do* it. You want to do it *well*." She smiled. "You told me Alan always wanted to be a star. You want more than that. You want to be a good actor." She paused. "Don't you understand? You want to be *good*. Don't you?"

"... Yeah."

"Most people just want to be *thought of* as good. But you want to *be* good. That's very different, Jake." She took both my hands in hers. "You're not like other men. You're not like your father. You're not afraid to touch someone. To hold them, just hold them. And you're honest, Jake. You're open. You're the most open man I've ever known."

"I feel open, with you."

"Good. I'm glad you do. I want you to be that way. I want you to feel you can trust me. 'Cause you can, Jake. You can."

"I know that."

I felt so warm now. So good. So strong. I leaned forward and kissed her on the forehead. Then I held her against me. I felt so comfortable with her. So secure. I could say anything in the world to her. She listened and understood and accepted and cared. But she didn't judge.

I wanted to give something back to her. I thought of all those questions I'd asked her the night before. In the car. She hadn't answered any of them, but I'd sensed she'd wanted to.

"Katie? You can trust me, too, you know."

"Yes, Jake. I know I can."

"Then will you tell me? About yourself? I'll listen, if you want to tell me things."

She looked up at me. But she didn't speak.

"Please, Katie. I'd like to know. I mean, if you'd

like to tell me. If there's anything you'd like to tell me..."

She hesitated. She touched my lips again. "I will, Jake. I'm just not ready yet. Give me a little more time. Please?"

I smiled at her. "Sure. Take all the time you want. I'm not going anywhere."

"Oh yes you are."

"What?"

She smiled. She looked at the card on the table. "You're going there. Tonight."

I started to feel cold again. "No, Katie. I don't want to."

She looked up. "You're going to make it, Jake. You are. But you can't make it by saying no to things. You can't make it by just sitting here and stapling pictures together. There's a world out there. Things are happening out there. So that's where you've got to be." Her eyes looked so deep into mine. "Stop saying no to things, Jake. Say yes."

IT was my first visit to that part of Malibu. They weren't too anxious for too many people to visit that part of Malibu. They gave you two hundred feet of brightly lit dirt road, then they gave you a gate. The gate was closed. Two hulking bruisers in tough-looking uniforms stood in front of the gate. The bruisers wore guns. The first bruiser came to the driver's window. The second one stood in front of the car. I could've tried driving over the second one if I'd felt like it, but I had a hunch he'd come out of it looking better than me or my car would. The first bruiser leaned a thick, flabby hand against my car door and growled. "Name, please." His voice was as thick and flabby as his hand.

I considered making up a name, maybe even a real name, maybe the name of a star, just to see what might happen, but neither of them looked to be in the mood for that sort of thing.

"Jake Bolin."

Another thick, flabby hand came up with a clipboard.

"May I please see some identification, Mr. Bolin?"
"You serious?"
"Driver's license will be fine, please."
The "please" made me smile. It didn't make him

smile. Probably nothing would. I gave him my driver's license. He looked at it, and then he looked at Katie. I realized the second bruiser in front of my car was also looking at Katie. When I looked at her I saw she was sitting absolutely still, staring at the dashboard, making no sound at all.

Something brushed my shoulder. I turned. The first one gave me back my license. He stepped away from the car and nodded at the second one. The second one moved back a step and pushed a button. The gate behind him buzzed and swung open. The first one said, "Up the hill. Second house on the right." He slapped one hand hard against the other for no reason I could figure out. It made a pretty loud slap. "Have a nice evening, Mr. Bolin."

I tried to breathe normally. I pressed my foot gently on the gas pedal and inched slowly through the gate like a dying man clawing his way through the desert. I figured they'd like that. That's right, Mr. Bolin. Go slow, Mr. Bolin. Drive carefully, Mr. Bolin. We both have guns, Mr. Bolin. Have a nice evening, Mr. Bolin. Please.

I heard the buzz again. The electric gate swung shut behind me. I wondered, now that I was in, would they ever let me out?

I turned and looked at Katie. She was still that same way. Staring silently at the dashboard.

I kept my mouth shut and drove up the hill.

There was lots of noise coming from the house. I didn't pay much attention to it. I was still too concerned about Katie. She looked really spooked now. I was afraid to touch her. I sensed it might make her worse. I drove along the line of cars. Lincolns. Cadillacs. A cream-colored Rolls. The leather on their seats probably cost as much as my car had cost when it had been new.

I found an empty space and parked. Katie got out of the car and began straightening her dress nervously. It was a new dress she'd just bought the day before. It had very simple, very clean lines. She looked great in it.

She saw me looking at her. "What's the matter? Don't I look all right?"

"You look terrific."

"I should've worn something else."

"You kidding?" I gave her a big smile. "You look fantastic."

Then she smiled. "Who can believe you? You're prejudiced."

"I'm also honest."

"Forget honest. Make me laugh."

It confused me for a minute, then I understood. I made a face. The turtle face. She kissed me.

Then she turned away and opened her pocketbook. She took out a small pill bottle. She took off the cap and I expected to see the blue-and-red capsules, but I didn't. She tapped a small yellow pill into her hand. She brought her hand to her mouth, threw her head back and swallowed.

"Katie? What's that?"

"Diet pill. It'll kill my appetite." She put the bottle back into her pocketbook. "If I don't take one before we go in there, I'll eat everything I see."

I tried not to think about it as I took her arm and fumbled for a joke. "You'll eat everything? Including the furniture?"

She laughed. "I would if it's seasoned right!" Her voice lowered. "If I start eating, stop me. Please. All right?"

"All right."

She clung to my arm. Halfway across the grass we passed a group of loud people. Alan came out of the group as if he were dazed. Then he saw me and threw his hand at me like we hadn't seen each other in years. "Jake! How are you?"

Maybe for him it seemed like it'd been years. For me it had only been a week and a half.

"Jake, I'm really glad you made it." He stopped short. He stepped back and took in what I looked like. "Hey! Must've looked in the mirror before you came! Look at this! Haircut! Clean shirt! Pressed pants! How'd I recognize you?"

Then he saw Katie. His mouth dropped open.

"Well. Good evening." Charm oozed out of him. His hand came forward again.

Katie hesitated a long time before she took it. I could see from Alan's face that he remembered seeing her that night at The Dancers. That meant he remem-

108

bered stopping at the bar to talk to her. And she hadn't been interested.

And now she was with me.

Good.

I had my arm around her and was smiling broadly now. "Katie, this is the one and only Alan DeVoss. Currently the brightest star in ABC's heaven. That'll last all the way till next week's ratings come out. Right, Alan?" He gave me a tight smile. I was sorry I'd said it. I spoke evenly again. "Alan, this is Katie O'Hanlon."

"Yeah. I think I saw you once, Katie. Down in Santa Monica. At The Dancers." He was using his killer smile for all it was worth. "Welcome to the house."

Katie nodded slightly. She kept her mouth shut and moved closer to me.

It surprised me. I didn't know if she was scared of him, or scared of something else, or what. Of course I knew she was a lot like me, she just didn't like them when they came on that strong. Or it could've been just that undercurrent of nervousness that always seemed to be part of her. It could've been the way we'd been stopped at the gate, or the pill she'd just taken.

No, it couldn't have been that. She'd only taken it a minute before.

I stepped in between them. As I did she held tight to my arm. I looked down the road toward the gate. "Impressive setup, Alan. Sure you can afford it?"

He looked down the road and winced. His eyes had a haunted look they'd never had before. "I'm sure I can't. So what? This is America. Doesn't matter if I can afford it or not."

I touched his arm. "No, Alan. This isn't America. This is Malibu."

"That's right. So it *really* doesn't matter!" He laughed. It was loud and a little strained. I didn't like it.

I could see the gate and the bruisers on the far side of it. They were questioning another car. "Love the security guards. Who's the unlucky guy with the job of throwing the raw meat at 'em twice a day?"

"They're necessary, Jake. Hostile city. Or ain't you heard?"

"Living up here, how would you know?"

He looked straight at me. "I know, Jake. Believe

me, I know." Then he smiled at Katie and flung his arm up with a jerk. He motioned toward the house. "Go ahead! Plenty of booze! Plenty of grass! Plenty of whatever you want!"

I didn't want to look at him anymore. I turned my face and smiled at Katie. "I already got what I want."

Alan squeezed my shoulder and pushed me toward the house. "All right. Enjoy yourselves. That's all we ask."

"That's all you're going to get." I swept Katie away from him, and we started toward the house. "Maybe we'll even get to see you again sometime tonight."

"Don't worry, Jake. You'll see me. Anyway, I'll see you." He paused. "I'll be everywhere."

I took one last look at him. He'd already turned his back to us. He was looking down the hill again.

He'd see us? He'd be everywhere? That probably meant he had closed-circuit TV in every room in the house and was putting the whole party on video tape so that after it was over he'd know which of his guests had stolen what. And whether or not it'd be worth the effort to try to get it back, or just write it off. Another expense of giving a party on a hill in Malibu.

Alan provided plenty of whatever we might want, all right, and plenty that we didn't. There was too much of everything, especially noise. People were dancing and singing and smoking everything but the carpets. In the living room they were doing things that should've been done in the bedroom. I assumed that meant the bedroom was already taken. There was probably a waiting list. There was an empty-eyed girl sitting on a couch in the corner. She had one man's hand hidden by her skirt and another man's eyes glued to the eighteen-inch opening in her blouse. Meanwhile she was busy flirting with a third man standing above her.

Katie didn't care for it any more than I did. We went to the bar. Katie got a glass of Jack Daniel's, no ice. I said nothing about it. By then I wanted something, too. They had no wine so I tried a vodka and tonic. I figured one wouldn't hurt me.

We wandered for a while. When we came back to the living room, the empty-eyed girl was gone from the couch. So were the three men. They'd been replaced by

110

another girl with only two men. A much duller show. There was a big, square cocktail table in the middle of the living room. People squatted on all sides of it. They were watching a stunning woman who had piercing blue eyes and blond hair pulled back tight and well-bronzed skin and as much of the skin showing as she could possibly manage. She had a small amount of white powder spread in front of her. It was very quiet around the table. Nobody breathed too hard. They didn't want to blow away any of the precious white power. The stunning woman's well-shaped hands knew what to do, and, as she went through the ritual, the expectation was so thick a buzz saw couldn't have sliced through it.

Katie was clinging to my arm again. "Jake? You don't ever use that stuff, do you?"

"No. Too expensive for me."

Her grip tightened. "Don't ever use it. It'll kill you." She pulled me away from the cocktail table.

As we turned, I saw Ruth. She was fifteen feet away, talking to a man.

Katie saw her, too.

I thought a moment, then started forward. If Ruth was here we'd run into her sooner or later, and I always figure if that's the setup, go ahead and get it over with. It's not that I'm brave about standing up to things. I'm not. But I learned a long time ago you get a lot less brave when you put it off.

Katie suddenly let go of my arm. I turned to see what the matter was, but she was only stopping to drink her Jack Daniel's. I didn't like it. She was gulping. That same kind of scary way she'd gulped at the bar at The Dancers.

She saw me looking at her and stopped drinking. She took my arm again and we went toward Ruth. Some people made way for us, and when they did I saw who Ruth was talking to. Jack Christolf.

Actually it was Christolf who was doing all the talking. That didn't surprise me. He had a girl on his arm. Usually he had two. Maybe he'd lost one earlier in the evening. No. Christolf didn't lose girls, they lost him. One who'd lost him recently had been a pretty decent young actress who'd been just starting out. When she lost him she killed herself. Slashed her wrists. It had led to a lot of talk. The talk lasted almost two weeks. Then a new movie opened and started breaking box-office records, and everyone forgot about her.

The girl Christolf had with him tonight belonged in high school. She had plenty of blond, sun-bleached hair. Her face had seen a lot of sun, too. Right now it looked okay, she was still young, but give her another ten years, fifteen if she was lucky, she'd have that worn leathery look. The look that makes men seem like they've lived and women seem like they've just been used. The girl was holding on to Christolf for all she was worth. Like she knew she wouldn't have his arm for long, no matter how lucky she got. Then something scared me. I realized Katie was holding on to my arm the same way.

Christolf was in midsentence when something he said made Ruth blow up. "Why the hell are you always such a prick at parties?"

Christolf laughed. "It's good business. Last time I got into a fight, someone wrote it up in the gossip columns. I was able to get another thirty thousand on my next picture. That's your trouble, Ruth. You never learned enough about the value of notoriety."

"You're just too damn hungry for it. You're too damn hungry for everything."

"I got to be. Got a lot of bills to pay."

She turned away and almost walked right into me.

I stepped back. "Hi, Ruth."

"Oh, hi, baby. How're you . . ."

Then she saw Katie. It was a bad moment.

Then Christolf saw Katie. When he did he smiled. "Ah!" He swooped at us like a sailboat that had the wind behind it. "Well! Here's one I haven't seen before!" His eyes shifted once quickly to check me out, then jumped back at her. "This one's worth seeing, too!"

His voice was drunk and loud, but that was the way it had sounded the other four times I'd met him—so maybe it was normal for him.

The main thing about Jack Christolf was, he wasn't handsome. He was ugly. Ugly as sin. The nose was the wrong size and bent, the ears flapped out, the mouth never seemed to close right. And his hair always looked like something should've been done to it. His eyes were pretty good. They squinted, but they were sharp. When he looked at you you knew you were the one who was being looked at. If you'd wanted to trade one of your features for one of his, there'd be nothing to pick. All of them were wrong. But the way they went together, you couldn't take your eyes off him. And he was sure of himself. God, was he sure of himself. And even more than that, he could act like a dream.

His arm beat the air ferociously. Suddenly it dipped toward Katie. "My name's Jack! What's yours?"

Katie's eyes narrowed as she shied away from him. Her mouth stayed closed.

But Ruth spoke right up. "Her name's Katie, Jack. She's just your type."

I gave Ruth a look. Christolf lurched at us again. "Hell, they're all just my type! I'm an equal opportunity employer!"

The girl with the blond hair tried her best to rein him in. "Come on, Jack. I want to go over and meet—"

"Hey!"

That shut her up. She wasn't going to say another word for the rest of the night. For the rest of the week, if he didn't want her to.

Christolf's eyes flashed and his teeth showed, and he moved toward us again. He stopped, and something seemed to register in his eyes. He cocked his head at me and his hand gestured, closed in a fist and tapped the side of his head. "Got it! Actor! Right?" I nodded. He smiled. "Pretty quiet for an actor! Aren't you?" I nodded again. He shook his head. "No. Must be wrong. Can't be an actor. Don't *act* like an actor!" He looked quickly at the people around us to see how many of them were watching.

"You mean I don't act like you."

I was surprised I'd said something, I should've said nothing. His eyes came back and his face lit up. "Hell, *I* don't act like an ac-tor! I act like Jack Chris-*tolf!*" He quickly looked around for applause. He didn't get any. The only one who would've clapped was the blond, and he'd just told her to keep quiet. He looked back at me and pitched his voice a notch higher. "Well! Keep plugging away at it, quiet man!" He threw two fake punches at my chest. "You can be like me, some day! Shoot your mouth off whenever you feel like it!"

"... No thanks."

"No? That's the wrong attitude! See life that way, you won't make it!" A smile crossed his lips. It stayed there. "Not in this business!"

I wasn't going to answer him at all this time, but I was trapped. They were all watching and waiting for my answer. Even Katie seemed to be waiting. It came out embarrassingly small. "Maybe I'll make it my own way."

"*Maybe*?" His hand dipped up and down like a yo-yo. "Maybe! Maybe!"

Ruth tried to get between us. "All right, Jack. Cool it. There're no columnists here tonight."

He smiled at her but kept his eyes on me. "You live in a world of *maybes*? Then the answer for you is, probably *not!*" He laughed again. "What the hell, you never know in this business! They're always looking for anything! Maybe you'll be a maybe who'll make it!" He stopped again. "Then again, maybe you won't. Want to put some money on it?"

I didn't answer.

"Want to *maybe* put some money on it?"

I breathed out sharply. "Not tonight. I left my money belt with my other pants."

"You *got* other pants?" He laughed. "That's okay, I take checks! Money orders! Credit cards! IOUs!"

I didn't answer.

It got quiet again. He looked me up and down. "Yeah. I've seen you around. Jay something, right?"

"Jake something."

"Huh?"

I gave it to him slightly louder. "*Jake* something."

"Yeah? Really?" He considered it. He looked at the blond. She considered it. He looked back at me. "You *sure* it's Jake something?"

"... I'm rarely wrong."

"But neither am *I!*"

It was getting touchy. I was almost at the edge. He was wearing sandals. I was wearing boots. I was thinking about the possibilities that gave us. But I wiped it out of my mind. I wasn't the type for that kind of thing, even if I wished I was for a second. Besides, I was beginning to understand. His eyes had that same scary look that had been in Alan's when he'd squeezed my shoulder and told us to go into the house. It was Malibu.

But then Christolf looked at Katie again and chuckled. "Katie, Katie, give me your answer true!" His eyes were stuck on her like a bug on flypaper. "You know, I've never slept with a Katie!"

Her fingers tightened on my arm again. That did it. Sometimes you won't do anything if it's just yourself that needs protecting, but when it's someone else, that changes things. I stepped forward hard and fast, so he had to step back and give me room. "I've heard you've never slept with a horse either, but I wouldn't put any money on it."

His eyes widened. Suddenly he grabbed my arm. "You got the right idea, Jake something! *I* sure as hell wouldn't put any money on it!"

I looked him straight in the eye. "Get your hand off me."

He didn't move. "Why?" He held a beat. "Going to do something if I don't?"

I held the look. "I'd rather we didn't have to find out."

Katie squeezed against me. Christolf's voice got loud and desperate again. *"I'd* rather we *did* find out!"

He was only a little bigger than me. I don't know if I could've taken him or not. But at the last moment I stopped. If I was ever going to hit someone, it would be because *I* wanted it to happen. And never just to get into some gossip column.

I pulled away from his hand. I turned my back on him and took Katie with me. I heard his laugh behind me, and for a second I wanted to turn.

But I kept on walking.

Then Katie spoke. "You didn't have to act like that to impress me."

"What?" I stared at her. "Act like what?"

She hesitated. "Like you just did."

What was she talking about? I'd thought I'd handled it pretty well. What was I supposed to have done? Back down from him completely?

Her hand touched my chest softly. "Jake, you don't have to be that way. I like you better when you're yourself."

"What's myself?"

"When you're quiet. Gentle." Her fingers came up and touched my cheek.

I stiffened. Didn't she understand? He'd been *right!* If I wanted to make it I *had* to be like him!

And I didn't know how.

We continued across the room. Then we bumped into Alan. I grabbed him suddenly by the arm. "Hey, Alan, I can understand your inviting half the town up here . . ." I took a quick breath. "But why the hell did you invite Christolf?"

He looked at my hand. I looked at it, too. I had his arm pretty tight. I shook my head and removed my hand. He looked at me a second and then looked over my shoulder and frowned. "Who invited him? There's some people even private guards can't keep out." He started to turn away.

Then Katie nudged me. She nudged me again. I knew why she was doing it. It was crazy. One moment she didn't want me pushy, the next moment she did. And this time I didn't want to be.

But I did what she wanted. I reached out and caught Alan's arm again, but this time I did it softer. Even so, he jumped at my touch. He was still full of that nervousness I'd seen in him earlier.

He settled himself quickly and faced me. I paused a moment. I felt uncomfortable saying it, but Katie was looking at me. "Alan, you're still shooting your show, couple more weeks. Think maybe you could get me something?"

He looked surprised. He hadn't expected to hear that kind of thing. Not from me. And not on a night like this.

Katie nudged me again. I had to stop her so I said, "Maybe something with some lines?"

Just then there was a big noise from the middle of the room. It came from the cocktail table where they were sniffing cocaine. A man with a red face and a chin covered with white powder stood up. The others laughed at him. He turned. They continued laughing. His face got redder, and for a second I thought he was going to hit someone, but then I could see he was obviously too scared

116

to. He walked out of the living room. The laughter followed him all the way to the door.

Alan took a deep breath. "Stupid schmucks. That guy's got money." I looked down. Alan's hands were in fists. His arms were shaking. "I been talking to him and some of his friends about backing a movie. Hell, I knew he wasn't the type for this kind of thing. I had to invite him, it would've been worse if I hadn't." His voice was staccato in a breathless way I'd never heard before.

He struggled to keep himself still. Then he looked at me and blinked once and remembered what I'd asked him. "Oh. Yeah. Sure. See if I can get you something." His head jerked around again. It shook back and forth. "Catch you later, okay?" He was looking toward where the red-faced man had gone. The laughter was barely fading. Alan's face had turned pale and his voice got thin. "Those idiots." He went quickly across the room.

I didn't like having asked Alan for a favor that way. I've never felt good about asking anyone for help. Maybe because the few times I've asked, the help hasn't come. You get so you'd rather not ask than take the chance, and ask, and get turned down again.

Sometimes they turn you down 'cause they can't help you. Those times it's all right. But sometimes they say they *will* help you, and then they don't. That's when it really hurts. And when it finally hurts enough, you stop asking. You know it's stupid, not asking. But you've been hurt so much, you're not willing to take the chance of getting hurt again.

It's not that I blame people for it. It's not their fault most of the time. They mean to help when they say they're going to. But we all have our failings. Our self-interest. Our own desires. And when we get caught up in the things we're trying to do, one minute we say we'll help someone and the next minute we forget all about it. So the other guy gets hurt. I didn't want to be that other guy anymore.

But Katie had kept nudging me. I knew she'd meant well, but she'd kept at it and hadn't stopped and my adrenaline had been up from that stupid scene with Christolf and what she'd said to me after. So I'd asked Alan for

117

the favor, even though in my heart I'd known it was a favor I'd never get.

I was mad. At myself. For asking. For getting my hopes up on something I knew wouldn't happen.

I was mad at Katie. For pushing me into asking.

The glass in my hand was empty. I went to the bar to get it filled. Katie followed me. She got more Jack Daniel's. I got myself another vodka and tonic. I was ready to try to get drunk. I'd only tried twice in my life up till then and neither time had worked. Just made me tired and sick and unhappy. But I was ready to try again for number three. I was ready to try for numbers three, four, five, six and seven, all in one night. Why not? If I was going to get sick, this was a fine place to do it in. There was plenty of vodka, and it was all free.

We were still at the bar when Katie stiffened. She entwined her arm around me in that clinging-vine way she'd been using ever since we'd gotten to the party. I turned to see what was spooking her now. It was Jill. She came over and did what she always did—put her arms around my neck and kissed me, the same way she'd done it that day on the street.

"How you doing, Jake?"

"Fine."

She gave me a look like she could read my thoughts. She knew how I felt about being around people like this.

I spoke quickly. "Katie, this is Jill. Alan's girlfriend. Jill, this is Katie."

Jill put her hand out. "Hello, Katie. Nice to meet you."

Just then Ruth came over to get a new martini. She smiled at Jill. "Nice house, baby. You can get comfortable in a house like this. Just make sure Alan doesn't try getting comfortable somewhere else."

Jill smiled. "He better not try it. I'll do surgery on him, below the belt."

Ruth laughed. "You do that, you'll break the hearts of four million teenagers."

"Better their hearts than mine."

Ruth bent her head farther toward Jill and spoke so quietly I could hardly catch the words. "He's acting pretty jumpy tonight. He going to make it?"

Jill's face hardened. "I don't know. He's . . ." Her

eyes shifted across the room to where Alan was talking to some people. I don't know what he was saying, but he was being very careful to keep his smile on his face every second. Jill ordered another drink. "Yeah. He'll make it."

Ruth collected her new martini and turned to Katie. I could almost see Ruth shiver. I could feel Katie do it.

Ruth looked at the tumbler of Jack Daniel's in Katie's hand. She put steel in her voice. "Well, baby. You're sure a good drinker." Ruth raised her own glass and toasted her. "Come to my office some time, I'll break open a bottle of something, we'll have a nice talk about things."

I could've said something, but I didn't. I was still mad about the way Katie had pushed me into asking Alan for that favor.

Katie pulled me away from the bar. "I don't like her." She lowered her voice. "She's always so pushy. She's more like a man than a woman."

I was still thinking of Alan. "You know, sometimes you're a little pushy yourself."

"What?" Her hand left me. "No I'm not. How am I pushy?"

"You pushed me into asking Alan for that job."

"But Jake—"

She stared at me a moment. I couldn't tell what was in her eyes. Or her mind. Then suddenly she turned away and walked across the room.

A second later Ruth was next to me. "Sure knows how to put it away. Hope you can afford her bar tabs."

I gave Ruth a look. She sipped her martini and draped an arm over my shoulder. Katie had turned and was just starting back, but now she stopped. She turned away again.

Ruth snuggled closer, as if she were hoping Katie would see it again. But she didn't. Ruth kept looking at her. "There's something wrong with her, baby."

"What?"

"I can feel it a mile away. This isn't just jealousy talking. There's definitely something wrong with her."

I breathed in deeply. I could see Katie opening her pocketbook and digging to get something out of it. I knew what the something would probably be.

I drank my vodka. I watched as Katie went through

a door. Just as she did, I saw the pill bottle in her hand.

Suddenly I didn't like the idea of her being alone. I left Ruth and went after her. But it took me too long to get across the room, and when I went through the door she wasn't there.

I spent fifteen minutes looking for her. She'd really disappeared. Then I found my glass was empty. I went back to the bar and got a refill.

I ended up sitting in a corner with George Harding, a young character actor. Luck had found George about a year and a half before, and he'd become that miracle of miracles, a working actor. He always had a new job coming up. Commercials, character bits in movies. Currently he had a running part in one of the top-rated TV shows. It was a secondary role. He was usually called for at least two out of every three episodes. That was good. There was no pressure on him the way there was on the stars. If the ratings went down, it wasn't his fault. The money was good. Apparently the money was very good. A nonworking actor like me should've hated his guts, but I couldn't. He was too nice. And he could act.

He was also a quiet guy like me and felt out of place at a party like this. Which was how I felt. We sat in a corner and talked about the business. We tried politics for about three minutes and then slid into the business again, and once we were back in that groove we stayed there. About five minutes later I looked up and Katie was there. She was smiling. Her fingers were snapping like crazy. "This is a really nice house, Jake! You should see the back! They got two pools!"

I watched her fingers carefully. "Sure. One for the people, one for the goldfish. Katie, this is George Harding. George, this is Katie O'Hanlon. She's not in the business."

George smiled at her and mumbled something which sounded like "Congratulations." Katie put her hand out and spoke loudly. "Nice to meet you, George! You an actor too?"

George nodded. Katie looked at me again. "You okay now, Jake? You seemed kind of down before."

"I'm okay." I paused. "You?"

"Me? I'm fine!" Her face beamed. She picked up my empty glass. "Want me to get you another?"

I thought for a second. No, I didn't want to try getting drunk tonight after all. Besides, I was feeling okay now sitting here with George. Back in my own depth, maybe. Anyway, I didn't need liquor. And I suspected it might be best not to take it even if I did need it. I shook my head.

Katie went away. I kept my eyes on her and talked some more to George. Then Katie came back and handed me a vodka and tonic.

I laughed. "Katie, I said I didn't want another one."

"Oh, it's all right, Jake. What the hell, it's a party."

She sat in my lap.

But she was quiet. George and I talked. She just listened. It was all still shop talk between George and me, and eventually she got restless. She kept rubbing her hands together, but she had stopped snapping her fingers. Suddenly she kissed my cheek and then she stood up. "Excuse me."

She walked away. I watched her again, but she just walked around looking quietly at people and stopping here and there to listen in on a conversation. After a few minutes I stopped worrying. I turned back to George.

Later I was talking to some other people and I felt a hand on my arm. I turned, smiling, and found Ruth.

"Come here a minute, baby. Want you to see something."

Before I could ask her what she wanted me to see she'd pulled me to the other side and was looking across the room. I followed her eyes and there was George Harding sitting in that same corner. Katie was sitting next to him. They seemed to be arguing. Or rather Katie seemed to be arguing. George was silent. Katie's hands were gesticulating wildly. George finally opened his mouth but Katie kept talking and George closed it again.

"You were talking to him before, weren't you?"

I shifted from one foot to the other. "Yeah."

"Looks like you were paying a little too much attention to him, baby. She didn't like it."

"You're crazy." But I was a little bit scared now. And more than a little bit high from the vodka. I kept my eyes on Katie. "You don't know what you're talking about."

Ruth's voice was even. "If I don't, this'll be the first time."

I looked at her. "Then this'll be the first time." I walked away from her.

When I got to the couch, George looked at me nervously. Katie turned and saw me and immediately smiled broadly. "Hi! Where you been?"

I laughed. "Looks like quite an argument you got going here. Can I get into it, or is it private?"

"Argument?" Katie laughed. "No argument! We're just talking!" She moved over quickly, making space for me on the couch. "Come on, Jake! I feel like laughing! Make us laugh!" She looked at George. "He's good at making people laugh!" She looked at me. "Come on, Jake!" She smiled and reached up toward me.

I made a small face and sat down next to her. George immediately got up. "I better be going. Shooting tomorrow. Early. See you, Jake." He nodded at me and then at Katie. "Nice meeting you, Katie."

"Yeah! Nice meeting you!" She gave him a big smile. "You're going home, drive carefully!"

I was still watching him leave when she took my face in her hands and kissed me hard. So hard it took my breath away. I finally got our mouths apart and took a quick breath. She laughed and giggled and leaned forward again. This time I was ready for it.

Then she got her hands inside my jacket, and she seemed so anxious that for a moment I was worried she was going to start ripping my shirt. But she just held her arms around me and we kissed some more.

I forgot all about George Harding. We sat there kissing and she felt so warm beside me, that was all I cared about. After a while she wanted to go to the bar for another drink. I went with her.

Two drinks later, we found a dark corner. We started going at it worse than two high-school kids in the back row of a movie theater. Then she nuzzled against me. "Let's go home."

I laughed and held her close. "Yeah, I think the sooner the better."

She smiled and took my hand and pulled my other arm around her. By the time we walked out the front door I think one of us was holding the other one up, but I wouldn't want to place any bets as to which one of us was doing the holding. It looked like I'd come pretty close to getting myself drunk after all.

We stopped halfway to my car. Alan and Jill were fifteen feet away, standing side by side with their backs to us. I took Katie's hand and went toward them. Katie swung my hand back and forth as we walked. We looked at each other and smiled.

Alan heard us coming and turned quickly with a jerk. He looked briefly at me and took a longer look at Katie. There seemed to be something funny in the way he looked at her, but I had no idea what it could be.

Suddenly Katie started giggling, and that made me giggle. Alan said nothing. He looked away again. He had a glass of whisky in his hand. He took a very long drink from it. When we came up next to him we looked in the same direction, and we could see down the road all the way to the front gate. The two guards were there. There were a bunch of kids, too. There seemed to be a lot of them. They had built a small fire and were grouped around it having their own party. Drinking, singing, fooling around. Looking up at us on top of the hill.

Alan stared at them. "They were trying to get in before. Gate crashers. Guards stopped 'em."

I laughed. "Looks like they got here a little late, Alan! Must be this isn't the first party on their list!"

He gave me a look. His hand rubbed the side of his jaw nervously. "Told you, this is a hostile city, Jake."

Jill wrapped her arms around herself. Alan moved closer to her and took her hand. "Don't worry. They'll keep 'em down there."

Jill nodded. "I'm not worried."

I wasn't worried either. Not about anything. I was holding on to the sexiest, most adorable, most warm and loving girl in the world. I was feeling very tall. Hell, I should've felt tall. I was standing on top of six vodkas.

I laughed again. "Such is the price of fame, Alan!"

His eyes slid toward me. "You're getting a little loud, Jake. You been drinking?"

"Sure! You said drink! I drank!" But suddenly I felt dizzy. I held on to Katie and yawned to see if that would make the feeling go away. "Getting late, though. Got to go." I looked around. "Nice house, Alan. Nice party."

"Yeah. Thanks." He looked briefly at Katie again.

Loud yells came up the hill from the gate below. The kids had broken away from their fire. There seemed to be a skirmish going on. Nothing physical, nobody touching anybody. Just the gate crashers splitting up and a few of them making a move toward the gate. But the bruisers seemed to have it under control. Besides, none of it seemed real. None of this night seemed real.

Then a lone figure ran forward. He went straight for the gate. He dove and grabbed onto the wire. He started to claw his way up. We all watched him silently.

But the bruisers knew their business. One of them faced the kids while the other calmly took the crasher by the back of the belt, pulled him off the gate and held him above his head like in a wrestling match.

The crasher began to yell. His friends had gone suddenly quiet. The yells carried all the way up the hill to us. They were sharp and scary and they were real enough. We all waited to see what the bruiser was going to do to him.

The bruiser did nothing. He walked several feet from the gate and put the crasher down and left him there. All very methodical and measured and disciplined. The world was safe after all.

The crashers slowly returned to their fire. Some of them began to dance.

But when I looked at Alan, he had the shakes. It took him another moment to get rid of them. He breathed in sharply. "Better wait a little before you drive down there, Jake. Give 'em a chance to try someone else's house. Looks a little risky right now."

I looked down the hill. I looked at Katie. I didn't want to wait. "Aw, what's a little risk?"

Alan looked at me. "Thought you were the guy who always said to stay away from that kind of thing."

For no reason at all except maybe six vodkas, I laughed as loud as I could. I tried to act like I knew what I was doing. "Who? Me?" I turned to Katie and made a funny face for her. She laughed.

Yeah. That was it. *She* was the reason I was acting like a fool. Forget the six vodkas.

Alan moved closed to Jill. "Your choice, Jake. If I were you, I'd wait a little."

"You're not me!"

Katie and I turned and swung hands as we walked to the car. We got in, I managed to get my key into the ignition, even managed to get the motor started. Then Katie was reaching for me. She had my shirt open and was kissing my chest. Suddenly her mouth began to move lower.

I pulled her face up to mine. Her mouth was open. I gave her a big kiss. Then I held her close. "We'll be home soon."

Her eyes shone in the darkness. "I know. I'm just getting ready."

"You're getting me a little bit *too* ready." I put my hands against her cheeks. "Let's wait till we get home. Okay?"

"Okay."

I turned front and put the car in reverse. I was still sober enough to remember to look behind me before I started moving. I backed slowly out of line, and then I saw someone standing in the shadows near the house.

It was just light enough for me to see who it was. I couldn't tell what kind of expression Ruth had on her face, but I could pretty well imagine what it would be.

I faced front and changed gears. I drove onto the road and started down the hill. Katie reached forward and turned on the radio. It blared rock at us. Her head leaned against my shoulder and her hand draped across my leg.

Driving fast down that hill with the wind coming through the windows at us, that loud crazy music, Katie sitting next to me, I felt as strong and powerful as I'd ever felt in my life. I pushed harder on the gas. The car went up along a small rise and then gently down. Now I saw kids again, on the far side of the gate. They were dancing around their fire. So free and uninhibited. I was feeling that way too. Katie's hand was beginning to rub up and down my leg.

The bruisers heard us coming, I was coming quickly. They didn't care. They weren't interested in whether or not I knew the password either. They had enough problems with the gate crashers.

I hit the brakes at just the right moment. The car

stopped on a dime. The bruisers weren't moving fast enough for me, so I gave them the horn. One of them looked at me for a second, then they both moved the crashers several feet down the road. When they'd cleared enough room, they opened the gate and motioned us through. Katie's fingers were fumbling with my belt buckle.

I laughed. "Katie! Not now! Please!"

Some of the kids began yelling. Katie stopped what she was doing and sat up suddenly and looked at them in confusion.

After coming so fast down the hill, now we were just standing there. Finally one of the bruisers yelled. "Come on, damn it! You're coming through, come on!"

But it all seemed so different now. Being so much closer to these kids. Seeing their faces and the expressions on them.

I touched the gas pedal lightly. I increased my speed but tried not to go too fast. But I couldn't control my heart. It was racing. I suppose half of it was because of what was out there and half was from what was sitting next to me, but I knew I really wasn't in control anymore.

I was scared to let any of it spook me into going fast. The hill road had been empty, but this part of it wasn't. All I needed was for one of these kids to jump in front of the car just as I stepped on the gas.

A new song came on the radio. A louder one than before. There was a strong drum behind the music playing an irregular beat. I didn't like the sound of it. I reached forward and snapped it off. Then some of the crashers made a run for the open gate.

They didn't get through it. The bruisers were too fast for them. So then they began to yell. The rest of them converged around my car. They didn't seem to mean any harm, they were just peering in the windows to see if either one of us was worth recognizing.

Then Katie began to laugh at them. I wished she'd stop. I couldn't move the car at all now. Suddenly she turned. She took my face in both her hands and leaped halfway into my lap. She kissed me hard on the mouth. Her face was covering mine and I could hardly see, but I could hear the kids saying things about us. I pushed Katie away. "Please, Katie, not now."

Katie looked at me, half hurt and half confused. Some of the kids outside the car were making comments they thought were funny. There were still too many of them in front of the car for me to drive forward.

Then a girl's hand came through my side window and threw a notebook at me. She was saying something I couldn't make out in all the noise. But I had the general idea. I wrote *Alan DeVoss, The Brightest Star in ABC's Heaven*. Katie saw what I was writing, and she laughed. The girl outside the car squealed in delight.

Writing anything was a big mistake. As soon as I gave the notebook back to her, more hands and notebooks came at me. My eyes caught Katie again, and she was leaning against the far door. She'd stopped laughing. "We better get out of here, Jake."

"Yeah." I looked at the kids in front of the car.

Hands and notebooks were shoved through the window. I shook my head and waved them off and honked my horn. I tried to drive forward. They didn't like that. They didn't know who I was, that I was nobody at all, but if I'd signed one autograph I'd damn well better sign the rest. When I kept shaking my head they started screaming. Some of them began rapping on the car with their hands. Katie was rapping the dashboard with hers. "Come on. Jake. Let's go." She looked worried.

I pushed slightly on the gas pedal. The car moved forward half a foot. More of them began to yell. Then out of the corner of my eye I saw a young boy at the side of the road. He looked like he couldn't have been more than ten years old. He was reaching down and picking up a rock.

Katie saw him too. "Oh God, Jake, come on! We got to get out of here!"

I leaned on my horn and looked into the rearview mirror. The bruisers were at the gate about twenty feet behind me. They were talking. They'd let me through, they weren't interested in me anymore.

The boy with the rock was coming forward. I could see his face clearly. It looked nervous, but it was smiling.

"Oh God, Jake! Look out!" Katie came halfway across me and slammed her hand on the horn. Then she grabbed the steering wheel. She tried to get her foot on the gas. Before I could stop her, the car had jerked forward almost a foot. The kids were yelling. I got her away from the steering wheel and back into her seat. Her face was full of terror. I had my foot firmly on the brake. An arm had come through the window and was circling around my neck. As I looked up, I saw how angry his eyes were. Over his shoulder I saw the small boy with the rock.

I twisted away from the arm and got my eyes front, and suddenly the gate crashers were crowding around the sides of my car. There was a goodsized opening in front of me. Not as big as it could've been but probably as big as it was going to get. I put my foot on the gas and floored it.

The car shot forward. Hands flew away from the sides of the car. The yelling got louder. It sounded like a big angry animal who was out for blood. I kept on going. I looked through the rearview mirror and saw the boy with the rock. His hand went up and behind him and then it flew forward. I stepped harder on the gas, but the pedal was already as far down as it would go. The moment seemed to take an eternity. Then I heard the rock hit the fender of my car. That was all it hit.

I kept the gas pedal down and screeched forward along the dirt road. Even though the car was swerving from side to side, I made no attempt to slow down till I reached the highway. I was much more sober now. I didn't feel so strong and powerful. I was aware of reality again. I wasn't in the house on the hill with the free vodka anymore.

I finally reached the highway. I stopped. I turned quickly and looked through the rear window. There was nobody behind us. I faced front and collapsed against the back of my seat. I breathed heavily. Tried to control it. Looked over at Katie. She was huddled against the door. I began to reach toward her. She saw my hand coming and turned toward me quickly. Her face looked bad. Then she saw my face, and mine must've looked worse. She shook herself. Sat up straight. Looked through the rear window, then back at me. Then she laughed as if nothing in the world had happened at all.

It took me a moment, then I laughed too. I wanted

to hold her hand, but I decided I'd better not. I'd better drive with both hands on the wheel.

I had reached the road leading up to my house when she said, "You jealous?"

"Jealous? Of what?"

Her voice was soft. "Alan. The way he's made it."

I thought about it. What had he made? What did he have?

He had everything. The house. The party. The people. The liquor.

The ability to afford it all.

The success. The adulation.

"Yeah, he's really made it, hasn't he?"

That above all. To have made it. To have *made* it. To *know* you made it! All the way! To the top of the hill!

He also had the shakes. The fear in his eyes.

But that didn't worry me. Alan was strong, he'd get over that. It was just a passing phase. Having made it, that was what counted. The top of the hill.

"I'm not jealous of him. I like him. I'm happy for him."

"You're just as good as him, Jake. No. You're better. *Much* better." She curled herself against me. "Just remember that. Don't let yourself forget it."

Then she was quiet.

I sat on the edge of the bed and took off my shoes. My head was starting to pound. It was a feeling I hadn't felt for a long time, but now that it was there I recognized it quick enough. The best thing was to try to keep as quiet as possible. I hadn't even had that much vodka if you consider what most people put away on a regular basis, but for me it had been more than enough. I lay back and put my head on the pillow and hoped the pounding wouldn't last too long.

Katie sat in the chair and stared at the wall. She had a glass of Jack Daniel's in her hand. She rubbed the bottom of the glass against her knee, then raised the glass and drank. She stayed quiet. I was willing to leave it that way for the night. I just wanted to fall asleep. But then she said, "I'm getting older, Jake."

"We all are."

"No. It doesn't matter with a man. Age gives you character. With a woman, it just gives her wrinkles."

I looked at her. She was drinking again. I tried to laugh. "With a man, it just gives him heart attacks."

I waited a beat for her to laugh. She didn't.

I turned on my side. "By the way, what was it you were arguing with George Harding about?"

Her eyes shifted. They tried to focus on me. "What? George who?"

"Harding." I yawned. "The guy you were sitting with. In the corner."

She stared at the wall again. She seemed to be in a different world. I waited a moment. She didn't move. I reached down and got my shoe off the floor. I held it near the edge of the bed, then dropped it. It hit hard. She turned and looked at the noise. "What?"

I hesitated. "You were sitting with a guy. The actor. George Harding. You were arguing with him about something." Her face stayed blank. "You were waving your arms at him, Katie. It seemed like you were almost yelling at him."

"What're you talking about?"

I looked at her. "Katie . . . I had to come over and stop you. You were scaring him to death. I came over and sat down next to you—"

"I don't know what you're talking about." She got to her feet and went out of the room.

I turned so I was sitting on the edge of the bed. I felt dizzy. I waited a few seconds. I knew I shouldn't stand, but I stood anyway. My head felt light. I waited. It cleared a little. I went into the living room. It was dark. None of the lights were on. I could hear her at the bookcase, pouring whisky.

I put my hand on the back of a chair. "A little before we left the party. You were almost yelling at the poor—"

"I don't know what you're talking about. I wasn't yelling at anyone."

I took my hand off the chair. I went toward the bookcase and reached for her arm. "About fifteen minutes before we—"

"Don't touch me!"

"What?"

"You heard me! Don't touch me!" She pulled away from my hand. "If I want you to touch me I'll tell you!"

I knew she didn't like me to touch her before she'd already touched me, but sometimes she'd let me do it. Why not now?

I didn't like it. I didn't like her saying it to me that way. I didn't like the sound of her voice as she'd said it.

I reached for her again. As soon as she felt my hand she slapped at it. Then her hand swung up and slapped me across the face. The sound of the slap scared me more than the feel of it, but then a second later I realized how hard it'd really been. A second after that, her hand was coming at me again. Somehow I got my own hand up and grabbed her wrist before she reached me.

We stood there a moment with me holding on to her, then she jerked her hand away. Her dark figure went quickly across the living room. Her voice was uncertain. "I told you not to touch me. Can't you understand English?" Then her breath hissed at me in the darkness. "Look! You ever treat me like that again, I'll leave you! I mean it! I've got my own rights! I've got rights just like everyone else!" She took a deep breath. "You remember that. I'll walk out of here right now." Her voice began to break. "I mean it! You'll never see me again! You understand?"

We both stood quietly. Finally I realized what it was. All the liquor. The party. The danger with the gate crashers. I was drunk. She was drunk. Probably neither one of us knew what we were saying or doing or what was going on.

I went back to the bedroom. I sat on the edge of the bed. My head was still bad. I tried bending forward and putting it between my knees like you do when you feel faint.

Then I heard footsteps. I didn't look up. The footsteps stopped.

"I'm sorry, Jake, I'm just . . . I'm a little scared tonight."

"What?"

"I have to do something with my life, Jake. But I can't.... I'm not good enough."

I turned my head and looked at her from the corner of my eye. She was in the doorway. She still had her glass.

"... We have to do it together, Jake."

I stared at her another second, then felt weak and bent my head forward again.

"Jake? ... I'm tired, Jake. Been a long day."

I answered very softly. "Yeah. Same here."

A moment passed, and then she walked around the bed and went to her side. I kept my head down. I could feel the bed shake as she sat on it. Then her hand touched my back. She moved. She was sitting behind me. Her hand came up to my shoulder and pulled me into a sitting position. Her lips brushed my neck. The side of my face. But I didn't respond.

"Please, Jake? Please? Don't be mad at me." She kissed my neck again. "Show me you're not mad at me. Please?"

I half turned to face her. Her mouth came against mine and opened. Her arms went around me. Then her fingers tore at my shirt.

She guided me back so my head was against the pillow. She lay beside me and swung her leg across my waist. She kissed me some more and then rolled on top of me so she had herself in her favorite position. Her mouth found mine again, then she seemed to be crying. I tried to push her back to see her face, but when I tried it she held on to me more tightly. "I'm sorry, Jake, I don't know why I did that. The other room. You're not mad at me, are you?"

"... No. It's all right."

Then her teeth bit lightly against my lip. I was scared she was going to bite harder. Then she was kissing me again. Then I was inside her. She started to moan.

She sat up suddenly so she could control her movements better, and then she withdrew slowly in that way she had till we were almost apart, then she came slowly forward again.

"Jake? Does that feel nice?"

I mumbled something.

She went back and then came forward, and when

our stomachs were touching she paused and did that smooth circular movement with her hips. She did it again. Then pulled back again.

"How's that, Jake? Is that better?"

I tried to speak. "I don't know. Maybe not tonight. I had too much too drink."

She came forward once more. Pulled back. Came forward. By then I was helpless to her slow, rhythmical rocking. My eyes were half closed. I knew I *could* do it. But I didn't say anything. I didn't want to break the spell. I felt warm and safe and on the edge of ecstasy. Then suddenly she reached beside my head. She took the other pillow in both her hands and lifted it up and quickly mashed it down hard against my face.

I couldn't breathe. She kept pressing down. I couldn't take it. I was terrified. I tried swinging at her with both my hands, but it was no good. I was too drunk. Too weak. It was killing me. The pillow. Cutting off my breath. What was she doing? I couldn't get her off me. I could feel her hips still rotating slowly, but the whole top of her body was pressed against that pillow. The darkness in front of my eyes was replaced by small explosions of light, as if fireworks were going off inside my brain. There was a horrible pulsing in my ears. I knew they would pop any second. All I wanted to do was breathe again. I knew I'd never breathe again. There was nothing I could do to stop her.

And then I came. It was overpowering. I knew even if this was going to be the last moment of my life, it was worth it. It was the most explosively magnificent orgasm I'd ever had. Nothing had ever been like it before. Not lovemaking, not even acting. The lower half of my body strained up toward her as if neither of us were on the bed any longer but instead were floating in space. For those few brief seconds I didn't care about the pillow. Nothing mattered at all.

Then it was over. I fell back again even weaker than before. Completely spent. Ready to die. It didn't matter.

Suddenly the pillow was off my face. Air hit me like a tidal wave. Just before I passed out, I saw her in the darkness above me. She was smiling like an angel.

THE next morning when I woke up she wasn't there. The phone was ringing. It was nine-fifteen. I picked up the phone, and it was an assistant director on Alan's show. He told me they had something for me and they needed me there by ten.

I didn't expect it to be much. It wasn't. Never expect much, they won't disappoint you. There were no lines involved at all. I was one of seven extras they were using that day, and none of us had any lines. Most of what we did was smoke cigarettes, share gossip, drink coffee and sit quietly, which we were all good at. We got the opportunity to watch Alan and several other actors with overstuffed wallets and overfed egos go through their paces.

The script was bad. The acting was slightly better. Actually, some of it was pretty good. The director ran through the whole thing like he had to catch a plane that left in five minutes. At one-thirty an assistant direcor talked to us. It was the first official contact we'd had with the production company all day. He told us where to stand, how to look, when to react.

We rehearsed the scene. The assistant director came back and gave us the director's notes. Don't stand here, stand there. Don't look like that, look like this. Don't react that way, react this way.

We took it all politely, with smiles. Each of us had one thing in mind. We wanted to be remembered as cooperative. So we were all as cooperative as robots. Nothing they told us could bother us. Nothing they wanted us to do was beyond our capabilities. We could stand as still as trees if they wanted us to. We could walk tightropes if necessary. We'd be happy to sit in electric chairs if they wanted, even while they tested the current. We were good little actors who were happy to be there. If we were ever asked to come back, we'd be just as happy the second time. If there was ever a third time and lines were offered, we'd be happy to speak lines. We'd speak the lines clearly. We'd speak them whatever way they wanted us to speak them. If there weren't any lines, that would be okay, too.

At twenty after three they were finished with us. They told us to turn in our wardrobe and go home. When the assistant director didn't look too busy I approached him and asked politely if anyone would mind if I stayed around a little longer. I promised I wouldn't get in anyone's way. Sure, I could stay around. I'd shown myself to be a good boy so far. I'd done everything they'd wanted me to do. I could stay all I wanted. But I wouldn't get paid for it, understand. Sure, I understood.

Another hour passed. They took a ten-minute break. Alan sat in a director's chair and listened halfheartedly to the director's notes.

I went over to Alan. He nodded at me wearily and opened an ice chest. He took out a beer. His shoulders were sagging.

"Just wanted to thank you, Alan. Didn't expect anything so quick."

"Sure, Jake." He opened the beer.

"Really appreciate it." I gave him my version of his smile. "What do you say, maybe next time . . ." I thought of Katie and forced myself to go on with it. "Maybe next time, you could get me something with a line or two?"

Alan's mouth opened savagely. "Sure, Jake! Anything you want! What the hell, put in your order! I'll see what I can do!"

He threw down his beer and got out of the chair and walked away. He went into a trailer and slammed the door behind him.

I didn't have any idea what it was about. I could've gone after him. We could've had it out. But this was his set. I knew the rules. You don't pick a public fight with a star. Not on his set. Not *off* his set either. Not even if he's supposed to be your friend. Not unless you're a star, too. And sometimes not even then. Unless you're a big star. As big as him. As big as Jack Christolf. Then you can pick a fight with anyone in the world.

Besides, I'd been on the set all day and I'd made a good impression. I didn't want to spoil that. And Alan, he'd had a long day, he still had part of it in front of him. He was edgy. He'd been edgy the night before. He had a right to be edgy. The strains, the pressures. For all I knew his anger had nothing to do with me. It probably didn't. I was edgy too. I still felt that pillow.

I looked around quickly. I was in enemy territory. I wanted to be remembered as polite and silent and cooperative.

I walked off the set and let it go.

I called my service as I usually did. There was a message to call Ruth.

"Hi, baby!"

"Me, Ruth. Been working."

"Oh. . . . Hi. Working doing what?"

"Alan's show. Nothing much. Extra bit."

"Oh. . . . Good for you."

"Only medium good. No lines. But I acted polite to everyone, maybe I'll get asked back some day." I thought again of Alan.

". . . Got a little news for you, baby. Thought you might be interested." She paused.

"What is it?"

". . . I was having lunch with some people today, Jake. Up at Scandia. Ran into a good buddy of yours. Antonio Calisi."

She paused again.

136

I didn't know if it was the pauses or her tone of voice or Alan's tone of voice, but something was getting to me. "So? What is it?"

"I told him I'd seen the proofs. Your pictures. Thought he'd done a fabulous job with you. He felt the same way. . . . I said it was awfully generous of him, doing it for free. Know what he said?"

I didn't answer.

"Pictures weren't freebies, Jake. They were paid for. In cash." She paused. "Want to guess who paid for 'em?"

I chewed my lower lip. "No."

"No? You mean you knew?"

". . . No. I didn't know." I searched my pockets for cigarettes. I found the pack and got it out. I tapped it against my hand. I stuck a cigarette in my mouth. "Not till just now." I shoved the pack back into my pocket. I got out my matches.

"Looks like she's trying to do some kind of number on you, baby."

I didn't answer. I struck the match hard. Its head broke off.

". . . Better watch yourself, Jake. I mean it."

"Yeah. . . . Thanks for the information. . . . I'll talk to you."

I hung up the phone. I got out another match. I lit it and lit my cigarette and took a big drag.

I sat in my car. I didn't want to go home. I didn't want to see her.

And then suddenly I did want to see her. Very badly. I drove quickly and got home as fast as I could. She wasn't there. I looked at my watch. It was earlier than I'd realized. She probably wouldn't be home for another hour.

But now I really wanted to see her. I didn't care what was going on. I wanted to hold her in my arms. Feel her burning beside me. Feel her mouth on mine. Her body pressed against me. If I couldn't have that, at least maybe I could hear her voice. Not even because I wanted to ask her anything. I just wanted to make contact again.

There was no number I knew of where I could reach her. I hardly knew a thing about her. Every time I'd tried to get her to talk about herself she'd shut up like a clam. And taken a pill.

But I knew Allstate. I looked it up in the phonebook. They had listings all over the city. I picked the address that looked like it would be their main office and called it.

They didn't know her.

They went away and checked some records. When they came back they still didn't know her.

I hung up. I sat quietly a moment. I checked the phonebook for another number and called that one. The second office didn't know her either.

My forehead was damp. I found seven offices that didn't know her. None of them could find a record of her. None of them knew who *might* have a record of her. All they could tell me was to try the main office, which was the first one I'd tried.

I was dialing the eighth office and had stopped midway through the number and was about to hang up and run into the bedroom to see if her things were still there, since she'd said that thing about never seeing her again the night before, when I heard a car pull up outside. I looked through the front window. I saw the side of the yellow Volkswagen. I hung up the phone.

She came in smiling. "Hi! How'd the day go? They give you any lines?"

I didn't give that a thought, that she knew I'd been working on Alan's show. I was too desperate and relieved to see her. "Katie, I've been trying to call you."

"What?" She stopped still, but kept smiling. "Call me? Why? Something the matter?"

"You told me you work for Allstate, I've been calling every Allstate office in—"

"I never told you I worked for Allstate."

". . . What?"

Her eyes turned away. She hesitated. "I told you I *sell* for Allstate. I didn't say I *work* for them." She took a deep breath. Her eyes came back. "I also sell for State Farm, for Prudential. I'm an independent broker, Jake. I don't work for just one company." She turned and went into the kitchen.

I went after her. The Jack Daniel's bottle was in the kitchen. By the time I got there, she had it. I stared at her a moment, and then I took it out of her hands with more force than I'd meant to. My voice came out with too much force, too. "You told me Antonio Calisi had an insurance policy with you. You said that's why he was doing my pictures for free. But they weren't free. You paid for 'em."

Her eyes narrowed. "You needed pictures. You said so yourself." She looked past me. "But you weren't going to get 'em. I had to make sure you did."

I put the Jack Daniel's on the counter. I took both her arms and turned her so she was looking at me. "Why'd you tell me they were free?"

She didn't answer. I shook her. Hard.

"Don't touch me like that."

I shook her again. "Katie, I have to know! Why'd you—"

She broke away from my hands. Her hands went back to slap me. But then at the last moment she stepped back.

I stayed where I was. I was scared. I could see she was scared too. I hadn't meant to shake her that way. And I knew I was getting ready to do it again.

Damn it, I'd been going over it in my mind for over an hour! How when I saw her I was going to keep calm and quiet and not touch her at all! Just ask her the questions that had to be asked! Listen patiently to her explanations! And then no matter what she told me, I was going to accept it! And kiss her! And make love to her!

But as soon as I'd seen her, it had all gone out the window. I'd ended up shaking her like she was nothing but a rag doll even though I knew that was the last thing in the world I should do with her.

But why had she paid for those pictures?

I turned away and went toward the table. I knew why I'd shaken her so roughly. She meant even more to me than I'd thought she did.

Then I heard her moving behind me. When I turned she was pouring Jack Daniel's into a glass. The glass was already half full. Her hands were trembling.

Something about it made me feel so angry. "Damn it! Why've you always got to have a drink?"

Her hand jerked. The glass fell. It broke on the floor and splintered. She gave a small yell. I thought a piece of glass must've hit her leg. But then she was quiet and stood absolutely still and breathed in and held her head up stiffly. "No. I'm excited." Her voice was cold and almost mechanical now. "I'm too excited. I've got to cool down."

She walked stiffly out of the kitchen.

I couldn't move. I looked at the broken glass. The spilled whisky.

Then it came over me again. The desperateness. I went after her. She'd gone down the hall to the bedroom, but she wasn't in there. I heard her in the bathroom. I knew what it would mean. She saw me coming and shut the door. I kept going forward. I heard the door lock.

I yelled at her. "No, Katie! Don't take a pill!" I pounded on the door. She didn't answer. Then I heard the water running.

I put my shoulder to the door and slammed into it. It wouldn't give. I knew I was acting like a madman, but I couldn't stop. I hit the door again. This time the lock broke. The door flew open. She was standing at the sink. She had the pills in one hand and a glass of water in the other.

I slapped the pills out of her hand. Before I even understood what I was doing, I had turned her around so her back was to the sink. I took her by the waist and lifted her so she was sitting on the edge. She slapped me, but by then I had her skirt up. Nothing was going to stop me. I grabbed the front of her pantyhose and ripped them down savagely. I got her wrist in my hand and let her other hand keep slapping at me as I undid my belt. My pants dropped. I wedged her legs open and then had to use both my hands to get myself into her. She was small and tight, but I didn't care. I had no control over it. I kept pushing myself at her. She had her hands up around my neck and was trying to choke me. I didn't try to stop her, I just put my hand under her and lifted her up and then she had to wrap her legs around me to stop herself from falling. I turned around madly, and the next thing I knew I had her back against the door. Her fingers were still digging at my neck. I was pressing farther into her and trying to kiss her. She bit me hard. Even that didn't stop me. Then I was screaming, and she was screaming too. I thrust one more time. I knew that had

140

done it. But then she hit me hard with her fist. I stumbled back. Suddenly we were apart. Even if I'd been able to get back inside her, it was too late for that now.

I lay on the floor with my back against the wall. She kept her eyes off me. She knelt down and carefully picked up her pills. They were the red-and-blue ones. The capsules. She put them all into her pill bottle except one. She put that one in her mouth and threw her head back and swallowed it without water. I hadn't tried to stop her. Then she looked at me a second. I looked away. She stepped over me and went out the door.

I finally struggled to my feet. When I got to the bedroom she was taking her clothes out of the closet and fighting to get one of her suitcases down from the shelf. I was almost ready to cry. "What're you doing?"

Her voice was a whisper. "Leaving."

"Katie. . . . No. . . . Please. . . ."

She jerked the suitcase down. It fell out of her hands and hit the floor. I reached for it, but she pushed my hands away. "Why shouldn't I leave? You don't love me."

"Yes . . . I do . . . Katie, I couldn't help what just—"

"I'm not talking about that!" She turned away. "It's what you said about Calisi. About Allstate." She shuddered. "You don't believe me. You don't believe a word I tell you."

"But how do I know what to believe? You never tell me anything about yourself!" I watched her throw the suitcase across the bed.

She pushed dresses into her suitcase. "Of course I don't. Men don't like to hear a woman talk about herself." She went back to the closet.

"I do! Katie, I want to know everything!"

She looked at me suddenly and then looked away. She ripped open a drawer. "No. Sometimes a man pretends he wants to hear. But he doesn't listen to a thing you say. He doesn't believe a thing you say. Ever." She stopped dead and looked at me again. "All a man cares about is getting between your legs. I don't want to tell a man anything. Not *any* man. I can't trust any of you."

I brought my hands up but made no move to touch her. "Please, Katie. I'm sorry. I didn't mean to do it. . . . I just couldn't stop! I love you!"

". . . Do you?"

"Yes!"

She hesitated. "No. You don't. Nobody does."

But she kept looking straight at me. Her breathing was heavy. I could tell something was in her mind, but I didn't know what.

Then her hands came out slowly and reached up to my shoulders. They began to press hard. I was confused for a moment, then I understood. I went down to my knees.

She stood there above me She took a big breath. She moved forward a step. Then she stopped. She reached down to her skirt and raised it slowly, an inch at a time. When she got it to her waist there was nothing under it. I'd already torn her panties anl pantyhose off her.

She moved another step closer. I kept my eyes on her eyes and touched her knees gently with my fingertips. She nodded.

I brought my hands up slowly. As slowly as she'd raised her skirt. After a moment she nodded again. I rubbed my left hand along the outside of her thigh. My right hand went between her legs. It rubbed her softly. At first she didn't move. Then her mouth opened slowly. She nodded again.

Her breathing quickened. I started to get up. She said, "No! . . . Please. . . . No. . . ." She shook her head back and forth and kept me down with one hand. She moved forward another step. As I began to kiss her, her hips began to rotate. That went on for a while and then she took my head in her hands, pressing me tighter against her. She began to moan and to murmur things. I stayed where I was. Then one leg came up and over my shoulder and she moved even tighter against me. She began to shake. I had to reach up and hold her from behind because I was sure she was going to lose her balance and fall, but she didn't.

When it was over, she moved away from me awkwardly, as if she couldn't understand what had just happened. She turned toward the dresser and reached for her bottles of perfume. Her fingers wouldn't close properly. She knocked the first bottle over and then the second.

She stepped back. Started crying. She went past me

and out to the living room. I heard something fall. When I got to the living room I saw she'd knocked over a chair. She was floundering like a drunk now. I took her in my arms because I didn't know what else to do. This time she didn't fight me. "Please, Jake! Don't get mad at me! I can't take it if you get mad at me!"

"Katie? . . . I'm not mad."

"Don't yell! Please!"

I didn't think I was yelling.

"You weren't going to get the pictures, Jake! If I'd told you I'd paid for them you still wouldn't have gotten them! Would you? Jake?"

". . . No. I guess not."

"I know! That's why I lied about it! I had to! Lots of people lie, Jake! I saw you needed help and I wanted to help you! Was that wrong?"

". . . No."

"I love you, Jake! That's not a lie!"

She looked so beautiful. I bent my face toward her, and her mouth opened wide. We kissed.

She moved away from me, back toward the bedroom. She seemed better now. But then she stepped forward and her leg went into the corner of the bed. She began to fall forward, put her hand against the bed and pushed herself back up. "Jake? . . . Jake, I gotta tell you something. . . ."

"No! Don't tell me anything!" I put my arms around her, then slid down her body till my knees were on the floor and my face was pressed against her waist. "Please, Katie, it's all right. Whatever it is, it's all right. You don't have to tell me anything."

"No, I gotta tell you. . . . Jim Cain. . . . You know who Jim Cain is?"

I looked up at her.

"Jake? . . . Don't you know who Jim Cain is?"

"He's a director."

"Yeah. . . . I gotta tell you. . . ." Her hands were in my hair. She was trying to smile. "Jim Cain. . . ." She began to tip to the side.

I stood up again and put my arm around her. I held her so she wouldn't fall.

"Gotta believe me, Jake. . . . Sometimes I lie, but

you gotta believe me. . . ." Her hand came up and clamped onto my shoulder. Her eyes widened. "Nobody believes me! That's what it is! Nobody ever believes me! Jake, if only you—"

Then she went slack, as if her legs had given out. I struggled to hold her up. Her arms swung around my neck. "Gotta make it, Jake! Gonna make it! Together! You and me! Our only chance!"

I got her so she was sitting on the bed. I was crying by then. I sat next to her and held her close. "What's the matter? Katie! Tell me!" Her eyes began to close. "Katie! I'll call a doctor!"

Her eyes opened. "No! No doctor!" Her hands came around me again, this time like claws. "Please don't call a doctor! Don't yell at me, Jake! I love you! I can't make it without you! We need each other! Don't you need me?" Her voice got louder. "Listen to me, Jake! Just listen to me! Jim Cain. . . ."

Then she stopped. She passed out.

She seemed to be sleeping peacefully now. I felt her pulse. It didn't seem fast, or slow. But I knew nothing about pulses. I felt my own pulse and counted against the second hand of my watch and then felt her pulse again and counted the same way. The counts seemed close enough. She looked peaceful. Just tired.

I didn't call a doctor. I was scared to. She'd told me not to, but that wasn't it. Sometimes we want to know things, but at the same time we're scared to know them. Then if we wait long enough we end up deciding we'd rather not call someone who might lead us to the answers we don't want to know.

Besides, she looked so peaceful now.

I sat there and watched her. I took her hand so she'd know I was there. Even while she slept her hand held me tightly in that way she had. Half an hour passed. Her eyes opened. She sat up with a start. "What happened?"

". . . You passed out. Fell asleep."

Her eyes jumped at me. "Did you call a doctor?"

"No. You asked me not to."

"Oh. Good. Good. I don't need a doctor."

She yawned. She stretched her arms and shook her head. It was very childlike and very innocent, the way she usually was. She smiled and stretched again, and then she laughed. "I didn't get much sleep last night. Been falling asleep all day." She stood up.

"I don't know if you should be on your feet yet, Katie." I paused. "You sure you don't want me to call a doctor?"

"No! I feel fine!" She smiled and bent toward me and kissed my cheek. Then she growled and bit playfully at my ear. She seemed so alive now. So herself. "Really, Jake. I feel fine. Just let me splash some water on my face."

She went out of the room and took her pocketbook with her. I followed her down to the bathroom but that was all she did. Splash water on her face.

We went into the kitchen and she saw the broken glass. She swept it up. I wanted to hold the dustpan for her, but she wouldn't let me do it. I took some paper towels to mop up the Jack Daniel's, but she wouldn't let me do that either. I sat at the table and watched her. When she finished the floor was spotless. She stood up and saw the Jack Daniel's bottle sitting on the counter. For a second I thought she was going to pour herself a glass, but as I started to get out of my chair she screwed its cap back on and pushed the bottle aside. Then she looked at the counter. It wasn't clean enough for her. It never was. She sponged it off. Then she cleaned the sponge.

She looked at me. "Okay, Jake. Calisi. You're right. I paid him. I wanted you to have the best pictures in town. That's what you got, right?"

I took a deep breath and spoke carefully. "You shouldn't have told me they were free, if they weren't."

She snapped her fingers at the air so suddenly that it startled me. "You're right! You're absolutely right!" But then she came to the table and bent over and kissed me. "Can you forgive me?"

I hesitated. Then she kissed me again, and I felt her electricity go through me. I nodded.

She went back to the counter and took the Jack Daniel's in her hand. "You don't want me to drink any of this right now, do you?"

". . . I think it'd be better if—"

"Then I won't. Simple as that. I won't do anything

you don't want me to do. I promise." She went through the door.

I followed her to the living room. She put the bottle on the bookcase and lined up the other bottles so they were all straight. She looked around the room and picked up the feather duster she'd brought with her when she moved in. She dusted the table in front of the sofa. She dusted another table at the side. She went back to the bookcase and took several swipes at it with the feather duster, then she put the duster down.

"I don't feel like making dinner tonight."

"That's okay, Katie. I'll make——"

"Not while I'm around you won't!" She laughed. "Come on, let's go somewhere. Get some food. Get some air." She came across the room and grabbed both my hands. "God, Jake, I paid for those pictures 'cause I love you! Don't you know that?"

I thought a moment, and it bothered me. Because she loved me?

But she'd paid for those pictures after she'd only known me a couple of days.

"Come on, Jake!" She giggled as she tugged me toward the front door. "Let's go eat!"

When we got to the restaurant she wanted a drink. I told her I didn't want her to have one. I reminded her she'd taken that pill earlier. She thought a moment and remembered. She said yes, I was right. She was glad I'd reminded her. She didn't want a drink after all.

I hadn't thought I'd be hungry for much, but then when the food came she was talking easily again and I couldn't eat enough. I started off with soup, then a salad. Then a steak the size of Texas. Green beans and a baked potato. Pie a la mode. Katie ate just as much as I did. She ate with one hand. The other was under the table and on my leg. I didn't want it to be any other place in the world.

All through dinner she couldn't stop talking. I sat there and listened. Her talking so much didn't mean a thing to me. I figured she was always talking like that, either too much or not at all. But that didn't worry me, I was making sure she had nothing to drink. She kept turning around to see who was coming into the place and who was leaving. I didn't give that much of a thought either.

We'd come there in my car because I hadn't wanted her to drive. But on the way back she wanted to drive so much and she gave me such a big kiss, like a fool I let her. Five minutes onto the freeway and she was going ten miles over the speed limit.

"Don't take it so fast, Katie."

"Don't worry, Jake. It's okay. I feel fine now." She had one hand on my leg. The other left the wheel for a second and slapped her forehead. "What am I thinking about? I almost forgot to tell you! I was—"

"You're over the speed limit."

"What?" She faced front. "Just five miles over. I'll take it down." She put both hands on the wheel and slowed a little and hit the speed limit and even dipped just below it. Her hand came back on my leg. Her head swung around. "Now listen. I was all over town today. All the way from Santa Monica up to Hollywood. I ran into this guy, Jake. He turned out to be in movies. He's an assistant director on the new Jim Cain film. You know who Jim Cain is, right?"

"Yeah." I kept my eyes on the road. "You started to tell me something about him before, when you—"

"I did?"

She speeded up slightly. She pulled out of line and passed a car and pulled back into line. She flashed her smile at me. "See? Perfect control. And only one handed, too." Her eyes darted at the speedometer. "Hey, and only one mile over the speed limit. Can't ask for more than that, can you?" Her fingers tightened on my leg. "There. Right *on* the speed limit." She frowned. "What was I saying? Oh! Right! The assistant director! I had your picture and résumé with me, like I always do—"

A car honked on our left. I looked past Katie and saw a startled face in a Buick beside us.

"Katie, get back in your own lane, you're going to crowd him off the road."

"What?"

The man hit his horn again. Katie moved right. I kept my eyes on the Buick.

"There. That better?"

The man was still looking at us. His head was shaking.

147

"Jake?" Katie's hand flew off my leg. It went up to her forehead and gave me a salute. "That better, sir?"

"Keep both hands on the wheel!"

"Yes, sir!" Her hand came down and grabbed the wheel. "So. This guy, he says to me, he can get you into Cain's new film. Three day's work, at least. He might be able to stretch it to a week. He said there'd be no lines involved, but Cain's supposed to do a lot of improvisation, and the guy said—"

The Buick honked again.

"Katie! You're going into his lane again!"

"Huh?" She stepped on the gas. We shot straight ahead.

But behind us the Buick went half off the road. It turned quickly, got back on, then had trouble straightening out. It looked bad for a moment. Then the Buick stopped swerving. I took a deep breath and turned front.

"So the guy said, with any luck, he might be able to get you some lines. He said—"

"Katie, don't tell me about it right now. Just keep quiet and keep your eyes on the road." She looked at me. "On the road!"

She faced front. I watched her another moment, then unclenched my fists.

A second later there was honking from the lane to our right. The Buick was there. The man's face was red now. He was glaring at us. He began to yell. His words got lost before they reached us, then they came again and this time they were clearer. He pulled closer to us, as if this time he was going to force *us* off the road.

Katie hit the gas. Then she cut to the right. We were in front of him.

He cut left, still honking. I looked through the rear window and could see the veins sticking out in his neck. He came up fast, right next to us again. He began to inch sideways.

"Don't worry, Jake, I'll get away from him." Katie swung left. It scared him. Then she jerked the steering wheel right and kept going on an angle. The next thing I knew, we were leaving the freeway and barreling down an off-ramp.

There was a stop sign at the bottom of the grade. Katie hit the brakes. When I looked around, the Buick was next to us again. The man was livid. He was shaking his fist and shouting. Katie leaned forward to see if the intersection was clear. Her hands gripped the steering wheel and we flew forward.

But suddenly there was no place to go. She had driven us into a dead-end street. As we slowed down, the Buick slanted in front of us, cutting us off. The Buick came to a stop. The man pushed his door open and began to get out. "You goddamn bitch! You could've killed me!" His hand flew up. In his hand there was a gun.

"I'm going to teach you a lesson, you goddamn bitch!"

I stiffened. Katie gave a small cry. "Jake! Make him stop yelling at me!"

I reached toward the steering wheel and tried to bring my foot across to the gas pedal. "Katie, put it in reverse! Quick!"

She didn't react.

The man came around the front of his car. He yelled at her again.

"No! Don't yell at me!" Katie gasped. "Leave me alone!"

The man kept yelling. The gun waved in the air.

Katie turned. Her hand flattened against my chest. It pushed me back into my seat as her other hand went into her pocketbook. I watched in horror as she pulled out her water pistol.

"Katie! No! He's got a real gun!"

She didn't seem to care. She pointed the water pistol through the window, and then I heard a gunshot.

The gunshot came from the water pistol. It wasn't a water pistol this time, it was a real gun. She fired it at the street right in front of his feet. His mouth dropped open. She fired again. He jumped back and dove behind his Buick. She fired two more times, into the side of his car.

Then it was quiet. She began to shake. I heard a police siren, far away. She said, "Oh my God! Police!" She dropped the gun into her pocketbook, put one hand on the steering wheel and threw the car into reverse.

She circled back behind the Buick. She went too far, and we ended up on somebody's lawn. She shifted gears again, turned the steering wheel savagely and drove to the intersection. Then she hit the brakes. The freeway off-ramp was directly opposite us. A sign said DO NOT ENTER —WRONG WAY. But we were already several feet into the intersection. Katie swung the wheel and turned right. A good ten blocks in front of us, there was the police car. Its siren was going, its lights were flashing. It was coming straight toward us.

Katie drove forward and and turned right. She drove faster and took the next left. Then a right. Then a left. Then another right. I heard the siren still going but didn't know where it was coming from anymore. Katie kept driving. Faster and faster. Making every turn she came to.

She got us back onto the freeway and drove all the way home. We pulled to a stop in front of my house. She was like ice. I was a wreck. She looked at me, saw how I was shaking and opened her pocketbook again. Her hand came out with her pill bottle. She snapped off the top and spilled two of the garish-looking red-and-blue capsules into her hand. She held the capsules out to me. "Quick, Jake. Take one. It'll quiet you down."

I stared at her hand. She took one of the capsules and popped it into her mouth, threw her head back and swallowed, then looked at me again. "Come on, Jake. It'll help your nerves. Take it."

I looked into her open pocketbook. I could see the gun butt. "Katie. . . ." I gulped air. "Katie! Where'd you get that?"

She said nothing.

I picked up her pocketbook and held it open in front of her. "Katie!"

Her eyes moved slowly down. She looked confused. As if she were seeing the gun for the first time. Then she grabbed the pocketbook away from me. She closed it with a snap, and a second later she was out of the car and going into the house.

I found her in the living room, sitting in the dark, on the sofa. There was just enough light coming through the window for me to see her in silhouette. I couldn't see her face. I went to her and sat beside her and took her pocketbook. She didn't move. I opened it and tipped it so I could see inside again. I started to reach for the gun and then changed my mind. I put the pocketbook on the table in front of us. I reached for her hand. It was closed tight, but I yelled at her and made her open it. She was still holding the bottle of red-and-blue capsules. I tried to take it away from her, but she wouldn't let me. She said, "No, Jake! Please! I need them!" Then suddenly she was crying.

I knew if I struggled with her anymore or yelled at her again it would only make things worse. I gently put my arm around her. Her arms came hard around me. We sat quietly for a long time, and then I said, "Katie, something's wrong."

"I know!" She looked up at me. "God, Jake, I know!" She started crying again.

I waited for her to quiet down. "Katie. . . . Something's very wrong . . . I think . . . you got to see someone. A . . . a doctor. A psychiatrist—"

"I know! You're right! Of course I do!"

The abruptness of it startled me.

She held on to me tightly. "Yes, Jake! You're right! I've got to do it! I'm going to do it! Jake! I'm scared, Jake! Hold me! Please!"

I held her quite a while. She sobbed, then she stopped. Then she started up again. When she quieted down the second time, she seemed more in control of herself. She said, "I'm tired, Jake. I'm tired. I'd better go to sleep." She picked up her pocketbook and went into the bedroom. She took off her shoes and crawled into bed without taking off her clothes. Moments later she seemed to be sleeping.

I knew I had to do something about the gun, but I couldn't, not then. She had the pocketbook under the blanket with her. She kept her arms wrapped around it all night.

I sat in the chair and didn't expect to fall asleep but I did. When I woke up it was light and Katie was gone. I was suddenly afraid she'd left me.

I opened the closet. Her clothes were still there. And her suitcases. I went into the kitchen. There was a note on the table. *See you tonight. Love, K.*

Her pocketbook wasn't in the house. She'd taken it with her.

I sat at the table and didn't eat a thing. I didn't

smoke any cigarettes, I didn't drink any coffee. My stomach was acting up.

Then the phone rang. Someone named Paul told me to come out to UCLA. They were shooting the Jim Cain movie there. They wanted me on the set by nine.

I went into the bathroom and tried to shave. I almost cut myself three times.

THEY were working in a large studio up at the Theater Arts Department. There were lots of people. None of them paid much attention to me. I asked someone where I should go, and he told me, so I went. I joined a crowd of twenty other actors. I only knew one of them. His name was Harry Brock. We shook hands.

"Long time no see, Harry."

"Been on the road. Touring company of *Godspell*." He looked around. "Long time since I seen anyone in dream town."

"Make any money on the road?"

"Not much." His hand wriggled back and forth. "Just a bus and truck tour. They weren't paying top dollar. Hell, they weren't even paying middle dollar. Most of the time it was one nighters and sleeping in the bus and food you couldn't feed to hogs, but I liked it. There were audiences out there." He laughed. "What do you want? I'm a masochist. Hell, every struggling actor is a masochist, right? And every actor is a struggling actor. We don't come in any other variety, do we?"

He laughed again. I looked away.

Then a voice said, "Bolin?"

The voice belonged to a young kid who was waving a clipboard at me. "Come over here."

When I'm asked to do something by someone on a movie set and the someone has a clipboard, I don't argue the point. I went to him. He took my arm and pulled me aside and spoke to me quietly. "I'm Paul. Just wanted to make sure we understand each other. You're here as an extra." His eyes hadn't left the clipboard.

"Sure. What's the—"

"Quiet!" His eyes flickered up. "Keep your mouth shut, and I'll see what I can do. But no promises. Right?"

". . . Right. Sure."

I was staring at the clipboard. He had one of my pictures and résumés there. But it wasn't my Calisi picture. It was one of the old ones.

I was about to say something about that when he nodded and walked off. Very short, very sweet.

I thought about it a moment, and then Harry was standing next to me. "What's up, Jake? Know someone worth knowing?"

". . . I don't know."

"You sure? He's got a clipboard."

I took out my cigarettes and lit one.

Jim Cain was a bear of a man. His lower face was hidden by a beard. His mouth was never without a cigar. He wore a baseball cap which said *Brooklyn Dodgers*. The cap must've been the closest he'd ever come to anything to do with exercise. He was, like Falstaff, not merely a fat man—he was an enormously fat man. But he knew his business. His business was film-making.

He was calm. He was cool. He knew how to talk to people so they'd do the things he needed them to do. He was a pleasure to watch. He'd worked with a lot of these actors before, and you could tell they liked him. Most actors want directors to *think* they like them so the directors will hire them again. It doesn't mean anything more that that. But this was different. These people really did like Cain. Even the technicians liked him.

At one point an assistant cameraman, who could've been replaced as easily as you replace a used cigarette with a new one, screwed up a scene so bad there had to be a retake. Another director would've spent half an hour chewing the poor guy out. Threatening to fire him. The result would've been a wasted morning. A movie set is a pretty volatile place. Too many people have too much riding on the end results. When there's an argument, no matter what it's about, who's concerned, it shakes everyone up. Apparently Cain was so secure in his work that he didn't need an argument to let off steam. All he did was give the assistant cameraman a look, and when the look was finished you knew the cameraman and Cain were still friends. They'd probably be working on more movies together. The screw-up was as good as forgotten. Cain was a rare one, you knew it immediately.

It was a good set. Even just sitting there as an extra doing nothing, you enjoyed it. These people weren't just shooting a movie. Shooting is the right word for the way most film companies go about it. When they've finished, the film they've shot is usually dead, or if not dead at least pretty well wounded. It was a different case here. These people were actually trying to *make a movie*.

I don't mean to make it sound like what they thought they were doing was art. It had none of that about it. It was just good, clean work. Work that was going to be done and done right.

They enjoyed watching each other work. They weren't the usual kind who hope everyone else will screw up so they'll look better. They all had egos, of course, and their stupid insecurities, like the rest of us, but they had a good handle on them. It doesn't happen that way too often in the business.

Now I felt terrific. Through some great stroke of luck I'd stepped into this strange world. A world I'd begun to doubt even existed. A world five million light years from Alan's house in Malibu.

And I knew exactly how I'd gotten there.

At one-thirty they took a short break. All of us extras ran to the pay phones to call our services. When I called mine, I had a message. An audition for an Ajax commercial. But it was no good. It was set up for that afternoon at five-fifteen. I hadn't had a chance to call Ruth and tell her I was tied up with the Cain movie. I hung up quickly, thought a moment, then searched for the young kid with the clipboard.

I found him with his mouth around a cheeseburger. I hemmed and hawed, then said, "Just wondered, Paul, you know how late you're going to work us today?"

"Five, five-thirty. Something like that."

I hesitated. I hated to ask something like this, especially the first day on the set. But I took a stab at it anyway. "I don't want to make any problems. It's just, I called my service, I got an audition for a commercial. Five-fifteen." No, it was too much to ask. I shrugged it off. "Never mind. I'll call my agent, maybe she can get it pushed up a little later. Sometimes they're still seeing people till six or later." I began to turn away.

"Yeah, I know what you're up against." He stood up. "Let me check around, see if I can spring you any earlier."

He went away.

Ten minutes passed and he didn't come back. I gave up on it and walked over to the other side of the set and sat next to Harry. My face must've looked troubled. He said, "What's the matter? You look discouraged as hell."

I was, but it had nothing to do with the Ajax commercial. I'd begun to think about the night before again. "No, it's nothing." I tried to smile. "Called my service, got an audition this afternoon. If I can make it in time."

Harry gave me what he passed off as his Irish accent. "Isn't it terrible? To be runnin' to appointments all over town that way. It's meetin' himself comin' and goin' he'll be doin', 'fore he knows it."

I said nothing. He leaned closer. "Jake? What's wrong with you?"

I pulled out a cigarette and played with it. "Nothing." I tapped one end against the back of my hand. "You busy for dinner tonight?"

"Why? Got something in mind?" His eye winked. "Like girls?"

I took a long time getting my match lit and then even longer getting my cigarette lit. "How about coming over to my place tonight?"

"Oh. Well, all right." His eyes narrowed to a squint. "But can you cook?"

Cook? I hadn't cooked a meal in weeks. She wouldn't let me.

"It'll be a free meal, Harry."

"Oh. Then I'll be there." He smiled and put his arm over my shoulder. "What time?"

Just then Paul came over. He told me it was all set. If they hadn't used me by four o'clock I should check with him and he'd release me for the day.

The electricity and confidence from the Cain movie must've rubbed off. At the Ajax commercial I wasn't as scared as usual. My stomach only bothered me a little. I could've done better if I hadn't had so many things on my mind, but their responses to my reading seemed pretty good.

That meant nothing. Often they'd act as if they'd liked you just to get you out of the room without your blowing up and hitting someone. There'd been a story going around the year before about an actor who'd been up for a commercial at one of the major ad agencies. They liked him and called him back for a second reading. Then a third. But the third time out he knew he'd blown it. His reading had been terrible. He'd lost his place twice. He'd gotten the shakes. He'd dropped the copy on the floor. He'd had to clear his throat. A nerve in his right cheek had started twitching. When it was over they tried to tell him it was okay—they understood—he'd done all right, but he knew they weren't interested in him anymore. He was still in the room with them and they were still acting polite with him when he opened his portfolio and took out a gun. He tried to shoot himself. There were four of them and they wrestled him to the floor. They took the gun away from him.

I wasn't sure if the story was true or not. I'd heard it three times and each time it'd been said to have happened to a different actor, so it probably wasn't true. Just one of those stories that make the rounds. Something for someone to tell, something for someone else to listen to, to pass the time. But whether it was true or not didn't matter. I'd been around long enough to know it *could've* been true.

I was on my way home and I stopped. I pulled over to the side of the road. I thought about the gun again. Katie's gun. I thought about trying to locate her at an Allstate office and not being able to do it. I thought about all the things she'd told me and how little I really knew about her. How little she seemed to want me to know. Where she'd been and what she'd done before she got to me. Then I opened my wallet, and the slip of paper was still there. The one that said *505 Federal Ave*. I stared at it for half a minute.

It was a small apartment house, about twenty units. I knocked on doors. Nobody answered. Finally I found a woman, but she only spoke Spanish and I didn't. I don't know what I would've asked her if I *had* spoken Spanish. I tried the manager's apartment for the second time. Still nobody there. I hung around another five minutes, remembered I'd invited Harry for dinner, gave up on it and drove home.

There'd been no reason for it anyway. Just something to do, to stop from going home. No reason at all.

When I got to the house, Katie's car was there. I went farther up the hill and made a turn and came back and kept going. I drove to the bottom of the hill and pulled into a side street. I stopped the car, I got out a cigarette and stuck it in my fingers. I stared at it. I didn't want to be alone with her. Not yet. I wanted a third person present when I saw her again.

I don't think I was scared of what *she* might do. It was of what *I* might say, or do, if I caught her alone.

Twenty minutes later, Harry drove by. I watched him start up the hill and gave him half a minute and then followed him. When I reached the house, he was parking on the far side of the yellow Volkswagen. I parked on the other side. He walked over and threw his Irish accent at me. "How'd it go, boy-o? Impress 'em, didja?"

"Went all right. They had me read the copy three times." His eyebrows went up. "Told me to do it a different way each time, too. Taped it the last time."

"Hey! Boy-o!" He looked like he was impressed. I would've been impressed, too, any other day, but that day I didn't give a damn. I took a deep breath and led him into the house.

She was sitting in the kitchen. She was reading one of my *Daily Variety*s. She was drinking milk. Munching chocolate chip cookies. She looked up and smiled. "Hi, Jake!"

It was loud and vibrant. It scared me a little. I hesitated and controlled my voice. "Hi. How you feeling today?"

"Fine! Great! How about you?"

I nodded slightly. Harry came through the door behind me, and when he saw her his eyebrows went up again.

We had a very nice dinner, the three of us. Good food, good talk. Candlelight. Music. Wine for Harry and me, but none for her. She hadn't even asked for any. She drank only milk. But then halfway through dinner she left the kitchen for a moment. I went after her to stop her from taking a pill, but she didn't take one. She poured herself a glass of Jack Daniel's and came back to the kitchen. The way she looked at me, I decided it was best to say nothing.

Then she did something I'd never seen her do before. She drank the Jack Daniel's, and the milk, alternating between the two glasses.

But she was charming. So was Harry. As for her, maybe she wanted to impress him since he was my friend. As for Harry, he was Harry. He was probably thinking, If she ever dumps Jake, maybe I'll have a chance with her. And since he didn't play the actor that night and didn't come on strong like he usually did, she liked him. They talked and laughed. I laughed, but I didn't talk much.

Around eleven o'clock, Harry said he had to go, much as he'd rather stay. Katie nodded and collected the dishes and took them to the sink. I knew her pocketbook was in the living room so I wasn't worried about her taking a pill. I walked Harry out to his car.

"What'd you think of her?"

He laughed. "You mean besides the milk and the Jack Daniel's?"

Something happened to me. I took his arm suddenly as if I was going to rip it off. "I mean it! What'd you think?"

He looked at my hand on his arm. "What's the matter with you? You been spooky all day." His eyes came up. "I thought it was just being on the movie. First day on the set. But you been jumpy all night, too."

I mumbled something. I released his arm. I took out my cigarettes.

I offered him a cigarette and he took it. We lit up and smoked our first puffs. I spoke more evenly. "I'm just curious. What'd you think of her?"

He shrugged. "What's to think? I wish I'd met her before you did, boy-o."

The scary part was, right then part of me was wishing the same thing.

She'd finished the dishes. She was eating the chocolate-chip cookies again. When she saw me, she closed the bag and pushed it aside. "I've got to stop eating these things. Why don't you ever tell me to stop? They'll make me fat."

I leaned against the counter and rubbed the back of my neck. I looked at the floor. "You aren't fat."

She laughed. "Maybe not to you. You're prejudiced. I'm glad you are, but if you were objective, you'd say I'm a little fat."

"No. I wouldn't." I stayed calm. At least on the surface.

Her fingers rapped the front of the sink nervously. "I got on the scale this morning, I'd put on two pounds. All that food we ate last night." She looked at the dishes in the drainer. "God, and look how much we ate tonight. And you didn't even stop me." She frowned at me. Then she frowned at the cookie bag. She punched at it lightly, sending it across the counter to the wall. "Now this. I'm going to be big as a house."

"For Christ's sake, Katie, you aren't fat!" It was starting to come out. "Will you stop saying you're fat? Damn it, you say it so much, pretty soon you're going to make me think you *are* fat!" I tried again to hold it in, but it was no use. "I mean, God! That's what you keep saying all the time, you'll end up making me think it's true!"

She didn't yell back. Her hand stroked softly down the front of my chest. When it reached my belt buckle, her fingers curled over it. "But you'll still want me anyway, won't you?"

I didn't answer.

She stared at me in surprise. Then she took her hand away. She reached up and pulled open the cupboard. She grabbed the bag of cookies and threw it high over her head. It landed on the top shelf. Even I couldn't reach it up there without standing on my toes. She slammed the cupboard and looked at me. "There! That settles it! I'm going on a diet! Tomorrow!"

It didn't settle a thing. I crossed my arms and looked at the wall.

"Jake? What's the matter?"

"Nothing."

"Yeah?" She laughed. "You're acting pretty funny, for nothing to be the matter."

I looked away. "The guy on the movie. Paul. The one you met yesterday. How come you gave him one of my old pictures?"

"What?"

"He's got my picture and résumé. But not the new one. Not the Calisi. He's got the old one. How come you gave him the old one?"

Her forehead wrinkled. "Didn't know I had." She shrugged. "That's funny. Must've got mixed up with the others. Why? Something wrong with that?"

I didn't know. Something seemed funny about it.

She tapped the front of the sink again. I felt like grabbing her hands to stop her. Then she stopped. She kept her eyes on me and went silently across the room and sat at the table.

She stayed quiet. Waited. A few more seconds passed. Then her hand came up to the table and her fingers started tapping again. "All right, Jake. You've been acting funny all night. What's the matter?"

I kept my eyes on her. "I just wanted to know. . . . You decided yet? What you're going to do? About seeing a doctor?"

"A doctor?"

I hesitated. "A doctor. A psychiatrist. . . . Last night, you said you'd—"

"Oh. God. I was stoned last night, wasn't I?" She laughed. A very high, very light laugh. Light enough to float on the air like a feather. She got up and came across the room and put her arms around me. "God, Jake, I'm sorry. Won't happen again. I promise."

I stayed as I was, my arms still in front of me. I looked straight into her eyes. "*What* won't happen again?"

"I won't get stoned again. I promise."

I took her into the bedroom. I made her sit on the bed. I told her about everything that had happened the night before.

I told her about her coming home. Going into the kitchen. Taking the Jack Daniel's. Dropping the glass on the floor. Running out to the bathroom.

It took me a second, then I told her about what happened in the bathroom. What I'd tried to do to her.

Then I went on with it. About afterward. In the bedroom. And after that. When she'd passed out. And then woken up. Splashed water on her face. Gone back to the kitchen. Cleaned up the broken glass.

She remembered everything except the passing out. She didn't remember that at all.

I told her about our going out to eat. She remembered that. I told her about what we ate and the things we said during dinner. She remembered that. I told her about her wanting to drive home and our going onto the freeway. She remembered that.

But when I told her about the man in the Buick, and how she tried to get away from him, and the dead-end street, and the gun—she didn't remember any of that.

I went to the living room and got her pocketbook and brought it back to the bedroom and opened it up. She looked inside. Saw a gun. I took the gun out and held it in my hands. I fooled with it and finally got it open and showed her that several of the bullets had been fired.

She told me she didn't like guns, to please put it away.

I went to the other side of the bed and put the gun in the drawer of my night table. I closed the drawer and came back to her. Then she said something that scared the hell out of me. First she looked away, toward the window. Then she said very quietly, "God, Jake. Where did it come from?"

She wanted to take one of her blue-and-red capsules. She said it would let her sleep. I told her I wouldn't allow it. But an hour passed and she still couldn't sleep, so I told her to take it. Twenty minutes later she was out.

I took the gun from my night table and stared at it. I'd had an air rifle once when I was young. At summer camp I'd learned to shoot a .22. That was it, as far as me and guns went. I knew nothing about them and wanted to know nothing about them. Now I had one in my hand.

I went into the kitchen. I made some coffee and drank it. I had the gun away from her now, but what was I going to do with it?

Something in my subconscious told me I had to be very careful. Something told me I knew something about the gun. What did I know? Where it might've come from? What it might've been used for? If it ever *had* been used?

I drank more coffee. I didn't want to think about it.

I made my thoughts theoretical. Here was a gun. Suppose this gun had once been used for something. *Before* the other night. Suppose this gun had ever been part of some kind of crime. Where someone might've been hurt. Or killed.

I lit a cigarette.

Fingerprints. Could the police really get them off a gun. Because if there was something on this gun—a print—that would connect the gun to her—and if this gun had ever been used for something—and if this gun were ever found—and traced to her—

I lit another cigarette.

What if I just threw the gun away?

What if, some day, someone found it?

What if, when they found it, there was still a print on the gun that could connect it to her?

Then I would lose her.

I had to keep the gun. Keep it in such a way that I could be sure it wouldn't be found.

They say if you want to hide something, you should put it in the most obvious place. Nobody will look there. So the first thing that occurred to me was the simplest, and the most foolish. That top shelf where she'd thrown

163

the bag of cookies. Within a second I realized what a stupid idea it was. Maybe nobody else would think to look there, but she'd go up there sooner or later for the cookies, no matter what she said. It was the last place in the world I should put it.

I thought about burying it.

But when you bury something, you can never do enough. The ground always looks like something's been buried there. And when ground looks like something's been buried where nothing should be buried, sooner or later someone comes along and starts digging.

Maybe I *shouldn't* keep it. Maybe I should drive down to Santa Monica and drop it off a pier.

Sure. Next Sunday I'd read about a Sunday-morning scuba diver who'd found a gun.

I lit another cigarette.

Finally, I put the thing in a paper bag and I went outside. There wasn't much of a moon. I got the flashlight from my car and went out back to the trees. Some of them were pretty big. I looked toward the bedroom window. It was dark and looked empty. I climbed into one of the trees and found a nice resting place for the paper bag and put it there. From the ground you wouldn't be able to see it. It was too high up. I'd lived in the house long enough to know there were never any kids fooling around out there, so that wasn't a problem. This way, if there was ever any need to produce a gun, I could do it. And if there was ever any need *not* to produce the gun, I could do that, too.

I got down from the tree and looked toward the bedroom window. It still looked dark and empty. I thought I was safe.

I sat in the chair in the bedroom and waited for morning. As soon as it got light, Katie began to move. When she was up on her feet, I called an actor I knew. I apologized for waking him and asked for the name and phone number of his shrink. He growled quite a bit but he gave me what I needed.

Then I called the shrink. The only one there was an answering machine. I left a message.

Time passed. Katie was nervous. She said she had places to go to. I told her to wait.

At ten minutes after nine, Dr. Samuel's receptionist called. I talked to her first and then gave the phone to Katie. She stared at it a moment and then made an appointment for that afternoon at two-thirty.

We sat next to each other on the sofa for quite a while. I had no idea what she was thinking. Then she put her hand into mine and held on to me tightly in that way she sometimes did. "I'm scared, Jake."

I tried to speak calmly. "Scared of what?"

"That I'm going to lose you."

"What?" I put my arm around her and drew her head against my chest. "Katie. You won't lose me."

Then neither of us spoke.

It got late and I had to be at the Cain film. We kissed and I left.

What happened that day on the Cain film made me forget about Dr. Samuels.

It was during a short break. We were standing around doing nothing. I was bugging Harry again about what he really thought of Katie. He was giving me strange looks and telling me he thought she was terrific. He said if I was planning to dump her I should let him know, he'd be happy to give her a nice soft place to land. Then a voice called, "Hey! Bolin! Over here! Quick!"

It was Paul. I went over to him. He had my picture and résumé in his hand.

Suddenly I had to know. "Paul . . ." I rubbed my hand over my mouth. "That picture and résumé. That's my old picture. . . . How long you had it?"

"Your picture?" He thought a moment. His eyes were looking in the distance. "I don't know. Couple weeks, maybe three."

"What?" I gulped. "You didn't just get it, two days ago?"

"No." He kept looking past me.

I rubbed my hands together nervously. "That means she must've given it to you before she moved in with me." A hollow feeling crept into my stomach. "Before she even knew me."

Paul took my arm. "All right, come on, let's go. Right now."

He took me across the set and introduced me to Jim Cain.

Cain smiled broadly and held out his hand. "Glad to have you with us, Jake! Kind of busy, yesterday! Didn't get a chance to talk, did we?"

I cleared my throat. I mumbled something. His hand was still out. I shook it. He did most of the shaking. He kept hold of my arm and started walking. He pulled me along with him.

"Paul told me you've done a little work back East! Broadway!"

That threw me. Why had Paul had to pick *that* out

of my résumé? It was nothing. It was three years ago. Why would Cain be interested in it?

I didn't think fast enough to answer like an actor. I picked and answered like an honest man. "That wasn't much, the Broadway thing. Just a couple lines, that's all."

When I heard what I was saying I could've shot myself.

But Cain was listening. He fished out a cigar. Lit it. Waited to see if I was going to say anything else. He was probably wondering how stupid the something else might turn out to be.

I went on. "Did some off-Broadway. A couple originals. For Papp, down at the Public Theater." My stomach felt queasy. "I did Norman in *Moonchildren*. Not in New York, it was a stock package. We did one of the circuits in New England."

I should've told him I'd done three seasons of Shakespeare in Stratford, Connecticut. The lead in a play that had tried out in Boston and Philadelphia but hadn't made it to New York. A supporting part in some really hot production. *The Great White Hope*. The Richard Burton *Hamlet*. Those were safe shows. They'd been years before. The casts had been so huge, actors who'd really been in them would never be able to swear for sure you hadn't been in them too.

I went on. "I been out here, the past couple years. Done a little TV. Not much."

I should've given him a list of credits and hoped he wouldn't really listen. Nobody ever did. Bluff was what was needed. Bluff was what I couldn't do. I'd never been able to. I was always too chicken to try.

Cain nodded and puffed his cigar. He draped his arm over my shoulder and kept walking. "Way it stands, Jake, I got a script, but the script's got some holes in it. You know how scripts are." He laughed. "What I need is some fire! Energy!" His hands slapped together. "Spontaneous combustion, that's what I need!"

He'd stopped walking. Tom McEnroe, the star of the picture, was standing in front of us.

"Jake? You know Tom? Say hello! Say hello to Jake Bolin, Tommy!"

McEnroe said hello. Nodded. Shot his hand forward.

I stared at the hand blankly and somehow came out of my daze and shook it.

Cain had his arm over my shoulder again. "Tommy's always coming to you, Jake! Always needs a favor! You're friends! Good friends! But he's been pushing it lately." Cain's head nodded several times as he worked it out in his mind.

"This time, he really needs you. Yeah. And we know that, but *you* don't know it. He tells you he needs you. You don't believe it." He exploded again. "Yeah! That's what we'll do! You figure it's the same's it always is!" He stopped a moment. Then his head nodded even more vigorously. "Yeah! Okay! Simple scene, that's the way we'll play it. Straightforward. You've had it, Jake. You're fed up. Fed up!"

Cain kept his arm across my shoulder and turned so he could drop his other arm over McEnroe's. It was a clean, uncalculated motion. It tied the three of us together just right.

"What you got to do, Tommy, you got to get some money from him. If you don't, you're screwed. But Jake, no matter what he says it doesn't matter. You don't believe he needs it."

I nodded as calmly as I could. I tried not to think too much about what it really meant. I tried to tell my stomach to settle down. I concentrated on the burning tip of Cains cigar as it bobbed up and down. I was tired. I hadn't gotten any sleep the previous night. I was glad I was tired. That might be the only thing that could get me through this.

Then Cain's hand tightened on my shoulder. "You're mad, Jake!" I almost jumped a foot. "You're ready to give it to him!"

Yeah. Mad. Ready to give it to him. Sure I was.

"Things have built up over the years! This is the time it's all going to blow!"

Built up. Going to blow. I was going to blow it, probably.

"Fire! Electricity! Spontaneous combustion!"

Spontaneous combustion? Yes, damn it, spontaneous combustion! Yes! Say *yes* to things! Stop saying *no!*

It would have to look good. I'd have to pull it out of

somewhere. I'd have to break through all my barriers and give it to him. I'd *have* to bluff!

I'd have to get past the shyness. The lack of confidence. The fear. The shakes. The hollow feeling in my stomach. I'd have to do it like he wanted it. I couldn't let anything hold me back. This was a chance to do what I wanted to do. To act. To do it. Yes. I had to deliver. I had to give him something. I had to!

"The guy that wrote the script, he didn't get around to writing this scene for us, Jake. We're going to have to write it for him."

No script! Oh God, that was right! No script to work from!

Then Cain smiled and looked at my face, and something in it made him laugh bigger than before. "Don't worry about the words, Jake! Going to be okay! Besides, words are just a load of horseshit anyway! It's not what you say, it's what you do! You got to do it with all you got! Intensity! Emotion! That's what I want! You can give it to me! Might even be we'll have some fun with it" He blew smoke into the air. "Just so we don't end up having *too* much fun with it, we'll put some film in the camera." His hand tightened on my shoulder and pulled me closer. He could've pulled me all the way to China, I wouldn't have stopped him. "Doesn't work the first time, we can try it again. We got plenty of film, Jake. The set is booked till midnight. We'll play with it, we'll push it around, we'll see what the hell we can do with it, okay?"

I didn't answer.

He let me loose, walked several steps away and shook himself. There was an awful lot of him to shake. He swung his arms so they stretched out wide, and then he looked up toward the heavens. He growled like the MGM lion. Then he shook himself again as if he expected the earth to rumble, which is what I expected, and then he turned and looked down at me again.

"Don't turn him down cold, Jake. I want some humanity in it. Compassion. Feeling." He stopped a moment, then laughed wildly. "I want all those emotions the money boys don't have, but they tell me I better put 'em in my films or I won't make any money! Emotions! Like they'd know 'em if they tripped over 'em!"

He laughed. I nodded. He blew more smoke into

the air. We all watched it float. His hands smacked together. "All right! Tommy! Jake! What do you think? Going to give me some spontaneous combustion?"

McEnroe said something. I don't know what. I stayed quiet. I was trying to hold everything down and bring it all up at the same time. Keep the fear down so it couldn't control me, but let enough of it up so I'd be on edge. Get the nervousness at a level where I could still ride it. Let it sail me into the scene.

Cain laughed his big laugh and put his hand on my shoulder again. "You're just what I been looking for, Jake! A little new blood! A little push, little shove! Going to give it to me?"

I looked him straight in the eye. "Put a camera on me, I'll show you."

"That's the ticket! That's the ticket!" He was laughing and pulling me back toward the set. He waved his other hand at McEnroe. "Going to blow the film right open, Jake! You and Tommy!"

Thank God we did it right away, before I had a chance to throw up. Cain put the scene together, they set the lights, tested voice levels, everything was quiet—then the camera was humming. Someone's voice told us to go. It was Cain's voice.

I was losing my concentration already. I was thinking—this is a two-shot—just McEnroe and me—no matter what they do to the scene in the cutting room—if it ends up in the film at all—which it probably won't—I'm going to be there. Just him and me. Me and him.

It was terrible. I knew it was happening. I couldn't do a thing about it. But then, just before I lost control completely, McEnroe turned and let me have it with both barrels.

"Three thousand!" I could've fainted. "Just three thousand!" He paused. The briefest pause possible. His timing was perfect. "Three thousand will pull me through! It'll be the last time—"

"Till when? The next time?"

His eyes opened wide. He was probably as surprised as I was that I'd managed to say anything at all.

"This isn't like the other times!" He grabbed me. "You got to believe me!"

He must've known I still wasn't with him. I was still thinking about the camera. The crew. What they must be thinking. What Cain must be thinking.

But McEnroe's concentration was total, and he wasn't going to let some stupid, scared schmuck like me screw it up for him. "Listen to me! I'm telling you—"

"You're a goddamn sponge! You suck up everyone! You leave us with nothing!"

I wasn't even sure if what I'd just said made sense. My mind was flying in too many directions. I was trying to remember not to move too much. If you were improvising on a stage you could move wherever you wanted to, but this was a movie. I had to stay where the camera expected me to stay.

Damn Cain! He hadn't blocked out a damn thing for us! If I lost control and got carried away and took one step in the wrong direction, it would be his fault, not—

No. I wasn't going to screw it up. I was going to do it.

I stared into McEnroe's eyes. "Don't you understand what I'm talking about? It's not just you and me!" I threw all my torment and worries and fears into it. "You're doing it to everyone! You—"

"I got guys after me—"

"No! I don't want to hear it! I can't take it anymore!"

I stopped short. I'd just cut him off. He hadn't expected it.

Oh God, McEnroe was probably going to stop the take right there and I was going to get a lecture about not cutting off the star.

But then I saw in McEnroe's eyes that it was okay. He didn't mind. He was giving it to me. He wanted me to go on.

Okay. I shifted gears and stopped still. I looked at the cigarette in my fingers. It was a great moment. I curled my upper lip and threw the cigarette at the ground like I was really disgusted but bothered by it, too. It worked out just right.

Now for the next thing. Cain wanted humanity and compassion. This was the moment for it. I lowered my voice and made it as much of a contrast to my last words as possible. "I always help you, so you always come back to me. Don't you realize . . ." I held it a second. No melodrama now. Don't muck it up with business. Keep it clean. Simple. "You always get into something else. You always come back. It never makes any difference."

It was right! I felt it! I even thought a second about deepening it further. Putting in the beginning of a small, cynical laugh to show the other side of the character. And then cutting the laugh off immediately.

Then I saw something in McEnroe's eyes, and I let him take it. His hands came up limply. "This is different. I'm really in trouble."

"You're always in trouble!" God! I was really rolling! "Damn you! Don't you understand what I'm telling you? What you're doing, it's killing both of us!"

It was even better than before! My voice had almost broken!

Except, for one brief moment, something about what I'd just said made me think of Katie.

But then McEnroe seemed to be sending me a message, and I caught it. I stepped forward and put my hands on his arms, and I was in the scene again. I was careful to keep the two of us far enough apart so the camera would catch both our profiles in cleanly defined lines. "It's got to stop."

"It'll stop! I promise!" His voice dropped slightly lower. He gave his next lines just the right inflection to break your heart. "But help me this time. Please. I need it. Don't walk away from me."

It was good. It was short and easy and simple. It was effortless. God, the hardest thing to do is always to make it effortless! He was marvelous!

Now *I* had to be marvelous. The only way it would work was if I could keep it as quiet and as simple and as effortless as he had.

I did it. McEnroe had been good, damn good, but suddenly I knew I could match him. I gripped him more firmly with my hands and shook him just enough so it would read for the camera.

"I can't help you. If I don't stop it now, it'll never stop." I paused for one quick second. I drew in a fast breath. "It'll just tear us apart."

I cut it there and held it.

We were silent. Both of us. We knew it was over. We held the pose, and waited. Stared at each other. Scarcely breathed.

Waited. And waited. It was hard. I couldn't hold it much longer. I became aware of other things. Someone was moving about fifteen feet to my right. The camera was humming. My mind wandered again. Again I thought of Katie.

Then Cain's laughter filled the air.

A rough, clumsy hand touched my shoulder and shook it. I opened my eyes. I was lying on my back, across the sofa. I felt dizzy. Harry was next to me, on the floor. He had a vodka bottle in his hand. It was almost empty. He poured half of what was left into my glass and the rest into his. He put the empty bottle on the table. When he took his hand away, the bottle tipped over. It fell to the floor. I just watched it. Harry shrugged and swung his glass against mine. I heard a loud click. I drank. I closed my eyes again.

Then I heard words. "Hey! You should've seen it! Boy-o was terrific!"

I opened my eyes. Katie was there. She was standing at the edge of the living room. Harry got to his knees and started to speak again, but he choked, then laughed. I turned on the sofa so I was sitting. I pushed myself to my feet and stumbled toward her. "Katie. . . . I was so nervous. . . . I didn't even know what I was doing. . . ."

"Jesus Christ, Jake! Why the hell don't you learn to blow your own horn! Tell her you were great! Fantastic!"

I stopped in the middle of the floor. I smiled and tried again. "I was . . . I was okay."

"You stupid son of a bitch! Carry a goddamn press agent around in your back pocket or something! He was great, Katie! Terrific!"

Katie stepped closer. "Jake? What happened?"

I could see it again. Cain putting his arm over my shoulder. Taking me to McEnroe. The three of us standing there. *I got a script with some holes in it, Jake. I need some fire. Electricity. Spontaneous combustion.*

I put down my glass. I brought my hands together. Then I let them flutter apart. As they separated, I made the sound effect of a small explosion with my mouth. Spontaneous combustion. Katie was looking at me like I was crazy. I smiled at her.

"I said *yes*, Katie! I said *yes!*"

And somewhere I thought I could hear Cain laughing again.

Except it wasn't Cain this time. It was me.

I felt dizzy again. I was lying on the bed. I heard a noise, far away. A car engine. Loud. Then softer. Moving. Moving away. Then gone.

I drifted off.

Then I felt fingers touching my shoulder. They were very careful fingers, touching me lightly. Soft, fragile fingers. I opened my eyes.

God, she looked beautiful. She was sitting beside me on the bed, and her soft, fragile fingers were stroking my cheek. I didn't care anymore how long ago it had been that she'd given that picture and résumé to Paul. Two days, two weeks, it didn't matter at all. I closed my eyes and began to drift off again.

Then I thought of something and suddenly I tried to sit up. "I forgot to call the service!"

She made me lie down. "Don't worry, Jake. I'll call."

She went away.

I lay still and tried to fall asleep, but the only part of me that was falling was my head.

It was throbbing. It wouldn't stop. It was falling into a dark pit of dizziness.

Then I felt something. I opened my eyes and she was there again, holding a cold compress against my forehead. "I called the service, Jake. Guess what? You got an audition tomorrow for Viva towels. I wrote down all the information." She stroked my cheek. "How do you feel?"

My head seemed to be blowing up like a balloon. I knew that when balloons blew up too big—

Her lips brushed my cheek. "Feeling any better?"

"... A little."

No better at all. Hard liquor. The vodka. It could

still do to me what it had always been able to do to me.

Then I felt her hand on my chest. On my stomach. At my waist.

Moving between my legs.

"No, Katie. Not tonight. I can't. Please! I don't feel well!"

She stopped. It was quiet. Then she left me again.

I rolled to my side. Kept changing positions. I couldn't get comfortable. She came back with a glass in her hand. "Open your mouth, Jake."

"What?"

"Your mouth. Open it."

Her fingers spread against the sides of my jaw. Her fingers didn't feel so fragile now. They pressed against me till my mouth opened. Then I felt something on my tongue.

"Katie! No! Don't! I had all that vodka!"

Suddenly the glass was against my lips. It tipped slightly. It was water. I swallowed it. And swallowed the thing she'd put on my tongue.

I felt her lying beside me. When I moved slightly, I realized she was awake. She nuzzled against me. "Feel any better now?"

I didn't answer. I felt terrible. It was bad. I was angry at something. And scared at the same time. I didn't like the dark. God, I was terrified of it. I wanted it to go away. I couldn't stand it!

It was fear. That's what I felt. It was as strong as ever.

It turned my head and saw a small, faint glow in the distance. I stared at it for several seconds before I realized it was my watch sitting on the night table. I couldn't read the numbers so I reached out to pull it closer. My hand hit something, knocking it to the floor.

I rolled on my stomach and swung my hand down to see what it was I'd knocked over. A book. I picked it up and put it back on the table. Then I looked at my watch again.

Three-thirty. Only the middle of the night. I'd never make it to daylight, not feeling like this. Still scared. Of *them*.

I wasn't even sure who *they* were, but I was scared

of them anyway. They were going to come and get me. I could hear them out there. I could smell them. They gave off an awful stink. They were sweating and laughing. Their laughter wasn't anything like Cain's laugh. It was big and inhuman and confident and loud. It was hungry and so damn sure of itself. It was out there, just waiting for me.

My hand was still on the night table. It felt something else there. Something small. A round thing. A bottle. I picked it up and brought it closer to my eyes. I shook it. It had something rattling around inside it.

Then I remembered what had happened! What she'd put in my mouth!

She moved closer to me. "I did what you wanted me to do, Jake."

". . . What?"

"I went to see Dr. Samuels. He was nice. We just talked a little today, but I made some more appointments with him. He wants to see me a couple times a week." She moved closer and put her head on my chest. It seemed to weigh a ton. "Don't worry, Jake. Everything's going to be okay. From now on. I promise."

I hated her! Damn her! How could she have done this to me?

Her leg rolled over my waist. Her hand was on my chest. I pushed her hand away and rolled out from under her leg and stayed on my side with my back to her.

The fear held me all the way till it got light. Then it left me. Just like that.

Maybe she hadn't given me anything but water? I looked at the night table. The pill bottle wasn't there. Maybe I'd just imagined it. Maybe it had just been the vodka that had done it to me.

Yes. It had to be the vodka.

I wasn't on call for Cain that day, so I went to the Viva towel audition. As soon as they saw me, they told me it was a mistake. I wasn't the type they were looking for.

But since I was still flying high from that scene I'd done for Cain, I was able to shrug it off. I said fine, I understood, I didn't mind. I smiled and started to leave.

They were so surprised by my reaction they told me to wait a minute. They took another look at my résumé. They asked me questions. Then they asked me to read the copy.

I knew I didn't have a prayer of getting it, so I read with no nervousness at all. When I finished, they said that now that they had an idea of what I was like and what I could do, they'd keep me in mind for other things. I thanked them and went out. In its way, it was the best audition I'd ever had.

I called the service. Another audition. A commercial for dog food. It was at a small agency down on Wilshire.

The waiting room was so big you could've rehearsed the triumphal scene from *Aida* in it. It was filled with actors. That was okay. Today I didn't mind. I had a little confidence, and I didn't care if half of Los Angeles was there. When they finally called me, it was an hour and a half past my appointment. They apologized for being so far behind. I surprised myself by laughing and saying it was okay. I understood how these things happened. It wasn't their fault.

We talked. I read for them. They talked among themselves for a moment. Then they asked me to read again. I did. We talked some more. They were taking an awfully long time with me.

Then we shook hands and I left.

I felt pretty good. I'd done that scene for Cain yesterday and it had been decent. I'd given two respectable auditions today. I hadn't cracked during either one of them. I was almost feeling like an actor. I was even doing a good job of making myself forget the awful way I'd felt during the night.

I had no right to expect another audition, but I called the service anyway. There was nothing. Since I was so far down on Wilshire with nothing to do I drove over to see how the Cain movie was going.

It was nice. It wasn't that anybody made a big thing about me dropping by the set. A couple of them nodded. All Cain did was nod. But it was nice. It felt like home.

Harry was there. He was in a scene. Just a small thing with a lot of other people. Not the kind of thing I'd gotten. But it was more than just standing around doing nothing. He got to throw in two ad libs and he'd be easily recognizable, unless the whole sequence got lost in the editing room. There was a good chance he'd make it into the final cut. He was glad to have what he had.

When they wrapped for the day, Harry and I went back to my place. We sat in the kitchen and talked. I gave him some wine, but I didn't drink any.

He lit up a joint and puffed it and then held it out to me. I declined. We talked some more and I watched him smoke. As he kept getting higher and higher, my mind went back to the night before. I left him suddenly and went into the bedroom.

It wasn't on the night table. But when I remembered how when I'd reached for my watch I'd knocked that book onto the floor. I looked around the floor. I found nothing. But then I searched under the bed, and there it was. I snapped off the cap and spilled the capsules into my hand. Those garish colors. Red. Blue. Ugly shades. They felt ugly in my hand.

She *had* given me a pill last night. No question about it.

I put the capsules back into the bottle. I put on the cap and put the bottle into my pocket. I'd throw it away as soon as I got the chance. If she asked me if I'd seen it, I'd tell her I hadn't.

Harry held out the joint again. "Come on. Have some."

"No thanks."

"Come on! What're you, a goddamn puritan?"

I stretched out my arm till my hand found the door frame. "Never does the right things for me, Harry. Just makes me sick. Same as drinking."

He laughed. "Way I remember it, you drank enough yesterday."

"Yeah." I shook my head. "I paid for it, too."

I pulled out a chair and sat across the table from him. I took out my cigarettes. I stuck one in my mouth and lit it.

"Jesus Christ, Jake! Those things are worse than this!"

"I know." I bit my lower lip. "But they're cheaper."

"Not in the long run." He laughed again. He held

the joint up to his eyes. "Me, I need it, this stuff. To keep me going. To make me forget."

"Forget what?"

"Everything! Being an actor!" His eyes dropped. "Boy, it sure eats it, being an actor. Everyone telling you what to do. Where to go. What to look like. How to stand. How to smile." He took another puff. "Still, we stick at it, don't we?" He laughed. "I guess we like it, being pushed around. Told what to do. Controlled. Manipulated."

I slammed my hand against the table. "Stop saying that!"

"Huh?"

I closed my hand in a fist and hid it in my lap. "Nothing. Never mind."

It was okay. He wasn't listening. He was holding a paper napkin in his fingers and folding it in quarters. "Heard Joan Evans is casting for Universal now. Ever read for her?"

I brushed my fingertips restlessly across the tabletop. "Once. When I first came out." My mind was wandering. "She said she liked me, but I never heard from her again."

"Well, she's at Universal now. Ought to give her a call."

"Yeah."

Then there was a noise at the front of the house. The front door. "I'm home, Jake!"

Suddenly I was tighter than a drum head. I took a long drag on my cigarette and kept quiet. I knew what I'd do. I'd let Harry answer her. That's why I had him here in the first place.

"Katie!" He put the napkin down and sang into the air. "Back here, Katie!"

I heard her coming. Through the house. Past the living room. Down the hall. I kept my eyes on the table.

"Hi."

I nodded without looking up. I made some kind of sound.

"Hey!" Harry said. "How's it going?"

"Pretty good."

I turned and looked at her. At her hands. I waited

to see if her fingers were going to start snapping. They didn't, at least not yet.

Harry held the joint out toward her, and when he did she moved back suddenly, toward the door.

"Hey. Come on, Katie. Don't be like boy-o. Give it a try."

"No."

Harry started to get out of his chair. "Come on. Just a little puff."

"NO!"

Harry shrugged and sat down. Katie stared at the joint in his hand. Then she stepped forward suddenly and opened the refrigerator. She took out the milk and poured herself a glass. I watched her carefully. Did she seem nervous? Was she in one of her calm moods, or the other kind? Had she taken a pill?

Harry started telling me a rumor he'd heard about one of the advertising agencies revamping its casting department. Katie left the kitchen. I waited a moment, then told Harry I had to get something in the bedroom.

I found her sitting on the sofa in the living room. She had a small bag of peanuts in her hand. She was eating the nuts one at a time, popping them into her mouth in a steady but nervous rhythm. She'd finished the milk. There was Jack Daniel's in the glass now.

"Jake? Is this going to be every night?"

"What?"

"Him." Her head jerked stiffly toward the kitchen. "No. Why?"

She didn't answer. She sipped the Jack Daniel's. She faced front like I wasn't there anymore.

I shifted from one foot to the other and watched her pop the peanuts into her mouth. She picked up the glass.

"Katie, I don't think you should be drinking all that liquor."

"Why?"

"You're worried about putting on weight, aren't you? Well, that's got calories too. That and all the milk."

"Oh. Yes." She put the glass down.

She was quiet a moment, but then she shoved her hand out with the peanuts in it. "How about these? These got too many calories?"

Her voice had a harshness to it that time. Suddenly she dropped the bag of peanuts into the ashtray and crossed her arms in front of her. "You want to talk about cutting down, you could start with your cigarettes."

I looked at her a moment, then I stubbed out my cigarette.

I kept looking at her.

"What're you looking at!"

I didn't answer. Her hands folded tightly in her lap. She looked at the far wall. "I'm sorry, Jake. I had a tough day today. I've just got to be by myself, a little while."

I wasn't sure what to do. Part of me wanted to give it to her. Seeing her drinking, hearing her voice suddenly harsh, the look in her eyes—all the signs were there. Someone had to tell her to stop it. The pills, the liquor—

"Can't you please leave me alone when I say I want to be left alone?"

There was anger in her eyes. I kept quiet and went back to the kitchen.

Harry started telling me something. I don't remember what. I wasn't paying attention. Then I heard the front door open and close. By the time I got outside she was backing the Volkswagen toward the road.

I called out her name. She didn't even look at me. She turned the Volkswagen so it was aimed down the hill, shifted gears and gunned it. Stones spun out from under the rear wheels.

After Harry left, the house seemed very quiet. I went outside and sat on the front steps. I smoked a cigarette. I started making excuses for her. The sharp way she'd talked to me? Maybe she *had* had a tough day. Maybe it was because she'd seen Harry smoking grass. She'd been upset that time she'd seen the cocaine at Alan's party, too.

I kept making excuses for her. I just wanted her back home. Soon I found myself feeling very empty, and alone.

I smoked my second cigarette on the sofa in the living room. My third on the front steps. My fourth in the kitchen. Half of my fifth in the bedroom. Then I stubbed it out and lay on the bed with my eyes on the ceiling.

An hour later I heard noises. The front door opened. Slammed shut. Then it was quiet. I started to get up. She came into the room, and her fingers began to snap. I kept my eyes off her.

She hesitated, then went across the room. Her fingers snapped again. I stood up and turned, and there was just enough moonlight for us to see each other's faces.

I looked away again.

She came to me suddenly and kissed me hard on the mouth. When I didn't respond, she pulled back. "Jake? What's the matter?"

I moved away from her hands. I knew exactly what the matter was. I'd gotten used to her being there. *Needed* her being there. Without her, everything seemed cold. Desolate. Empty.

I stepped forward. It didn't matter how she was sometimes. Didn't matter that she'd given me that pill the night before. Nothing mattered. I was really in deep. She kissed me again, and this time I kissed her. I wrapped my arms around her as tightly as I could. She said, "Oh, that's nice." We rocked back and forth.

I had a "call-back" the next morning for the Ajax commercial. I seemed to read as well as I'd read the first time. They seemed to like me more than they'd liked me the first time. But you never know.

An hour later I had a "go-see" up on Sunset Boulevard. On a go-see, you go so they can see you. Sometimes when they see you they want you. This time they didn't. I shrugged it off and shook their hands and left.

When I came out of the building I saw a sparkling black Jaguar parked across the street. I was still admiring it when he came out of a jewelry store. He'd probably just bought everything they had.

"Alan!"

He turned and saw me. He didn't yell or wave back. There was no traffic coming, so I started to cross the street. He walked to the Jaguar. I wasn't surprised. I came up next to him and made a big show of being impressed with the car. I patted the hood reverently. "Nice. *Very* nice." I paused a beat. "But it isn't a Rolls."

He smiled. "Too hard to get parts for a Rolls."

His eyes looked me over. I looked pretty good. I

was wearing the new suede jacket I'd bought just a couple days before. Katie had talked me into it. She'd said now that I was getting auditions more regularly I ought to treat myself. And she'd been right for another reason. When you walk into an audition looking poor and out of work, it scares them. They worry. If they associate with you too long, maybe *they'll* end up poor and out of work. They very quickly give the job to someone who's dressed better. Eventually you either shoot yourself or realize it would be smart to buy a new suede jacket. It may not get you the job, but it makes them feel much more comfortable.

"Well, Jake. You look prosperous."

"I know. It's a bluff. Like everything else in L.A." I was about to lean on his car since he was a friend, but since the car was a Jag, I changed my mind. "They called me in to be an extra on the new Jim Cain film. I got lucky, Alan. Got to do a scene. With McEnroe. Just him and me."

"Yeah, I heard about it."

"What? How'd you—"

"Small town, Jake. Lots of people in L.A., but it comes to gossip, still a small town."

I laughed. "Smallest town in the world. Just didn't know I was worth gossiping about." I cocked my head to the side. "What'd you hear?"

"Heard it's a good scene."

"Yeah?" I felt anxious. "Who'd you hear it from?"

He shook his head. "Couple people. One who's connected to the film, one who isn't."

"Yeah?" I slapped my hands together. I was starting to feel like something. Starting to feel bigger than I had a right to feel. Sometimes you can't help yourself. "Hey, if it's beginning to get out that maybe I can actually act, maybe next time you could get me something on your show that's got some lines to it?"

"All right, damn it! I got you what I could, didn't I?" He turned his back to me and put his keys into the door lock.

I didn't like the way he'd said it. I hadn't liked the way he'd talked to me that day on the set, either. Now it was just the two of us. It was time to settle it.

"What's the matter, Alan?"

He didn't answer.

"Alan? What's bothering you?"

He started to open the door.

I moved closer and put my hand on his arm. "If something's bothering you, let's—"

"Let me go!" He ripped his arm away and drew his hand back in a fist.

I didn't move. We stared at each other.

Finally his hand opened. It swung slowly to his side. Then he spat out more words. "I didn't like it one damn bit, Jake!"

"You didn't like what?"

"Sending the broad after me to get you some goddamn work!"

It caught me off guard. "What are you talking about? I didn't ask Ruth—"

"I'm not talking about Ruth!"

That stopped me cold.

I stood there silently and watched him get into his car. Put his key in the ignition. Start the motor.

Then I breathed in sharply. "All right. Tell me what happened."

He ignored me and put the car in gear.

"Alan. I don't know what you're talking about."

He looked up. I was beginning to burn inside, but I still controlled my voice. "Tell me what happened."

He stared at me. "The party."

"Well?"

"The girl you were with."

"What about her?"

His face changed. He turned front. He tapped his fingers on the steering wheel. "You didn't know?"

"Know what?"

He looked away. "Hell. I should've realized."

"That's right! You should've realized!" I got my voice even again. "If you didn't realize, you should've had the brains to talk to me about it. Now tell me what happened."

Alan wiped his hand against his mouth. He kept his eyes off me. "The party. I went into the study. To get something. She was in there. All by herself." He realized his motor was running, and he turned it off, pulled the keys out of the ignition and looked at them. "She asked me, was I really going to get you some work, or was I just talking. I told her I'd do it. Something would come up. But it might take awhile." He looked up. "You know how these things are, Jake."

I didn't answer him.

"She said, how long would it take. I said I didn't know. Maybe a month or so. She said that wasn't good enough. It had to happen right away. She said if we were friends then I ought to get you something right away." He tapped the steering wheel again. "We're friends, Jake. You know that. It's just . . . you're on a show like this, you got to be careful. You start pulling your friends in for jobs, they start thinking you're a prima donna. Besides, I'd just gone through that thing with them about holding out for a bigger salary. I had to give it time to cool off, before I made any more demands."

He paused. Maybe he was waiting for me to say something. I didn't.

"She said you were depressed. You needed something. Some work. She started yelling at me, Jake."

"What?"

"She said that if I told you I was going to get you something, it didn't mean anything unless I actually did it." He rubbed his mouth. "She was really getting loud, Jake. I didn't know how to handle her. Hell, I've never known how to handle women. I'm scared of 'em. I always have been. I guess we all are. I mean, how do you handle a woman when she starts yelling and—"

"You mean to tell me she was really yelling at you? I mean, *really yelling?*"

"She slapped me!" He took a deep breath. His eyes had that look they'd had at the party. "She slapped me right across the face."

"No!" I turned away. "I don't believe you."

"She did it twice, Jake. I didn't know what to do. You can't hit a woman. What can you do when they . . ." He gulped air again. "I told her I'd get you something. I promised her I would. I was going to do it, too, but the next morning—I hadn't even left for the set yet—she called me at the house, just to make sure I was going to do it." He paused. He was looking at me again. "You must be strong, Jake. You must be a hell of a lot stronger than I thought you were. To handle someone like her."

The yellow Volkswagen was parked in front of the house. Ruth's car was parked next to it. That was all I needed.

I went into the house. They were both in the living room. Katie was sitting on the sofa with her hands folded in her lap, and Ruth was sitting in a chair on the other side of the room. As soon as I came in, Ruth said, "Hi, baby. Long time, no see." Her voice was soft. She looked very tired.

"Hello, Ruth." I stopped at the edge of the room. "Ruth . . . I'm sorry, you don't mind, this is a bad time to—"

"No it isn't, Jake. It's a pretty good time."

Ruth snapped open her pocketbook. She took out a pack of cigarettes. She tapped the pack against her hand, took a cigarette and lit it. She puffed. Exhaled. She waited for the smoke to break apart in the air. She wasn't going anywhere. Not till she was ready to.

"You gave 'em a good reading on the Ajax commercial, Jake. They called me this afternoon. They want you."

My bottom jaw fell open so far it must've ended up somewhere near my waist.

The Ajax commercial. I'd thought I had done well. They'd said they liked me. But I hadn't allowed myself to think I actually had a chance to get it. It was a jinx to think that way. You only ended up going through the same old agony when the time came to find out you'd been rejected again.

But this time I *hadn't* been rejected!

I began to go crazy. I started going through the *ifs*. *If* the commercial worked. *If* they liked the way it worked. *If* they liked it enough to play it on some test station. *If* their market surveys showed that people responded to it well. *If* they decided to run the spot. *If* they put it on the networks.

IF!

If enough of that happened—

A good commercial usually led to more. More meant big money. Enough to live like you wanted to live. For years. I was going haywire! It was happening so fast! I was seeing new deposits in my bank account! New clothes in my closet! New car! New house! Tickets to Europe! Weekend trips to Acapulco!

"Only one problem, Jake. The Ajax people thought someone from the office sent you to them. They were wrong. We didn't."

Then I knew it all.

Ruth looked toward the sofa. Her eyes were burning now. "Very cute girl you got here, Jake. Found herself a nice game she likes to play. Calling up people, all over town, getting 'em to listen to her by telling 'em she's part of the agency."

Ruth stubbed out her cigarette. She got to her feet. She walked slowly across the living room and stopped five feet short of the sofa. "Got news for you, baby. Talent agents got to be franchised."

Katie looked away and stared vaguely at the floor. "I just wanted to see him get somewhere."

They were the first words Katie had said since I'd come in the door.

Ruth's shoulders sagged. "Against the law, baby. Illegal misrepresentation. Getting an actor work? Taking a commission—"

"I haven't taken one cent from him." Katie paused. Bit her lip. "I don't plan to." Her voice was shaky. As thin as cellophane. But she kept on. "I'm not interested in him for money, the way you are."

Ruth straightened suddenly and laughed harshly. "You think I'm handling him for money? Come down to the office sometime, I'll show you my records on him."

Then she stopped short. She was mad, but she shouldn't have said that, no matter how mad she was. And she knew it.

She looked at me a second and slapped her hand against her leg, then she turned quickly back toward Katie. "You just want to help him, huh? You think you know this town and this business so well, you're going to show him how to do it?"

"He's going to do it." Katie was barely whispering now. But then her eyes came up. "Yes. He's going to do it." She jumped to her feet. "I got him the Cain movie. I got him the Ajax commercial. When's the last time *you* got him a job? *Any* job?"

Then Katie ran past Ruth and halfway to me. "And the Viva towel interview, Jake! The dog food interview! *I* got 'em for you! Not *her! Me!*"

Katie looked around wildly. I thought of what Alan had told me about the way she'd been with him. She focused on Ruth again. "I've seen the way you work! You're making deals every second of the day! But none of them are for him!"

Ruth stared at her. "Shut up."

Katie stepped back. It was quiet for a moment. Then she faced me again and spoke weakly but rapidly. "I've seen her, Jake. That time I was in her office. She picked up the phone, she talked for just a minute, then she hung up and said she'd just made a deal for twenty-five thousand dollars. In less than half an hour, Jake! She's getting work every minute of the day! For other people! Not for you!"

Ruth suddenly grabbed her by the shoulder and turned her around. "I told you to shut up!"

For a second I was sure Katie was going to slap her. But then she didn't. She pulled back out of Ruth's reach and kept moving till she reached the wall. Then she stayed there as still as stone.

Ruth balled her hands into fists. She turned to me. "Jake? Aren't you going to say anything?"

I looked at Katie.

Ruth stepped forward. Her mouth opened savagely. "Well? Say something! Come on! Say something, damn it!"

I couldn't. Too many things were going through my mind. Katie was scarcely breathing now, but what scared me most was the look in her eyes. I'd seen it before. It made me think of night, and a dead-end street. A man with a gun in his hand, yelling threats and obscenities.

Katie moved toward Ruth.

I stepped between them. "Katie. Easy."

She stopped.

I turned to Ruth. "Please, Ruth. Don't yell at her."

"What?"

I couldn't explain what I meant. I looked at Katie. Then at Ruth. "Please, Ruth. Just don't yell at her."

Ruth stared at me.

Then she ran out. She slammed the front door behind

her. I turned. Katie had her back pressed tight against the wall again. Her eyes were blank as marbles. She looked like she'd never move from that spot.

I turned and ran after Ruth. When I reached the front yard, Ruth heard me and swung around. Her face looked vicious now. And desperate. Something about it scared me. I brought my hands up, flat and open, like I would've if a man had stepped forward to hit me and I'd wanted to reason with him.

But before I could speak, the front door flew open and Katie came out. "He's got talent! He can make it! Where was his career going before I came along? Nowhere!"

Ruth screamed at her. "Shut up, you little bitch!"

I stepped between them. "No! Hold it! Both of you!"

But Katie grabbed my arm and jerked me off balance. She went past me and straight at Ruth. "He's going to make it! I want him to make it! Between the two of us, it's going to happen! Just leave us alone!"

"What?" Ruth laughed in her face.

I started forward, but Katie was already moving. Then her mouth began to open and her hand started up.

"Katie! No!"

She turned suddenly. "Don't you tell me—"

Then her hand started down. Before either of us could stop it, she'd slapped me hard across the face.

Her hand flew up again. Then it came down again. She'd slapped me a second time. I still hadn't done a thing to stop her.

Katie and I moved apart. Her mouth snapped shut. Her hand was at her side now.

There were tears in her eyes. Tears in mine, too. Ruth was staring at both of us. I didn't even want to guess what must be in her mind.

But what scared me most was the slap. The way I felt about it. It hadn't hurt me at all. Instead I was excited by it.

The passion behind it. Her uncontrollable passion.

Katie struggled to speak. "Jake. . . . I didn't mean to—"

"I know. I know."

Her hands came up. She began to plead with me. "I love you, Jake."

"I know you do."

"And I know you can make it!" Her eyes shut tight. "You just don't trust yourself. You've got to trust yourself." Suddenly her eyes opened. "All you have to do is take it with both hands and give it all you've got, Jake!" Her own hands came up and grabbed at the air in front of my face. "And I can handle it, Jake! It's what I've been looking for!"

"What?"

Her head nodded up and down. "Believe me, Jake! We both want it, don't we? We want it, we can make it! Just believe me!"

Her eyes blazed. Her face was desperate, but unconquerable.

"I see what it's like, Jake! It's a great business! A wonderful business! It's tough, but it's exciting! It's what I've been looking for! What I've always dreamed about! The business is wonderful, Jake! We're going to make it!"

Ruth and I looked at each other for a quick but very cold moment. We both knew what it was. The thrilling intoxication of someone new in the business who saw all the good things and didn't yet understand the bad.

But then Ruth stepped past me toward Katie and spoke in a small shaky voice. "I don't know what you think is going on here, but you're a little mixed up. Doesn't work that way. Handling an actor. He's got a contract with me. With my boss. When we handle someone—"

"But you *aren't* handling him! You aren't *pushing* him!"

Ruth stepped back. "Don't you tell me what I'm doing."

"I'll tell you whatever I want to tell you!" Katie's hand went up high above her head again. It stayed there for a second as if it were going to swing like a club. This time I moved toward her, but before I could reach her the hand did come down. But it only grabbed Ruth's arm, and as it did, Katie saw my eyes, and then she let Ruth go. She drew her hand back quickly as if she'd touched fire.

Katie looked confused. She began to cry again. She moved away several steps and looked at the ground. When she looked up, her face was white.

Ruth was trembling. I could see she wanted to move into my arms. But she was afraid to try.

I was afraid, too. I didn't know if I would've held her or not.

It was a terrible moment. Each of us wanted to touch someone, but none of us wanted to take the chance to do it. None of us was sure what was happening.

Or maybe it was the opposite. We were all too sure.

Katie spoke so softly her words seemed to float like dead leaves on a weak wind. "You aren't pushing him. You aren't . . ." Then she gulped in air like she couldn't get enough of it. Her lips began to tremble. Her body shook. Like she was having a convulsion. She could barely control it.

I looked at her in horror. She faced me again. "Don't you understand, Jake? She doesn't *want* you to make it. She thinks if you make it you'll leave her, just like Jack Christolf left her."

The three of us stood quietly in the middle of the yard. Katie wasn't looking at either of us now. Her face had set in a cold icy stare.

Finally Ruth breathed in deeply. "I'm your agent." She inhaled again. Her voice fought to be strong. "You've got a contract with our office. When we handle someone . . ."

Then she was quiet.

I walked across the yard to the edge of the road and stood there. When I finally turned, Katie hadn't moved at all. Ruth was standing next to her car. Her hand was on the door handle. Her hand was shaking. A tear was dripping its way slowly down her cheek. It reached the end of her chin and thickened and fell. Then she realized I was looking at her. She pulled the door open, but she didn't get inside.

I went over to her slowly. When I spoke, I did it very softly. "She's right, isn't she?"

Ruth didn't answer. Her fingers rubbed lightly along the edge of the car door.

"Neither of us have wanted to admit it, Ruth. But it's true. We better face it." I stopped. Waited. Then I went on with it. "I've been with you over a year and a half. What's it done for either of us?"

Another tear came out of Ruth's eye. Now I wanted to touch her very badly, but something stopped me. Part of it was anger. Knowing how true Katie's words had been.

Ruth straightened. She set her mouth tightly and spoke in a dull monotone. "You're signed to us for another eighteen months. You better remember that."

I almost lost control and yelled at her then, but at the last second I held it in. I continued speaking softly. "We've got to face the truth. It's hard, neither of us wants to hear it, but it's there. You've never wanted me to make it, Ruth. You've wanted me to give it up. Come into the agency and work with you. But I can't do that. It's not what *I* want."

Ruth's fingers moved along the top of the open car door and gripped the edge. The skin on the back of her hand drew taut and whitened. "I love you, Jake. Don't you know that?"

"Of course I know. That's the problem."

She looked at me. "Problem? Is that what it is? A problem? What've I got to do to stop it from being a problem? What've I got to do to make you love me, Jake? Slap you around a couple times?"

I froze. I gave her the hardest look I'd ever given anyone in my life.

Then I walked off toward the house and sat on the steps.

Ruth jumped into her car. She started the engine, pulled the door closed and drove toward the road. She made the turn and was about to drive off when she jammed on the brakes. Her face swung around and she looked through the driver's window at me. "Jake! Don't you see what she's doing to you? She's controlling you! She's taking over your life! You going to let her do it?"

I leaned forward. I rested my elbows on my knees and stared at the ground.

"Jake! Don't be crazy! Don't let her . . ."

She was silent. Then suddenly she drove off.

When I looked around, I realized Katie wasn't there. I found her sitting on a big rock in the back yard, looking toward the woods. She seemed so small and helpless, perched there. Like some kind of fragile, wounded animal. Her shoulders were shaking a little.

I walked closer. I knew what she needed. Some kind of strength. Support. From someone else. The kind of support she was always giving me. I didn't have much to give her right then, but she needed something. I put my hand on her shoulder.

"I'm sorry I slapped you, Jake. I didn't mean to—"

"It's okay. Just be quiet."

She didn't move. She didn't look at me. "I didn't think about it. That you're signed to her. I ruined it for you. Everything."

"You didn't ruin anything. It'll work out." I rubbed her neck gently. "You said some things. Ruth and I have known 'em for a long time. They were going to come out sooner or later. You're not responsible for it." I stood behind her and put both my hands on her shoulders. I tried to force a light laugh. "Your only trouble, sometimes when you get going, you're such a tough cookie, you get carried away and—"

"No, Jake. I'm not tough at all. I'm very insecure. I always have been. That's why I . . ." Her hand came up and covered one of my hands on her shoulder. "I do get carried away with things. Because . . . I've never believed in myself. It's not good, when you don't believe in yourself. Then other people don't believe in you. That's why I keep telling you . . ." Her fingers tightened, grasping at me. "You can do it, Jake. But you've got to believe in yourself. You haven't got a chance if you don't believe in yourself."

I sat beside her on the rock. "I know. There isn't a thing about self-confidence that I don't know. I know I haven't had it. I've *known* I haven't had it, ever since I came out to L.A. I was never able to do anything about it, before."

"Before?" She finally looked at me. "You feel different, now?"

"Yeah." I put my arm around her, and her mouth broke into a tiny smile.

I finally knew one thing for sure. No matter what she was, no matter what she did, I loved her.

We taped the Ajax commercial two days after that. I was pretty nervous when I got there. They expected me to be nervous. They knew that whether I was a young struggling actor on his first time out or an old established star on his hundredth, the one thing they could count on was my being nervous. They knew it was their job to make it as easy for me as possible. And they did it.

It was really something. Here I was, working for the same people I'd had to face for years across tables at auditions, but this time it was different. We were all on the same side of the table. We weren't two teams anymore. We were one.

He rehearsed. I went through make-up. They checked the lights, the audio. We rehearsed some more. Checked the lights some more. We prayed and crossed our fingers and our toes, and then we started shooting.

We made it almost all the way through, letter perfect, but then, as I reached my final line, one of the lights popped. It spoiled the whole take.

We immediately started again. In the middle of this

take, someone opened a door on the other side of the studio. The door knocked over a folding chair. The chair hit the floor with a sound like a gunshot. We all turned to look at it. That ruined take two.

On the seventh take, one of the extras started laughing. Soon we were all laughing. We couldn't stop, not for three more takes. It was beginning to turn sour. That made it scary. I felt it first in my stomach.

When we were ready for the eighteenth take they gave me a new can of Ajax but nobody remembered to check it. I went through the lines, smiled into the camera, tipped the can upside down, and shook it. Whatever was in there, none of it came out.

I shook and I shook. Nothing came out.

They brought me a new can. This time we checked it. But this time the lines went badly.

We tried it again. A dozen times again. It wasn't any good. We broke for lunch.

Some of us could eat. I couldn't. We told stories of other horrendous shoots we'd been on. Commercials. Movies. TV shows. We told the stories to convince ourselves that this wasn't unusual. That the shoot wasn't jinxed. But we all believed it was.

Someone said we all ought to get stoned. The crew was very much for it. The director was on the fence. The producer was nervous and frightened and turning gray from worrying about the mortgage on his house. He said no.

We finished lunch and talked as long as we could, then finally someone suggested we ought to get back to work. We stood up uneasily. We all shared the same thought.

We were going to go back there and shoot the whole damn commercial in one take and be finished with it.

Everything went wrong. Some of the lights had been moved by mistake and were now out of focus. I skipped a line at the beginning of the copy, then reversed two lines and covered it, but then when I picked up the can of Ajax, it was upside down. Then someone started to laugh. It was a disaster. You'd have thought we *had* gotten stoned at lunch. My legs were like Jell-O.

We kept on going. When we finished the forty-third

take, there was a long moment of silence. For some reason which none of us could quite understand, it had seemed to go right.

Finally the director said, very quietly, "Do it again, please."

We did it again. Number forty-four seemed to work, too. We did number forty-five. It was even better. The director told us to keep going. We kept going. Number forty-six was a total fiasco.

We threw up our hands. We laughed. We cried. The producer told someone to bring in a case of beer.

One beer never does much to me. If I have two, I feel the second one halfway through. That's where I stop. But I didn't stop. I had four. It may not sound like much, but I could feel each one of them.

I drove home slowly. Stop lights would turn green. I'd forget to move. Cars would honk at me. Then I'd move. I'd try to move in a straight line. I must've done all right, 'cause nobody in a uniform bothered to pull me over. I drove up the road and parked in front of my house. The yellow Volkswagen was there. Next to it was a blue MG I'd never seen before.

I walked to the front door and pulled it open silently. I don't think I meant to do it that way. I was just moving slowly because of the four beers. When I came into the living room, Katie hadn't heard me coming. She was sitting on the sofa with Paul, the guy from the Cain movie. She was laughing. So was he. She had her wallet out. She was giving him money.

Then she saw me. Her head jumped back. Her lips tightened against her teeth.

Paul looked up and saw me. "Hi, Jake. How you doing?"

I just nodded. I watched as his hand took out his own wallet and tucked the cash Katie had just given him into it.

"Katie said you were out shooting a commercial today. That's great."

I put my hand across the back of a chair to steady myself. I felt weak and sick. It wasn't just from the beers anymore. Katie's hands were folded in her lap. She was looking down at them.

198

Paul stood up and stretched. "Had a long night. Shooting over at Stone Canyon Reservoir. Up there till one in the morning."

Paul looked at Katie. She still had her head down. He tugged at his belt and pulled it away from his waist, then let it fall back into place. "Seems like Cain really liked your scene, Jake. I shouldn't be saying it, but he said a couple things about using you again. Another movie. Could turn into something."

Could it? For how much money could it turn into something?

"Just don't say I told you about it, okay?"

I nodded. I felt ready to throw up.

Katie still had her head down. Paul looked at his watch. "Better get going. Got to be on the set by seven." He started moving.

"Wait a minute." I brought my hand up. "What did you come over here for?"

He didn't answer.

I spoke again. "Just to say hello? Long way to come just to say hello." I raised my voice slightly. "Come on, Paul. Say it. Why'd you come over here?"

He hesitated, then he gestured toward the table behind him. "Brought you some film you might be able to use. Just make sure nobody knows where you got it."

Then I saw the large brown envelope on the table in front of Katie's knees. I was still staring at it when Paul put his hand on my arm. "Just want you to know, Jake. Far as I'm concerned, it was worth it."

"What?"

"You delivered. You really surprised me."

I breathed in heavily. "Did I?"

"Sure. Hell, I'd never seen you do anything before. I figured if you'd been around town this long and you were any good, I'd have seen you in something. I was taking a big chance, you know. Sticking my neck out. But you were great. You scored a few points for me with Cain, too. He figures I must be pretty sharp if I found you. Good work, Jake. Worked out just right for both of us."

I stood on the front steps and watched him get into his MG. As he backed toward the road, he waved to me.

I didn't wave back. When I returned to the living room, Katie wasn't there. I reached the kitchen in time to see her swallowing a small yellow pill. She jumped when she realized I'd seen her take it.

"I'm getting fat again, Jake. Got on the scale this morning, I've put on almost five pounds." Her words were jumpy. Her eyes slid quickly away from me. Her fingers drummed the edge of the counter nervously. "Take me a day or two, I'll take it off. Don't look it, do I? Hard to tell on yourself. Five pounds—"

"Stop eating all the chocolate-chip cookies and drinking all the goddamn milk."

I don't know what made me say it that way. Maybe it was the nervousness of the day mixed with the four beers. Maybe it was seeing her pay him. Maybe I was just scared.

Katie only giggled. "Milk is good for you."

"You don't need two quarts a day!"

She opened her mouth. Then closed it quickly.

I slammed my hand against the counter. "God! You know I don't like it when you keep telling me you're putting on weight! I don't see you putting on weight, I wouldn't even give it a thought if you didn't keep telling me about it!" I tried to stop, but I couldn't. "If you think you're putting on weight, don't eat so much! And for God's sake, stop taking those damn pills! You can't count on them to kill your appetite, you got to do it yourself!"

It had nothing to do with her weight, and I knew it.

It wasn't even so much that I'd seen her paying him. It was *how* she'd paid him. In cash.

Ruth had told me Calisi had been paid for the pictures in cash. It had struck me as strange. Katie always paid for everything that way. I'd never seen her use a credit card or a check for anything. It was always cash. I was afraid I knew why. Checks were traceable. Cash wasn't.

I turned suddenly and went into the living room. She came after me. She was laughing again as if nothing had happened. "You see what Paul said? He was surprised how good you were. He couldn't figure out why he hadn't seen you in something if you'd been in town this long. It was Ruth's fault, Jake. Not yours. You had the talent, she just didn't know how to sell it."

I kept my mouth shut, and kept moving. My stomach felt like it was ready to collapse.

"How was the commercial, Jake? Come on, I want you to tell me all about it."

I stumbled to the table. I picked up the brown envelope and shook it at her. "How much did it cost for him to get this for you?"

"What? It's not for me." She stepped back. "It's for you."

"How much did it cost!"

"Not much." She walked quickly across the room. "It'll be worth it, Jake. To show people, so they can see how good you are."

I fought to stay standing. I held one hand over my belly. "You've got to stop buying things for me!"

She nodded. Then she moved with a jerk toward the bookcase and the liquor bottles.

"No!" I started toward her. "You just took one of those pills! Don't drink anything now!"

She stopped where she was. Her arms hung stiffly at her sides.

"God, Katie, how much did this film cost? How much did you have to pay him to get me into the film in the first place? What are you going to pay for next? Getting me into Cain's next film?" My eyes were full of tears. "Or maybe next time you'll buy me my own movie! That what you're going to do?" I finally said it. *"Where's the money coming from? Where, Katie? Where? Selling insurance?"*

Neither of us had mentioned the insurance for a long time. I'd stopped believing she'd ever sold it at all. But I hadn't called her on it. I hadn't wanted to. It had seemed easier that way, not knowing for sure.

But I'd known. I just hadn't known where her money was really coming from. Hadn't wanted to know. But now I was scared, and desperate, and I almost didn't care what I might find out.

"Just how much money have you got, Katie? Where's it coming from?"

"We had to get you started, Jake. So we did it." Her

eyes lit up. "And I didn't buy you that Ajax commercial! I got you that interview by using my brains, and you got the job because of your talent!"

"Talent? How do I know that? How do I know anything? How can I be sure I've gotten anything without you paying for it?"

Then I couldn't stand anymore. I went down to my knees and held my stomach in both hands. I was sure I was going to be sick.

I felt her hand on the back of my neck. I pulled away from it. "No! Don't touch me!"

She stepped back.

"Don't you understand, Katie? I thought it was my credits! My talent that got me onto that film! But it wasn't! It was money! Your money! And I don't even know where the money is coming from!"

I jumped to my feet. "What are you doing to me? What do you want from me? Who are you?" I grabbed her by the shoulders and shook her. "Who are you! Every time I ask you anything, you just shut up and take one of your goddamn pills! Katie, who are you? Where's the money coming from?"

Her face was white. She was petrified. But she made no effort to pull away from me.

I kept shaking her. "Tell me! Where's the money coming from?"

Her head shook back and forth. Suddenly she was gasping. So was I.

"Katie, what do you think you're buying with it? What do you think you *can* buy? Me? My love? Katie, you can't buy love!"

"I'm not trying to buy . . ." Her voice faded away to nothing and her eyes got larger. They were glistening now. "Jake? I thought you already loved me. You said you did." She went limp in my hands as if she were about to faint. "You said you wanted to marry me. Didn't you mean it?"

"Of course I meant it! I *do* love you! But I . . ."

I was still shaking her. I was enraged.

I understood now what was happening. It wasn't the beers, the money, where the money was coming from. It was the spell of love. It was breaking.

The spell of love always breaks. The blindness

starts to leave you, and for the first time you see things more objectively, the way other people see them. Then you have to decide. Can you live with that vision? Love someone in spite of it? Because it's dangerous, that moment. The relationship can start getting better and deeper. Or worse. Much worse.

You always fool yourself that this time it won't happen—then it leaps at you out of nowhere when you least expect it. It's what you do then, without thinking. What you say before you can stop yourself. If you do and say the wrong things, suddenly it's over, there's no way to get it back.

Sometimes it should be over, but it's a mistake to force it before you're sure. There's always the chance the relationship can be saved. Maybe it's just a step you're taking, the two of you, so that everything can be better. And then if the relationship holds—

It's still dangerous. You'll have more of those moments. The only thing that ever ends them is the end of the relationship.

I knew all that. Knew it right then. And wasn't sure enough of anything to take a step in any direction. I let her go and stepped back and looked at the floor. I saw the large brown envelope. I picked it up and put it on the table and stayed by the table. I knew if I started walking toward her I'd have to go all the way. Or not go all the way. Touch her, or not touch her. Kiss her, or not kiss her. And I wasn't sure which of those choices I would make.

She must've realized what was happening. She turned suddenly and went down the hall to the bedroom. She didn't come back.

She stayed in the bedroom all night. I spent the night in the living room. No choices were made by either of us. We let it blow over. We'd wait till the next time.

TWO days passed. We both managed to act like everything was all right. Katie called the Ajax people. They told her they were very pleased with my commercial. They planned to test it in six cities starting the following month. If the results were good, they'd go national one month later. Katie and I were both relieved by the news.

When we made love that night I was lying sideways across the bed with her on top of me. Suddenly she pushed me so my head was over the edge. The blood began to rush to it. I began to see spots. I tried to get back up, but she put both hands against my chin and wouldn't let me. I was almost unconscious when I came. But when I came, it was magnificent. It shook my whole body out of control. She laughed when it was over and began kissing me softly on the chest. I liked it. God help me, I liked it. So it went on.

A week passed. We were still all right. Katie got me a couple of movie interviews. The first one didn't pan out, but the second one sounded good. They made me an offer to do a short character bit. It would be a small scene. Maybe ten lines at most. Unless they rewrote the scene, in which case there might be a few more lines. Or a few less. However many lines it would eventually amount to, it would still be only one day's work.

We thought it over. It was a big-budget movie. We figured, a day's work, lines, a major film . . .

Two seconds later we told them it was fine. They said good. They'd mail us the contracts.

We went driving that night. She suddenly told me to pull over to the side of the road. There were cars driving by but she said not to worry. She laughed as she hiked up her skirt.

Another car stopped on the road beside us. She just laughed again. By then I didn't care either.

I got another commercial out of the blue. A producer called and said he'd seen me shooting the Ajax spot. He'd liked me and wanted me for something he was doing, if I was interested and available. It wouldn't be a spokesman deal like the Ajax commercial had been, but would I be interested?

We checked my schedule. I was available. And interested.

The guy turned out to be the one who'd opened that door and knocked over the folding chair and spoiled the second take. What he wanted me for was a spaghetti-sauce commercial. There were ten words involved. I had to say them all in less than three seconds. The money was very good for ten words in three seconds.

It only took two and a half hours to get it right.

That was the night we did it in the parking lot outside Tulley's Bar. It was crazy. I don't know why I went along with it. As we came out of the bar, a car screeched into a space and people jumped out singing and laughing. One of them, an actor I knew, saw me and waved. Then his girlfriend threw her arms around him and kissed him.

A second later, Katie did the same thing to me. She really made a show of it.

Then, when they'd gone into the bar, she pulled back and laughed. I laughed too. I unlocked the passenger side for her, but instead of getting in she turned me around and started undoing my belt.

205

I tried to stop her, but she was too determined. Then she grabbed me, and I didn't have the control to stop her. The best I could do was to do it as fast as I could.

Something about the speed of it and the danger of being seen was very powerful. It made it different than ever before. Then a couple came out of the bar. They came straight across the parking lot and got into the car next to us. They drove off. But they'd been too late. They hadn't seen a thing.

So the lovemaking was usually terrific. And the work was finally starting to come. I was beginning to make it in the business, in a small way. But I wasn't enjoying any of it quite the way I should have. It didn't feel right. There was no music in it anymore.

Ever since I'd brought up that thing about the insurance, Katie had stopped making any pretense that she was selling it. She stayed home much of the day now, making her calls from the house. She'd go out sometimes to see people. She'd come back and tell me about it. None of it resulted in any work.

Every Tuesday and Thursday she left the house at nine forty-five and drove over to Hollywood to see the psychiatrist, Dr. Samuels. She said talking to him seemed to help.

And she did seem better in some ways. I'd gotten her to stop taking so many pills. But occasionally she'd take one.

We hit a ten-day dry spell. I couldn't get an interview for love or money. Then I got one, but they took one look at me and didn't even bother to have me read.

On top of that, the contracts for the big-budget movie still hadn't arrived. Katie called them. They told her they'd had to postpone production. One of the stars was in the hospital. It was serious. He might be back, he might not. They might have to recast. If they recast they might have to rewrite huge sections of the script. They might have to do half a dozen things. Any one of them might mean they wouldn't be using me at all. What it all added up to, though they weren't insensitive enough to say it, was that the last thing in the world they gave a damn about right then was a small-time actor named Jake Bolin.

It was tough. We'd thought we had the job. Now we didn't. There wasn't a thing we could do about it. We had no signed contracts.

It wasn't a big thing. Only a day's work. Only ten lines at most. But right then it was the only thing I'd had, and now I didn't have it.

We didn't make love that night. Neither of us seemed to want to.

I ran into Jill one afternoon over in Century City. I must've looked sort of down. She was sympathetic. We had lunch together. I got a call from Alan that night. We talked for twenty minutes about nothing much at all. I think he felt guilty about the way he'd thought I'd put Katie up to cornering him at the party to get me some work. Before we hung up, he said how his TV series was going to try to get me something decent in one of their opening shows. I laughed and said that would be fine. I wondered exactly what Jill had said to him. I didn't believe he'd actually get me anything. Katie didn't think so either.

I still wasn't able to reach any decision. I still seemed to care about her, but it wasn't the same. I was seeing her that different way now. I wasn't sure if things were getting better, or worse.

I'd drive home some days half hoping she wouldn't be there. That maybe she would've left, like she sometimes threatened to. She was doing that a lot lately. Threatening to leave. And getting into depressions about my lack of work. And wandering through the house restlessly.

One night she yelled at me as if she hated me for not having gotten another job yet.

And suddenly I found myself yelling at her for not having gotten me one.

I went driving the next day. I stayed away from the house all afternoon and into the evening. I didn't even call the service in case she'd left a message.

But then around nine I finally did go home. When I walked into the kitchen and saw her, she was smiling. I smiled too. We talked and laughed and ate a late dinner, then we went to bed. I was damned glad she was there.

But still, it wasn't the same. I just didn't feel the same way about her as I'd felt that night in the car when I'd asked her to marry me. I didn't feel the same way I'd felt that first night we'd made love. I didn't even feel the same way I'd felt that first night I'd seen her, at the bar at The Dancers.

It was getting worse and worse. It wasn't just the lack of work that was getting to me. Or her depressions. Or the arguments. It was that there were so many things I wanted to know.

And I still wasn't brave enough to ask her about them.

I came home one day and she was gone. Her clothes were gone. Her suitcases. Even her bottle of Jack Daniel's. I sat in the living room for half an hour in complete shock.

Then suddenly I felt a surge of elation. It was out of my hands now. There was no decision to make. It was over.

I felt so relaxed. I went into the kitchen and made dinner. I put up a big pot of chili and sat there for three hours smelling it cook.

I had no wine with dinner. I had no urge to get drunk. When I finished eating, I was all set to wash the dishes like I always used to do, but then changed my mind. *She* had always been so immaculate about the dishes. They always had to be washed *immediately*. And *spotlessly*. I wasn't going to do that. I'd leave them till morning.

I didn't wash them the next morning. I sat in the back yard and read. Around noon I felt tired for some reason, so I went into the bedroom for a nap. When I woke up it was dark.

The third morning I didn't bother to shave. I looked at the dishes in the sink and left them there. I made coffee and sat in the living room and smoked half a pack of cigarettes. I looked at the phone. No matter how long I stared, it didn't ring. Of course it didn't. There was nobody out there trying to get work for me. I opened a book. I couldn't get past the first paragraph.

The fourth afternoon I called Ruth. It rang twice before it got picked up. "Hi, baby!"

I didn't answer. I hung up the phone.

I went into the kitchen and made another pot of coffee. I ripped open a new pack of cigarettes. The coffee was taking forever, so I took a walk out to the yard. My head felt light and I bumped into the corner of the house. I stepped back, then swung my leg out and kicked. I kicked again, as hard as I could. I don't know how many times I kicked. Soon I could hardly feel how much it hurt anymore.

But then something made me realize that though my foot wasn't broken yet, it would soon be, so I stopped.

I hobbled into the kitchen. The coffee was boiling over. I turned off the burner and went into the bathroom. I took off my shoe and sock. It wasn't as bad as I'd thought. Only my big toe was bloody. I washed it and dried it and put a bandage on it. After a couple of hours I didn't limp too much. But I couldn't wear a shoe for the rest of the day.

At least I'd proven one thing. I sure didn't need her. I knew how to slap myself around.

The next day I ran out of cigarettes and had to go down the hill. When I came back the yellow Volkswagen was there.

I must've looked terrible when I walked into the kitchen. My hair, my beard, the clothes I'd slept in for the past two nights. She didn't look much better. Her hair was unwashed. Her eyes had dark circles under them. She was at the sink, putting on an apron, getting set to wash the dishes.

We didn't say a thing. We didn't talk during dinner. We didn't talk till we were in bed. She surprised me suddenly by starting to reach for me, and then trying to get on top of me like she always did. But I stopped her. I pushed her back so she was lying on her back. She said, "Jake? What're you doing?"

"I'm making love to you."

I got on top of her and put my hands between her legs. I didn't know what I was doing. I mean, if it was love, or just sex. But as soon as I was inside her, it felt so right. I could barely control myself. "Wrap your legs around me."

"What?"

"Wrap your legs around me! Quick!"

She still didn't seem to understand. I pulled her legs around my waist. I put my hands under her and pulled her up against me. "Hold me tighter!"

"What?"

"Your legs! Hold me tighter! Squeeze me!"

Her legs tightened like a vise.

I got my mouth on hers. Just as her mouth opened I began to come. She felt it and arched her back against me. She screamed. I held her against me and thrust hard.

I felt exhausted. I pulled her head against my shoulder and began to stroke her forehead. Then I realized she was shaking.

"Katie?"

"It didn't work."

"What?"

There were tears in her eyes. "It didn't work."

"I'm sorry. I did it too fast. I couldn't help it."

"No! That isn't it!" Her whole body was trembling. "That time we did it outside Tulley's, that was fast too, but that time it worked! This time it didn't!"

It took me fifteen minutes before I thought I might be ready to try it again. Then I reached over and began to pull her on top of me.

"Jake? What're you—"

"Shh. Come on." I had her knee pulled across my stomach. I drew it farther till it rested against my right side.

"No, Jake, it's all right. Not if you don't want to do it this way."

"It's all right. Come on." I put my hands on her waist and waited.

She just sat there a long time and looked down at me. Finally I began to rub myself against her.

"I'm sorry, Jake. It's the only way that ever works for me. I don't know why."

"It's all right, Katie. Come on."

Her hips began to sway. Circle. Withdraw. Then she pushed down.

And I knew I'd been wrong. I wasn't ready. Not yet.

But she couldn't stop. Her head came forward and her lips kissed my ear. "You're nice, Jake. You're so nice."

She began to move faster. Back and forth. Back and forth. She was moaning in ecstasy. But I was dying.

Then it happened. It surprised me. I'd been sure it wouldn't. Even as it was starting, I didn't think it was going to be very strong. But it was. I lifted her right off the bed.

I was sure now it was love. It had to be.

The next day something ridiculous happened. We got a call from the big-budget movie people. It turned out they'd recast their movie and now they had a rising young star named James Montgomery for the lead. They'd had to rewrite the scene they'd told us about. Now it would be twenty lines, not ten. There would also be a second scene with more lines. Both scenes would be with Montgomery. It was going to be three days' work. Maybe even four. And they wanted me for it.

Katie played it like ice. She told them that since the postponement I'd gotten a couple of new offers. One of them was very definite. We still wanted to do their picture, of course, but it would cost them a little more now. Not much more. But a little. Twenty-five hundred dollars more. Otherwise we'd have to go with one of the other offers.

I was listening in on the phone in the kitchen and was almost ready to smash my fist through the wall. But before I could explode, they said sure, we could have the twenty-five hundred extra. They'd send out the contracts in the afternoon mail.

Five seconds after I hung up the phone, Katie came into the kitchen doing a little dance. "We're rolling, Jake!" She grabbed some spoons and started drumming the counter. They she put them down and did the dance again. As she danced she began snapping her fingers. She smiled at me. "Oh, baby, now we're really rolling!"

I turned away suddenly.

Katie did some drinking that night. She was excited because of the way she'd pulled off the deal. I let her drink. I wasn't sure how to stop her. After dinner I wanted to make love. But she didn't. She said she felt too drunk.

Then she started talking. She told me a story about a girl she'd known several years before. She lost the thread right in the middle of it.

She sat on the bed and put her head in her hands. She couldn't for the life of her remember the rest of the story.

It started driving her crazy. To get her mind off it, I said something about the movie deal. She stared at me. For a moment she couldn't remember having set it.

After she fell asleep I checked her pocketbook. I didn't find any pills. Only an empty bottle. I put it in my coat pocket. The next morning, when I went to an audition, an old friend went with me—fear.

It was just as bad as it'd ever been. I seemed to have no confidence at all. My stomach was gurgling and doing flipflops. I thought I was going to faint. I knew what was happening. So did the casting director.

We both got through the interview as fast as we could. Then I left without even shaking his hand. That was one job I sure wasn't going to get.

Fear. I couldn't let it grab me again. I was going to have to do something about it.

IT was the middle of the afternoon, two days later. I was sitting in a booth at Tulley's. Ruth came in.

It was the first time we'd seen each other since that day at my house. I was sitting in the booth so I was safe. It wasn't my move, it was hers. She stood near the door a moment, then walked across the room. She smiled at me. "Well. Nice to see you."

"Nice to see you."

"Uh huh. Use some company?"

"I could use all you got."

She sat down. We were quiet. She looked at the half-empty glass next to my hand. What the glass contained was vodka.

She slid a cigarette pack onto the table so it was flat on its side. She twirled it with one finger.

"I got three, four days' work coming up. That movie they just signed James Montgomery for." I paused.

"That's good. Good part?"

"Two scenes. Both with him."

She nodded. She lowered her eyes. A moment passed.

Her eyes came back up, and her smile was back too. "I got someone else on that film. Tim Garrison. So I saw the script, couple days ago. Looks like a good project to be part of."

"Yeah, looks like it."

Her eyes went down again. "Sounds like your boss is doing okay for you."

"Yeah. . . . Okay." I was controlling my voice. I hadn't liked the "boss" part. I watched Ruth's finger play carelessly with the cigarette pack. "Beginner's luck, I guess."

Ruth snapped a cigarette out of the pack and stuck it in her mouth. "Luck comes two ways, baby. Good and bad." She clicked on her lighter. She grinned stiffly at the flame. "Could be, you're playing with the proverbial fire, you know. Don't start thinking you're made of asbestos. You're not."

I didn't answer.

Suddenly she leaned forward. "How'd she get you onto that Cain movie?"

"What?" I jerked back. I was flat against the booth.

"Cain always uses the same actors, over and over again. How'd she—"

"She met an assistant director. He—"

"Met an assistant director? And he got you on the film? Just like that?"

I straightened my face. "Yeah. Just like that."

Ruth took a deep breath. "And that's what you like about her. She knows how to meet assistant directors."

I stared at her grimly. "No. I like her 'cause she's always so sure she can do something. So sure she can pull it off. So willing to go after it. So confident."

"You mean so naive." Ruth laughed.

"Whatever you want to call it, I like it. She's got guts."

"We all had guts, once. Wait'll you see how she is when she tries to make a couple deals and something goes wrong with 'em and she loses 'em. See how much guts she's got then."

That got to me. I'd already seen what happened when Katie lost one. The first time with the big movie deal, she'd lost it. *We'd* lost it. Then she'd started yelling at me.

And I'd started yelling at her.

And then she'd left.

Ruth's head nodded up and down. "Knowing how to roll with the punches, Jake. That's what it's all about. That's something it takes time to learn, if you can learn it at all."

The flame on Ruth's lighter was still going. We both looked at it silently. Then Ruth lit her cigarette and shook the flame out with several quick waves of her hand. We watched the smoke straighten and thin out.

Her mouth tightened and grimaced. "All right, I don't want to fight with you. Let's forget it." She leaned back in the booth. "The Montgomery picture. That sounds good."

I tried to relax. "Just set it verbally, so far."

Ruth's eyes snapped wider open. "Better get the contracts right away, baby. They already came close to canceling it once. You could get burned."

My right hand closed in a fist. "I know."

"What?" She looked at my hand. "Oh. I see. Almost *did* get burned, huh?"

"Almost." I opened my hand. I kept my eyes down. "On this deal, you're still my agent. You still got me exclusive. I mean, you'll still get the commission."

Ruth's hand slapped the table hard. She stabbed her cigarette into the ashtray and killed it. I thought she was going to get up and leave, but I was wrong. She looked straight into my eyes and stayed sitting. "Look, baby. I was excited that afternoon. We all were. But you want a release from your contract, just tell me. I'll talk to Mel, we'll release you."

"No. I don't want that." I stared at my vodka. "There's lots of actors in this town, Ruth. Some of 'em have agents. Some have managers. Some have both."

She said nothing. It got awfully quiet. It stayed that way for longer than I wanted it to.

Then she said, "Yeah, I've heard it's done." Her thumb rubbed the table so hard I thought she wanted to take off the veneer. "Sort of like having your cake and eating it, too, huh?"

"That's not what I meant!"

I swung out of the booth and stood up. I took two steps, then stopped.

I held it in. I turned and sat down. I picked up my glass and put it to my lips. Then I put it down again without drinking.

Ruth's fingers played nervously with the cigarette pack. Her voice whispered at me. "I just don't know what to say to you today. Or how to say it."

Her hand came slowly across the table. It touched my hand, and then her fingers closed around mine and squeezed slightly. "Friends? But I guess not lovers? Huh?"

"... We could try."

"Yeah. We could try." She looked at my vodka again. She took the glass, put it to her lips and sipped. "Not wine, is it?"

I shrugged and said nothing.

She put the glass down, keeping it on her side of the table. "I'm here for lunch, baby. You?"

I looked across the room. Tulley was in the middle of pouring a large Coke for a man at the bar. I caught his eye. He stopped and waited for me to speak.

"Two bowls of chili, two salads, one martini."

"Comin' right up, Jake! Want another vodka?"

"No." I turned back to Ruth. She looked tired now. I was tired, too. "Except for the movie deal, been a slow week."

"Story of Hollywood. Too fast or too slow. Can you handle it?"

"I got a choice?"

"Yeah, but we better not get into it again." She took another cigarette. "Okay. So you and I keep going down the road we both know too well." She paused. "I just don't want to see anything bad happen to you."

"Like what?"

"I don't know. Can we talk, without you getting mad?"

I tried to laugh. "Sure. I never get mad."

"Since when?" She tried to laugh too. "Look, we're going to yell at each other, it's okay to do it up at your house. There's nobody up there." She paused. "Except her." Then she went on quickly. "But here—" Her eyes scanned the room. "Here we got to keep it civil."

This time I really did laugh. "Since when?"

She smiled. She tipped her head slightly to the side

and lowered her voice. "I'm not just talking, Jake. I really do think there's something wrong with her. Maybe something serious." Her expression changed. "Aw, I knew I couldn't say anything to you about—"

"No, that's not it." I held up my hand and took a quick look across the bar toward Tulley. He was setting two bowls of chili on a tray. I turned back to Ruth. "It's not her, Ruth, it's the pills."

"What?"

". . . She takes pills."

Ruth's look sharpened. "What do you mean? What kind?"

I lowered my eyes. "You name 'em, she's got 'em. Mostly blue-and-red capsules. I took some to a pharmacist to see what they are. Sleeping pills. Tuinal. But she takes diet pills too. Something called Ritalin. The Ritalin —when she gets nervous, she overeats. I've seen her go through a whole bag of chocolate-chip cookies in half an hour. She dumps 'em in milk to make 'em soft so she can chew 'em. She's always drinking milk. Sometimes a couple quarts a day. She puts on weight, then she thinks she's getting fat, so she takes the Ritalin to kill her appetite. But the Ritalin are uppers, and sometimes when she's up she takes more of 'em to keep her up. She's very insecure. About her weight, about her looks. About dealing with people. Sometimes, when she's getting ready to see people, like that night at Alan's party, she takes the Ritalin to take her up so she won't be scared. The Ritalin makes her hyper, and she starts talking really fast. And loud. And then she can't keep her hands still. She starts snapping her fingers. And sometimes when she's really excited about something and can't calm down, she takes the sleeping pills to—"

I cut it short. Tulley was there.

He smiled at us and put down the chili, the salads and the martini. I stayed quiet and waited for him to go away. Ruth chewed her lower lip. "You're talking about prescription drugs. Where does she get 'em?"

"Who knows? She gets 'em. It's not even the pills that does it. I mean she's always taking pills, to take her up, to bring her down, to take her up again—but it's the drinking that does it. She's always drinking Jack Daniel's, and when she mixes that with the pills . . . " My hands were shaking. I put them under the table. "God, Ruth, I've been trying to get her to stop, but—"

"Stop trying, damn it. Get her to a doctor."

"She's seeing one. A psychiatrist. But I don't know if it's helping or not. Dr. Samuels. I got his name from Bill Hutchings."

"Hutchings?" Ruth snorted the name like it belonged to a disease. *"He* ought to be going to half a dozen shrinks."

"The thing is, I don't know if it's doing any good. She seems to be taking fewer of 'em, the pills, but I can't be sure."

Ruth wrapped her arms around herself and looked down.

I grabbed my spoon and gulped down a mouthful of chili. I couldn't taste a thing. But I needed time to decide what else I could tell her.

"She has blackouts, sometimes."

"What?"

Now I wanted to take it back, but it was too late. I went on quickly. "Sometimes she does things, and later on she doesn't remember she's done 'em. She's completely blank."

"Christ. Dump her, Jake. I mean it."

"No! I need her!" I stopped. "She needs me. I've got to get her off the pills."

"You need her for what? Jesus Christ, Jake. Look at yourself. You're a mess. Your hand's shaking so bad you can hardly hold that spoon. You can't sit still, you're talking like you can't think straight. You need her? You don't need her. You need to get away from her. Fast."

"No! Whether I need her or not, she needs me! I've got to get her off the pills!"

"She needs *some*thing, that's for sure. What do you think, you're married to her?"

I stopped and caught my breath. "It's not that bad. She's been better, this past week." That was a lie, but I felt I had to say it. "She's been really cutting down, Ruth. . . . It's just . . . I can't get her to stop completely."

"Don't give me that! It's nothing to do with pills!" Ruth came halfway across the table at me. "It's *need,* all right! That's exactly what it is! *You need her*! Too damn much! You're dependent on her! And she's dependent on you just as bad! I've seen the way she's always looking at you! Holding on to you! And you're just the same! The two of you, you act like neither one of you could stand up by yourself!"

I looked away quickly.

She'd pegged it all right. Dependence. I'd been acting like an idiot, the way I'd been depending on her. It was as simple and foolish as that.

Sure it was simple and foolish. It was love. Love turns all of us into idiots. If only it weren't so wonderful, it would be a damn good thing to do without.

I sat up straight. I took a deep breath and leaned forward. "I'm not dependent on her at all. I just happen to love her."

"The hell you do. You love what you think she's doing for your career." Ruth's lips curled in and her teeth showed. "Don't tell me about what you love. I've been around this town too long. I've seen too much of what happens when people like you are trying to make it. *That's* what you love."

We both stared quietly at our uneaten bowls of chili.

"Listen to me, Jake. This is important. You can make it now. You believe in yourself. You know you do. That's all you ever needed."

"But she's the *reason* I believe in myself."

"No!"

Ruth leaned back in her seat and put the fingers of both hands around her martini. "Okay. Maybe she's part of the reason. *Maybe*. And the thing with the pills. . . . You're a nice guy, Jake. You're worried about her. Okay. I can understand that. But I wish to God you'd worry about yourself. Her and the pills, they'll drive you out of your mind. I know what I'm talking about. I've been through it."

"What?"

Her hand waved at the air. "Forget it. It doesn't matter. I'm talking about you. She's hurting you. I mean, in the business. She doesn't know how to talk to people, Jake. She's making enemies. All over town. I've been hearing things."

"What? What things?"

"Let's just say she's not making friends the way she

ought to be. There's something crazy about her. People see it. You weren't so blind, you'd see it too."

"She's making enemies, huh? She's getting work for me. You never did."

"How could I? Look what you were!" Ruth's hands gripped the table. "That's my point. You've changed. Now you've got it. You want it now. And you think you can get it. So you *can* get it! What're you going to do now? Let *her* hold you back?"

She waited for an answer. I didn't give her one. She reached across the table for my hand.

I pulled both my hands off the table and dropped them in my lap.

Then something happened to her. Her eyes drifted away and her mouth clamped shut. Her head dropped down. Her eyes closed tightly, and her face hardened as if it were going to crack.

I reached across the table and covered her hand with mine. Her hand tightened and pulled away. She turned and buried herself against the inside of the booth. A moment later she wiped tears out of her eyes.

I got out of my side of the booth and went quickly around to her side. I slid in and put my arm around her. She tried to move away, but I wouldn't let her. She looked up at me. "I just don't want to see anything happen to you!"

I began to say something. Her hand came up and covered my mouth. "I'm scared of her, Jake! I'm scared I'm going to pick up a paper some day and read she's put a knife in your ribs!"

It hit me with enough force to knock me through the back of the booth.

"Jake, it happens every day! How do you know it couldn't happen with her? There's something wrong with her!" She gasped for breath. "What do you know about her? I mean, *really* know? About her background? Do you know where she came from?"

I stiffened. I knew plenty. I knew what she'd told me that night in the car, when I'd asked her to marry me.

I was married once. I don't want to be married again. I'm afraid of it.

And the part that came after.

He's dead now. My husband. Someone killed him.
"Jake! What is it?"
". . . Nothing."

God! That's what I'd remembered that night I'd hidden the gun in the tree! That's why I'd been trying my best not to find out anything about Katie's past! Or where her money was coming from! Or why she paid for everything in cash!

Ruth spoke again with very little breath behind it. "You're scared, Jake? What is it? Tell me! Please!"

I said nothing.

Ruth moved away from me. "I was wrong about you. I thought you'd changed. You haven't changed at all. You're still just as scared as you've always been. You've got yourself into something, you don't know how to get out of it, and you're too scared to get out of it."

I put my hand on her shoulder. She pushed it away. "No, Jake. I can't take any more of this. The way you're acting, you're killing me."

I was silent awhile. Then I swung across the seat and got out of the booth. I looked down at my bowl of chili and my salad. But I didn't want them anymore. I began to turn away.

"Jake! Wait a minute!" Ruth took another deep breath. "It's just, the Montgomery picture."

"What about it?"

"When you get the contract, better go over it with a magnifying glass. The producers, they're real sharpies. Sometimes they play games, just to prove it."

I stared at her. I put my hands in my pockets. "Yeah. Well. . . . I told Katie, soon as we get the contract we ought to show it to you. Get your opinion."

I hadn't told Katie anything of the sort.

Ruth spread her fingers on the table. Then she picked the spoon out of her chili. "Well, if you want to do that, I'll be happy to take a look. I'm still your agent."

"Yeah."

But her eyes were off me, and they stayed off me.

I burned a lot of gasoline on the freeways that afternoon. From Hollywood to North Hollywood to Encino. From Encino to Westwood. From Westwood to West Hollywood. I had nowhere to go. I had plenty of freeways to take me there.

When I finally got home, Katie was on the phone. She smiled at me and winked and kept talking. It sounded like she was talking to a movie producer. I didn't stay to listen. I went into the kitchen.

There was some ground meat on a plate. I looked at it for two minutes, and then took out a frying pan. I got out a can of tomato sauce and a can of tomato paste, and started chopping an onion. It felt good to be doing it. Besides, I needed something to do with my hands.

I was just putting the onion in the frying pan when she came in. "Jake, don't do that. I'll do it."

She took the frying pan away from me.

I sat at the table and watched her start the spaghetti sauce. Finally I said, "I talked to Ruth today. We—"

"Ruth? What did you talk to her for?"

I watched as she carefully scraped tomato paste out of the can. "I was having lunch at Tulley's. She came in."

"Oh." Katie stirred the contents of the frying pan and lowered the flame.

"I told her . . . about the Montgomery picture—"

"I bet *that* surprised her!"

"Yeah. It did." I waited a moment. "We got to talking. About the contract. I told her we'd let her see it when we got it." Katie didn't move. "Ruth's used to contracts. She knows what to look for to make sure—"

"You don't trust me at all, do you? Don't you think *I* know how to read a contract?!"

It was a silent dinner. A silent evening. But she didn't take any pills. And she didn't drink.

Around eleven-thirty I asked her if she was coming to bed. She said no, she was reading a book. I stayed up another hour watching her. Then I was too tired. I lay down on the bed. Soon I was asleep.

It was dark when she woke me. She snapped on the overhead light, and when I opened my eyes she threw a paper at me.

"What's this?"

"Read it."

I took the paper in my hand. It was a personal management agreement. It said that I, Jake Bolin, agreed that she, Kate O'Hanlon, would manage my career. I agreed to take no work unless she approved it. I agreed to uphold the agreement for three years.

I blinked my eyes to see if I was really awake. I tried to think. "Katie, this is no good."

"Why not?"

"You aren't franchised to be a personal manager."

"I don't have to be. An agent has to be franchised, a personal manager doesn't have to be anything." She looked nervously at the wall. "I checked with some people, Jake. All a personal manager has to have is a written agreement with a client. A nice, simple, written agreement."

I sat up and fixed the pillow against the headboard. "Why do you want me to sign this? So you can have a cut of the money I get from the Montgomery picture?"

"Money?" Her eyes narrowed. Her words hissed at me. "How much do personal managers get? The same as agents? Ten percent?"

I watched her carefully. "Sometimes. Sometimes more. I don't think it's regulated."

She reached forward suddenly and took the agreement back. She leaned over the bureau and wrote something, and then when she gave it back to me there was an additional line. Now I was to agree to pay to her one percent of all my earnings.

I laughed. "Katie, you know how much one percent is going to amount to? Peanuts!"

"That's right." She smiled. "Now you know it's not because of the money."

". . . Then why?"

"To show me you trust me."

Then she kneeled beside the bed and put both hands on my arm. She was different now. So soft. Vulnerable. Almost helpless. "Jake? Haven't I been doing a good job for you?"

"Yes, you've been doing—"

"Then show me. Show me you trust me. That you think my judgment about your career is good. As good as hers." She got off the floor and sat on the bed and put both her arms around me. "I want to know that you trust me, Jake. That you won't take a job that's bad for you. That Ruth won't be able to talk you into something that's not right for you. I want to protect you. We've got your career going now, we've got to make sure we keep it going. The right way."

"I don't need that kind of protection. And certainly not from Ruth."

"Then just sign it to show me you trust me!" There were tears in her eyes. "I need to know that, Jake! I really do! Please!"

I signed the agreement.

The next morning she decided it wasn't good enough. She wrote the whole thing over so it looked neat and proper, and then we went to a notary public. We signed it in front of him.

When we were back out on the street, Katie threw her arms around me. "Thank you, Jake! Now I know you believe in me! That's all I wanted!"

She kissed me. And I kissed her. But it was the weakest kiss I'd ever given any one in my entire life.

She had to leave then. To go see Dr. Samuels. She'd set up an audition for me at Paramount. I went to that. I didn't have to sit in the waiting room for long, I don't know if I could've sat for long. My stomach, as usual.

I read for the director and the producer. I read fairly well, but not like I should've. Then I got in my car and drove. I drove twice as much as I'd driven the afternoon before. It was four before I realized I'd forgotten to call the service. I called. There were no messages. I drove some more.

Something kept popping out from the middle of my thoughts. That management agreement. Something bothered me about it. But I wasn't sure what.

When I got home around seven, I found Katie in the kitchen making dinner. She didn't ask me why I was so late. She threw her arms around me and kissed me the same way she had that morning on the street. And I kissed her the same way. Weak. Very weak.

But she wasn't weak at all. I didn't like how much energy she was putting into it. Then she started talking quickly. I didn't like that either.

"I've been reading this book, Jake. *Brownsville Station*. It's wonderful. It's all about—"

"I know. I read it." I moved slowly out of her arms and went to the table. A paperback copy of *Brownsville Station* was folded open somewhere past the middle.

"They're going to make a movie out of it, Jake."

"Yeah. I know."

She was really talking fast. Whenever she talked that fast, it was bad.

"I'm going to find out who's producing the movie. You'll be perfect for the younger brother. It was written for you."

I sat down. I felt very tired. "I couldn't get the part of the younger brother if my life depended on it. Jack Christolf owns the book. He's going to make the movie through his own company."

"Jack Christolf? So what?" She came over and sat in my lap.

"Jack Christolf, Katie. Remember? At Alan's party? Christolf isn't going to use me for the second lead. He isn't going to use anybody like me. He's going to get himself a name that—"

"No! Don't give up so easy!" Her fingers closed around my chin. She tipped my head up and made me look into her eyes. "You're right for the part, Jake. And it's a game, right? You got to play the game. You can't give up on it."

She kissed me. I didn't want her to, but her tongue forced its way into my mouth. She had my head bent back, and her arms were tight around me.

Then her head drew back suddenly, and she laughed. Her eyes twinkled. Her fingers snapped. There wasn't a single thing about it that I enjoyed.

She got out of my lap and went to the counter. She laughed again as she started fixing the casserole. Then her hand reached out, and I saw the glass of Jack Daniel's.

I got out of my chair and went out the back door quickly.

I sat on the grass with my back against the tree, several feet away from the tree where the gun was hidden. It was quiet. A good fifteen minutes or more must've gone by. Then the back door creaked open.

She looked out at me. She was so small and helpless and weak. How could she be a threat to anyone?

I reached into my pocket and found my pack of cigarettes. There was only one left. I'd gone through the rest during my ride on the freeways. I stuck the cigarette in my mouth and lit it.

She came down the steps and into the yard. "I saw Dr. Samuels today."

I nodded.

She took another step. "Do you want to hear what we talked about?"

I stared at her. She'd never told me anything about what they talked about. She always told me when she was going to see him, and later she'd tell me if it'd made her feel any better or not. If he'd said anything that seemed to help her. Or hadn't said anything. But she'd never told me *anything* they'd talked about.

"I told him some things I never told anyone before." She paused. "Jake? You want me to tell you?"

". . . All right. If you want to."

She nodded. She came halfway across the yard toward me. I killed my cigarette against the tree.

"My mother died in a car accident. When I was young. Three. Three years old. I don't even remember her. My father, he had to bring us up. He . . ."

She broke off. She began to pace back and forth in front of me. "It wasn't good, Jake. Growing up like that. So I ran away. I mean, when I was older. I went to New York."

She went quiet again. She stayed near the edge of the yard as if she were trying to make some decision.

Then she spoke quickly. "I got in with some people. In New York. Some kids. My age. I needed money, we all did, so we did some things. But then I got caught. They put me in jail." She breathed in sharply and looked at me.

I didn't move. "For how long?"

"Just a couple of months. That's all. When they let me out, they made me go on a methadone program. And I had to see a psychiatrist, every Monday, Wednesday and Friday. He didn't want to see us, but he didn't have any choice. It was part of his residency." Her voice caught. "He hated me, Jake. Because he wanted me. I told him things, and he pretended to listen, but then . . . he tried to do something, and I didn't let him."

I started to speak, but she cut me off. "I reported it, but they didn't believe me. He said I was lying, and they believed him. They made me keep seeing him."

The timer went off inside, the kitchen. It seemed to freeze both of us in place.

"It can stay in the oven a couple more minutes, Jake."

"Sure. Go on."

She nodded and began to move. "I went back, the next time, like they said I had to, but as soon as we were alone, I told him if he ever touched me again I'd kill him." She paused. Her eyes floated up toward the sky. "And he knew I meant it. I *did* mean it. He'd thought he was really something. So pushy. So sure of himself. But I scared him." Her eyes came down slowly. "But I had to keep seeing him. I couldn't get out of it. And I had to tell him things because he had to make notes and turn them in. So at first I made up things, but later. . . ."

". . . Yes?"

"Later, he seemed different. Like maybe he really *was* listening. So then I . . . I started telling him the truth. And then . . ."

I was straining forward. My forehead felt damp. "Yes?"

"Then when he heard what I told him, he wasn't scared of me anymore. So *he* started saying things. About what I'd told him."

"What did you tell him?"

She looked at me quickly, then turned away. "He started tearing me apart. Kept saying what was wrong with me. That I was insecure, that I always had been. That I'd gotten in with those kids 'cause I was scared to be by myself. Always needed someone else to depend on." She stopped. "Or some *thing*. Like the heroin. Or the Jack Daniel's . . . or the pills."

She threw her head back and looked at the sky again.

"What did you tell him, Katie?"

"That's when I started taking the Tuinal. I'd take two every time I had to see him. They relaxed me, I could get through it that way. No matter what he said about how insecure I was, it didn't get me scared, not as long as I'd taken the Tuinal." Her voice seemed to choke.

"But it didn't work. One day he tried it again. He attacked me. And I was tired because of the Tuinal. I hit him, but I was too tired. I yelled for someone to come help me, but I couldn't yell loud enough. And nobody came. Nobody ever comes, do they? You yell for help, but they don't want to help. I guess they don't care."

Then her voice got stiffer. More definite. "But I'm helping you. Aren't I, Jake? I'm getting work for you."

"Yeah, Katie. You're helping me a lot."

"Yes! I have to! Nobody else would! *She* wouldn't! I helped you right from the start, didn't I? With those kids in the parking lot?"

"Yeah. You helped me then, too."

"Sure. I had to." She smiled at me.

Then she turned and went into the kitchen.

I went after her. She was standing by the table, looking at the oven. Her hand was on the back of a chair. "Jake? Can you turn off the oven? I feel so tired."

I turned off the oven and took her in my arms.

"I want to go to bed, Jake. Is that okay?"

"Sure."

As we walked to the bedroom, I kept one arm around her.

She lay on the bed and looked up at me. "Maybe ... if I took a Ritalin. That might wake me up."

"No, Katie. You're tired. Go to sleep." I gently closed her eyelids with my fingertips. "And don't worry. Nobody's going to hurt you."

"I know that, Jake. I'm not worried. I'm never worried, when I'm with you." She took my hand and kissed it.

I sat in the chair and watched her sleep. She began to toss and turn, but it only lasted a minute. Then she seemed calm.

I wasn't calm. She'd finally started to tell me things. What was she going to tell me next?

THE next day I opened the mail and there was a check from the Ajax people. Katie had been so down that morning that I made a big thing of writing out a check for one percent of the fee and giving it to her. She giggled as she held it.

We went to the bank. I deposited my check, and she cashed hers. That night she used the money to take me to a restaurant we'd never been able to afford before, down on Wilshire Boulevard. We ignored the prices and ordered like there was a host of Ajax commercials waiting in the wings. Neither of us ordered a cocktail. She insisted I have some wine. I had a glass of house wine. Then she told me to order another, and I felt pretty good, so I did. She finally asked me if she could have a little. I gave her a sip. That was all.

After dinner we went driving along the coast. It was a dark and beautiful night. She was sitting against me with her arm behind my neck. We had the radio on, and she was singing along with it. I'd never heard her sing before. She had a nice light voice.

We went through Ocean Park and Venice, and

then we were back on the freeway when another song came on. It had a strong, pulsing rhythm. As she sang with this one, her hand dropped in my lap. Suddenly both her hands were there, and she was undoing my belt.

"Katie. Stop that."

She laughed. She unzipped my pants.

"Katie!"

I was going over fifty. I was in the middle lane. There were cars on both sides of me and one right behind me. I tried to swerve toward the right. There was no opening. I tried to push her away, but I couldn't. She wasn't singing now. Her head was down in my lap.

I got my left hand on her mouth and stopped her. I floored the gas pedal. I didn't know how fast I was going, and I didn't care. I shot ahead of the cars on my right and found space and changed lanes. She was off the seat now and kneeling on the floor. She was reaching for me. I didn't know what else to do, so I slapped her.

She stayed there, on the floor. When I reached the next exit, I screeched down the off-ramp and stopped at the bottom. There were no cars around me. I shifted into park and turned off the motor. I was breathing like a steam engine. Her dark eyes looked up at me.

"Katie! What were you doing?"

She didn't answer. She leaped up at me and straddled me. Suddenly I felt like slapping her again, but when I brought my hand back to do it, she slapped me first.

Then it didn't make any difference what I felt like doing. It had been four days since the last time we'd made love. I wanted it as bad as she did.

Then, when I was almost there, she seemed to realize. She forced my head back against the top of the seat so far she almost choked me.

My climax was as powerful as it'd ever been.

She leaned against the inside of the passenger door. She smiled at me. I could hardly speak. "Did you take any pills tonight?"

Her face seemed confused. "No. Why?"

I shook my head. "Sometimes you're absolutely crazy."

"I know." She giggled. "I don't know what happens. I don't plan to do it, but suddenly, it just happens." The giggle grew bigger. She laughed. "But it was fun, wasn't it?"

"It wasn't fun when we were in the middle of the freeway!" I tried to breathe normally. I searched my pockets for cigarettes. "God, Katie, sometimes I think you want to kill me." I was excited and nervous and wasn't thinking straight. "I'm not that psychiatrist that raped you, Katie. If you want to do something to *him*, don't do it to *me*."

She gave me a look that froze my blood.

I didn't think she was going to say anything to me for the rest of the night. But then when I was driving back up through Santa Monica I stopped at a red light and suddenly her hand was in mine. When I looked at her she was smiling. She nodded toward my left. I looked and saw the sign in the distance. The Dancers.

"Let's stop in." She nuzzled against me. "Just for a little while."

I didn't want to, but I didn't want to lose her again that night. "All right, but no Jack Daniel's. Not even wine. Okay?"

She kissed me lightly on the cheek.

The Dancers was crowded. We found places at the bar. The bartender seemed to recognize me. It was from that time I'd come in there trying to find out if he knew who the girl had been that I'd seen at the bar.

I ordered a glass of wine for me and a Coke for her. We drank and watched the action. We'd almost finished when Katie bent her head closer to me. "How do I look?"

"What? Terrific. How else could you possibly look?"

"You're no good, you're prejudiced." But she smiled. Then she lowered her voice. "Come on, I mean it. I really look okay? Dress doesn't make me look too fat, does it?"

Katie. She was put together as perfectly as anyone had a right to be, but nothing in the world would ever convince her of that.

"You look absolute terrific." I leaned over and kissed her. But as I leaned, I found my head was a little light. Then I remembered this was the third glass of wine I was polishing off that night. "All right, I told you how you look. Now what else you want to know?"

Her eyes slid past me. I followed them all the way down to the other end of the bar. And I saw him. Jack Christolf. He was with a girl. Not the one he'd had at Alan's party, but this one was just as young.

"I'm going over there and talk to him." Katie straightened her dress and picked up her drink.

"Talk to him about what?"

"*Brownsville Station.*" She slipped off her stool.

I grabbed her arm and pulled her back. "Oh no you're not."

"Jake? Let me go! I want to see if I can—"

"No!"

I looked toward Christolf again. He had the girl laughing her head off. You could hear her all the way across the room.

"He's rotten, Katie. I don't want you going near him." I made her sit on the stool. "Anyway, he's all booked up for the night. So forget it."

She started to say something, but then she stopped. She changed her expression and suddenly smiled. "Hey! You know what? I like you when you're jealous!" She put her hand on my neck and kissed me softly. "Okay. I'll catch him some other time."

"No you won't. Finish your Coke."

"Yes, sir!" She picked up the coke and gulped it down.

But then before we could get out of there, Christolf came by with the girl hanging on to his arm.

Up close I could get a better look at what she was. Underage. Undernourished. And before the night was over, probably under him. He'd split her in two.

When Christolf saw us, he stopped. His head swiveled quickly to see who was around. Then he cocked his thumbs in his belt and threw a big smile at Katie. "Well, now! Hello!" God, he was so *sure* of himself. He licked his lips with the subtlety of a fox in heat.

He bowed toward Katie. "Think we've seen each other before."

Katie smiled at him. "Good evening, Mr. Christolf."

"No, no, no. We've met. Shouldn't be calling me Mr. Christolf." His lips pulled back so we could get a better look at his teeth. They were a dentist's dream. "It's Jack, to anyone that looks like you."

We all looked at each other. Then he looked right, and left, to check out his audience. He drew himself up taller. All I could think of was how my right fist could've sent both his confidence and his molars sailing across the floor.

The jailbait on his arm gave him a tug.

He raised a finger toward her but kept wearing his smile. "Uh uh uh. Careful, careful."

She was very careful. Very careful.

Christolf smiled again at Katie. "My friends *always* call me—"

I was all set to cut him off right there, but Katie beat me to it.

"You seem preoccupied, Mr. Christolf. You ought to stick with what you already have. Seems to be about your size."

I stared at her. Then at Christolf. His head turned slowly, and his eyes ran up and down the girl. Then he dismissed her like she was just a piece of meat. He turned back, laughed and moved closer. "Hell, they're all my size. Seems you're a little more sure of yourself than you were last time we met. Think I like it."

"Maybe it's that I'm just not interested." Katie picked up her glass and toasted him with her final drops of Coke.

Christolf's tongue played restlessly across his lower lip.

God, what a peacock! What an egotist! What a swaggering self-assured—

Actor.

His eyes finally left her and found me again. "Well! *Jay* something! Right?"

I was pretty tight. Pretty close to the edge. But not quite close enough. I shrugged.

He waited for me to way something. So he could say something.

But I stayed silent.

"What's the matter, little mouse? Cat got your tongue?"

I was on the edge again. But I leaned against the bar and smiled at him peacefully.

It got to him. He had no idea what to do with me.

Finally his eyes went back to Katie. But she didn't seem any more interested in him than she'd seemed before. It was driving him nuts.

"Well. Maybe I'll be seeing you, sometime." He looked briefly at the girl on his arm, then leaned toward Katie. "See you sometime when we're both not so preoccupied."

Katie yawned.

His eyes narrowed to slits. "Ought to check me out, sweetheart. I got great staying power. If you know what I mean." He looked sharply at the girl. "Right?"

I think the girl blushed. Maybe it was just the lighting.

Christolf laughed at her and looked around again, then turned back to us. "Sometimes I got *too much* staying power! Sometimes, you *can* believe everything you hear!"

He curled the edges of his mouth as close to his ears as he could get them. But that didn't get him anywhere either.

He must've finally gotten tired of listening to himself talk. He winked and smiled sweetly. His eyes flashed right, then left. Then he turned away and left. I was almost sorry to lose him.

Katie let out a long breath. "Well. I handle him okay?"

"This time I think we both did."

But I didn't know. Had I played him right? Or had I just been too chicken to play him any other way?

I faced the bar again. "Give him a couple minutes to find his way out of the parking lot, then we'll go home." I finished my wine in a single swallow.

Katie slid off her stool and went across the restaurant toward the rest rooms. When she was gone the bartender came over. He asked me if we wanted another round. I told him we didn't.

"Didn't want to say anything in front of the girl. But I remembered you came in here that time. Asking about that broad. You ever find her?"

I nodded.

"You did? Good for you!" He studied my face. "Wait a minute. *This* one?"

I nodded again. He laughed and turned away but

234

then suddenly turned back. "Wait a minute. How'd you find her? You didn't even know her name."

"Kismet."

"What?"

"Fate."

I didn't notice Katie when she came out of the rest room. I was facing the bar and looking at my reflection in the mirror, just like any other actor would've been doing. Then I saw her reflection. She was behind me, working her way through the tables. I turned and smiled at her. She didn't look at me at first. Then her eyes shifted and caught me. Her hand waved. I waved back. She came and sat on the stool. "Whaddaya say? Buy you a drink?"

I froze.

She laughed. She put her hand on my shoulder and looked toward the bartender. "Give him another! I'll have a Jack Daniel's, straight up!"

I didn't say a thing. I just wanted to see if she was really going to do it. Drink it. In front of me.

The bartender came over. He poured the two drinks. Wine for me, Jack Daniel's for her. I waited.

She didn't drink it. She left the glass sitting on the bar and opened her pocketbook.

She didn't take out pills. She took out money and spread it in front of her. She smiled at the bartender. He took it. Then she yawned. She covered her mouth to hide it. She shook her head several times very quickly. She still hadn't touched her glass. If she had, just then, I think I would've hit her five times as hard as I'd been ready to hit Jack Christolf.

"Listen, baby, remember that actor I was talking to you about?" She turned to face the tables. "You remember, right? You said you'd try to set up an interview with him for next week."

I stared at her. Her eyes were like fire. She went on. "Listen, baby, we're in luck. He's here tonight." Her eyes swept the room again.

I felt cold and shaky. I wasn't sure what to do. The wrong thing might only make it worse.

"He's here somewhere. Good chance for you to meet him." Her smile broadened. Her hand touched my arm just above the elbow. "You know the one I mean. Just did the part in the new Jim Cain film. Gotta meet him, baby." Then she leaned close. "Didn't wanna tell you, onna phone." She put a finger to her lips and dropped her voice to a whisper. "I got a print of the scene he did for Cain. Don't say anything, I'm not supposed to have it."

And she sat there, grinning at me.

I held my breath. "How'd you get it? The scene?"

"Doesn't matter how I got it. Point is, I got it." Her hand came up. Her fingers rubbed together, as if they were feeling dollar bills. Then her hand patted my arm. It moved down to my forearm. "And if I got it, that means you can see it. I can bring it over to your office tomorrow. Wanna do that?" Her hand traveled all the way down to my wrist and past it and then took my hand. Her fingers opened my hand gently. They snuggled into my palm. "You see the scene, you're gonna want him, baby. Give you my word on it."

My stomach began to flutter. "Which film was it you thought he'd be right for?"

"You remember. The Dunaway film." Her voice purred at me. She took my hand in both of hers and began to stroke it. "I'm telling you, baby, you take one look at that scene . . ."

Then she stiffened. Her head shook back and forth. Her voice exploded. "It's you! . . . My God, it's you! . . . I'm talking to you!"

She opened her mouth wide and laughed. "Jake! God, I must be stoned! I thought you were—"

I grabbed her arm suddenly and jerked her off the stool.

"Jake! What're you—"

"Shut up."

"What?"

"I said shut up!"

And before I knew what I'd done, I'd slapped her.

I looked around. People were staring at us. I grabbed her arm and dragged her toward the front door. I shoved the door open and yanked her through it. When she tried to get away, I slapped her again.

I threw her into the car. I took her pocketbook and tore it open. I found a clear plastic bottle with liquid inside. I twisted off the cap, smelled it and took a sip. It was Jack Daniel's. I threw the bottle across the parking lot.

I got in on my side and pushed the key in the ignition, but the engine wouldn't start. I hammered my hands against the steering wheel, then stepped down hard on the gas. This time the engine caught. I put the car into gear and swung out of the parking lot onto Santa Monica Boulevard.

I wanted to go fast but there were too many traffic lights. I found a freeway entrance and took it. When we reached the San Diego freeway, I switched to that one.

I went faster. I wanted to burn up the road. But finally the fast driving wasn't enough for me either. I pulled off the freeway. I found a dark street and followed it up a hill. When I reached the top, I hit the brakes. I pulled over to the side. I turned off the engine and pulled my keys out of the ignition turned to her and grabbed her and brought my hand back one more time.

This time I didn't do it. I let her go and turned away and pushed the door open and got out. I walked away from the car and went to the edge of the road. The city was below me. A gigantic pool of darkness dotted with a million spots of light. I wished I knew how to dive into the middle of it.

I went down to my knees. I buried my face in my hands and cried.

I heard the car door open behind me. I looked toward the sound. I'd turned off the car lights, so all I could see of the car was a big shadow in the road, and a much smaller shadow moving away from it. The smaller shadow came toward me.

"Jake—"

"You lied! Before we left the house I asked you if you'd taken any pills today! You said you hadn't! And you promised me you wouldn't have anything to drink!" I jumped to my feet and shook my fist at her. "But you lied! All you ever do is lie to me!"

"No! Jake, I didn't take any pills today! Not till—"

"You always lie to me! You don't care about me, about my career! I don't know what you've been doing!

But you haven't been doing it for me! You've been doing it for yourself!"

"What?" The shadow stopped moving.

"You started doing it before you ever knew me! You broke into my house that night, and you stole my pictures! You gave one of 'em to Paul to get me on the Cain movie! But you didn't even know me then! We'd hardly even talked!"

"But Jake—I love you!" Heavy breathing came toward me through the darkness. "All right. You're right about the picture. When I gave it to him. And maybe, maybe I didn't love you then, but I love you now. I do, Jake! I do!" Her voice broke. "And you're right. About the pills. I took two, this afternoon. I was nervous. I needed them. We were going out to dinner. I had to take a diet pill or I'd—"

"Don't blame it on going out to dinner! If I'd known you'd taken a pill today—"

I took a step toward her. Both my hands were still in fists. I was trembling. "You were supposed to be cutting down since you started seeing Dr. Samuels! You haven't! You've been taking the same amount, you've just been doing it behind my back! Dr. Samuels hasn't helped you at all!"

Then I realized. She was quiet now. Very quiet. And I understood what it had to mean. My heart seemed to stop.

"You haven't been seeing Dr. Samuels at all. Have you?"

She didn't answer.

There was a large patch of dirt at the side of the road where cars could make their turn. I went slowly across it and toward the edge of the hill. It was a gradual decline that sloped away and fell gently into darkness. It looked like a nice, soft fall. You'd probably find yourself rolling across sharp rocks and fallen trees and God knows what else down there, but whatever was along the slope was hidden by blackness now. It looked nice and gentle.

I stepped closer to the edge.

"I went to see Dr. Samuels, Jake, I made that appointment. I went to his office. I just couldn't go in. I told you what happened to me in New York. With that other one. I'm scared of them. All of them."

I heard her moving somewhere behind me but not coming closer. I kept staring down the hill.

"I lie, Jake, I know I lie. But what difference did it ever make? Nobody ever believed me when I told the truth. So I lied. It always seemed to get me further."

Her voice came from quite a distance now. She'd moved farther away than I'd thought. I turned to see where she was. "I know you lie! Katie. . . . How do I know if you ever *don't* lie?"

I saw movement, far away. Thirty feet. Maybe forty. The darkness and the wine and my anger and fear confused my sense of distance. But I could tell she was moving. Walking back and forth, somewhere back there.

Then I lost her completely. I couldn't even make out her silhouette.

I searched my pockets. I found a loose cigarette. It was pretty well bent out of shape. I didn't care. I just wanted an excuse to light a match. I stuck the cigarette in my mouth and opened a matchbook. I pulled out two matches and struck them together so they'd make a bigger flame. It showed me where she was. Across the road and only about twenty feet down.

She didn't react to the flame. She was looking into the distance, as if there was something there to look at. I kept the matches going as long as possible, then shook them out. When it was completely dark I said, "How do I know any of that about New York is really true?"

She didn't answer. Maybe she hadn't heard me.

"Katie? New York. The psychiatrist. How long ago? What year? Give me the year."

". . . I don't know. . . . Nineteen seventy-four. . . . Summer . . ."

I gave her another question fast. "The clinic. What was the address of the clinic?"

". . . I don't remember the address."

God. It was a lie. Another one.

I wanted to run down there and grab her and shake her—

"Somewhere on West Thirteenth Street. It was part of Saint Vincent's Hospital."

I tried to remember. What street was Saint Vincent's Hospital on?

I tried another question. "What about your mother, dying in a car accident? Was that true?"

". . . No. . . . No. She didn't die." She was pacing again. "There wasn't any accident. She ran off. Left us. Me. My father. My . . . brother."

She paused. Then she spoke quickly. "I was three. He was only two. My brother. My father had to bring us up. But he was always working, my father. In construction. His hours were very long. He was hardly ever there. There were always other people. Women. . . . He always had a woman, but he never had one for very long. He always got tired of them. Or they got tired of us. My brother and me. So they left him, my father. Like my mother had. And my father, he always blamed us for it." She stopped again. Her breathing, heavy and quick, filled the darkness. "Except . . . he never blamed my brother. He always blamed me."

I'd gone into the road. I could almost make her out now. She was farther down the hill, at the side of the road.

"When I got older, I could've taken care of them. Both him and my brother. But they never let me. Everything I did for them was wrong. They didn't like the way I cooked, they didn't like the way I kept the house, nothing I ever did for them was right . . . I wasn't any good in school, either. Or I wasn't good enough. Even when my teachers said I was doing all right, it wasn't good enough for my father." Her voice grew louder. "See, Jake, I understood! When you told me about your father! It was the same with me! The same!

"But with my father, he used to hit me. So . . . I didn't care anymore. What my grades were. No matter what they were, he was going to hit me anyway." Her voice began to choke. "Jim. My brother. He got good grades. But even when he didn't, it didn't matter, he never got hit. He was always so sure of himself, my brother. Because my father always complimented him. Told him how good he was. With Jim . . . nobody ever told him he ever did anything wrong. But he told me what *I* was doing wrong. He used to put me down as much as my father did. And when I told him to stop it, he . . . he hit me,

240

Jake. He hit me, the same way my father hit me. And my father . . . knew it. And he never made Jim stop. And I . . . I wasn't strong enough. To make him stop."

She stopped then and was quiet. I thought she was finished. But then she started again, and her voice was sharper. "They never believed a thing I told them. Neither of them."

I waited for her to start again. But she didn't.

"Katie? Never believed you about what?"

"About anything! They never believed anything I told them! They always said I was no good, I was rotten, I was lying! Just making things up! They always had to ask someone else! They never believed a single thing I told them unless someone else said it was true!" Her voice came closer. "Why did they hate me, Jake? I didn't make her leave! I needed her! She left me, too, didn't she?"

She stopped again. Her voice lowered. "I was too young, I didn't know what to do. How to take her place." She sighed. "They didn't love me. Of course not. Why should they? I didn't know how to do anything for them. I couldn't. . . . God, I'm tired. . . . Jake? I feel so tired. Why do I always. . . ."

"Katie? Are you all—"

"When I got old enough, I ran away. So now I never have to see them again, do I? And they don't have to see me. Ever." Then she gasped. "God! If I ever see either of them again, I'll kill them! I will!"

It was quiet again. It stayed that way. I thought I heard her moving. I couldn't tell for sure. I knew it wasn't the time for it, but maybe there never would be a time. I had to ask.

"Katie? *Did* you ever kill anyone?"

I got no answer.

I waited. I called her name gently. Nothing. Finally I walked down the hill to where I thought she was. I took the matches from my pocket and lit one.

There she was, ten feet away, sprawled helplessly at the side of the road.

I parked my car in front of the house. I got her in my arms and carried her inside, took her to the bedroom and put her on the bed. I fixed the pillow under her head but decided not to put her under the covers. The movement might wake her. I got a blanket from the closet and draped it over her. I sat in the chair and stayed quiet.

She rolled to her side. Rolled back. Sat up with a jerk. She looked around quickly and saw me in the chair.

"Jake?" She looked around again as if she were lost. "We weren't here, were we?"

"No. We were. . . . You were tired. You fell asleep. I brought you home."

"Oh." She turned so she was sitting on the edge of the bed. "We were talking. I was telling you . . . about something . . ."

I rubbed my hands slowly along the sides of the chair.

"What was I telling you, Jake?"

I said nothing.

She rose slowly and came across the floor. "Are you mad at me, Jake?"

"What? . . . No."

"Good." She smiled. "Make love to me."

I didn't move.

"Jake? Is something wrong?"

". . . No."

"Make love to me, Jake. Please. Show me you're not mad at me."

"I'm not mad at you." I squirmed slightly in the chair. "It's late, Katie. We're both tired."

She stopped. Her head nodded up and down. "I see. You don't want to." She nodded again quickly and turned away. "I'm tired, too. But I can't sleep."

"Where are you going?"

". . . Nowhere." She kept moving. "There's nowhere to go. There never is."

I got out of my chair. I was in front of her before she could reach the door. "No, Katie, no pills. Not tonight."

"What?" She stopped and looked into my face with a blank stare. "What did I *tell* you?"

I put my hands gently on her arms. "You just told me about your family. Your father and your brother. And your mother." I tried to turn her toward the bed.

"No! I don't have any family! I never did!"

Her hands gripped my shirt. Her fingers dug into me. I got my hands on her wrists and pulled her off, then one of her hands ripped free and slapped me. Her fingernails scratched across my left cheek.

"It's none of your business! It's my family, not yours! I don't have any family!"

I grabbed her hand before she could scratch me again, then she tried to slap me with her other hand. I twisted her so her back was against my chest. Her feet kicked at me, but she wasn't wearing shoes and it had no effect. I got my arms around her and pulled her to the bed. I forced her down across it. There were tears in my eyes. "Please, Katie! Please! Stop it! Be quiet! Just be—"

I didn't have to finish the sentence. She'd already passed out.

I went out to the kitchen and smoked a cigarette. I came back to the bedroom and sat in the chair. I watched her for a while, but I didn't feel comfortable. I went into the living room and sat on the sofa. I lit another cigarette.

It was the cigarette that woke me. I'd fallen asleep with it still in my hand. The ash had gotten long and fallen off. It had landed on my leg and burned me. I slapped at my leg. I found the cigarette on the floor and stamped it out. Then I realized I wasn't alone.

I heard her fingers snapping only a few feet away. The darkness magnified it. Made it sound like small explosions going off.

Then I heard feet slapping against the floor. She went into the bedroom, but suddenly she was back. She was standing in the dark snapping her fingers again.

She went away, this time to the kitchen. I wasn't worried yet. The Jack Daniel's was here in the living room. I heard the refrigerator open, then shut. She'd be taking out the milk.

I tried to settle down. I looked around in the darkness and found my cigarettes on the table. I took one from the pack. I heard her open a kitchen cupboard. That would be for the chocolate-chip cookies.

I took out my matches and lit one. Raised it. Then blew it out. I kept the unlit cigarette in my fingers and played with it nervously.

Several minutes passed.

Then she was in the archway, snapping her fingers again. I could see her only in outline. I put the cigarette in my shirtpocket and got ready. She'd be coming for the Jack Daniel's now.

I moved slowly between her and the bookcase. I kept my hands at my sides. She came forward two steps and stopped. It was silent, then her voice broke it viciously.

"You don't want to make love to me! You don't love me!"

Suddenly her right hand flew up. It was holding something. She had a pot from the kitchen.

I tried to move out of her reach, but it was too late. Her hand swung down toward my arm. I felt sudden pain. I grunted. Reached for my arm. Hunched my shoulders together as if that could make it hurt less.

"I hate you! You're no different than any other man!"

Her hand swung the pot again. I tried to block it with the flat of my left hand. My hand burned, then there was no feeling there at all.

"You bastard! Without me you're nothing! You better remember that!"

Before I could move, she was swinging again. The pot caught me on the side of my head.

I stumbled. Fell. Tried to get to my hands and knees. My left hand had no strength. I felt dizzy. Weak. I pushed against the floor with my right hand and got to one knee. She hit me across the back. I lost my balance and rolled to my side. Suddenly she was on me.

"You don't believe me! You don't love me! I'll kill you!"

I knew she would, but I couldn't stop her. My head was spinning. Her fingers were ripping open my shirt. I reached up toward her, I was gasping for air, my hand felt her face, I tried to push it away.

"No! Don't do that!"

She bit down on my fingers.

I was barely conscious. She was straddling me now. Her movements were savage. For a second I saw her eyes—they were hungry and desperate. Then I felt her hands on the sides of my face. Her fingers dug into my cheeks, her lips were against my mouth, she was making sounds like a frightened animal. Her tongue came out and pushed its way into my mouth. I couldn't stop anything she was doing. My face felt wet, and for a second I was scared it was blood, then I realized it was tears. Her tears. She was crying. But still kissing me.

Then I passed out.

I don't know how long it was before I opened my eyes. I saw a light. One of the table lamps. It was lying on the floor. She was standing over it, and her hand reached down slowly. She picked the lamp up and set it on the table, but I could see it was too near to the edge. I tried to say something, but my voice wasn't there. Her hand went away and the lamped tipped and fell. This time it broke. The light bulb exploded. It made a sound like a gunshot, then everything was black. She gasped and moved and something else fell against the floor. She stood still, then moved again. She went to the bookcase where the liquor bottles were. I could see her silhouette against the window. She was drinking straight from the bottle. I closed my eyes again.

"Jake! Jake!"

A hand slapped my face. I opened my eyes.

"Oh God, Jake! Don't be dead! Please!"

She slapped me again. I tried to speak. All that came out were vague sounds that had nothing to do with words.

"Jake?" Her hands shook my shoulders.

"Katie..."

She froze. "Jake? Are you all right?"

I groaned. I felt pain in my arm and the side of my head.

"Oh Jake! Oh God! I thought you were dead!" She sat on the floor and put my head in her lap.

Her breathing finally slowed. She began to rub my forehead. She rubbed too vigorously and I tried to stop her.

"No, it's all right, Jake. Everything's all right. I'll help you, Jake. I will. Like I did in the parking lot when the kids had you." She stopped. "The kids...."

She was quiet.

After a minute I tried to sit up, but when I did she

forced me down again. Her hand rubbed my forehead. "Bob and me. We went to a party. And when we came home, there were some kids. They were across the street from our apartment house. They were following an old lady. I stayed in the shadows, but I had to do something. Before they . . ." She paused. "It was so dark, they couldn't tell what I was holding. It scared them. They ran away."

She shifted slightly and moved closer against me. Her fingers dug into my chest. "It got me excited. Nervous. I couldn't settle down. When we got upstairs I took some pills, but I must've taken too many. When I woke up, I was lying on the floor in the bathroom. I'd been there all night. It was almost morning." She pulled me up so my head was against her breast. I could feel her heart pounding. "I went into the living room and Bob was there. On the couch. He was lying across it. I tried to talk to him, but he didn't answer me. I thought he was asleep and I tried to wake him up, but I couldn't." Her breathing got fast and rhythmic. "The kids did it! It *must've* been the kids! They found out which apartment I was in! They came after me! But they didn't find me! I was asleep in the bathroom! They found Bob, and they . . ." She took a deep breath. "Yes. *They* killed him. It *must've* been them."

She began to shake. Her voice quivered horribly. "I was alone again! I was scared! What if they were still looking for me? What if they found me? I had to get away from Phoenix and . . ." She took another deep breath and held it. "I had to make sure they couldn't find me. Because if they did. . . . I was alone. You're helpless, when you're alone."

She looked down at me. "You don't have to worry about that, Jake. You'll never be alone. I'll never leave you."

She kissed my forehead.

When it started to get light, she got to her feet. She went across the living room and down the hall to the bedroom. When she came out, she was dressed. She walked past the arch toward the kitchen. She didn't look at me once.

I heard her moving in the kitchen. I smelled eggs cooking. Coffee. I felt a little stronger and sat with my back against the sofa and looked at my left hand. The whole side of it was black and blue. I touched my face and expected to feel dried blood, but couldn't locate any scabs. I got my shirt all the way off and looked at my arm. A dark bruise ran from my shoulder to my elbow.

Then I heard her moving again. She went past the arch without looking at me. The front door opened and closed, she was outside in the yard, then her car door opened and closed. The engine started.

Then she was gone. Thank God, she was gone.

When I got to the bathroom, I looked at my face in the mirror. It was pretty bad, especially the scratches on my cheek. I ran the water till it was warm. I held a washcloth under it, then touched it gently against my face. I dried my face with a towel. I stood still a moment, then went into the bedroom and lay down on the bed. I tried to fall asleep.

The phone rang and woke me up. I stumbled to the living room and grabbed it.

". . . Hello?"

"Hi, baby! Guess what!"

"Hello, Ruth. . . . What is it?" I sat on the floor and leaned my back against the wall.

"Ford's looking for a new spokesman for a whole set of commercials they're doing for the fall. They want to use a new face. Someone nobody knows. I took your Ajax commercial over to 'em yesterday and they liked it. And they said if that's the only one you'll have going, they want to meet you. How's that sound?"

I didn't answer. I felt my neck gently.

"I set it up for this afternoon, Jake! Three o'clock!"

I thought of the way my face looked. "No, Ruth. Not today."

"What?"

". . . I can't see 'em today. I can't see 'em for a couple days."

"What?" She hesitated. "What's the matter, Jake? You sound funny."

"Nothing's the matter. It's just, I cut myself shaving. Real bad. I need a couple of days for it to heal. Can you tell 'em I'm out of town, I'll be back next week?"

"Jake.... Sure. Okay. If that's what you want."
"Please."
"Jake? Are you okay?"
"... I'm okay." I hung up the phone.

I fell asleep sitting there with my back against the wall. Then the phone rang again.

"Hello?"

"Hello, Jake! Wonderful day out! Just wanted to make sure you were up!"

God, even the sound of her voice scared me.

"Would've woken you when I left, but I thought I might as well let you sleep! You didn't have anything scheduled this morning! Oh God, Jake, I've been seeing people today! Lots and lots of people! Got to go now! Just wanted to be sure you were up! Been any calls?"

"No. Nothing." I felt my throat carefully with my fingertips. I wasn't really thinking. "Just Ruth. She got me an interview for some Ford commercials. That's all."

There was a long pause. "What did you say? Commercials?"

"Yeah." I closed my eyes.

There was another long pause. "I'll talk to you later, Jake."

The next phone call was from Ruth.

"Jake? What's going on? She just called me. She said to cancel the interview with Ford."

"What?"

"She said she's got an agreement with you. She said you can't take any work unless she okays it, and she said she doesn't want you doing any more commercials. Just movies and TV."

I jumped to my feet. "She said what?"

"She said I shouldn't set up any interviews for you unless I set it up through her first. Jake, she said you won't go out for anything from now on unless she agrees to it." Ruth paused quickly as if she were trying to catch her breath. "Jake? Is it true? Does she have an agreement with you? She said you'd signed something. Did you?"

I spread the contract on the table in front of me and stared at it for fifteen minutes. Then I called Ruth back. When I read it to her, she said what I already knew.

"You were an idiot to sign that thing!"

"I know." I felt sick to my stomach.

"It's not that the Ford thing's a commercial! It's that *I* got it for you! Not *her!*"

"I know."

"Jake? Don't you understand? She's going to ruin you in the business!"

"I know. I know."

"What're you going to do?"

"Break the contract."

"You can't break it!"

"I'll find a way!" I slammed my hand against the table.

She could slap me, she could hit me, she could try to break my arm. But she couldn't do this. Not to my career. I couldn't let her get away with that.

I was an actor. Whatever else I was, I was an actor. I had to protect that.

I went into the bedroom and started going through her things. There wasn't much. All she'd brought into the house had been two suitcases, three armfuls of clothes, a bottle of Jack Daniel's and her pills.

And the gun.

The gun. It had come from some place. It had been used for something. Her husband?

There was nothing in her clothes. Nothing in her drawers. Her suitcases weren't locked. When I opened them, they were empty.

But then I checked the ribbing on the insides and found old identification cards. The first one said *Kate Hanley, 16 East 4th Street, New York, New York*. The second one said *Kate Hanley, 304 Harvard Street, Denver Colorado*. The third one said *Katie Linowes 1214 Jackson Street, Phoenix, Arizona.*

And then I remembered that other address. *505 Federal Avenue.*

I'd gone there once before. This time I had more luck. I rang the bell next to the door that said MANAGER, and a thin scrawny woman opened up. She looked at me like I was the wild man of Borneo. I'd put on make-up to hide the bruises, but it hadn't hidden them very well. The thin woman scowled at me. "No apartments. Maybe next month."

I fought to control my voice. "I'm looking for someone who used to live here. A girl. Katie O'Hanlon."

She looked like it meant nothing to her. She still didn't like my looks. She cleared her throat loudly several times without bothering to cover her mouth. "Don't know where you'd find her. She moved out."

She started to shut the door.

I put my hand up suddenly to stop her. It was my left hand, and when it touched the door it ached. "No. It's something else. I'm just trying to find someone who knew her. Did you know her?"

Her eyes turned sour as lemons. "I'm paid to collect the rent. I'm not paid to know people."

I put my good hand against the door and held it open. "She had a roommate. The roommate got married. You got a forwarding address on the roommate?"

The woman gave me another one of her priceless looks. Then she stared disgustedly at my hand on her door.

I removed my hand. She shook her head and cleared her throat again. She stepped forward and pointed up some stairs. "She lived up there. Apartment One-K. It's a studio apartment. She lived alone."

It didn't surprise me. Not a bit.

When I turned, the woman had moved back and was already in her doorway.

"You got an address on where Katie O'Hanlon lived before she moved here?"

The woman put her hand against her forehead. Ran her fingers up through her hair. Then her eyes half closed. "Look. I'm a busy woman. This is a clean place. I keep it that way. I expect people who live here to keep their apartments that way. Most of 'em do. That's all I care about. That and the rent. I want the rent, I want it on time. I want all of it. Long's I get that, and nobody

251

makes too much noise at night, I don't care where they come from or where they go to. Understand?"

I started to say something but then bit it back. I turned and started down the walk. If she'd ever known where Katie had come from, she wasn't going to give that information to me. And she probably didn't know even as much as I did. Phoenix. Denver. New York.

"You can stop coming here and bothering me. I told the other guy. I don't know where she is now, so just leave me alone."

I turned fast. Not fast enough. Her door was already closed. I ran to it and rang the bell and began pounding with my fist.

She opened up. "What is it?"

"The other guy! Who was he?"

Her eyes narrowed. "I don't know. Police or something. Aren't you?"

"I've got to find him! Did he leave a card? Did he leave a number?"

"No." She tried to shut the door.

I kicked the door open. "When was he here?"

She stepped back.

"Tell me! When?"

". . . A long time ago."

"What do you mean? Days ago? Weeks ago?"

". . . Yeah. I guess so."

"He hasn't been back?" I stepped into the apartment. "You haven't heard from him again?"

"No!" She put her hand up and kept moving away from me in fear. "No, I haven't heard from him!"

I stopped. I looked at my hands. They were at chest level. They were in fists.

Phoenix. Denver. New York. That was all I had. There had to be something. Somewhere. But where?

Then I drove by a pay phone. No matter what condition an actor is in, no matter how much of his world is falling apart, if he's passing a pay phone and he's still sane and breathing, he calls his service. I did, and there was on message. Call Ruth. Important.

I dialed and it rang and got picked up before it could ring again.

"Hi, baby."

252

"It's me, Ruth, Jake. What'd you—"

"Hold it." She was quiet. "Can't talk right now. Caught me at a bad time. Maybe I could meet you. Pick a place."

". . . Tulley's?"

"Meet you there in an hour."

She hung up.

Something was wrong. I'd never heard her sound quite like that before.

Tulley's was empty. I sat in a booth all the way in the back. Tulley came over to make small talk. He asked me if I wanted a drink. I said I didn't. He offered me a drink on the house. I thanked him but turned it down. He stood there and finally asked me if I was okay. Had I been in a fight, or had I gotten myself a seven-hundred-pound bear for a pet?

I told him he'd gotten it on the second guess. I'd gotten myself a seven-hundred-pound bear for a pet.

He got the message. He nodded and left me alone.

Half an hour later Ruth came in. She looked nervous. She walked across the bar and sat down next to me. Then she saw the way my face looked. "My God, Jake! What'd she do to you?"

". . . I'm all right."

"Jake!" Her eyes filled with tears. "Jake. . . ."

She was in worse shape than I was. I put my arm around her and held her as she cried.

Tulley came over to see what the matter was. I waved him away. So did Ruth. I gave her my handkerchief, and she mopped her face. She sat up straight. I kept my arm around her and she nodded several times.

"Reason I couldn't talk to you on the phone, she was there. In the office." Ruth began to choke. Her shoulders shook.

"It's all right, Ruth. It's all right."

Her eyes were haunted. They looked at me for barely a second and then looked away. "She came barging in, Jake. Said she had to see me. Something important. She . . . she told me, she hadn't liked the way you looked this morning. Now I see you, I can understand what it was she didn't like."

A tear ran down Ruth's cheek. She brushed it off with the back of her hand. "She said you looked depressed. Said you're on the verge. You can hit, now. All you needed was a break. One good break. The right kind. Not a commercial."

I studied the tabletop and remained quiet.

"She said maybe if she and I put our heads together, we could get the one good break for you. I said, all right, maybe we could. What did she have in mind?" Ruth's voice broke. "She looked spooky, Jake! I was scared of her!"

"I know. I know." I held her closer.

Ruth's head nodded several times. Then she went on. "She took a copy of *Brownsville Station* out of her pocketbook. She said it would make a pretty good movie. I said I thought so, too. She said she'd heard Jack Christolf was going to make it. I told her she was right. She said you'd be perfect for the younger brother." Ruth paused half a second. "I said yes, you were right for it, but it wouldn't make any difference. Christolf is out to get a name for that part. He can't get a name, he'll have to settle for an unknown. But the last thing in the world he's going to do is use some unknown who's good enough to turn in the kind of performance you could turn in."

Ruth's mouth tightened. She rested her head against my shoulder and kept her eyes down. "No newcomer's ever going to get himself discovered in one of Jack's movies. That happens, it won't be one of Jack's movies anymore. It'll be the movie in which so-and-so got discovered." She laughed bitterly. Her hand touched my chest. "God, Jake, it's such a rotten business. Always has been. Always will be. I tried submitting you, week and a half ago. Jack's such a sweetheart. He had some teenage hooker he's currently using as a production assistant call me up. She could hardly speak English. She told me they were terribly sorry, but they weren't interested in anyone who didn't have a very good track record. Took me five minutes to get that much out of her." Ruth moved tighter against me. "Sounded higher than a kite. Nice way to put a movie together, huh? Using kids who don't know a damn thing except how to shoot something, or smoke something, or lie on their backs with their legs open."

Ruth began to cry again. I held her and waited. She breathed in sharply. "I called Jack directly. His private line. I gave him the pitch on you. He thought about it a minute, then he figured out who you were. He told me to go to hell."

I nodded. Then I shut my eyes.

"I told her the whole thing, Jake. She said it didn't matter. She said he'd have to give you a chance. At least let you read for it. She said it was important to you. Driving you crazy. All you could think about."

"I hadn't been thinking about it at all. She brought it up. Yesterday. And when she did, I told her to forget about it."

"She said I better help her do something. I said there was nothing I could do. She said what if we slid some money under the table. Maybe that would have some influence with Jack. I told her, aside from it being a rotten idea, it wouldn't work. Jack already owns the table and anything anyone could find to slide under it. And you can't count on any good will, 'cause he hasn't got any."

Her whole body stiffened. I looked at her now, but she was only staring at the other side of the booth.

Something occurred to me. "You said she was in your office when I called."

"Yeah."

"But you left a message on my service, to call you. An hour before that. You said it was important."

Ruth nodded. She brought her hands together on the table, intertwined her fingers, and stared at them. "You didn't get the contracts on the James Montgomery picture yet, did you?"

"Should be in the mail."

"No." Her eyes widened slightly. "They didn't have Montgomery. They just thought they did. Turns out he's signed to do something else. They've postponed the picture again, but between you and me, it's as good as canceled."

That made it perfect. Absolutely perfect.

Ruth's hands flew apart. One of them slapped the table. "I sent a messenger down there a couple of days ago for Tim Garrison's contract! I made sure everything was signed and filed with SAG so we'd be covered in case it fell through again! I should've done it for you! Least you'd get some money out of it!"

Her hand came down hard on the table once more.

I looked across the bar at Tulley. He was wiping the bar mirror. He used long, even strokes. Getting it as clean and shiny as possible.

Katie wiped everything that way. Till it was spotless. And shiny. Like it was a compulsion with her.

Everything was a compulsion with her. To clean a glass. To drink milk. To drink Jack Daniels. To lose weight.

To push me. Till I made it.

To control me. So I made it her way.

And only her way.

And her way was no good.

Ruth moved tight against me again. "When I told her it was no use going to see Jack, she got pretty excited. She started yelling and she threw some things. A couple of manuscripts I had on my desk. She knocked a chair over, and then she came around the desk at me. I thought she was going to do something to me, Jake. I screamed, and Donna came in, and Mel, and Bob, from down the hall. When she saw them, she grabbed her pocketbook and ran out, but if they hadn't come in just then, I don't know what she would've done. Her eyes, Jake. The look in her eyes."

Ruth began to cry again. It took me a long time to get her quiet. Tulley started over, but he'd been in business long enough to know not to butt his nose in when people didn't want him to. He went all the way to the front. He stood by the door and looked through the window at the street.

I stroked Ruth's forehead gently. I kept my voice low. "I know something about her. I just don't know what it is I know. She tells me things, but sometimes they're all mixed up. She does things, she doesn't remember she's done 'em. Or exactly what it was, that happened."

"I know. . . . You told me. . . ."

I looked at Tulley again. He still had his back to us.

"She told me about someone. Someone who's dead now."

"What? Who?"

"Her husband. She said someone killed him. A bunch of kids. She *thinks* it was the kids."

Ruth looked up. "You think *she* killed him?"

"I don't know. She had a gun one night. I took it away from her. I hid it. But she didn't know where she'd gotten it. This morning I went to the place where she used to live. I was trying to see if there was anyone there who knew anything about her. I couldn't find anyone, just the manager. But I found out there's been someone looking for her. Trying to find out where she's living now. Someone from the police."

Ruth's eyes opened wider.

Tulley turned away from the front door and started back toward the bar. As he swung around, his eyes caught us for a second. He was looking at me. From the look on his face I knew what I must look like.

I sat at the table in the kitchen. I wasn't smoking. Wasn't drinking coffee. My stomach couldn't have taken it. It was way after five. If only she'd get there.

Then I heard her car. I put my hands in my lap and sat quietly. I had to pull it off.

She came into the kitchen and stopped when she saw me. I thought it must be the way I looked, the scratches and bruises, but it wasn't that. She went quickly past me, across to the back door. She put her shoulder against it and kept her face turned away. "The movie's been canceled."

I said nothing.

"Didn't you hear me? The movie's been canceled! The Montgomery movie! I should've gone over there and gotten the contract myself! Why did I wait for them to mail it again? I was stupid! So stupid!" Her right hand beat against the counter. As she turned, I saw tears running down her cheeks. "I should've made sure you had it this time, then they'd have to pay you! Now they don't have to pay you anything! I was so stupid!"

She huddled against the counter. A few days before, I would've put my arms around her, but not today. I sat stiffly in my chair. I didn't know how much longer I could last. I only needed another minute.

Then I heard Ruth's car. A moment later there was a pounding on the front door. I was already out of my chair and going toward it. Katie was right behind me. I made sure I didn't look at her.

I pulled open the door and Ruth looked at me. She kept her eyes off Katie too.

"Jake! Did you hear about Bill Starrett?"

"No." I kept my face blank. "What about him?"

"He was in a car accident! Up in San Francisco!"

"What? Oh my God!" I took a step back. I waited a beat. "How bad?"

"I talked to his wife, they don't know if he'll make it or not!"

Ruth was too nervous and too scared to say it convincingly so I cut in on her fast to keep it going. "I got to go up there!" I took a step forward, then stopped. I looked toward the bedroom. I kept my eyes off Katie. "I better pack a suitcase!"

I ran to the bedroom and pulled out my suitcase and began to throw stuff into it like I wasn't thinking straight. I heard two sets of steps behind me.

"I called the airline, Jake, there's a flight at four-forty. I can drive you to the airport."

"Good, Ruth! I'll be ready in a minute!"

Then Katie spoke. "No. I'll drive you."

She insisted on coming into the airport with me, so I had to buy a ticket for San Francisco. I figured if I could get rid of her quick enough I might have time to exchange the ticket, but she wouldn't leave. She held tightly to my arm like she'd never let me go and told me not to worry about losing the Montgomery picture. She had lots of other ideas. She'd tell me about them as soon as I got back.

She kept on talking. When they were boarding, she put both arms around me and looked into my eyes. "It's Friday, Jake. We don't have anything set up for you for Monday or Tuesday. Maybe you should stay up there a couple days. You've been on edge, the change might be good for you."

I was surprised. It was what I'd wanted to say to her, but I'd thought I'd better not.

"Call me when you get back. I'll come pick you up."

She kissed me. Hard.

When I went through the gate, I turned for one final look at her. Suddenly I felt sick. I hated her now, but not for anything I'd seen about her. It was what she'd shown me about myself. I was ambitious. Determined. I wasn't going to let anyone get in the way of my career.

I was an actor. No different than any other actor.

When I got to San Francisco, I bought a ticket on the next flight to Phoenix. I got to Phoenix at eleven. I rented a car and drove to a motel. I checked in and tried to sleep, but I couldn't. When the coffee shop opened at seven, I was there. I ate breakfast quickly and then sat there, staring at my second cup of coffee. Suddenly I was in no hurry at all. I wanted to stay sitting at that table all day.

But at seven forty-five I paid my bill. I went outside and got into my car.

It was a good-sized apartment house. I stood in the parking lot and looked across the street. Private houses over there. Lots of trees. A few street lights. Not enough to light the street too well at night. Just the right spot for a bunch of kids to go after an old lady. The parking lot would be just the right spot to see it from. If it had really happened.

I was walking toward the entrance when a man in a light gray uniform came around a corner. He was pulling a garden hose out behind him. He turned for a second and gave me a disinterested look. The red stitching over his shirt pocket said *Manager*.

I curled my upper lip against my teeth and went over to him. "Morning."

He grunted. He gave me a look. His look let me know that my bruises still showed. His arm swung in a big arc and snaked the garden hose out across the grass.

"Sorry to bother you."

"Ain't bothering me yet."

"I'm trying to find a woman I used to know. A couple of years ago, in New York. I think she lives here now."

He grunted again. He was pretty good at it.

"Her name was Kate Hanley. Heard she got married out here. Some guy named Linowes?"

He kept his eyes on the hose. "Katie don't live here anymore. Don't know where she's gone off to."

I started to open my mouth. He turned his wrist and looked at his watch. "Still early. If you want to talk to her husband, try his apartment. Six-C."

He aimed the hose across the grass and shot water at some bushes.

I got out of the elevator on the sixth floor and walked slowly down the corridor. I found the door that said Six-C. The name plate that said Linowes. I thought about turning around. Walking back down the corridor, pushing the button for the elevator, going down to the lobby, getting into my car, driving out to the airport. Because he wasn't dead. She hadn't killed him. There was nothing to be found out here.

Except one thing.

I took a long breath, put my finger on the buzzer and pushed hard. I heard the buzz inside. I waited. Listened for sounds on the other side of the door. Maybe he wasn't there. Maybe I hoped that he wasn't. Because if he was there, what kind of man would he be, the man she had married? And what would that tell me about me?

I was about to ring a second time when a voice said, "What is it?" with enough force to knock the door off its hinges. The voice had come from deep inside the apartment. When I couldn't answer quick enough, it came at me again. "Who's there?"

It was closer and louder now. It was still ringing in the air when a lock turned and the door opened.

I couldn't believe it. Antonio Calisi couldn't have improved on him if he'd had all day. He was tall. Six and a half feet at least. Well built. People that height always seem well built. He had sandy hair and light blue eyes, a firm jaw, well-tanned skin. He would've been unbelievable on film. He would've made it big in the business, guys like him always make it big. It hardly even matters if they have any acting ability or not. He had that tough, indomitable look that never goes out of fashion. He's called Wayne, or Mitchum, or Hudson or Lancaster, Eastwood or Bronson, Reynolds or Stallone. When the story is over, he's the one we've been cheering for. He's the one who's come through. We run to every picture he makes because he makes us feel all the things we want to feel. And this was Bob Linowes.

If I'd been born to look like him, I wouldn't have been a struggling two-bit actor living in a ramshackle house hidden away in one of the cheapest canyons Los Angeles had to offer. I would've been sitting by a pool outside a mansion in the hills of Beverly, spending half my time sifting through film scripts and the other half talking to tax accountants.

God, what kind of world did a guy like that live in? A world where you never had to be scared or shy about anything. You were never unsure of yourself. You never worried about whether they liked you or not. They liked you from the first second they saw you. You were so gorgeous, you never even had to be self-conscious about how gorgeous you were. You stood there strong and silent, like he was standing there now, and you knew there was absolutely nothing wrong with you.

You had the greatest thing in the world. Confidence.

His voice boomed at me again. "What do you want?"

". . . I'm looking for Mr. Linowes." It came out so weak it seemed to limp through the air on crutches.

"Bob Linowes. You got him." He smiled. It wasn't the studied and calculating killer smile Alan used all the time. It was open and honest. Enough to melt the heart of an undertaker.

". . . I'm trying to locate a girl I used to know. . . . Her name was Kate Hanley then. I heard—"

"Katie? When'd you know her?"

". . . Three . . . four years ago."

"Yeah? Where was that?"

"New York." I put my hands in my pockets, and tried to stop my feet from taking me down the hall. "She moved. I lost track of her. Someone told me they'd heard she was living out here now. I was passing through, I—"

"Come on inside!"

He stepped back and pushed the door farther open. He brought his hands toward me as gently as a lover.

Bob Linowes led me into the living room and gestured toward the sofa. He sat in the chair opposite me. He was still dazzling. His eyes were as clear as a summer sky. He rubbed a hand against his cheek and smiled again. "Who told you she was living in Phoenix?"

"Friend of hers . . . girlfriend . . . in New York."

"You heard we got married?"

"Yeah." I turned my eyes away. "Just thought I'd stop by. To say hello. Since I was in town."

"Yeah. Sure." His hand moved to his neck and massaged it firmly.

Suddenly he stood up. "Wait a minute, I'll be right back."

He went out through a door.

His voice. It was wonderful. Actors took years of voice lessons to develop a voice like that.

But there was something wrong. I knew Katie wasn't here. And he was acting like she was.

I looked around the living room. Maybe I'd see some sign of her that she'd left behind. If there was one, I didn't see it. I could've been sitting in any living room in any apartment in the world.

And then I realized that if you looked at my living room, you wouldn't see much of her either. The only place you'd see her was in the bruises on my face and across my hand.

Several minutes passed. He didn't come back. I found myself sitting on the edge of the sofa as stiff as a board. I closed my hands in fists and clenched them hard. I held them like that a moment, then opened my fingers slowly. It was an old relaxation exercise. One of the things actors sometimes use before they start a scene. Something to drain the tension and nervousness out of you. As much of it as will let itself drain.

He still didn't come back. I did the exercise again. I held it longer this time. I was just relaxing my fingers when the door swung open and he came in with coffee cups in both hands. He had them by their saucers. They looked like dollhouse toys in his oversized hands. He set them down on the coffee table and nudged one in my direction. He sat in the chair opposite me and waited for me to say something. I took a sip of coffee, then put the cup down. I was about to open my mouth when he leaned forward.

"How well did you know Katie?"

"Pretty well. . . . Off and on."

He smiled and looked down at his coffee cup. His hands covered his knees as he leaned forward again. "You liked her?"

I hesitated, then nodded. It was a small nod. I was beginning to wonder what he was after.

His eyes seemed to brighten. "Sure. Everybody likes her. That's the kind of girl she is. When did you say you knew her? Couple years ago? Can't forget her, can you?"

Why was he being so friendly to me? What was he up to?

"You did know her pretty well, didn't you?" He stared straight into my eyes. He spoke again very softly. "I mean, you knew her pretty well."

I didn't answer.

"It's okay. I understand. You don't have to be nervous about it, I never thought I was the first man in her life."

His eyes traveled over me quickly. They came back to my face. "It's just, I didn't think she went for your type. Don't get me wrong. No offense. It's just, you don't look like the kind she'd go for. But you can't go by me. I don't know how women think."

He was so strong. So solid. He'd never let anyone push him around.

Yes. Her father and brother. They'd dominated her, too. And that psychiatrist in New York who had raped her.

Sure. After them I'd been exactly what she was looking for. Someone different, and weaker. Now I understood why she hadn't been interested in Alan that first night at The Dancers. He'd seemed so sure of himself. He'd gone over to her and made the advance. And of course she'd recognized him from his series. She'd admitted that once. She'd known he was a star, someone who'd made it. And I was someone who hadn't.

Yes. She'd never loved me, not even at the start. She'd loved my failure. It had given her something to control. Manipulate. Push around.

Bob Linowes coughed. He coughed again. "She's not here anymore. She left me."

His voice sounded hollow. His face wasn't quite so composed anymore. His hands searched his pockets, and when he took out cigarettes it was the first I noticed his hands were shaking slightly.

"You're not surprised to hear that? That she left me? Why? You think I'm not her type?"

"I don't know. I don't know what her type is."

"I know *exactly* what her type is!"

Then he was quiet. He offered me a cigarette and took one for himself. He scooped a lighter off the table, and when I leaned forward so he could light my cigarette I had to put my hand on his to keep the lighter steady. He picked up his coffee and almost spilled it. He put it down quickly without drinking. "So what are you doing? Trying to find her?"

"No. I just heard she was in Phoenix. It happened to be—"

"*I'm* trying to find her." He got up and walked across the room. He sat in a chair against the far wall and began to chew the edge of his thumb. "Got a private detective on it. He traced her to some address in Los Angeles about two weeks ago, but he was too late. She wasn't there anymore. Doesn't know where she is now. But I still got him looking." He got out of his chair and walked to the window. "Costs a little, the private detective. Costs more than a little." He turned suddenly. "That what happened to you? She walked out on you?"

I nodded quickly. His eyes opened wider. "Yeah? Well! Then maybe that's the way she is, huh? I mean if she left you, too . . ."

"Maybe that's the way she is."

He kept his eyes on me. "Yeah. Maybe." He seemed to relax slightly. "It's worth the cost, you know? To find out where she is. Not knowing, that's what costs too much."

Yes. I remembered how I'd felt, those few days she'd left me.

He came back to the chair opposite me and sat. He reached for his coffee cup but then only ran a finger around its rim. "You want any more?"

"No, thanks."

"Yeah. Me neither."

He sat there like stone.

Another moment passed, and his mouth tightened. "What the hell. You went to bed with her, right? I mean, you know what she's like, right?"

I hesitated, then nodded.

He laughed, very forced. "Brother. I didn't know what to do at first. I mean, she started getting a little kinky and . . ." His eyes went away. "But . . . it was kind of interesting . . . and after a while. . . ." He seemed lost. "After a while I even got to . . . like it . . . a little. . . . But then I had to put my foot down. I mean it was really getting out of hand. I told her she had to stop it!" He looked at me. I kept my mouth shut.

Suddenly he stood up. "Here. Let me just take these things out to the kitchen."

He picked up both cups and went through the door.

Three minutes passed, and he didn't come back. His cigarette was dying in the ashtray. I put it out of its misery and gave him another two minutes. Then I went to the kitchen door. I was just about to tap on it when I heard something. A loud slap.

I don't know if I knew then what it was or not. I pushed the door open. He was standing in the far corner by the wall. His right hand was hanging loosely at his side. There was blood on his hand. There was blood on the wall.

His eyes looked at me weakly, then slid away. His right hand went up and back. Forward. It hit the wall again. He took a small chunk of plaster out of it and left more blood behind.

I went forward and grabbed him by the other arm, but I couldn't budge him. He was a full head taller than me and fifty to seventy pounds heavier. He hit the wall again.

I lowered my shoulder and drove it into his stomach. I slammed him right up against the wall. He turned and reached down to push me away, but his right hand was so far gone by then that he could only push with his left. I grabbed onto his arm.

He turned half a circle to shake me off. I felt the wall hard against my back. I groaned and let him go.

He was in a complete rage by then. He didn't seem to know where he was. He stumbled and seemed off balance, and then he cried out suddenly and brought his hand up once more and then down across the kitchen table. There was a terrible crack.

I don't know how I did it, but there was no time not to do it. I went straight at him. I tackled him from the side. He must've been off balance because I knocked him off his feet. I was yelling my head off by then, and it must've scared him as much as he'd scared me, because he stayed there on the floor and stopped moving.

I took a dish towel and gave it to him. I told him to wrap it around his hand. He nodded and did it. He sat there huddled in the corner with his knees bent up in front of him and his eyes still on me. I got both my hands around the edge of the sink to keep myself standing. I was beginning to feel the pain in my back from where he'd thrown me against the wall.

Suddenly he spoke in a rush. "I don't know what happens. One minute everything's all right, you wouldn't know there's a damn thing bothering me, then all of a sudden something happens. I can't control it. I feel like I'm ready to kill myself." He gripped his knees with his good hand. His teeth were clenched, and all the tension showed in his face. He started to break again. "God, is that the way it happened with you? When she left you? Always changing quick like that? One minute you think you got it under control, the next minute—"

"Yeah. The same thing. Exactly the same." I felt dizzy and saw spots. "It would come and go, just like that."

"Yeah. Yeah. I keep thinking I got it licked, but I don't. Every time I think it's over, a couple days pass, something happens, I feel like I'm ready to kill myself again!"

He screamed it. I shook my head to clear it and moved forward. "You can't let it beat you. You can't."

His eyes jumped at me. "No, I wouldn't do it, I'm not the type, but sometimes I find I'm actually *thinking* about doing it!"

"You think it, but you won't do it." I tried to steady myself. I was ready to leap on him again if I had to.

"I like to exercise. I jump rope. Fifteen minutes every day. Two days ago, all of a sudden, no reason at all, I started thinking what it would be like to wrap the rope around my neck and pull it tight, just to see what it would be like!"

"No. You wouldn't do it." I moved closer and braced myself with whatever strength I had left. *"You wouldn't do it!"*

His head swung up suddenly, and he looked at me in fright. His voice changed. "No. No. Don't worry. I'm not going to do it. I'm not the type. It was just, for that moment . . . I got scared. I kept thinking if I *were* that type—"

"You're *not* the type. Listen to me! You're not the type!"

He stared at me.

Then he winced and looked down at his right hand. Blood was starting to soak through the towel.

I turned back to the sink and got another towel. I made him wrap that one around his hand too.

It took about an hour at the hospital. When he came out, his hand was in a cast. He was very quiet now. He got into the car by himself. I got in on the driver's side and started driving. He only spoke to give me directions. We were stopped at a light when he looked at me and held up the cast. "Stupid, isn't it? Crazy. The whole thing was so—"

"We all do crazy things when we get mixed up."

"Yeah?" He shook his head and looked at the cast. *"You* ever done something like this?"

"Something exactly like that."

"What?"

"My foot. Not my hand. I was wearing a shoe, so it wasn't as bad as for you."

He looked at me a long time before he seemed to realize I really was telling him the truth. Then he began to smile. "Really, huh?"

"Really."

Then I laughed. A moment later he laughed, too.

"I don't know what's going to happen. I mean, if I'm going to be able to find her or not. The detective, he said there wasn't any forwarding address. But he's supposed to be good. If she can be found, he'll find her."

I didn't know what to say to that.

"The thing is, why'd she leave me? I thought I was giving her what she wanted. She moved in on me, I didn't move in on her. I thought that's what she wanted. A commitment. That's why I married her. First night I met her, she borrowed money from me. Ten dollars. Just ten dollars."

I looked at him. She'd borrowed ten bucks from me. That night she'd come over for dinner.

He went on. "I always figured, only reason she borrowed it, she wanted a reason so we'd have to see each other again. Then, we got to know each other, she moved in with me. Said it would be cheaper. And easier."

Sure. I could've told his story myself.

"The thing I don't understand, if she was ever going to leave me, why did she move in on me that way? It was her choice, not mine. I didn't ask her to do it. She didn't like it, she could've moved out any time she wanted, but she didn't, she stayed." His left hand closed in a fist. "I was never one of those guys who thought he had to get married. I figured I might never get married. I was doing okay by myself." His hand opened slightly. "Well, pretty much, okay. But once she was living with me, it got so I really needed her." His hand opened all the way and pressed against the dashboard. I took a long swallow and stayed quiet. "So we got married. It was never the same, after that. She said she felt trapped. I don't know why. I gave her all the freedom she wanted. She could've done anything. Anything she could've done before we got married. But it was no good, it did something to her. Did something to me, too, I guess. Ruined everything."

He laughed. A quiet laugh. So quiet it could've been nothing more than a trick of my own imagination. But whatever it was, it wasn't very pleasant.

"Sure didn't last long, the marriage. Three and a half months. A hundred and seven days. Then she left, just like that." His hand slapped the dash, and this time his laugh was much louder. "She was screwy. Always making things up. You were lucky if you could get the right time of day from her. Always making things up about everything. She that way with you?"

". . . Yeah."

"I don't know about you, but I couldn't take it."

He was silent. I kept my eyes straight ahead. "She ever tell you anything about her family?" He didn't answer. "Her father? Her brother?"

"Didn't even know she had a brother." He thought about it a second. "You sure she *does* have one?"

"No. I'm not." I felt very cold.

"That's Katie. Maybe she's got a brother, maybe she's got twenty brothers. Maybe she hasn't got any. Why'd you ask?"

I shook my head and said nothing.

"It really got to me, all the lying. I told her to stop. It didn't do any good. Doesn't matter now, I guess. All that matters is she left."

"Why do you think she left?"

His hand reached for the dash again. "She took those damn pills all the time. I tried to get her to stop. I didn't know how to do it."

"You think she left you 'cause you tried to get her off the pills?"

"I gave her an awful hard time about 'em. Maybe I shouldn't have. Didn't do her any good. Didn't do either one of us any good."

His voice trailed off, but then after a moment he started in again very quickly. "Say one thing for her, once she got her teeth into something, she was hell on wheels. She had a real head for business. I got my own appliance store, downtown. She came in there, started working the floor for me, you should've seen the way she took the place over. Pretty soon she was doing everything.

The books, writing newspaper ads, she even talked me into making a commercial for radio. She was good. Profits jumped fifteen percent. Imagine that?"

I could imagine it only too well.

"Actually, the store hadn't been doing all that well before. I mean, up to when she came in there. But once she started working with me, brother, we really started to do business."

I could imagine that, too.

He had some trouble trying to unlock his apartment door. I almost helped him but then decided it might be better if I didn't. He tried it again, and this time his left hand figured out which way to turn the key. The lock clicked open.

When we were sitting in the living room, I spoke as if asking nothing more than an idle question. "The day she left you, anything strange happen?"

"What do you mean?"

I started to dig for my cigarettes, then changed my mind and left them where they were. "When she left me, it wasn't till night. She'd been acting nervous all day. Like she was scared of something." I was really groping. "She anything like that, the day she left you?"

"One thing she wasn't that night was scared." He laughed. He leaned against the arm of his chair. "We went to a party that night. Friend of mine. She drank a lot over there. I did, too. Really tied one on. It was pretty bad." The fingers of his left hand touched the cast carefully.

"Did something happen? At the party?"

"No. She talked a lot, that's all. Telling stories. It was afterwards, when we came back here. I was trying to get into a parking space downstairs. I was really plastered, and she had to get out to tell me if I was far enough over. When I finally got the car parked, I saw she was over near the street, looking at something. There were these kids over there, a whole bunch of 'em, and some old lady. Looked like the kids were following the old lady. Katie went a couple of feet into the street. She had her back to me, I couldn't see what she was doing. Then one of the kids saw her, and all of a sudden they stopped following the old lady and started coming across the street toward Katie. Then they stopped, right in the middle of the street, and took off. I figured it must've been 'cause they saw me coming, but when I got to Katie, she had this water pistol in her hand. I guess she'd had it in her pocketbook, and she'd taken it out, and it was so dark, the kids must've thought she had a real gun."

"A water pistol?"

"Yeah. Looked just like a forty-four. Don't know why she had it."

"The kids. Did they come back?"

"You kidding? They weren't going to come back. The water pistol must've scared the hell out of 'em."

I rubbed my hand against the sofa cushion. "What happened then?"

"We came up here. I told her she was crazy to get herself into something like that. I was really mad at her. I was trying to . . ." His mouth closed tightly. His eyes lost their focus. "I was trying to act strong with her, I guess. I never knew how to handle her. I didn't know if she wanted me strong, or not so strong. She needed *someone* strong, a hell of a lot stronger than me." He paused another moment. "I told her we ought to call the cops, but she wouldn't let me. She didn't like cops. Never liked anyone with any kind of authority. She was a little nervous, and she went into the kitchen. I was pretty drunk, so I sat down on the sofa.

"I was sitting there, and she came out, and she wanted me to go into the bedroom with her. Well, I knew what that'd mean, the way she always was, in bed, and I was real tired, I told her to wait a minute. I was drunk, I didn't feel too good, I didn't know if I was up to it. The kind of things she liked to do. So then she went into the bedroom herself, and I guess I fell asleep or something, 'cause the next thing I knew, she was there again, and she wanted to do it. She went wild. She hit me and started yelling. I didn't know how to stop her, so we did it. Made love. Right there on the sofa. She was pretty excited. More than she'd ever been before. It got pretty scary. She seemed like she was going to go crazy for a second."

"How bad did she hit you?"

"Bad. I probably would've felt it worse if I hadn't

been drunk. The next morning, my whole jaw ached. I didn't even remember her hitting me on the jaw. Hell, I probably didn't remember it 'cause I was so used to it by then."

His left hand covered his eyes. I gave him a moment. "What else happened?"

". . . Nothing. I must've fallen asleep again. When I woke up, it was morning. After six. She was gone. No note. Nothing."

He sat there with his left hand on his knee, opening and closing it like he'd done earlier in the car.

It was close enough to the way she'd told it to me. She'd fallen asleep on the floor of the bathroom. When she'd woken up it'd been almost morning. She'd come out to the living room. He'd been asleep on the couch. She must've tried to wake him up.

"What kind of sleeper are you, when you're drunk?"

"Huh?"

"You said you were here on the sofa. She must've come through and made noises when she left. You didn't wake up?"

"Me? She could've driven through here with a ten-ton truck, she wouldn't have woken me up. Better chance trying to wake a dead man."

Bob Linowes opened the door and came out to the corridor with me. He seemed much better now. I'd spent another hour with him, listening to him talk about Katie. About his appliance store. About anything he'd wanted to tell me about.

"We had a joint savings account. Opened it when we got married. She cleaned it out. I mean, half of it." He laughed. "Half, to the penny. Over eight thousand dollars."

"That why you're trying to find her?"

"The money? No, she can have it. The money she brought into the store, while she was helping me, it came out even enough. I don't want the money, I want her. Only reason I got the detective on her, I want to know where she is, that she's okay." He looked down the hall. "All the lying. All the pills. And if she came out of that elevator right now, I'd be the happiest guy in the world."

He looked at his apartment door. He reached down

273

suddenly and closed it. "Come on, I'll walk down to the elevator with you."

He turned quickly and started down the hall. I went with him. He said, "You know, all any of us wants, you know what it is? Someone we can love. And who'll love us. Doesn't even matter what they look like. I used to think it did, but it doesn't. Dark hair, light hair, good body, bad body, it doesn't matter. If you care about 'em, and if they care about you, that's what matters. But if you care about 'em and then they leave you . . . Christ. It's enough to kill you." He pushed the button for the elevator. "I've never been honest enough with people. To show 'em that I care. I wasn't honest enough with her. I guess I wasn't strong enough."

The elevator came. When the door opened, I didn't get inside. I was worried about him again. He was six and a half feet tall. He had the build, the voice, the eyes, the warmth—everything I'd ever wanted in my life. He could've walked into any bar in the world and walked out with anyone he wanted.

And it didn't matter. His heart was no tougher than anyone else's. He was in the same boat as the rest of us.

The elevator door started to close. He put his left hand against it to stop it. "Aren't you going to get in?"

I put my hand on his arm and spoke softly. "You going to be all right? You want me to stay here a little longer?"

He hesitated. His eyes slid away. "No. I'll be okay. It's been six months. I got through six months, I got through this morning, I'll get through the rest." He looked down. Up. Then he stepped inside the elevator. "I'll ride down with you."

We rode in silence. As we walked across the lobby he said, "Maybe getting married was too big for her. Scared her too much." He shook his head quickly. "No, it must've been the pills. The way she kept taking 'em when she knew I wanted her to stop. Maybe she couldn't take the way I rode her on it." He shook his head again. "It could've been the store. Things had started getting tough again, business was falling off, it was looking pretty bad."

"You think *that's* why she left you?"

"I told her it was just the time of year, the month

was always bad—but with her, you always had to keep doing better and better. So when we finally hit that stretch when business hadn't kept improving, she started going nuts, and it just got worse, with the pills and the booze."

My heart seemed to stop. Suddenly I wanted her again. In spite of that hate I'd felt before.

And now, hearing him talk about business falling off, I was sure she wouldn't be there when I got back.

But then he spoke again. "No. It probably wasn't that either. She hit the pills and the booze pretty bad then, but she stuck. Worked even harder. Got things back to where they'd been the month before, and everything was going real well again. *Then* she left. Hell, I don't know. Doesn't make sense."

When we reached my car, I dug out my keys and opened the door. He touched my arm. It was the first time he'd touched me. "Funny. The way you seemed at first, I didn't think she'd go for your type, but I can see it now. You're probably a lot more her type than I am."

I looked at him in disbelief.

"You're quiet. That's part of it. And you listen pretty good. I wouldn't be surprised, the next guy she finds, that's the kind she'll look for." He laughed sadly. "Look for? For all I know, she's probably already found him."

That hurt bad. I wasn't built for this kind of thing. I kept my mouth shut and got into the car.

I reached out for the door, but he was holding it open. "I was just thinking, you're going to be in town for the day, we could get together for dinner. What kind of food you like?"

"I can't." I looked at my watch. I didn't want to look at his face now. "I got a flight out of here at two."

"The thing that scares me, wherever she is, she's probably taking those damn pills. She'll never get off 'em."

"You never know. She once told me she'd been on heroin, and she got off that." I put my key in the ignition. "That's if she was telling me the truth about it."

"No, you're right, she did kick the heroin."

I froze with my hand still on the ignition key.

I looked up at him. "How do you know she kicked it? How do you know for sure she was ever on it?"

"She was on it. She had to write some clinic in New York. She needed a letter from 'em so she could get methadone out here."

"Wait a minute." I could feel my heart racing now. "How do you know she needed a letter? How do you know she didn't just make it up?"

"The letter? I saw it. Saw the one she sent, and the one they sent back."

I stared at the steering wheel. The heroin had been true.

If the heroin had been true, maybe the psychiatrist raping her had been true.

Her father and brother dominating her? Her mother running off?

He started to laugh. "You know, you're right about the letter. I wouldn't have believed it myself, if I hadn't seen it. The way she was always making up stories. That's why we had to leave that party."

It took several seconds before it hit me. "You had to leave the party?"

"The one I told you about. The night she left me."

I shrugged to control my voice. "Why'd you have to leave it?"

"I told you. She'd been drinking." His eyes wandered off toward the apartment building. "She was telling all these stories. About herself. Me, I was used to her lies, I used to let 'em go in one ear and out the other, but these people, they were my friends. I couldn't let her go on that way."

"What did you do?"

"I tried to stop her. I couldn't, so I pulled her out of there. I was pretty mad, and I tried to act tough. I told her she better not do that kind of thing anymore. Ever. I mean, once I started going, I really gave it to her. Yelled at her. I told her I'd had enough of her lies." He turned and looked at me again. "You think that could've been it? Yelling? I had to yell, I didn't know how else to do it." He paused. "But I yelled at her other times, and she didn't leave me. It doesn't make sense."

It made sense. She left because she thought she'd

276

killed him, but now I knew *why* she'd almost killed him. He'd yelled at her to stop lying.

Sometimes a man pretends he wants to hear. But he doesn't listen to a thing you say. He doesn't believe a thing you say. Ever.

Yes. She wanted him to believe her. She wanted him to care enough about her that he'd believe anything she said, no matter *what* she said. When she found out he wouldn't, she almost killed him.

When she went wild and hit me with the pot—it was the only time she'd ever hit me that it seemed like real anger. Hatred. It was after I'd pulled her out of The Dancers and told her *I* didn't know if *I* could believe anything she told me.

Linowes shut the car door. "I'm glad you came by. Gave me a chance to get some things off my chest. Maybe it'll help." He touched my arm again for a brief moment, and then he stepped back. "My detective ever finds her, you want me to contact you? Let you know where she is?"

"I'm going to Los Angeles and look for her myself. If I find her, I'll let you know. So you won't have to worry anymore."

He nodded. "Yeah. Figures you'd go. I couldn't. I'm scared to. Scared to see her again. That's why I had to send someone else. But not you. Yeah, you're her type all right. You're strong. A hell of a lot stronger than I am. You're probably *just* what she needs."

A hell of a lot stronger than I am? Someone else had said something like that to me.

Alan. When he'd told me about being scared when she'd slapped him at the party. He'd said how *I* must be strong, to be able to handle her.

No. It was crazy. I wasn't strong. I wiped it quickly out of my mind. I still had one final question. The one I'd been putting off. "You said she used a water pistol to scare away those kids. Are you sure? Could it've been a real gun?"

"A real gun? What would Katie have a real gun for?"

"You're right. She wouldn't."

I turned front. I started the engine and put the car in gear. All I wanted to do now was get back to Los

Angeles as fast as I could. Because if the gun had nothing to do with him, it must've had something to do with something else.

But before I stepped on the gas, I gave him one more look. He was holding his cast in his left hand, looking this way, then that, switching from one foot to the other, constantly fidgeting. Something about that worried me greatly.

IT was almost four when I got back to L.A. I called the house, but there was no answer. Finally I called Ruth. It was Saturday afternoon and she was at her apartment. She wanted to know everything about Phoenix. I told her a little and said if she'd come pick me up, I'd tell her the rest. Then I hung up the phone quickly. I felt tight again. I went into the men's room and almost threw up, but didn't. I couldn't. I hadn't eaten in hours and my stomach was empty. I splashed water on my face and looked in the mirror.

My eyes. They had that same desperate look Linowes's eyes had had. That's what had worried me.

I dropped to the floor and put my head between my knees.

When Ruth picked me up, I wanted to get home fast to see if Katie was there. Whatever had to be said and done, I wanted it over with. Ruth shook her head. "Won't do you any good, Jake. It's not just the gun you got to worry about. It's the pills, the liquor. The way she is. Face it, Jake, you're not a doctor. You can't help her."

"You want me to give up on her."

"That's right. I know what I'm talking about. I've been through it."

I took a deep breath. "Sure. That's you, Ruth. That's you all over. You've wanted me to give up on a lot of things, haven't you?"

Her head turned. "I don't want you to give up on anything. I just want you to do what's best for you." Her eyes swung off me and back to the road. She hit the gas harder. She shot up the hill toward my house. "Listen, baby, all I care about—"

"Stop calling me baby."

She hesitated. "I call everybody baby."

"Maybe it's time for you to stop!" I looked up the road, half hoping I'd see the yellow Volkswagen, half hoping I wouldn't.

It wasn't there.

Now I felt even worse. I realized I was shaking.

Ruth pulled into the yard. She hadn't even turned off the engine when I threw the door open and jumped out. I heard her opening her car door.

"Jake? What's wrong?"

I couldn't control it. I turned and yelled at her. "We're not babies! We're people! We've got our own feelings, our own minds! Our own desires! You got a job where you spend a lot of time trying to persuade people! Maybe you forget, people like to think for themselves!"

"Jake—"

I moved toward her. My hand was waving viciously at the air. "You told me once if I wanted a release from my contract I could have it! All right! I want it!"

"What?" She stared at me. "You're crazy. What for?"

"Because I don't want to depend on you anymore!" I looked toward the spot where the yellow Volkswagen was usually parked. I filled my lungs with air. "I don't want to depend on her, either! From now on, I'm in charge! I'm going to do whatever I have to do! The pills? The liquor? I'm going to make her stop! And my career? I'm going to take care of that, too. I'm going to show her she can depend on me, and I'm going to show *myself* I can depend on me!" I hardened my voice. "Goddamn it, he was right! I *was* strong! I *used* to be strong! I used to

280

have confidence in myself, but I came out here and I met you! You knocked it out of me."

Suddenly she was angry. "I didn't do a damn thing to you! Whatever happened, you did it to yourself!"

I looked at her. "Your right. God, you're absolutely right. *I* did it!" Then I stopped. "But you saw me doing it, Ruth. And you let me."

Then I realized I wasn't yelling anymore. There was no need to. I was finally looking at myself and seeing exactly what had happened to me.

I *had* to look at what had happened. It was my only chance to change it.

I walked slowly toward Ruth. My voice was soft. "I had a reason for coming out to L.A. I wanted to make it. I still do. And I'm going to make it. I'm not going to let this city, or anyone in it, stop me. Not anymore."

Then I laughed. I could laugh now by myself, without needing anyone else to give me a reason to laugh.

Ruth smiled at me. "You've got it, Jake."

"What?"

"You're not just talking now. You really believe it."

"Believe what?"

"In yourself."

I sat on the sofa and watched Ruth pace nervously. She loosened her scarf and rubbed her throat. "Mind if I get myself something to drink?"

"No. Help yourself."

She walked to the bookcase and filled a glass with vodka. "So now you want her again."

I shuddered involuntarily, took a quick breath and nodded. Ruth pulled off her scarf and mopped her face with it. She raised her glass and sipped vodka, then walked halfway across the room. "You were wrong, Jake. About why I didn't want you to make it. I wasn't scared of losing you. The day I came over here and she'd moved in, I saw the way you looked at her. I knew it was over, you and me. It didn't make any real difference. I still cared about you as much as ever. The reason I didn't want you to make it wasn't the reason you think."

"What do you mean?"

She raised the glass and drank all that was there

"I love you a lot, Jake, but you're not the great love in my life. You couldn't be. I had that love a long time ago, and I lost it."

"Christolf?"

"Sure." She went back to the bookcase and poured more vodka. "You never knew him before he made it. You see Jack the way he is now. He talks loud, he's always putting on an act. He's a bastard and he doesn't care who knows it. He *wants* people to know it, 'cause bastards are what the public is buying right now. As long as they'll buy, he'll be one, but he wasn't a bastard before. He was as clean as they come. He cared about other people. Respected 'em. He was nice. And he had talent."

She drank again. "He always had talent, and it was a damn good talent, but now it's starting to turn lousy. When he loses enough of it, there's going to be a million knives in this city, ready to slice him apart. He's scared, Jake. He's older than he wants to be, he's always hanging around with these young girls, he wants to show everybody he's got what it takes to get 'em. The ones he picks, it doesn't take much. But he knows he hasn't got it in him to maintain a relationship, so he dumps 'em, 'cause he knows if he doesn't, they'll dump him. He couldn't stand for that to happen.

"He's still got a lot of magnetism and surface bluster, but don't let that fool you. There's not much behind it anymore. There's been too many nights I've gotten a phone call, two in the morning, asking me to come out there right away. There's been too many doctors I've had to call at two-thirty in the morning, to come and get him fixed up again."

"You mean after the way he treated you, he still calls you to—"

"He calls me 'cause he's so bad off he can't call anyone else. You think Katie's on pills? That's nothing. You ought to see what's in Jack's medicine cabinet. He's not going to last long. He doesn't even care. We've talked about it enough times. He says he's going to stop, but he doesn't. None of 'em ever do. Jack won't, Katie won't. Once it gets 'em, they're finished. And it's got both of 'em."

She finished her drink and left the glass on the bookcase. She began to move aimlessly around the room.

I moved to the edge of the sofa. "Ruth? Are you all right?"

"I'm sorry for Jack. He used to be something, but he won't be much longer. And it's not just him, Jake. This town is full of 'em. Look at Alan. It's coming to him awfully fast. I don't know if he's going to be able to handle it or not, but he might. You know why?"

"You think that much of Alan?"

"No. Of Jill." Ruth smiled at me. "I know, you think she's pushing him, getting him to go out to Malibu and everything, but you're wrong. She wanted him out there so she could watch him like a hawk. She's looking after his money, too. Making sure no business adviser comes along and loses it for him. Surprised, huh? You know Jill pretty well and she's never told you about it, but she's told me. We don't always tell men the same things we tell each other." She laughed. "With Alan, there's another reason I think he's got a chance to come through it all right. He's just not going to last that long. Right now he's one of the three current rages of the country, but next year there'll be three others, and within four years his series will be canceled. He's going to find he can't get the same kind of breaks anymore. He's hit it now 'cause he's fresh. The thing he doesn't realize, he's not on his way up. This is it for him. Alan's not a long-distance runner. Not enough talent."

She looked at me for a second, then looked away. "But when he falls, he's going to be lucky. Jill's going to be there. I've talked the whole thing out with her—what's going to happen—when he falls, he's going to find out she's invested his money pretty well. The day comes he can't even get himself arrested, she's going to be there, making sure the bills are paid. Unless he gets stupid and leaves her, she's always going to be there. 'Cause she's that kind of person, Jake. And so am I. And the hell of it is, so are you.

"But Jack, he's not going to fall like Alan. Even now, Jack's talent is still so massive that he thinks it's indestructible. Thinks he'll be able to write his ticket for the rest of his life. And he probably could, if he could keep his talent up, but he won't be able to do it much longer. He's destroying his insides, and his talent is going to go right along with it. When it does, there's going

283

to be nobody around to take care of him, except me. And that's not going to do any good. Because he won't let me help him. He's too scared."

"Maybe when it happens, he'll get scared enough to let you help him."

"No. Not Jack." Then she laughed sadly. "And you, Jake? Your problem is, you're not like Alan either. You've got as much talent as Jack. As Jack ever had. And Jack knows it. He can smell an actor with talent and potential anywhere within a hundred miles of him. Talent always recognizes talent. You pay attention from now on, you'll see those are the guys Jack goes after—every time he sees 'em. But someone like Alan? You'll never see Jack stick his fangs into Alan's neck. You're a different story. You see, Jake, you've got it. I knew it the first time I saw you. You were in that workshop production up on Hollywood Boulevard."

That made me shudder. "I was rotten in that."

"The play was rotten. You were pretty good. Jake, you were very good. So I signed you. Mel thought I was crazy, he didn't think you had anything, but Mel never knows. That's why he's got to have people like me working for him. If he didn't, he'd be finished." She moved away again. "Then I got to know you, and I saw something else. You didn't have the confidence to make anything out of your talent. I was going to try to give you that confidence, but then something happened, and I got so I was glad you *didn't* have any confidence."

"Why?"

"'Cause you were an awfully nice guy. 'Cause I started to fall a little bit in love with you. And when I did, I realized what it was. You were the same kind of guy, had the same kind of talent, as Jack. And by then I'd seen what Jack was turning into. What his success was doing to him. How he couldn't handle it. How it was killing him. So I made a mistake. Every time I looked at you, I started seeing you ten years from now. Successful. And dying. Like Jack. Killing yourself. I wasn't going to let it happen to you. So I held you back, just like you said. To save you from it. Not to stop myself from losing you. I knew I could live through losing you, 'cause I'd lived through losing Jack. And no matter how much I loved you, I could never love anyone as much as I loved him."

She walked to the bookcase and stared at her empty glass. "Why do we all pick the wrong ones? You and Katie. Me and Jack. And some of us can't let go, even when we realize it. Ridiculous, isn't it?" She shook her head. "That's why I've been trying to stop this thing with you and her. She'll kill you, one way or another. I've been through it, I know. Maybe it's no use. When it comes to love, we're all crazy."

I just sat there and looked at her. I was shaken by what she'd said.

"You were right, Jake, we didn't have to be lovers. Probably never should've been. We could've been friends. Guess it's too late now. Afraid I've blown it."

I went to the bookcase and put my arms around her. I held her tight, and we both began to cry. I was trying to find the right words to say when I realized we weren't alone. Katie was standing at the edge of the arch.

She hadn't come in through the front door, she'd come in through the kitchen. Ruth and I pulled apart quickly. Then Katie spoke and her words stung the air.

"What are you doing back here already? You said you'd stay up in San Francisco for a couple days!"

"I didn't go to San Francisco. I went to Phoenix."

"What?"

"I saw your husband, Katie. He isn't dead."

It stopped her cold. She didn't move at all.

"He's alive—you didn't kill him. If you thought you killed him—"

"I don't know what you're talking about!"

I took one step forward and kept my voice low. "You told me you fell asleep in the bathroom. When you came out to the living room he was on the couch. You tried to wake him up, but you couldn't. You thought he was dead. But he wasn't dead, he was just asleep. Drunk. That's why you couldn't wake him up."

Her mouth fell open. I thought she was going to cry, but then something happened and her eyes glazed over. "*You* thought I killed him."

Halfway to her, I froze. "You had that gun. You

didn't know where you'd gotten it. You kept telling me someone had killed him."

Her eyes seemed to clear. She looked toward Ruth. "What's she doing here?" Katie's arms fell to her sides. "God, Jake. You hate me, don't you? You don't trust me. You think I'm no good for you. I didn't get the contracts for the Montgomery picture. I can't get you work. You think you need her. Jake! I'm sorry you lost that movie!"

"It doesn't matter." I moved a step closer.

"It matters! It was an important part!"

"They wanted me, Katie. That's all that matters. If they wanted me, other people will want me." I reached for her. "A job fell through, that's all. They fall through all the time. It's just part of the game. There'll be other jobs."

I had her in my arms.

Suddenly she tore away from me. "Other jobs? You think she'll get them for you, don't you? You don't trust me! You hate me! You think you need *her!*" Katie's hand dove into her pocketbook. It came out with a piece of paper. "Here!"

I didn't react. Her hand came farther out and slapped the paper at me. "Here! Take it!"

I took the paper. As I did I realized what her blouse looked like. It was torn away at the neck. Torn again at the sleeve.

She followed my eyes and looked at herself. She held the blouse where it was torn open. "He got a little rough. I gave him what he wanted, and he gave me what I wanted. But he got a little rough."

"What?"

She pointed weakly at my hand. "Read the paper."

I felt a chill go through me.

"Read it. Please."

I unfolded the paper.

TO WHOM IT MAY CONCERN,
I agree to hire Jake Bolin to act the part of the younger brother in my forthcoming production of *Brownsville Station*. Financial terms and billing shall be as already agreed to verbally. All terms shall be set forth in contracts which

I agree to deliver to Mr. Bolin within the next three working days.

The letter was written in longhand and dated. The handwriting was Katie's. The signature at the bottom was Jack Christoff's.

"It's only a letter, but it's okay, it's as good as a contract. You'll have the contract by Wednesday. Registered mail."

I felt dizzy. "Katie? What did you do?"

She exhaled slowly. "I did what had to be done. You had to have that part. Now you've got it."

Ruth was at my side. She took the paper from me. After a moment she groaned.

I was staring miserably at Katie's clothes. "Did he do that to you? My God! I'll kill him!"

Katie shook her head. "He didn't do anything to me. I did it to him. He didn't want to give you that part, but I made him." Her face hardened into a mask of stone. "I was with him all night, all morning. He thought he could outlast any woman in the world, but he found out he couldn't."

Then she laughed.

I had a horrible sinking feeling. I reached for the chair. "God. Why did you do it?"

"For your career, Jake. That's all you care about, isn't it?"

Before I could answer, Ruth screamed. "What did you do to Jack to make him sign this thing? Did you hurt him?"

Katie's face came alive again. She breathed in hard. "It was your idea, sending him to Phoenix. Yes. You said he had to go up to San Francisco, his friend was in a car accident. It was a trick. You planned it. You hoped I *had* killed him! You wanted to get rid of me!"

I moved forward. "No, it wasn't her idea, it was mine."

"You?" Katie moved backward. "You don't love me. You never loved me. You just used me. But I loved you." She pointed at the paper in Ruth's hand. "I proved it, didn't I!"

Katie turned and went down the hall toward the front door.

Ruth screamed again. "What did you do to Jack?"

By the time I reached the front yard, Katie was running down the road. I saw her car parked in the distance. I kept walking. I was scared that if I ran I'd panic. I watched as she reached the car and pulled the door open. Suddenly she turned toward me.

"You're like all men! You don't love me! You just think you need me! You do need me! Without me you're nothing!"

"No, Katie, you're wrong. I'm something." I kept walking. "I'm me. With you or without you, I'm me. But I want it to be with you."

"No! You need me! You still need me!"

We were only a couple of feet apart now. She was breathing as hard as I was.

"No, Katie. I don't need you that way. Not anymore."

She stared at me with confusion on her face. Then her right hand flew back and came straight at me.

I caught her hand by the wrist and stopped it. "No, Katie. Don't do that. Not anymore."

She didn't move. She was holding her chin out and waiting. Then I understood. She was expecting me to slap her, like I had at The Dancers.

I didn't do it. I wasn't going to.

As she realized that, there was panic in her eyes. "Jake?"

"No."

"Jake!"

She struggled to get free. I let her go. She pulled away and her hand went back again.

But I stood my ground and shook my head.

She was crying as she leaped into the Volkswagen.

When I got back to the house, Ruth was standing by the phone. I walked slowly past her and collapsed on the sofa.

"She's poison, Jake. Why can't you face it? The girl you picked is the wrong one."

"We're all the wrong ones. We all pick the wrong ones. Maybe there is no right one. It's just a matter of how long it takes before we realize it. But we finally do realize it, and sometimes it doesn't matter."

"You're crazy."

"And you aren't? You just called Christolf, didn't you?"

She stood there quietly.

"God, none of us have got any brains when we pick who we're going to love, but once we've picked, we've picked. We can't get out of it. We've made a commitment. We stick."

Her hands flew up. "No!"

"Yes! Everyone's got something wrong with 'em, but you don't turn your back on 'em, not if you really love 'em!"

She was quiet again. She came to the sofa and sat beside me.

"Is Christolf all right?"

"I didn't even get to talk to him. I talked to one of his girls. She said he's fine."

Ruth lowered her head. I took her hand gently, put my arm around her and held her against me.

All I could do was wait. Roam around the house. Sit here. Sit there. And wait.

Ruth waited with me for about an hour, but then I sent her home. It was better that way. If Katie did come back, I didn't want Ruth there.

Finally I realized it was after ten and I hadn't eaten a thing since breakfast except for the coffee Bob Linowes had given me. I wasn't hungry, but I knew I had to try to eat something. I made soup and toast. I ate them very slowly. Half an hour later I vomited them up.

Another hour passed. I was still in misery. I was sitting in the kitchen, drinking coffee, smoking, when it happened. I found myself looking at the stack of old newspapers sitting on the floor.

It seemed strange. That they were still there. Katie always kept the house so immaculate. Normally she would've thrown those papers out a long time ago. But for some reason she hadn't.

My mind flew back. The week I met her. The day she came to the house. I made dinner for the two of us. Baked chicken. We'd finished dinner, she's washed the dishes, she'd come back toward the table, then she'd stopped. She'd picked up the top newspaper.

She'd read something to me. When I'd reached across the table to look at the article, she hadn't let me see it.

I dug quickly from the top down, searching from day to day in reverse. It was like a film run suddenly backward. Each day's news abruptly replaced by the news from the day before. I ripped through the papers in a rush, and finally it was there, staring up at me from the extreme right-hand column.

MIDDAY ROBBERY ON FAIRFAX
Butcher Held Up With Own Knife

Samuel Adler was having a quiet afternoon until a young woman came into his butcher shop, held a knife to his throat, and stole $3.43 from him.

The woman, in her twenties and well dressed with shoulder length brown hair, smiled at Adler as she entered his shop. She claimed she had bought two steaks from him the previous week and the meat had been spoiled. She demanded her money back.

But when she reached into her pocketbook, Adler was alarmed at the suddenness of her action. He has been held up three times during the past year. He reached under his cash register for his .38-caliber pistol. The gun is legally owned and registered.

When the woman's hand came out of the pocketbook empty, Adler was so embarrassed he immediately lowered his gun and began to apologize.

But then the woman screamed at him. She came to his side of the counter and, apparently unafraid of Adler's gun, picked up a carving knife and held it to his throat.

The woman was absolutely calm now, as if in a trance. Terrified, Adler opened the cash register. The woman said the steaks had cost $1.75 each. Adler put $3.50 on the counter.

The woman shook her head and screamed again. "No! I want the exact amount! $3.43!"

When Adler gave her the correct amount, she took the money and his .38-caliber pistol and put both into her pocketbook. She walked away, and as she reached the end of the counter she drove the carving knife point-first into the wood.

The woman went out to the street and got into a yellow Volkswagen. Adler told the police the car had out-of-state plates, but he was unable to give the license number.

When I finished the article, I read it again quickly. Then I threw the paper onto the stack.

It was nothing. Nobody had been hurt. The butcher hadn't gotten the license number. There was no way for anyone to know who she was.

The only thing was the gun. I could get rid of it now. It was safer to get rid of it than keep it around any longer. I could take it out to the woods and bury it. It wouldn't matter if anyone ever found it. What was the crime? A robbery? For $3.43? It was nothing.

I went out to the back yard and climbed into the tree. The gun wasn't there.

I looked at the bedroom window. She'd seen me that night after all. I went into the kitchen and heard someone at the front door. I ran through the house and found her going toward the bedroom. She looked at me with empty eyes. "It's okay now. Everything."

"What?"

"But I feel so tired, Jake." She yawned. Her fingers fumbled uselessly with the buttons of her blouse.

She walked into the bedroom and unzipped her skirt. As she stepped out of it, I noticed something I hadn't noticed before. There were scratches on her face.

"I'm so tired. I better go to sleep." She sat on the bed and picked up her pocketbook. "Don't be mad at me, Jake. For sleeping with him. It didn't mean anything, you were the one I was doing it for. I love you."

I stared at the scratches on her face.

Then her hand came out of her pocketbook holding a bottle of pills.

"No!" I grabbed the pills out of her hand and swung my arm as hard as I could. The bottle flew across the room and hit the far wall.

"Jake? What's the matter? I was just going to take one so I could sleep."

I grabbed the pocketbook away from her and looked inside. I found another pill bottle. I held it in front of her and shook it back and forth. "Damn you, Katie, you take these pills, you do things, you don't even remember what you've done! I can't take it anymore! You've got to stop! You take any more of these things, you'll kill yourself!"

". . . What?"

I cried as I turned savagely and threw the second bottle against the wall. "Katie! You've got scratches on your face! Where'd they come from?"

She didn't react.

I was going crazy. I turned the pocketbook upside down and opened it wide so everything came out and fell across the bed. And there it was. The gun.

Wrapped around it was a scarf, and I knew whose scarf it was.

I ran to the living room and dialed Ruth's number. There was no answer. I hung up and dialed again. I let it keep ringing, but it did no good.

"Jake?"

She was standing in the archway. She had one of the pill bottles in her right hand and the scarf in her left. "What's the matter, Jake?"

"That's Ruth's scarf! What did you do to her?"

Katie stared at me blankly.

I threw down the phone. As I ran by her, she reached out for me. I ripped past her hands and went through the front door. I jumped into my car and drove down the hill as fast as I could.

I drove wildly. I couldn't think straight. When I screeched into the parking lot I heard a scraping noise, and realized I'd driven right up against a guard railing. I got out of my car without stopping to look at the damage and ran across the lot and into the lobby.

I hit the elevator button several times, then turned and went through a door and up the stairs. I ran up two flights, onto a walkway along the outside of the building. When I reached Ruth's door, I rang the bell. Then hammered against the door with both fists. Tried to force it. But it wouldn't open.

I ran farther along the walkway and turned at the entrance to the pool. I ran across the courtyard toward the back of Ruth's apartment. I banged against the sliding glass doors. There was a light on somewhere inside, but it wasn't enough to show me anything.

I took a chair from the patio and lifted it over my head. I threw it against the glass. When the glass broke I reached inside and unlocked the doors and slid them open. I stepped across the shattered glass and turned on a standing lamp.

The living room was empty.

I looked into the kitchen. That was empty. I ran down the hall into the bedroom, then ran down the other hall to the study. That's where the light was on.

The chair behind the desk was overturned. A low table lay on its side. An ashtray had been knocked on the floor.

Then there was a sound. It seemed to come from the living room. I ran down the hall and found someone coming slowly through what was left of the sliding glass doors.

It was Katie. She was dressed in pants and a shirt. The shirt was only half buttoned. Her face was a mess. She was clutching her pocketbook. Her hand came forward holding a pill bottle.

"I did what you wanted me to do."

"What?"

She came farther into the living room. "You thought I did something to Bob. You thought I killed him. You think I did something to Ruth. God, you must hate me!" She held up the pill bottle. "You said the pills would kill me. And you left them." She opened the pill bottle. "So I did what you wanted me to do, Jake. I took all of them."

She turned the bottle upside down. Nothing came out.

"What? How many did you take!"

"All of them." The bottle dropped from her hand.

I went to her and grabbed her. "How many? How many were left?"

". . . Three, four . . . I would've taken more, Jake, but that's all there were. Please don't hate me. I can't stand for you to hate me."

Three or four. That wouldn't kill her. Three or four was what she usually took.

Then there was a sound behind me. The front door. I turned and expected to see the apartment manager or the police, but when the door opened it was Ruth.

She stepped into the dark apartment and closed the door behind her. When she turned on the overhead light, she saw us. She moved backward with a jerk, but the closed door stopped her.

"Jake! . . . She broke my arm!"

Ruth's shoulder was bandaged. Her arm was in a sling.

"She said she wanted to talk to me! I wouldn't let her in! She pushed her way in and started yelling at me! She slapped me, she kept hitting me!"

Katie stepped away from my hands and moved toward the broken glass doors. "No! I didn't! She's lying, I didn't do that!" Her eyes swung toward me. "I didn't slap her, Jake!" She gulped in air and looked around wildly as if she wanted to run off, then she looked again at Ruth. "No, Jake. *She* slapped *me*. . . . Yes! I just wanted to talk to her, but she slapped me! She kept slapping me! I couldn't get away from her!"

Ruth had her back against the door. "She's lying, Jake, she tried to kill me. I had to go to the hospital. The police know, they're looking for her."

"Police?" Katie jumped back. "No! No police!" She came forward suddenly. "You've got to believe me, Jake! She made me do it! I couldn't stop her, she was hitting me!"

There were sounds outside on the patio. When Katie turned, I could see people out there. Neighbors, trying to see what was going on inside.

Katie's hand jumped into her pocketbook and came out holding the gun. She aimed it at them. "Get away from here!"

Suddenly the faces were gone.

Katie turned and looked at Ruth. "Tell him the truth!" She stepped forward. Her mouth tightened into a flat slit across the bottom of her face. Her voice was like ice. "Tell him!"

The gun came up and aimed at Ruth.

I said, "No, Katie! Don't do it! Please!"

Katie looked into my eyes. "You don't believe me. Nobody ever believes me. You don't love me. You love her."

I heard Ruth moving behind me. As Katie's hand moved, I moved with it. Suddenly I was in front of the gun. "Put it down, Katie. Please."

I heard a noise at the front door. Katie jumped aside. The gun was no longer on me, and it fired. I turned and saw the top half of the door splinter. But Ruth had jumped away from it in time.

I stepped forward and reached for the gun.

The gun swung away. It swung back quickly. I couldn't catch her wrist this time, and the gun hit me so hard I lost my footing. I stumbled against the wall.

When I looked up Katie said, "Jake. . . . I'm sorry. . . . God. . . ."

I reached toward her with my hand open. "Please, Katie. Give me the gun."

She turned and aimed at Ruth. "Tell him the truth!"

Ruth moved. Katie fired again. Paint chipped off the wall barely three inches away from Ruth's head.

Katie stopped still. She half turned to me. "Jake! . . . Do something! . . . Please! . . ."

I stared at her. Then I started moving again.

Ruth yelled. "No, Jake! She'll kill you!"

The scream scared Katie, but when the gun moved this time, it moved toward me. "You don't believe me, you believe her!" Her voice went cold again. "You're like every man. You don't believe me."

The gun fired.

I saw sparks coming out of the barrel. I felt some kind of horrible force pushing at my left side. I didn't connect the two things for a second, then I connected them, but they still meant nothing. All I could think of was Bob Linowes. I couldn't be like him. I caught my balance and stepped forward again.

"I believe you, Katie. Listen to me. I believe you."

My left arm felt very warm, then seemed to go numb. I felt weak. I thought I was going to pass out. "Ruth hit you. I believe you."

Katie's face showed confusion. "Don't hit me, Jake! I need help! Help me, please! Don't hit me!"

"I won't hit you."

"No! You're lying! Don't come near me." Her eyes were full of tears. "Oh God! Please! Don't!" She began to shake. "Do something! Jake! Do something!"

I could hardly stand. I saw spots, then something else. The way Linowes would've yelled at her and yanked her out of that party.

Linowes. He'd thought I was strong. Maybe I was. Even if I wasn't, I had to be. It didn't matter what it might cost me.

I shook my head and my vision cleared. I stared at the gun, the way her hand was tight around it. The way she was shaking. I stepped in front of the gun with my hands at my sides, and in that brief second I realized that I had no fear of anything. It had finally left me.

"I believe you, Katie. The way you say it happened. I believe you."

"What?"

"The way you say it happened." I spoke calmly and softly. "I believe you."

Katie blinked "You do?"

"Yes."

"God! You believe me?"

"Yes."

Katie's hand lowered slowly. The gun pointed at the floor. "No, Jake. I was lying. It happened the way she said it happened."

The gun made a dull sound as it hit the carpet. Neither of us looked at it. Katie was still now. She was standing near the sofa. She sat, closed her eyes, and made no sound at all. I looked at my arm and found she'd hit me just above the elbow. I told Ruth to get me a towel. It took her a moment, then she got it. I held it against the wound and looked down at Katie.

"We're going to have to call the police."

Her eyes fluttered open.

"The police, Katie. We've got to call 'em."

Katie remained silent.

Ruth said, "Somebody has probably already called 'em."

I looked at Ruth quickly. She understood and was quiet. I looked back at Katie. I wasn't going to ask her again. She had to make the decision herself.

She looked up finally and took a long slow breath. "Yes. Call the police. Do it fast. Please."

Ruth went to the phone.

Katie breathed in and out heavily, then looked at me again. "I'm worried about you, Jake. So many things you got to do. Your career..."

"It's all right."

I sat beside her. She shivered as I put my arm around her.

"I'm very scared, Jake."

"I know. So am I."

"You really believed it happened the way I said it happened?"

"Yes."

She was quiet again. Then her eyes closed and her head rested against my shoulder. "Will you hold my hand?"

I slowly got my hand around and into her hand. I must've squeezed her tighter than I meant to. She said, "You don't have to hold it so tight, Jake. Just hold it."

I loosened my grip. She turned on the sofa and put her other arm around me, but she didn't cling to me the way she usually did. I guess it was because she finally knew what I knew. That she didn't have to worry, I wasn't going to let her go.

It didn't come to an end with Hammett and Chandler. The tradition of the tough guy detective survives and flourishes on the typewriter of Brad Solomon.

THE GONE MAN
By Brad Solomon

"THE GONE MAN is a descendant of the classic private eye novel, and it marks the debut of a talented writer."
The New York Times

Jamie Stockton, the son of a Hollywood film tycoon is missing and his father hires Charlie Quinlan, ex-actor turned private eye to track him down. It's a case made to order: simple and very lucrative. But Jamie has been swallowed whole somewhere in the seamy Hollywood of gambling dens, raw booze, and hard-gunning sex. And from the outset what seems like a detective's dream is fast becoming a nightmare involving Quinlan in the biggest challenge of his career.

AVON Paperback   49577/$2.25

THE OPEN SHADOW
By Brad Solomon

"Easily one of the best private eye novels in years."
Washington Star

Fritz Thieringer and Maggie McGuane are the tough-minded, usually broke and often bruised partners in a Los Angeles detective agency. Thieringer is a witty, street-wise hustler with a slightly shady past. McGuane is a soft-hearted divorcee who reviews movies on the side. Investigating the murder of a crooked entrepeneur they become ensnared in a web of betrayal and blackmail stretching back twenty-five years.

AVON Paperback   50633/$2.50

Available wherever paperbacks are sold, or directly from the publisher. Include 50¢ per copy for postage and handling: allow 4-6 weeks for delivery. Avon Books, Mail Order Dept. 224 West 57th Street, New York, N.Y. 10019

B. Solom 12-80